THE EXTERN
A JASON RODGERS NOVEL

David Perry

Pettigrew
ENTERPRISES

PO BOX 687
CARROLLTON, VIRGINIA 23314

ACCLAIM FOR DAVID PERRY'S THRILLERS

The Cyclops Revenge

"David Perry is in a league with James Patterson. *The Cyclops Revenge* is a page-burner, fast action and a great story line. Love this author can't wait for his next book!"

-Barbara Rippel, Amazon Reviewer

"…is an intricate and extraordinary read that will keep you up late at night feverishly reading until the end. An absorbing and intricate cast of characters…Perry's mastery of story-telling will keep you on the edge of your seat…"

-Mary Dunnigan- Amazon Reviewer

The Cyclops Conspiracy

". . . a pharmacist's death turns into an adventure of international proportions in this fast-paced thriller…Perry builds—and deftly sustains—a momentum that will have readers engrossed in this page-turner."

—ForeWord Clarion Reviews

"David Perry has written a fast-moving, engrossing book. . . Action is fast and riveting. . ."

—Paul Lane, Net Galley

". . . a top-notch thriller that you won't want to put down!"

David Compton, best-selling author of Executive Sanction

"*The Cyclops Conspiracy*. . . ramps up the pace revealing a new twist and a new turn by the page. I will be adding him to my must-read list."

—Alan Williams, Book Reviewer

". . . Perry . . . gives an extra zing to an already interesting story . . . there are so many lovely twists and turns . . . kept thinking of Robert Ludlum novels . . . I couldn't put it down at night until I started seeing double. If you like political conspiracy thrillers, then check this one out!"

—Popcorn Reads

Second Chance

"There are not many books that keep me up reading all night but this one I could not put down. It had my interest from the very first page. This is the best I have read so far this year. Looking forward to the next book from Mr. Perry. Shame I could not give it more stars than five."

—Julie's Reviews, GoodReads

". . . a wonderful read if you are not checking into a hospital anytime soon."

—Rosemary Smith, NetGalley

". . . fast-paced and kept me awake all night long."

—Theresa Nelson, NetGalley

ALSO BY DAVID PERRY

The Cyclops Conspiracy
Second Chance
The Cyclops Revenge

THE EXTERN

A JASON RODGERS NOVEL

The Extern
Published by Pettigrew Enterprises LLC
PO BOX 687
Carrollton, Virginia 23314

For more information about our books, please visit the website at
www.davidperrybooks.com

Published in the United States by Pettigrew Enterprises, LLC
Cataloging-in-Publication date is on file with the Library of Congress

Library of Congress Control Number: 2020921775
ISBN: 9780998853253(softcover)

PRINTED IN THE UNITED STATES OF AMERICA
First Edition

10 9 8 7 6 5 4 3 2 1

FOR THE NEXT GENERATION OF PHARMACISTS...

You are the future of a profession steeped in history and with a mission dedicated to the well-being of humankind. Our profession is under siege from every direction…protect and guard it well.

"A feeling of sadness that is not akin to pain, resembles sorrow only as
mist resembles rain."
— Henry Wadsworth Longfellow

"Spurn not a seeming error but dig below its surface for the truth.
And beware of seeming truths that grow on the roots of error."
— Martin Farquhar Tupper

ACKNOWLEDGMENTS

I extend my deepest gratitude to the folks who have assisted me in my journey to see this work published:

To Dexter Morgan, my friend, your guidance and assistance in all things related to my website and your wise counsel in matters of marketing;

To David Compton, editor and mentor, your narrative principles resonate in every scene;

To Leah Spradlin, my social media manager and copy editor, your insights and suggestions on the manuscript were spot on;

To Kristy Williams, one of my biggest supporters, for being a reader and offering your advice and encouragement;

To Mary Freeman-Stauffer, a friend and confidante; for always listening and offering wise counsel in pharmacy matters and for "talking me down off the ledge" on more occasions than I'd like to admit.

To Anne, for your support and love;

To my two beautiful daughters Katlyn and Sarah, and their significant others: Brandon and Alex. Your love and support mean more than I can express in words, written or spoken. The physical distance between us creates an incessant stream of yearning. Anne and I are so proud of all of you and we greatly miss the family dinners;

To my brother Scott, for always being a sounding board;

To my parents, Betty and Walter, once again, for always being there.

CHAPTER 1

Jason Rodgers peered intently at the source of his mounting anxiety through the dirt-speckled windshield of his rusting blue Honda Civic. The aging car idled as he sat behind the wheel, its inefficient air-conditioner struggling to cool the cabin against the sweltering mid-August heat. It was after nine on a brutal Monday morning. Newport News and the surrounding cities of the Hampton Roads area had been mired in the relentless clutches of one of Virginia's ritualistic heat waves for the last seven days. With no relief in sight, the stifling humidity lent the air the quality of a hot, viscous soup. Sweat had erupted from every pore, soaking his clothing. The cotton of his Navy trousers was glued to his thighs. The starched white cotton shirt had lost its stiffness an hour ago.

But it wasn't just the brutal summer weather causing Jason's physical discomfort. The nature of the meeting he was about to undertake contributed significantly. He rotated his wrist and checked the black Casio watch with resin strap--a fifteen-dollar cheapie from Walmart. Rodgers wasn't sure what he wanted to happen: to speed up the advancing numerals so he could get the interview over with or, if it was somehow possible, to go back in time and rethink his choice. Nonetheless, the inexpensive timepiece of this intelligent but poor college student continued to serve its unremitting purpose: counting down the minutes and seconds with pinpoint precision, shrinking the interval between him and destiny.

Someday, he promised himself he would own a truly magnificent watch. One that reflected the success he planned to achieve as a result of his work in the world. He'd spied a gleaming silver and gold Tissot on the wrist of a ruggedly sophisticated male model in a men's magazine. One day, he told himself. One day.

He lifted his eyes and peered through the grimy windshield once more. The object of his scrutiny was a short stretch of storefront in a shopping center at the busy intersection of Jefferson Avenue and Denbigh (pronounced Den-bee) Boulevard in the northern stretches of Newport News. The glass door, framed in a faux bronze metal with a matching hand bar stretching across its width, opened every minute or so. At some point during each arc, the glass captured the morning sun, sending a sunlit laser beam into Rodgers's eyes. He hazarded a third glance at the trusty Casio again. 9:23am. Seven minutes to go.

In four minutes, he told himself, he'd get out of the car and walk to the door. *Don't want to appear too anxious by being too early*. But he also didn't want to make the fatal mistake of being late. To distract himself and pass the infinitely long quartet of minutes, he continued his examination of the exterior of the aging pharmacy.

Four large plates of tinted glass streaked with grime and dotted with dried water spots flanked the front door, two on each side. The massive window immediately to the right of the door had been stenciled many years ago with the massive words "The Colonial Pharmacy" arcing regally across the glass. The stenciling had occurred years earlier. He knew this because the "r" of "Pharmacy" had gone missing and the gold of a few of the other runes had flecked and cracked like the oil pigment of an ancient Caravaggio. The store's hours were also posted, equally aged, horizontally beneath it. Faded from years of wind and weather, the earth-toned wall encasing the large windows possessed a pasty white-yellowish hue. The dark outline of water stains traversed the stucco creating continent-like images on an old-world map.

A covered sidewalk stretched the length of the outdoor shopping center allowing patrons to stroll and window shop out of the sun and rain. On the overhang of the section of the breezeway in front of the pharmacy a tall cursive neon lettered sign rested. It, too, spelled out, The Colonial Pharmacy. Despite the morning sun, Rodgers could see that the sign was illuminated. As if coordinated with the stenciling on the glass below by the cosmic gods of decay, the "h" in Pharmacy blinked off for long periods…recovered for a moment…then went dark again. The wanting appearance of the business suggested a healthy measure of neglect.

Despite the faded façade, what lay inside was a granite bulwark of respectability and influence in the profession of pharmacy. The uniniti-ated would never know to look at it, but this strip mall pharmacy was one of the most sought-after training experiences for pharmacy students in all of Virginia. Those that managed to be accepted into and survive the six torturous weeks…or if by some stroke of good fortune… somehow elicited a few glowing words of recommendation from the owner and preceptor, were heralded as the cream of that year's apothecarial crop.

The Colonial (over the years its moniker had been shortened by its devoted patrons) anchored a stable of retail shops and restaurants. But this independently owned enterprise sat like a beleaguered out-post across the wide expanse of Jefferson Avenue, hunkered against the onslaught from a corporate fortress of one of retail pharmacy's behe-moths. A Walgreens had laid siege to The Colonial five years earlier.

Often when a large chain store popped up beside a mom-and-pop drug store, it was only a matter of time before the owners caved to a solicitous offer from the greedy giant under the promise of total obliteration. If they refused, they were promised a slow, agonizing death by a barrage of over-the-counter promotions, cheaper prices and supposedly faster service.

But, despite the persistent threat from across the way, The Colonial, continued to flourish, nurturing a large, devoted clientele and consistent, exemplary personal service that the chains just could not deliver.

Regardless of its outward appearance, Rodgers refused to speak any criticism concerning The Colonial aloud. Karma was a bitch, he thought. And he needed every milligram of luck, kismet and fortuity the cosmos offered. He wanted this externship badly. No, he didn't want it. He needed it. In fact, he was consumed by it. At night as he lay in bed, his gut ached thinking about it. His deep competitive nature and the desire to do things right and see them done right by others was both a passion and, at the same time, a curse. Passing—no excelling at this particular rotation—would validate to the pharmacy gods that Jason Rodgers had the goods.

Pharmacy students that had gone before him said if you landed an externship at The Colonial—and came out clean on the other side--you could write your own ticket. Rumor also had it that the big pharmacy chains like Walgreens and CVS paid better for successful Colonial trainees.

Jason had heard the stories from former students. The Colonial's reputation had been established fifteen years earlier when the owner, Thomas Pettigrew, had been asked by the Dean of the Medical College of Virginia in Richmond, a good friend, that he become a site for training pharmacy students. Pettigrew had agreed with two stipulations. He would take only the best, most dedicated students. He also demanded that he be able to choose the candidates himself. This had been in direct conflict with long standing tradition that the candidate be assigned to a site by the pharmacy school. Attempts to get Pettigrew to soften his position proved fruitless. After much grumbling, the Dean granted Pettigrew his terms. In return, Pettigrew promised to deliver well-trained, dedicated super-hero like pharmacists. If he failed, he would withdraw from the program. And in the last decade and a half, Pettigrew had made good on his promise.

During each school year, The Colonial hosted only eight externship rotations. Hundreds applied. Of those, only twenty-five were granted interviews. The twenty-five "lucky" ones endured a rigorous ninety-minute interview with Thomas Pettigrew himself. The relentless taskmaster insisted on the right to turn away any student he did not think possessed the mettle to withstand his withering expectations. Then based on the interviews, the list of candidates was ranked in order with the top eight students being accepted into Pettigrew's program. Each candidate entered the program one at a time with the first beginning in September. They were thrust into six weeks of intensive, mind-numbing, one-on-one training. If a candidate bowed out of the program, or they did not please Pettigrew in the first few days, the next candidate in line was offered the opportunity to step in.

After the first year of The Colonial's participation in the program, each of the eight candidates had received multiple job offers. Every employer had contacted the school to inform them that they were the most prepared pharmacists they had ever seen. The college contacted each candidate and asked what the most influential part of their training was. To a person, they all credited Thomas Pettigrew. He was a bastard, they complained. But if they had to do it again, they said they would not hesitate. And thus, The Colonial's—and Pettigrew's—reputation had been born.

Requirements were stiff. If your GPA was less than 3.5, do not bother to apply, the students were told. In fact, last year all the students selected for placement had possessed a perfect 4.0 GPA or better. Their resumes had to be exemplary with references from the most demanding professors and indicate that the student was active in at least two pharmacy-related organizations or activities. Mediocrity was tantamount to incompetence.

Can't be late! Jason checked the Casio again. Tardiness was a self-inflicted, mortal mistake. Last year, a female student had become bogged down in the heavy traffic on Jefferson Avenue because of a three-car fender bender. She arrived two minutes late for her appointment. Thomas Pettigrew had chastised her for a full three minutes about the need for punctuality, never raising his voice or using profanity. He kept his voice low and even. But the message had been monolithic and resolute.

"Pharmacies could not open unless a pharmacist was present. Every second you were late was one more second a patient could not be served!" He'd informed her. "You will not be an extern here. Please leave my pharmacy immediately."

Jason had learned of the dressing down from an acquaintance. He told him in gory detail the blow-by-blow description of the defrocked young woman. Reduced to a blubbering mess, the student had hit another car from behind on the way back to school because she couldn't see through her tears.

As a rising fourth year pharmacy student--a P4, as it were-- Rodgers's didactic course work had been completed in his first three years of pharmacy school. These next eight months from September to April would be consumed by a handful of six-week-long graded and unpaid rotations. This allowed the future druggists to sample different types of pharmacy practices from high-volume retail chains, independent drug stores, hospital and compounding pharmacies. It also served as an opportunity for the candidates to show off their pharmacy skills and academic acumen to potential employers. For the privilege, students were charged regular tuition rates even though they never set foot inside a classroom during their final year.

He regarded for the fifth time the black rubber watch. 9:26am. He jerked the door handle, leaned his shoulder into the door and pushed it open with a loud shriek. He grabbed his leather briefcase and exited the car, shaking his creased, sweat-laden pant legs away from his skin and smoothing them with a hand. After a long, deep breath, Jason strode across the heat-softened pavement, through the palpable mugginess toward his appointment with the monument of a man named Thomas Pettigrew. Though he'd feel a massive relief when this interview was over, a sense of destiny swelled within him. Something huge lay in his future. He could feel it.

And something massive did lay in Jason Rodgers's future.

It would devastate his life and career.

CHAPTER 2

The rental car, a gray Ford Taurus, sat nestled among several other vehicles at one end of the parking lot near the McDonald's. It had been parked in such a way as to provide a perfect view of anyone walking toward the pharmacy. The driver, a short, round, balding man named Victor with the thick arms and hunched shoulders of a weight-lifter, puffed on a thin black cigarillo. The blue, acrid smoke floated just below the roof of the cabin. His black watery eyes buried deep in their sockets beneath two bushy black eyebrows, darted back and forth every few seconds recording every passerby, every face entering the pharmacy. So far, he had counted no less than five employees, their lab coats draped over their arms arriving for work, including the tall, lanky pharmacist with the shock of mangy, white hair. Thomas Pettigrew.

Victor's partner, Simon, a slightly built man who appeared so leafy it seemed a strong gust would send him wafting skyward, gazed out upon the same scene from the passenger side as a Nikon D3500 with a 300mm lens rested in his lap. A pair of blue-tinted Maui Jim sunglasses rested on a thick crop of sandy pale hair. His thin face and pointed nose gave him the appearance of a tanned waterfowl. Now, he grimaced at the cloud of blue smog engulfing them. He coughed and depressed the button, lowering his window a few inches.

"Who's that?" Victor asked, impervious to his partner's discomfort.

A slender young man in his early twenties with a thick tousle of chestnut hair dressed in a navy suit and bright red tie marched toward the front door of the pharmacy carrying a leather briefcase. His quick but tentative gait belied an air of phony bravado.

"I dunno," Simon replied, lifting the camera to his face. He depressed the shutter and the Nikon recorded a video of the young man as he strode toward the pharmacy. "His face is covered in sweat. He looks like he's walking to his own execution."

"Salesman?"

"Nah," Simon answered. "Too young to be a drug rep. Maybe a student. Could be an extern. It is that time of year. Pettigrew should be starting his interviews 'bout now."

"Never seen him before," Victor muttered to himself. He slid a small notebook from inside the console of the Taurus and jotted something in it. "Did you see which car he got out of?"

"Yeah, it's that blue shit box...Toyota or a Honda." Simon swiveled the lens and captured stills of the license plate.

"You gotta love these cake assignments," Victor smiled, drawing a long pull on the cigarillo. He exhaled another plume of blue smoke into the cab that was quickly dissipated by the car's fan, which Simon had pushed to its limit along with several waves of his narrow hand.

"Cake assignments?" Simon whipped his head in Victor's direction. "You do realize we're being punished for screwing up in Italy. We're in goddamned spook Siberia. No, this is a bullshit assignment. I didn't leave the legal profession to sit in the sweltering heat to watch a God forsaken pharmacy while sitting in your cloud of poison. I should have stayed in law. The only good thing about this is at least we're back in the field," Simon declared, wiping beads of sweat from his forehead with a small hand towel he'd brought from their nearby safe house. Next, he swiped moisture from the back of the camera.

"I was trying to take a positive outlook," Victor countered.

Simon pushed out a cheek full of air through lips pressed tightly together. "Face it," he declared. "We screwed the pouch." Another ten seconds elapsed.

"That wasn't our fault. Who knew they'd switched backpacks and hoodies? It was an honest mistake."

"Doesn't matter," Simon retorted. "They blame us for DeMarco being tipped off. The whole op collapsed because of what we did." Simon cleared his throat and let the thought hang in the air like the acrid smoke. Then he decided to change the subject. "How long do we need to watch this shithole?" He returned the camera to his lap and removed an expensive Mont Blanc pen from his shirt pocket. He twirled it in his hand, a nervous habit that helped him pass time and allay frustration.

"Dunno that either. All I been told is The Colonial has been tagged as a possible cover for a future op. All the employees and the owner need to be vetted."

"What's the op?"

"I told you I don't know."

"This is bullshit," Simon whispered. "How many employees again?"

Victor removed a folded piece of paper from his shirt pocket and opened it. He read a moment. "State Corporation Commission records say he has six employees. Thomas Pettigrew, the owner and pharmacist; there's also a staff pharmacist named Kyle Griffin and four technicians plus a delivery driver. One of the technicians is Pettigrew's daughter. Name's Christine."

"I'll give it a minute," Simon said. "Then I'll go in and see if we can determine what boy wonder is doing here.

CHAPTER 3

Christine Pettigrew perched herself on the tall, uncomfortable wooden stool behind the prescription counter, peering out over the sales floor like a lioness scanning the spreading savannah. Even though her butt had gone numb a minute after sitting down on the flat wooden seat, she loved this vantage point. It was high. Tall enough to allow her to look out over the short, frosted glass in front of the pharmacy. From it, she could see the entire sales floor laid out before her: shelves brimming with merchandise, arranged and faced in perfect rows. Two customers casually roamed the aisles, browsing lazily beneath the slowly rotating dust-covered ceiling fans. Sunlight filtered through the tinted windows creating honey-colored trapezoids on the tiled floor. The front door equipped with a small bell chimed every time it swung open. Whenever she heard the familiar tinkle, she automatically lifted her head. Chrissie loved to watch her father's patients and customers come and go.

Out of the corner of her eye she watched and admired her father. At six-four, he towered over the computer terminal, as he typed. A stack of square paper prescriptions lay on the cluttered counter beside him. He was a giant man both in stature and reputation. Chrissie respected and idolized him. She cherished his tough love, most of the time, and his work ethic. Thomas Pettigrew had established a deep respect in the pharmacy community in Newport News area and the state. Chrissie didn't remember the names of the organizations he belonged to, but the list was long. He traveled to Richmond periodically to meet with members of the General Assembly when important pharmacy and healthcare laws were being debated. Her father had once told her he'd been invited to sit on the Board of Pharmacy by the governor. But, citing time constraints, he had declined. On more than one occasion, local politicians had invited him to run for the House of Delegates. Again, he'd refused.

His frame carried little flab. His unbuttoned knee-length lab coat draped from his wide shoulders like a cape trailing behind a superhero as he maneuvered about the pharmacy. His glacial blue eyes narrowed at the first hint of bullshit. This was often quickly followed by a direct and unfettered admonition to the person delivering said excrement. People noticed two things about him upon first meeting him: his mop of unkempt silvery hair and his massive hands. Pens, stock bottles and counting spatulas looked like dollhouse miniatures between his fingers.

Christine had worked for her father since she was ten years old. In high school, she filled in after school and on weekends. In college now at Virginia Tech in Blacksburg, she could only work summers. In fact, this would be her last summer working at The Colonial. She was about to begin a paid internship with a local accounting firm in Newport News, part of Tech's work-study program. These two facts left her with a deep sense of nostalgia laced with a euphoric sense of anticipation.

Chrissie had loved numbers for as long as she could remember. Thomas had recognized this early on. Since her sophomore year at

Menchville High when she'd first taken an accounting class, he'd allowed his daughter to manage his invoices and prepare The Colonial's books for his accountant.

Two days hence, she would begin an internship and leave The Colonial behind. She wanted to live up to his expectations and show him she was as good as he was…maybe better. She hoped to one day be the type of dedicated career woman that would make him beam with pride.

"Are you going to start counting, honey? Or are you going to sit there watching me all day?" Thomas said in his low baritone as a quick, but expectant smile flashed across his face.

"Yes, Daddy," she replied, hopping off the stool.

In addition to serving as his bookkeeper, she had developed the skills and knowledge to be a competent pharmacy technician. Chrissie picked up a counting tray and a spatula as Thomas plopped a large round stock bottle, a prescription label and paper prescription in front of her. Chrissie poured some of the long thin capsules onto the tray just as the tinkle of the bell pierced the stillness out front once more.

Instinctively, Chrissie lifted her head. A young man about her age strode into the sun-dappled space. He carried some sort of leather satchel and his eyes were held high, peering into the pharmacy area. She could always tell when they were headed for the pharmacy department. Expectancy gripped the eyes.

The young man appeared to be looking for someone. He stepped tentatively through the oral care aisle, trying to look casual and failing miserably. His shoulders and torso moved awkwardly holding tension like a leaden shroud.

"Are you expecting a drug rep today?"

Thomas looked up at the young man and checked his watch. "No, that's my first interviewee for the externship for the fall. And he's right on time."

"Why didn't you tell me you had an interview today? This one's cute!"

Thomas spread his lips in a conspiratorial smile. "That's exactly why I didn't tell you. Now get those drugs counted so I can check them. Sarah will be here at ten and she can help you. If anyone calls, take a message and tell them I will call them back."

"Where's Kyle? You normally don't work the bench when you have interviews."

"Kyle's taking the day off to play golf. I can handle it as long as you count those drugs." Pettigrew's mouth spread into a paternal smile directed at his only child. It was as if he'd just noticed that she had grown from an awkward, spindly girl into a vibrant, intelligent and attractive woman. "Damn! Where have all the years gone. You've graduating soon and then you have to study for the CPA exam. I can't believe you won't be working here anymore."

Chrissie smiled and shook her head. "I know. You keep reminding me."

The young man approached the counter and asked for Thomas. The silver-haired apothecary descended the two steps from the prescription department to the lower counter area guarded by two cash registers and an assortment of shelved sundries not available on the sales floor.

"Jason Rodgers, I presume," Thomas said extending a large, beefy hand.

Thomas grinned as the young man's eyes widened for an instant as Pettigrew's massive mitt moved toward him. The pharmacy student's thin fingers appeared like that of a child's in Thomas's.

"Yessir, thanks for meeting with me."

"Follow me," Thomas instructed.

The pair climbed the two steps into the prescription department as Chrissie slipped into one of the bays lined with stock bottles. As she faced the shelves, she glanced toward the young man following her father. He was lean with an athletic build. He moved with a stiffness that shouted nervousness. But Chrissie sensed he was normally confident and composed. The thick almost riotous brunette locks on his head invited fingers to run through it. His forced smile curved cutely up to the right. The hazel eyes were intelligent and sharp. As he slid past like a lamb following the shepherd, she noticed that his suit coat had rumpled upward exposing his trousers clinging to a perfectly formed backside.

Thomas led this Jason Rodgers into the narrow hallway behind the department where he kept his office. Her father had not bothered to introduce this man to her. He had finally learned his lesson with one of the candidates last year. Chrissie's playful character did not always mesh with Thomas's staid, professional demeanor. She often played small pranks on her father and his visitors.

Chrissie had been so busy and preoccupied with her upcoming departure from her father's employ and preparation for the upcoming internship she had completely forgotten that it was extern season. Over the next few weeks, her father would interview more than two dozen wide-eyed, naïve pharmacy students who had heard about the tough externship at The Colonial but had no clue that they were about to be hit by a pharmaceutical locomotive.

Chrissie had witnessed her father's demanding and unyielding methods for the past twelve years. She knew the pharmacy students he trained hated the experience while they were going through it, but they also knew that her father made them better pharmacists…and she believed better people. Her father had earned the nickname the "Old Man". In this densely populated military area, Chrissie quickly learned it was a moniker normally associated with high-ranking officers and was used by their underlings to demonstrate respect and toughness, not necessarily advanced years. Of course, no one called Thomas Pettigrew "Old Man" to his face.

As they filed past, Chrissie poked her head out of the bay and watched Jason Rodgers's backside disappear into the hallway. "Oh yeah," she smiled to no one in particular. "I'm going to have some fun with this one."

CHAPTER 4

What Jason did on the uncomfortable gray, vinyl and metal chair could not be called sitting. Sitting implied some measure of relaxation. It was as if he was propped on some medieval torture device like rigid stocks. His back ramrod straight, he refused to lean against the backrest. There were two reasons for this. He did not want to give the appearance of being a slouch and his nerves would not allow it. Instead, he sat uncomfortably on the edge, his hands grasping his leather case like a life preserver as it rested on his knees. His elevated heels placed pressure on the balls of his feet as his knees rubbed against the cream-colored, dented, metal desk. It was all he could do not bounce his leg up and down.

Thomas Pettigrew read over Jason's resume and seemed to be studying it like it would reveal every misdemeanor he'd ever committed, or any lie Jason had ever told. The document, apparently, was the Rosetta Stone to unravelling the mystery that was Jason Rodgers. Pettigrew had been studying it for an interminable amount of time and seemed to be in no hurry to engage this potential extern in any form of verbal communication. For a moment, Jason wondered if Pettigrew remembered he was sitting before him. Then sweat flowed over him again gushing forth like the murky brown waters of the James River.

While Pettigrew took microscopic scrutiny to his educational career, Jason scanned the surroundings. The tiny office held barely enough space to hold the metal desk, the chair in which Jason now sat and an identical one for Pettigrew. The desktop sagged under the weight of stacks of reports, computer printouts and pharmacy and medical journals. Pettigrew had carved a valley among the stacks to view the prey sitting across from him. A circular receptacle held pens of various colors, emblazoned with assorted logos of various drugs and their manufacturers, no doubt offered up as tribute from the endless line of ass-kissing drug reps. The blotter was one of those large calendars upon which each day was represented by a large square and inside which were scribbled appointments and reminders in Pettigrew's hieroglyphic handwriting. A flimsy desk lamp sat near the blotter on the desktop. A cone of yellow light provided the only illumination in the window-less, coffin-like room.

A four-drawer filing cabinet had been crammed against the wall. It, too, seemed to strain beneath the burden of a blinking console which looked like some kind of computer server, more documents and weighty, bound volumes. Jason recognized the blue *Physician's Desk Reference, Gray's Anatomy*, and a weathered copy of a tome on medicinal chemistry. Two frames hung on the wall over the filing cabinet. One was Pettigrew's diploma from the Medical College of Virginia in Richmond, Jason's own school which was now known as Virginia Commonwealth University but was frequently referred to as MCV. The second was an inspirational poster that read: "If you think you can or you think you can't, you're right."

With the scan of the office complete and taking no more than a minute, Jason turned his attention back to Pettigrew, studying the man through the paper canyon. The pharmacist was not an old man, but he had crested the hill of life and was beginning his descent into his golden years. When stretched to his full height, Pettigrew stood no less than six -four. This human being consumed the space of the small, cramped office like King Kong in a steamer trunk. Jason could not but help noticing Pettigrew's massive hands., dwarfing his two-page resume.

The pallor of his skin and its mottled nature told Jason that this man worked long hours behind the counter and rarely took vacations and the only time he was exposed to sunlight was to walk from his car to the pharmacy. Such was the nature of being an independent business owner, especially of a pharmacy. Your work was your life.

At the corner of Pettigrew's eyes, barely perceptible crow's feet framed a pair of intelligent, ice blue eyes. The mop of flowing white hair hung to his shirt collar and looked like it needed to see the business end of a strong comb. But, Jason guessed, Pettigrew found little time for either a trim or a comb. The bushy salt and pepper eyebrows lent him an Einsteinian aura. His brows furrowed as he read. The sterile blue eyes moving over each word as a long, slender finger scratched the side of his nose. This was followed by a quick inhaled snuffle.

Jason deftly rotated his wrist and dropped his gaze without moving his head to check his Casio without being noticed. Just over two minutes had passed.

"I'll be with you in just a moment, young man. You're mine for the next ninety minutes," Pettigrew intoned without taking his eyes of the resume.

Pettigrew flipped to the second and last page of Jason's resume, absorbing every word, rolling them about in that harsh, cement-mixer like brain.

A rough sound emanated from Jason's throat. It was an involuntary act caused by a sudden dryness climbing up through his chest;

something akin to clearing his throat. Almost three minutes now. Jason found himself wishing he were at the dentist for a root canal. Then without warning Thomas Pettigrew placed the resume on his calendar-blotter and said, "Let's begin."

CHAPTER 5

Chrissie managed to fill the thirty or so prescriptions her father had put into the system since the pharmacy had opened. He always arrived an hour before opening to input the refill prescriptions that had been called in overnight by patients or new prescriptions sent in electronically by physicians. Each patient's orders had been placed into a small rectangular plastic basket. While Thomas was in the office with the cute extern candidate, Chrissie had retrieved various stock bottles of medications from the wide bays of shelves and held their barcodes up to a small counter-mounted scanner, generating prescription labels which hummed from the small label printer.

She then counted them on a plastic counting tray and poured them into appropriately sized prescription vials. Each label was then affixed and set in the basket for Thomas's review. She had performed this task countless times in her twelve years working for her father. The morning's prescriptions had all been counted and labeled. The baskets stood stacked on the prescription counter awaiting her father's approval. And so, it went day after day, typing, filling, calling, counting, billing uncooperative insurance companies, checking vials and dispensing them to sometimes rude and arrogant patients. And Christine Pettigrew had grown to hate it. Though she did not care for the profession, she viewed all pharmacists with a profound respect. They toiled long hours and sometimes endured hellish patients and working conditions. She also knew her father loved it. He worked the prescription bench and counseled his patients with dedication and an attention to detail unrivaled by anyone she'd ever met.

Chrissie had inherited her mother's sense of organization and order and preferred the quiet confines of office work, spreadsheets and corporate ledgers to the fast pace and hurried nature of her father's world. With this batch of prescription work done and having earned a brief respite from the onslaught, her mind turned to her future. Only a few more days, she told herself. Then it was back to school for her final year at Virginia Tech to complete her accounting degree. Like the pharmacy student her father was interviewing, Chrissie had been accepted into a paid accounting internship with a well-respected firm in the City Center district of Newport News by the name of Collins, White and Casper.

The co-op program with Tech allowed the student to work for credit. The beauty of it was that they were in Newport News and Chrissie would be able to stay at home with her parents while she worked. She couldn't wait for that day to arrive.

The ten o'clock technician had arrived early to start her shift which meant Chrissie was now freed up to take care of the books, entering wholesaler invoices and insurance company reimbursement checks into her father's accounting system. This is what she loved. Numbers. Spreadsheets. Profit and Loss Statements. Trial balances.

Before she could retreat to her desk, the jangle of the single bell on the front door snatched her from her reverie. A slim man with a pair of sunglasses with deeply blue tinted lenses over a long, slender nose entered. A thick, unkempt thatch of sandy blonde hair and narrow, aquiline features gave him the appearance of a heron or an egret.

He was not here for a prescription; Chrissie determined that right away. The ones with prescriptions always turned their eyes first to the pharmacy department to see who was working or how long the lines were. No, this man entered, hesitated and checked aisle signage and seemed to find the section he wanted. He marched to the oral hygiene section located right in front of the pharmacy. It was then that he shot a quick glance in her direction. He smiled at her then nodded. Chrissie returned his smile. A weird tingling sensation slithered down her spine. This guy gave her the willies.

As he returned to scanning toothbrushes, Chrissie sipped her coffee, greeted Gloria, the technician and walked back into the small desk area at the head of the dark hallway leading to her father's office.

℞

Simon lifted the sunglasses onto his head once more and pretended to scan the toothbrushes, toothpastes and mouthwashes. As soon as he'd entered, what he saw — or rather, what he didn't see — told him what he needed to know. The man-boy that had entered The Colonial was nowhere to be seen. It had been nearly thirty minutes since he and Victor had watched him enter. If he were an employee of the pharmacy, he would most likely be in a smock or lab coat filling prescriptions or stocking shelves. He was not on the sales floor nor was he visible behind the counter. The only people Simon saw was the daughter, Christine, who had just made her way into the back and out of sight and the newest arrival, a technician named Gloria. A cashier named Ethel stood at the far corner of the sales floor placing feminine products in neat rows on a shelf. Thomas Pettigrew was also nowhere to be seen.

The need for this type of physical surveillance would soon be unnecessary. At present they did not have ears inside the pharmacy. But it had been decided from on high by their spymaster at Langley, a boorish, unimaginative man named Carl, that they would be inserting listening devices into The Colonial. This would allow them full access to the mind-numbing conversations that infected the building. For now, they were stuck with extrapolating; a fancy spy word for guessing.

As he pulled a package of dental floss from the peg on the wall, the phone in the pharmacy area rang. That should be Victor, Simon thought. Gloria picked up the receiver and greeted the caller. She listened a moment and turned to ask someone a question, presumably the out-of-sight Christine. Gloria put the phone back to her face and said, "He's in a meeting right now. Can I have him call you back?"

She listened for a moment then hung up. Simon and Victor had counted the arrivals so far. Seven people had entered The Colonial. Four of them, employees, had been expected. Thomas Pettigrew and his three female assistants. Two customers were not expected but their presence was not surprising. Those two elderly women now shopped, roaming the aisles with hand baskets. The Colonial had a handful of regulars who showed up as soon as the key was turned. The young man in the blue suit and red tie had been a surprise...and warranted further scrutiny.

They had been watching The Colonial, its owner and employees, for more than five weeks. There was no end in sight to this operation. It had not been said aloud, but Simon knew the assignment had been given to them because they were at the bottom of the pecking order. The result of their perceived incompetence in the last operation in north central Italy.

So far, they had thoroughly documented and established Pettigrew's routine and the regular comings and goings of employees. There was an operation in play, but Simon and Victor had no idea what it was. Their assignment was to study every employee, learn as much as possible about them, their personality types, education, family backgrounds, the works.

After a week on site in southeastern Virginia, they had quickly tired of the data collecting. These folks were not terrorists or criminals. Nothing remotely interesting had come up on their background searches except for a few traffic violations or late payment to utilities. The pair of covert watchers had fallen into a coma-inducing, mundane routine over the last thirty-six days. During the day they surveilled the pharmacy. During the evenings after Pettigrew left the store or on his days off, Simon would tail Thomas Pettigrew, following him as he traveled around the area. Victor had been assigned to Kyle Griffin, Pettigrew's staff pharmacist, who filled prescriptions at the store on days Pettigrew was off. Victor had confirmed that Kyle Griffin was at the Deer Run golf course, probably teeing off at that very moment. Instead of sitting in the parking lot for five or six hours waiting for Griffin to finish his round, Victor had opted to join Simon this morning. He would catch up with Griffin later in the day. After all, these people weren't spies. They didn't think like spies. Hell, they didn't even know they were being watched.

It hadn't taken long for these intelligence gatherers to accumulate notebooks and logs filled with addresses, the makes and models of cars, banking institutions, social security numbers and daily and weekly habits of the staff of The Colonial Pharmacy.

The appearance of the young, suited man entering the pharmacy with the leather satchel created a new and animated sense of urgency in both men. It was as if a new suitor had called on their subject. And everything that could be known about him…would now have to be known. There was new information to be gathered, reports to be filed and searches to be conducted. The as-yet unnamed male had injected a new sense of purpose into their duties. The appearance of this new player at The Colonial would be passed along to the analyzers in Washington who would pour over the information and, no doubt, compile summarized reports for the suits on the seventh floor. Then undercover agents posing as salesmen or delivery persons would knock on doors and speak to neighbors, friends or family members, and pose seemingly innocent questions about the subject, gathering as much intel as possible. An extensive dossier would be compiled and, if necessary, appropriate interventions made. What those interventions would be, Simon nor Victor might never know. Their job was only data collection.

"How can they not use us," Simon mused one afternoon. "We've collected all the data. We know them like no one else. You watch," he explained to Victor. "If there's an op in play, we'll be included."

The government entity for whom they worked was not supposed to operate on American soil. The Central Intelligence Agency's charter by law was to gather and evaluate intelligence on America's allies and enemies outside of American borders. What they were doing could end them up in prison. Though they did not fear being caught. The work was tedious but not highly stressful. They just took notes and stayed invisible. They were serving their sentence and staying out of trouble.

Simon took the floss and a tube of toothpaste to the counter. Gloria, the technician, descended the two steps from the prescription department and searched for Ethel, the cashier. She appeared to consider calling her from her stocking duties but reconsidered. She smiled at Simon and rang him up. After bagging the items, she wished him a good day and handed him the bag. Simon smiled back and nodded. "You, too."

He marched to the door and pushed it open. Resisting the urge to throw the bag in the trash receptable just outside, he held on to it. No sense raising suspicion by such an act. He clutched the bag tighter, marched to the Taurus and climbed into the passenger seat.

"He's meeting with Pettigrew," he told Victor. "Did you pull up the license plates?"

Victor grinned, readjusting the computer on his lap and said, "Sure did."

PHARMACY PHACT:

There are 60, 594 pharmacy students in doctoral programs across the United States as of the fall of 2019.

American Association of Colleges of Pharmacy

CHAPTER 6

For the first fifteen minutes, Pettigrew had lobbed several softball-type questions at Jason. He asked personal questions about Jason's life: where he lived; were his parents still alive; were they married; did he have brothers or sisters (he had one, Kathleen, who lived in Florida with her doctor husband). He inquired about whether Jason had had any run-ins with the law (he had not, at least, not in the United States). They were personal and pointed inquiries that bordered on being intrusive and inappropriate. But Jason answered truthfully. He had nothing of which he should be ashamed. He certainly had nothing to hide.

Pettigrew adjusted his large frame in the chair, indicating the interview was taking a more serious turn.

"It's time for me to delve into your knowledge of pharmacy, drugs and clinical issues. I'm going to ask you a series of questions. I want you to give me the first answer that pops into your mind," Thomas said, removing a thick sheaf of papers from the middle drawer of his desk.

Pettigrew had placed Jason's resume on his desk and taken a few minutes to explain the how's and why's of the externship he was offering. The pharmacist explained facts with which Jason was already familiar.

"Colonial Externships are the most sought-after in the state of Virginia," Pettigrew explained. "Employers such as large chain drug stores and a few hospitals all considered this experience to be a large, colorful feather in a candidate's cap."

"You will work harder than you have ever worked before," he continued. "You will be quizzed daily on your knowledge of pharmacy procedures, clinical knowledge, dosing parameters and pharmacy law among other things. You have been an exemplary student. But you will come out on the other side stronger and more prepared than most of your colleagues if I choose you. Are you afraid of hard work, Jason?"

"No sir," he croaked over a parched, desert-dry tongue.

"Good."

"First," he explained. "I have prescriptions to check. I will be right back."

Jason thought he saw a smirk flash over Pettigrew's mouth. The older man was somehow enjoying the discomfort he was inflicting on this anxious candidate. The pharmacist circled the desk and squeezed past Jason's chair. The tail of his long white lab coat brushed Jason's shoulder. A whiff of generic aftershave and hand sanitizer hit him squarely in the face. Pettigrew disappeared, leaving the door open. Jason sat frozen for thirty seconds as if he were a bronze statue. When the hard vinyl of the chair began to send shooting pains through his butt and legs once more, he decided to get the blood flowing again. He checked the Casio. He'd been perched rigid in his seat for almost thirty minutes and his ass felt like it had been injected with lidocaine.

℞

Chrissie heard her father exit the office. He marched toward her station just inside the doorway leading into the hallway. A small computer rested on a counter, providing just enough workspace to enter the bills and invoices.

"How many are there?" Thomas asked, pausing but not stopping as he approached within a few feet."

"There's about thirty. You have two doctor's offices that want you to call back and a patient's insurance wants a prior authorization for the blood thinner," she replied.

Thomas patted her on the head and headed straight for the leaning mountain of baskets loaded with prescriptions waiting to be checked. Chrissie watched him for a moment, made sure that he was fully engaged in his work before she silently slid her chair back. She turned and crept down the hallway.

Time to meet the cute new candidate!

℞

Jason removed the leather case from his lap and placed it beside his chair. Then like a defendant about to face a verdict, he stood up. He shifted his weight from one leg to the other, allowing blood to flow once again into his feet. After several deep breaths, a renewed sense of anticipation hit him. But the exhilaration was short-lived, interrupted by someone at the door.

One of the technicians, the cute one with caramel hair and deep caramel eyes happened past the open door. He had noticed her as he entered the prescription department. She was a looker. But Jason had other things on his mind. Facing the open door now, he saw her pass, walking deeper down the hallway. She had glanced quickly into the office as she passed but made no indication that she saw him. A few seconds later, she passed again this time going in the other direction now holding a file. She cast a quick glance into the office and smiled. She took one more step then stopped as if struck by a notion.

"Hi," she said. Her smile held a playful, mischievous quality.

"Hi."

She appeared to be about Jason's age, perhaps a year or three younger. Her eyes moved up and down, assessing him. The smile widened, curving up one side of her face. The flawless skin flowed over her cheeks, as soft and supple as milk and honey.

"Don't worry," she advised. "The pain only lasts a little while. Eventually, you get over it. Have fun!"

Then she turned and was gone...vanished.

Jason let out a short, exasperated sigh and shook his head. *Was she talking about his numb backside or the interview itself?* He turned in a full circle, assessing the room once more, his nerves on edge again. He picked up a pharmacy journal, *Pharmacy Times*, and flipped through the pages without seeing the photos or words.

Then his bladder seemed to suddenly fill. He needed to urinate. He tried to suppress it. But the three cups of coffee he'd sucked down had exerted their effect. He stuck his head out the door and checked both ends of the hallway. To the left--toward the hallway entrance--the brown-haired woman who'd just passed was seated with her back to him at a small counter with a computer. A stack of invoices lay spread near the keyboard. The one doorway he'd passed had been open. Jason had seen that it was a supply room filled with boxes of vials, caps, paper and all the other supplies needed to fill and package prescriptions and operate a pharmacy.

He checked to his right and saw another doorway deeper into the hall. Stepping out, he marched four steps and stood before it. Turning the knob, he pushed it open and was relieved to see it possessed a toilet and a sink. Jason stepped in, quickly unburdened himself and returned to the office.

Thirty seconds after returning to Pettigrew's office, the owner reappeared. They both took their seats and the interview resumed.

"Ready?"

"Shoot," Jason replied in a dry whisper, suddenly regretting his choice of words.

"Okay. Here we go."

Pettigrew started slowly. "Why pharmacy?"

Jason answered honestly, "I'm good in chemistry and math. And I want to help patients."

Pettigrew nodded as if to say, "I've heard that one a million times before." He flipped a page and fired another question. "What kind of pharmacy do you want to practice?"

Jason pretended to think for a moment. He'd anticipated this question. "I'm not sure. I will decide after my externships."

"I see from your resume that you worked in at a pharmacy in York County all last year as an intern."

"That's correct."

"But you stopped when school ended?"

"Yes."

"Why?" Pettigrew challenged.

"I wanted to continue working on the weekends. But the position was cut."

"Ah," Pettigrew sympathized. "There's a lot of that going on in the chains these days." Pettigrew paused. "Yet, you did not pursue other jobs?"

"Yes, I did."

"What happened?"

"I applied for several positions, but they wanted more hours than I could give. And I did not think it would be fair to take a job knowing that I would have to cut back on my hours once the externships began. It would not be fair to them."

Pettigrew nodded. *I may have scored a few points*, Jason thought.

"Plus, I was away for two weeks on a trip during the summer--"

"Jason," Pettigrew interrupted. "Let me explain. Being a pharmacist cannot be learned just by taking externships. If you want to be a competent pharmacist, you must practice your craft from the time you hit P2 until you graduate. We are always learning and perfecting our practices, every day. You can never stop learning. So, what did you do with your time this past summer?"

"I had the opportunity to travel to South America."

"Vacation?"

"Charity work."

"What kind of work?"

"I went to Ecuador with a local Rotary club to help build footbridges so residents could have access to healthcare, food and water."

"Ecuador, huh?"

"What did you learn?"

"That I'm incredibly lucky to live in the States. And I'm even luckier that I don't have to wonder where my next meal is coming from."

Jason still cringed at the memory of his trip to Ecuador. He'd interceded when he saw a man roughing up his wife. Jason's actions had insulted and infuriated the husband and almost caused the trip to come to an instantaneous halt.

Pettigrew gave him a satisfied nod. "Very good," the pharmacist said. "Okay, those were the softball questions. Here's the meat of it."

For the next forty minutes, Thomas Pettigrew fired questions at Jason like a prosecutor cross-examining a hostile witness. His tone was professional but firm. He wanted succinct, to-the-point responses. His queries tested Jason's knowledge of chemistry, pharmaceutics, drug therapy, pharmacy law, pharmacy calculations, ethics and pharmacokinetics. He read from a prepared document that was a half-inch thick. The dog-eared corners told Jason that it had been well-used and

Pettigrew had posed the questions therein to many previous victims. Some of the pages looked to be torn and taped back together.

At first, the pace of the questioning was slow and relaxed. After the first few questions, Pettigrew paused, allowing Jason time to compose his responses.

Then, in an effort to test not only his knowledge but his composure, Pettigrew shifted into a higher gear. Pettigrew did not ask a string of questions from one discipline. Instead, he jumped from topic to topic, asking a clinical question about a specific drug therapy in a specific medical condition then would follow that with a more mundane question about pharmacy law and paperwork requirements. The technique kept Jason off balance and uneasy. The acid in his belly churned hot and fast.

Jason perused the file cabinets of his mind trying to retrieve each answer. The varied nature of the topics queried caused him to have to run from file cabinet to file cabinet at opposite ends of his brain, locate the correct drawer, run his fingers over the files and finally pull out the correct document. Then he had to run to next imaginary cabinet. Pettigrew's questions shot from his lips, harder, faster and with more intensity. And several times, he had to stop and think about his answer. As the interview progressed, Jason found himself simply gasping "ums" and "ahs" unable to answer before the next interrogatory spewed from Pettigrew's lips.

When Pettigrew fired the last volley across his desk, Jason was mentally and physically exhausted. The thin shred of unstable confidence he'd carried into the meeting had been sandblasted into oblivion. He sat now with a deer-in-the-headlights, unfocused gaze at the owner of The Colonial, the monument of a man who held the roadmap to Jason's future. *Would Pettigrew allow him access to his externship and possibly a rarified opportunity? Or would he be relegated to the heap of other undeserving applicants who would merely go on to become minnows in an enormous pharmacy ocean?*

Jason wanted to ask, "How did I do?" But he was too exhausted—and too afraid of the response--to deliver the question.

Pettigrew tossed the sheaf of papers onto his desk with a breezy thud. He peered at Jason for an excruciatingly long moment. "I have one more question for you," he said sotto voce.

"Yessir."

"What philosophy should dictate your practice of pharmacy?"

Jason opened his mouth instinctively to answer, expecting that only a second would be allowed for him to respond. But he had no idea what answer to give. Pettigrew raised a long hand, cutting him off before any sound belched awkwardly from his lips.

"You and I," Pettigrew declared in a deep, powerful baritone, "have undertaken a very respected profession. Did you know that pharmacists are often more respected than doctors and clergy?"

"No."

"They are. We are a respected bunch. I've had patients tell me that their doctor instructed them to do such and such. But they wanted to ask me before they did anything."

Jason nodded. A fiery anxiety burned in his chest. In one of his professional practice classes, he had briefly considered his professional mantra, but whatever ruminations had bubbled into his mind in the past failed to appear now. Pettigrew held up his hand again as if he were reading Jason's mind.

"I want you to think about your answer for a few minutes. I must check more prescriptions. When I come back, I will hear your response. If I'm pleased, I will consider taking you on as one of my externs. It should be one short sentence, appropriate and succinct. Then be prepared to defend it." Pettigrew stood, brushed past Jason and left the small office.

Jason sat confused and perplexed for a moment. He felt as if he'd run five miles at a full sprint. Drained and perspiring, he puffed out two long breaths. He stood, again straightening his cramping leg muscles.

That's when he heard the words, "Are you the pharmacy student?"

CHAPTER 7

Jason spun at the sound of the voice behind him. It was the same young woman who had spoken to him earlier, taunting him about how the pain would not last long. And then she had tossed a teasing and playful, "Have fun!" at him. Jason stood transfixed and responded with a vacant, desultory stare. He was not confused by the question. Just mentally exhausted. He was not interested and did not possess the capacity to engage in any kind of banter, flirtatious or otherwise, with this woman. She seemed only interested in having a laugh at his expense.

She ignored or seemed not to notice Jason's lack of a response.

"Has he asked you the question yet?" She asked. "You know the same one he asks every intern—"

"If I get it, I would be an extern, not an intern," Jason replied, recovering some of his energy.

"Whatever," the woman retorted. "Did he ask you?" she repeated. "You know, 'How are you going to be the best pharmacist or something like that?'" She added air quotes around the word "pharmacist".

A thought struck him. He had sought out a handful of now-graduated pharmacists who had been selected by Pettigrew for externships in previous years. Jason had asked for their feedback and advice about the interview process. Why had Jason not been given any forewarning about this last, apparently vital question? Perhaps it was because, like Jason, they had all been flabbergasted by the process. But there was no time to ponder the issue now. He was here and the question had been posed, casting its lengthening shadow over Jason's future.

He was a desperate man in an endless desert stretching in every direction searching for an oasis with an answer. This woman stood before him. Perhaps she could help. She did after all work here. "He's coming back in a few minutes. Got any advice?" Jason asked.

"I sure do," she smiled. Her eyes brimmed with a devilish sparkle. Then she spun and walked away, disappearing from the doorway for the second time this morning.

It was as if a mirage had appeared and then suddenly evaporated. The confidence and cocksureness with which she'd delivered her reply sent waves of anticipatory hope through him. Adrenaline surged. His exhaustion evaporated. Now he stood on the edge of salvation. *Was an answer in sight? Or had it melted away as quickly as it had come?*

Was all this just his imagination?

His next act was not a conscious one. It was something one did instinctively, desperately, when one's life was on the line. A fight or flight response; failure to act would jeopardize one's existence. Jason took two long, hurried strides into the hallway.

The young woman had not gone far. She leaned against the wall, beaming. "That didn't take long."

"Are you having fun?" Jason hissed, instantly angry with himself, certain he was being played.

"I sure am. So, do you want the answer?"

"I want this externship. If you have information that will help me, I'd like to know what it is."

This girl with the pristine skin and the face of cherubic innocence betrayed by mischievous eyes lurked on the cusp of full womanhood. Like him, she was in her early twenties and had passed through the wispy, nebulous teenage years into adulthood. But small remnants of youthful exuberance still clung to her like tinsel from a Christmas tree in early January about to be stored for the coming year. He cast a furtive glance at her. The pharmacy smock failed to hide her ample breasts and tightly curved hips.

"I like a man that goes after what he wants."

Jason smirked. "You're just playing games. You don't have any advice." He turned to re-enter the cramped office.

"Oh, I have the exact answer he's looking for," she persisted.

Jason hesitated, now, wondering who this woman was. "And how do you know that?"

"Because he told me."

"Who are you? Do you work here?"

"You can call me Chrissie. And I work here in a manner of speaking."

Jason glanced toward the end of the hallway where light from the prescription department spilled into the darkened space. The sound of ringing phones and muffled conversations drifted through the opening like faint whispers.

"So, what's it gonna take to get the answer?"

"Dinner."

"Dinner? Do you do this to all the externs, Chrissie?"

"No, as a matter of fact, you're the first."

"I have two questions. Why am I so privileged? And why don't I believe that?"

"You better decide," she declared, her tone turning serious. "He's gonna be back soon."

"First, tell me why you want to help me."

"Because you're cute. I saw you come in. You've got a nice ass," she declared as a faint blush reddened her cheeks.

Jason huffed, glancing away. Then a smile spread slowly over his face. *She's playing me*, he thought. Her audacious ability to dangle this golden morsel in front of him had somehow dulled the sharp edge of his anxiety. Still, anxiousness ebbed and flowed like violent gusts of storm-laden winds. Yeah, she was playing him. But for some reason, he liked it.

"So, what's it gonna be?"

"Okay, I'll buy you dinner. But only if I get the externship. Deal?"

"Uh-uh. Maybe you won't use the answer I give you. Or you won't deliver it correctly. It's dinner or nothing regardless of the outcome of your interview. What you do with the information is up to you." She twirled strands of hair around a finger. "Deal or no deal?"

Jason sighed. A genuine smile formed on his lips for the first time this morning. "Okay, deal."

Chrissie stuck out a hand. Jason pumped it once. Her skin was soft and cool. She leaned in and placed her mouth near his right ear. The lavender scent of her perfumed shampoo enveloped his face and head. As the words slipped from her lips, gentle wisps of breath caressed his ear.

Jason nodded. Of course, he thought. It makes perfect sense.

"Don't tell him I told you. He'll be pissed and you won't get the spot."

Jason smiled. He made a motion of locking his lips with a key. Then he said, "That is of course, as long as I get the spot. Otherwise, who knows? I might have to squeal."

"I wouldn't do that," she cautioned.

"Why not?"

"Then he'll know you didn't come up it with on your own. And if you don't get the externship and then tell him I gave you the answer, my father will report you to the school for having cheated on the interview. Then you're really screwed." Chrissie made air quotes around the word "cheated".

Jason screwed his lips to one side.

Chrissie smiled. She'd trumped him. "Oh, one more thing. I translated the phrase into Latin. I think he'll be impressed." She leaned in again. Her soft auburn locks brushed his cheek as she whispered again. Jason repeated the words incorrectly. Chrissie corrected him. Jason repeated them back twice and Chrissie nodded her approval.

She moved back to her computer terminal. Three minutes later, Thomas returned to the office doorway. Jason stood near the wall, waiting.

"Okay," Pettigrew asked. "Do you have an answer to my question?"

Jason smiled, glanced toward Chrissie at her computer station, engrossed in something on the screen. "I think I do," Jason responded, his tone exponentially more optimistic. "I think I do."

CHAPTER 8

Chrissie had just finished inputting invoices into The Colonial's financial software program which would later be delivered via disk along with the hard copies to The Colonial's accountant when the door to her father's small office swung open. She caught the tail end of the conversation.

"...must say," her father bellowed. "You are the first extern who has given me an answer like that. It was spot on. How did you come up with it?"

'Well, sir," came Jason's reply. "I must admit I was a little flustered earlier. All the rapid-fire questions caught me off guard. The time you gave me to think about it allowed me to clear my mind. It came back to me as if it had been whispered by an angel."

"Well, Jason, retail pharmacy is a pressure cooker. You must think on your feet. You are going to be presented with all kinds of unexpected questions and requests. That's the purpose of the questions and the machine gun technique. I will tell you I especially liked the Latin translation."

Chrissie smiled as she pretended to study the computer screen. She could feel Jason's gaze burning into the back of her neck. The two men made their way down the hall and passed her location on their way back into the pharmacy.

"When do you think I'll know if I have one of the spots?" Jason asked.

Thomas Pettigrew paused and let out a resigned sigh. "I don't usually do this, Jason. Normally, I get back to the school in seven days with my list. But I am so impressed with your interview, especially your last answer, that I am going to give you your choice of the slots. Do you have a preference?" Pettigrew produced a paper with the dates of the available externships for the year.

"Well," Jason began, "there are a couple of hospital externships I was interested in taking early in the year. I was hoping for the spring?"

"Done," Pettigrew pronounced. Her father leaned over the paper he'd placed on the counter, clicked his pen and scribbled Jason's name into the second to last opening near the end of the school year.

Chrissie watched them shake hands. Jason cast her a glance as her father turned to walk him out. He winked in her direction and mouthed "thank you". She smiled and winked back.

CHAPTER 9

Simon scribbled an answer into one of the crosswords he was working in the thick, soft-covered, magazine-like publication: *A Thousand Crossword Puzzles*. In the weeks he and Victor had been handed this bullshit assignment, he had finished half of them--recently graduating to the medium-hard difficulty level.

Beside him in the driver's seat, Victor lay back in the reclined seat and had been in that state of repose for the last fifteen minutes. Currently in a coma-like slumber, his snoring sounded like the rumble of a passing freight train.

To avoid being noticed or having anyone call the police, every thirty minutes, they moved, repositioning the car in different locations. Since eight this morning, they had spent time in the parking lots across the street from The Colonial at the Walgreens, the nearby credit union and finally, they'd found their way to the Sonic fast-food joint because Victor needed a second breakfast. He'd scarfed down two breakfast sandwiches, two orders of hash browns and a massive cup of black coffee before falling asleep. Simon was relieved that he had some time to himself—and relief from Victor's incessant smoking.

The scrawny agent glanced across Jefferson Avenue and witnessed the young man in the blue suit and red tie leaving the pharmacy. He threw down the crossword puzzle and lifted the long lens of the Nikon to his face. He did not click off any frames. They had enough photos of him. He just wanted to see the look on his face. Expressions told much.

Now, this young man appeared to be walking on clouds. His gait was erect, unstressed and possessed a cheery spring had materialized in his step. A wide smile spread across his lips involving his entire face. The dour, ominous look from earlier had vanished. He tossed his car keys into the air several times. Each time catching them as if he'd just won the lottery.

In the next few days, the dossier would be compiled.

As the young man reached his piece of shit Honda, the pharmacy door swung open and Christine Pettigrew, Thomas's daughter, exited, making a beeline for the young man. Simon pulled the Mont Blanc from his shirt pocket and began twirling it.

℞

Chrissie caught up with Jason as he reached his car. "Hey, there," she called out.

Jason had unlocked the doors with his key fob and was about to open the driver side when he stopped. "Well, hello again."

"I overheard you coming out of the office. Very impressive."

"Yes, I'm quite happy. Thank you very much."

"You weren't trying to escape without getting my number, were you?"

"No," Jason replied. "I didn't think it would be appropriate to ask you where you wanted to have dinner right after the interview in there. I'm sure Thomas would have figured it all out."

"True," Chrissie countered. "I just wanted to make sure you didn't get away."

"I always pay my debts, Chrissie."

"Is that what this is...a debt payment?"

"Didn't we make a deal? You lived up to your end of the bargain. Now, I'll live up to mine. Where do you want to have dinner?"

Chrissie nodded. "Yes, we did make a deal. But I prefer to think of this as a date?"

"A date!?" Jason grinned, more to himself than her. "I get the impression you get whatever you want, don't you?" A thought struck Jason. "By the way, what are you going to tell Mr. Pettigrew about why you came running after me as soon as the interview was over. You're going to give me away!"

"No worries. He's back in his office taking a phone call from a state senator about some legislation about reimbursements or something. He didn't see me leave."

"What about all the other employees?"

"Fear not, they're all cool. They think I'm giving you the form for your background check. Here it is." Chrissie handed Jason folded piece of paper.

"Very inventive. You should have been a spy." Jason breathed a relieved sigh. "So where do you want to have dinner?"

Chrissie cast him a knowing smile. "Vintage Tavern."

"Vintage Tavern. Never heard of it."

"It's in Suffolk across the JRB. Just opened. Very..." Chrissie held up her hand and rubbed her thumb and first two fingers together. "And very chic. I hope you saved up," she said with a cautionary tone. "Do you have a pen?"

As a new round of perspiration dribbled down his spine, Jason fished a Bic from the inside of his suit coat and handed it over. She motioned for his hand. Jason extended it. Chrissie placed his hand in hers. An electric surge coursed up his arm as she scribbled her number on his palm.

"This is my cell phone. Call me or text me. Do not call me on the store phone. If my Dad finds out we have a date, you can kiss your externship good-bye. Got it?"

"Do you want my number?" Jason asked.

"No. I'll get it off your resume in his office when I have a minute."

Jason yanked open the Honda's door with a squeal. He stopped and asked, "Dad?" Did you say, 'Dad?'"

Chrissie grinned like Jason had unlocked a long-sought after mystery. "Another reason you can't tell him. Do...you...get...it?"

"Ah...yeah. Got it," Jason said with a slack jawed smile and a quick shake of his head.

She spun and strode back toward the pharmacy. He sank onto the hot vinyl seat, oblivious to the stifling heat of the cab, too pre-occupied with watching Christine Pettigrew trek back inside. Beneath her pharmacy lab coat, her slender hips moved with the fluidity and grace of a model on the catwalk. He watched the door for several moments after she disappeared inside. The memory of her scent and the soft lilt of her voice in his ear consumed him. Then his mind turned to the atomic bomb she just dropped.

Thomas Pettigrew was Chrissie's father!

Jason whispered aloud, "Jason, Jason, what the hell have you gotten yourself into?"

CHAPTER 10

Cloaked in the elegant charm of a southern plantation, the Vintage Tavern restaurant greeted drivers speeding along Bridge Road and those electing to enter the exclusive Governor's Pointe subdivision in Suffolk. It served a chic, decadent combination of American and Mediterranean fare delivered with in a nineteenth century ambience of a Scottish castle. Though the construction was new, it exuded an antebellum seductiveness laced with an upper crust aura that the well-to-do found satisfying to their discerning palates and overstuffed pocketbooks.

Jason pulled off Bridge Road and onto Governor's Pointe Drive. The first hundred yards were lined with mature, blooming crepe myrtles of white and crimson. Verdant, foliage-draped limbs arched lazily over the roadway, covering the lush median in shade. He negotiated the Honda onto the rich black and sun-and-shade dappled asphalt of the parking area and looped along the circular drive fronting a gabled portico supported by pristine, white tapered columns set on field stone pedestals.

The rusted, aging Civic seemed like the cheap prize from a box of Cracker Jacks compared to the gleaming, sleek BMWs, Cadillacs and

Mercedes Jason's rattle trap glided noisily past. The door of the restaurant was a round-topped, walnut affair bordered by glass and wrought iron and set in an elegant fieldstone wall, flanked on either side by two matching bronze sconces. Beside the entrance, an oversized stand held an equally oversized menu touting tonight's fare.

Alighting from the vehicle, he hurried to the passenger side. With a stiff yank, the door screeched open. Jason held out his hand. Chrissie clasped it as if exiting a royal carriage. He escorted her under the portico. Chrissie waited there as Jason returned to the Honda and slipped the car into an empty spot between a large black Audi and a spotless white Cadillac Escalade.

Hurrying back to the entrance, Jason allowed himself a moment to soak in Chrissie's natural beauty. She possessed a curvaceous, enticing physique: ample breasts, slim waist, trim rounded hips, and the long, toned legs of a ballerina. Her caramel eyes and blushed cheeks held a fading quality of adolescent exuberance which was rapidly yielding to the piercing, confident bearing of a poised woman who would have her pick of available men. Jason could see that she used extraordinarily little make-up. There was no need. The perfectly smooth skin of her face glowed in the fading summer light.

Chrissie wore a white lightweight floral print summer dress with a plunging backline crisscrossed with straps. Her bare legs flowed from the ruffled high-low skirt into a pair of white ankle strap heels. The whole outfit hugged the waving curves of a perfectly proportioned body now much more apparent without the lab jacket. The evening dress accentuated the swell of her breasts and slender legs. Her physique-to which it tantalizingly clung-radiated a cool, comfortable sexiness.

Jason swung open the restaurant's heavy door. Chrissie tucked a few strands of caramel hair behind her ear. With a downward tilt of her head, she cast him a sideways peek. Her caramel eyes twinkled.

"Thank you," she said. "You've been quite the gentleman so far, Jason. I'm impressed."

Jason smiled and made a small wave inviting her to enter. He followed her into a vaulted dark-wooded foyer and they were greeted by the wide smile of a pleasant maître d' behind a small podium. She pulled up the reservation and led them into the expansive dining area. Tables of various sizes were artfully arranged in the center while wide, comfy booths hugged the perimeter. The Old English country motif possessed a regal air. Large rectangular windows embedded in the dark wood filtered the pleasant late afternoon glow. Jason felt like he had stepped into a different era: that of a long-gone golden epoch of European castles, knights and maidens. To his left, a gorgeous, gigantic stone fireplace sat idle as the din of comfortable conversation, the clink of heavy flatware on expensive china and easy laughter perfused the space.

They were seated near the center of the room at a small square table for two. Their server, a middle-aged woman with a warm, easy smile clad in a white button-downed shirt and black trousers, appeared instantly, welcomed them and efficiently accepted their drink orders. A second server materialized, filled both water glasses and placed a basket of bread and butter wrapped in cloth between them. A minute later, the waitress returned and placed the drinks before them: a gin and tonic with a lemon and a lime for Jason and a glass of chardonnay for Chrissie. She asked if they had ever dined with Vintage. Jason and Chrissie both replied in the negative. She welcomed them and moved off. When she was out of ear shot, a moment of awkward silence yawned between them, so they busied themselves with their menus.

"So," Jason started, filling the quietude. "Thank you for your help with the externship." He raised his gin and tonic. Chrissie clinked hers against it.

"My pleasure," Chrissie replied. "And by the way, we ran your background check. Thanks for getting it back so quickly. It came back clean."

"I wasn't worried."

"Just remember, you didn't hear that from me."

"Roger that."

On Monday, Jason had been stymied by Pettigrew during the interview. His normally cocksure confidence had been shaken under the man's withering onslaught of machine gun questions. He'd feared that he had not impressed the pharmacist. Jason doubted his performance would have landed him an invitation for one of the precious eight slots.

Luckily, Chrissie had shown an interest in him and had negotiated dinner in exchange for the key phrase that seemed to change his fortune. She had given him exactly what he needed to get a leg up on the competition: a well-crafted, four-word phrase about what it meant to be a pharmacist. And, to boot, she'd translated it into Latin. Thomas Pettigrew had been floored. After Chrissie's lateral, Jason had thrown the game-winning touchdown pass with just seconds left on the clock.

Their server returned, explained the day's specials and asked if they were ready to order. They decided against appetizers and recited their choices.

"Considera aegrum totum," Jason said when they were alone again, repeating the phrase he'd dropped on her father four days earlier. "The Latin was a nice touch. Even your father didn't know what it meant."

Chrissie's smile widened. "Consider the whole patient!"

"Do you know what it means?" Jason asked.

"Yeah, think of the whole person."

Jason nodded. "That's right. Take everything about the patient into account: their lifestyle, family, their financial situation, their cognitive abilities, their habits and not just their disease states and medications.

Consider the whole patient." He paused then said, "I have a question for you."

Chrissie nodded for him to continue.

"I asked as many people as I could about the interview for your father's externship. People who had been externs with him. Not one of them mentioned the question he asked me at the end of the interview. You know, 'What philosophy will dictate how you practice pharmacy?'. Why? I would think they would have warned me."

"Well, I guess I'm glad they didn't, otherwise we wouldn't be sitting here right now on this date, would we?"

"Good point," Jason said with a shrug. "Do you know why no one mentioned it?"

Chrissie nodded. "He added the question late in the school year this past spring. So maybe you didn't ask any of those candidates. There were only three or four. Two were last minute replacements for folks that dropped out."

"So why did you do it?"

The answer to the question was put on hold as their waitress appeared with a massive, circular tray on which rested two plates of steaming food. A thick Delmonico steak and a side of French fries the size of railroad ties for him and a heaping bowl of Fettuccini Alfredo ringed with steamed broccoli for her. When the waitress departed, they agreed their meals looked and smelled fabulous. They ate in silence for a few minutes, forgetting for the moment Jason's question. As he chewed on the steak, he continued to wrestle internally with his dilemma.

Chrissie's comment about the fortuitousness of their serendipitous encounter at the pharmacy that led to their current "date" rustled an uneasiness in Jason. She was correct, of course. Had Jason known about the question in advance he might not have needed her help with the answer. Or so he hoped.

The issue that bothered him now--and which had for the last few days--was Chrissie's underlying assumption that this was a date. He'd not bothered to push the issue with her at the pharmacy. Mostly because he needed her answer and he had not wanted to poke this proverbial she-bear and potentially, ultimately steer her away from giving it to him.

But here she was using that word again. *Date.* Obviously, Christine Pettigrew was in the market for male companionship. And a target was painted squarely on Jason's back.

It wasn't that Jason wouldn't normally be interested. He was as much a testosterone-charged, twenty-something as the next guy. And she was, without a doubt, a knockout. If she were anyone else except the progeny and current employee of one Thomas Pettigrew, the high priest of pharmacy in the Tidewater and Richmond areas, Jason would pursue her with relish and abandon.

"So no boyfriend?" he asked.

Chrissie pressed her lips into a tight line. "I wouldn't have asked you for dinner if there was."

"That's good to know. But I'm wondering why not?"

"I broke up with him about four months ago."

"What went wrong?"

Chrissie's eye narrowed. "Getting personal, aren't we?"

"Just curious."

She shrugged as if to say what the hell then continued. "If you must know, Blake was a first-rate, dyed-in-the-wool ass kisser. He had no spine. Gave me everything I wanted. Never disagreed with me. After six months, it got old."

Jason smiled.

"What?" Chrissie asked.

"I thought that would be the case."

"Oh really? Are you some kind of relationship guru?"

"Women like you don't want it easy. You want a challenge. Most women do for that matter."

Chrissie shook her head. "And what about you? There's no girlfriend I need to worry about?"

"No," he replied.

A delighted glint flashed in her eyes. "Would you still have taken me to dinner if there were?"

"Yes, I would have told her the truth and still paid my debt."

In the days since his interview and after much internal deliberation, Jason had decided he would fulfill his obligation to Chrissie. But that's all. She was an intelligent, motivated, mischievous woman with the magnetic bearing of an up-and-coming actress. But when this "date" was over, he was going to send her--as politely and as gently as possible--packing. In fact, he had thought about telling her that he had a girlfriend or that he had just gotten out of a long relationship and was not ready for another. It would have been the easiest way to disentangle himself from any future "dates". But that was not his style. She was trying to coax him into a relationship. He knew he should set her straight now. But it was too early in the evening and he did not want to spoil the mood.

He had called the number Chrissie had scribbled on his palm on Wednesday, two days after his interview. It was a calculated but riskless move on his part. In the dating world, women held all the cards. Like the male peacock and the colorful mallard or the male of any species, they showed off for the females, trying to impress them into taking them as mates. It was no different, Jason thought, with the human species. Males pursued. Women decided. Like everything else in the natural world, dating and the pursuit of romance were a Darwinian competition.

But these days, those norms were changing and beginning to erode the natural order of such things. As was evidenced by Chrissie's forwardness on Monday. Jason liked it. Generally, though, men tried to impress with their witty repartee, their dress, their earning potential and, ultimately, their attractiveness and suitableness for procreation. Astute suitors picked up on subtle and not-so-subtle feminine clues. Women learned from a young age how to signal potential mates that they were interested, with come-hither looks and cute flirtatious responses. They also learned how to deftly dodge men that did not interest them. It was a difficult and hard-to-understand game of cat-and-mouse. Men, when they were interested in a woman or thought they'd received the telltale clues, approached the meticulous female, placing themselves in a no-man's land of uncertainty. If the woman agreed to a date, their days and weeks, no matter how bad, were transformed into utter successes. If they were rejected, it could be a crushing blow. There was no more personal triumph or rejection. And during his life a man would experience both.

But Chrissie had made it clear to him she was interested. She'd taken all the guesswork out of it. *Here I am,* she'd said. *Come and get me!*

Chrissie, obviously beautiful and seemingly intelligent, was anything but subtle. And she had negotiated her way into it. Romantically and socially, Chrissie had done his work for him. At the same time, her overture had taken the pressure off Jason.

He hadn't been looking for a date on Monday. Jason *had* noticed Chrissie that day in the pharmacy. You had to be blind not to. But he had been so pre-occupied by his interview, trying to talk her up and getting her number was the last thing on his mind. Hell, it wasn't even on his radar. And even though she was now a blinking icon on his screen, Jason was not about to bring this sleek, gorgeous plane in for a landing.

So, knowing she wanted to go out with him and that their date was a forgone conclusion, Jason had flexed this rarely used male muscle. He waited until Wednesday, late Wednesday, before calling her, making her wait more than forty-eight hours.

The thought had occurred to him to call her and postpone the evening until next week. But two things prevented him from doing so.

First, to say Jason wanted this externship badly was like saying that a hurricane was just another storm. If he hadn't completely failed during the initial part of his interview with Thomas Pettigrew, he had been nothing more than perfectly mediocre. He'd done nothing to stand out from his competitors – of that he was certain. Chrissie had saved him.

Second, Jason now owed her. He needed to make good on his part of the deal. His father had taught him from a young age to be in-debted to as few people as possible. But when you were, he told his son, pay them quickly and put it behind you. Even though he'd been arm-twisted into it, this was a debt Jason was happy to pay. If he per-formed well months from now during the externship, this debt would pay dividends for years to come. But he told himself, there would only be one dinner. He didn't need the complication of romance right now, especially with the daughter of Thomas Pettigrew.

Nonetheless, he couldn't help but notice her simple, enticing beau-ty now. It was an allure that couldn't be hidden behind a lab coat, a pair of slacks or the hum of a busy pharmacy. But tonight, it really shone. Chrissie was a knockout. She had all the goods, at least physically. And she seemed to have the smarts and personality to match. The combi-nation was enchanting, endearing and captivating. He'd recognized it as soon as she descended the stairs of her family home in the Hiden quarter of Newport News.

Chrissie had called him late Friday afternoon and said that she would be home alone all evening. Jason knew that Thomas would be working at The Colonial. And evidently, her mother, Eleanor, had made last minute plans. So Chrissie told him he was free to arrive at her doorstep like any other man picking up his date. This would probably be the only time in the near future it would happen, she warned.

After he rang the bell, Chrissie texted saying that she was still getting ready and to let himself in. So Jason pushed open the door and waited nervously in the small foyer at the base of the stairs.

After several minutes, she appeared at the top of the steps. Jason's heart gave a sideways lurch as his eyes absorbed the exquisite vision of her in the summer dress hugging her tightly in all the right places and flowing everywhere else, the silky, auburn locks, curled and smooth, framing the flawless skin and dark, moist eyes, bouncing as she navigated the stairs. It was a vision Jason knew he would not soon forget.

He'd also caught glimpses of her as they chatted on the drive to the restaurant and as he strode toward her at the front door of the restaurant. He wanted to stare at her and soak in the whole visual tableau but doing so would have been awkward and creepy.

Jason shook his head, clearing the notion from his mind.

"You okay," she inquired. "You were a million miles away."

"Ah...yeah. Just remembered something I needed to do."

"So, do you want me to answer the question?"

"What question?"

"About why I gave you the answer?"

"Yeah," Jason said.

"I told you," Chrissie replied. "I think you're cute."

"And I have a nice ass," Jason added with a grin.

"Maybe," she hedged.

"But that's what you said on Monday."

"A girl can change her mind."

"Oh, I see. So can a guy," he countered. After a beat, he added, "So do you always ask out your father's students?"

Chrissie grinned in spite of herself. "No, but I do mess with them once in a while."

"Like you did with me?"

"No, you're different."

"So, how do you mess with them?"

Chrissie leaned over the table as if she were revealing state secrets. "Last year, one of the candidates was a complete moron. He thought he had a spot sewn up. He came on to me ten minutes before his meeting with my father. He was an Italian named Manny McLean. A real greaseball."

"No shit? McLean sounds Irish."

"Must be Italian on his mother's side." Chrissie nodded. "But I took care of his ass," she grinned.

"Don't keep me in suspense."

"Daddy has a small compounding section locked in one of his drawers under the pharmacy counter. There are some old amber bottles with yellowed labels on them. One of them is croton oil." Jason sensed that Christine Pettigrew was a strong, self-assured woman. Her use of the word "Daddy" did not make her sound or appear weak, dependent or spoiled. The word simply conveyed her love and respect for the man.

"Croton oil?" Jason had never heard of the compound.

"Yeah, it's a purgative. My father offered the idiot some coffee and he said yes. Daddy asked me to get him a cup. I did. But I added two drops of croton oil and some cascara sagrada to Manny's cuppa Joe."

"So what happened?"

"You know what a purgative is?"

"Yeah, a strong laxative."

"Yeah, but croton oil acts very quickly. It's an irritant to the GI system. So evidently, he sucked down the coffee. By the end of the interview, my father said he started smelling a foul odor coming from across his desk. Good ol' Manny had shit his pants. Had to run to the bathroom. We found his soiled undies in the trash can in the bathroom."

Jason's eyes widened in shock, then he laughed out loud. "Remind me never to piss you off." His thoughts shifted to the unpleasant news he would deliver to this woman later tonight. "Did your father know?"

"I told him that Manny had asked me out and acted inappropriately. That guaranteed he wouldn't get a spot. I didn't tell him about the croton oil until a few months later. He was furious with me. Made me promise never to do anything like that ever again. Of course, we told no one in the pharmacy. And I'm swearing you to secrecy. It could get him in trouble with the school or the Board of Pharmacy."

Jason showed her the palms of his hands. "Forgot about it already. Anything else?"

"Yeah, there's been a few others. You remember the papers he used to ask you the questions?"

Jason nodded. "They looked old and tattered."

"He's never reprints the questions. Just make notes about new questions in the margins or adds pages. Two years ago, I glued the tops and bottoms of the pages together. He had to rip the pages apart one by one. Messed them all up."

"And he knew it was you?"

Chrissie nodded. "Most definitely. He locks the questions in his desk now. I just gave him my best eye flutter and 'I'm sorry, Daddy'. Eventually, he got over it."

They each sipped their drinks and fell into a comfortable silence.

"You have nice eyes," Chrissie said. "I do think your cute. There must be something about you if I'm giving up secrets over our first dinner."

"Thanks," he replied. "I'll keep your secrets safe."

"So, what about me?"

Jason's forehead wrinkled. "What about you?"

"Do you think I'm cute?"

Jason shook his head. He noticed a flush swim over her features. "Did you tell me I'm cute just so I could give you a compliment?"

"No," Chrissie pouted. "I don't do that."

"Then why did you ask me if I think you're cute?"

She frowned and shook her head. "Never mind."

The uncomfortable silence returned. Finally, Jason spoke. "Fine, I'll give you an answer."

"Fine," she replied, not looking at him as she fingered her fork.

Jason waited another moment until she looked up. He smiled. "The truth is I don't think you're cute."

Chrissie shoulders deflated. The edges of her mouth dipped into a frown. Her lips pushed out a tortured pout. He could see a frustrated hurt building in her eyes.

Jason hesitated, letting her disappointment fester thoroughly, enjoying the small amount of torture he was inflicting. Then he leaned toward her. A wide smile inched across his face. "I think you're much more than cute."

Chrissie's face lit up again. "Oh, yeah?"

"Yeah."

"Well, don't keep a girl in suspense." Chrissie studied him. She leaned in. Her head moved closer to him.

"I think you are D-D-F-G."

"D-D-F-G? What does that mean? Is that even a compliment?"

"On believe me," Jason continued. "It is a compliment. A very nice compliment."

"Tell me."

Jason smirked. "Maybe later. If you're good."

Chrissie sighed. It seemed to Jason to be a mixture of frustration, relief and anticipation. Then her mouth slipped into a knowing smile.

At that moment, the waitress reappeared once again to check on the quality of their food and ask if there was anything else they needed. When she departed, Jason decided it was time to change the subject.

"So, you aren't going to be a pharmacist and take over your father's pharmacy?"

"Hell no," she retorted. "I hate chemistry and medicine... too much memorization. I'm a numbers girl. Love them, in fact. I'm studying to be an accountant at Tech. I graduate next May and then I'm taking the CPA exam."

"But you work as a pharmacy tech with your father?"

"Only because he needs the help. I can count, pour, lick, and stick like the rest of them. But I also handle his books and invoices and pay the bills. And I did work for my father."

"You did?"

"Yeah, my time working at The Colonial is over. I'm starting as an intern at an accounting firm in City Center. My first day was Wednesday. The day you called me. I've been there all week. As a matter of fact, I have to go into the office tomorrow morning for a while."

"Oh," Jason answered. "What firm?"

"Casper, White and Collins."

"Good luck."

This news surprised Jason. The fact that Chrissie was still working for The Colonial was one of the arrows in his quiver he had planned to deploy in his argument against them dating. To his consternation, the weight of that quiver just lightened.

"Thanks, but I don't need luck. Luck is simply hard work that meets opportunity."

"I see. Did you come up with that?"

"No, I read it somewhere. But it's true. Hardworking people get more chances to succeed."

"Your father is hardworking. He's a very well-respected man in pharmacy. Many students scratch and claw to get an externship with him." Jason moved his gin and tonic to his lips and sipped.

"I know. But he's really a softie."

"To you, his daughter, maybe. Inside the walls of the MCV, he's prosecutor, judge and jury. A glowing review from Thomas Pettigrew means you can write your own ticket."

"Is that your goal, to write your own ticket?"

"Of course. If you're going to do something, why not be the best? I want to be successful, don't you? Isn't that why you're studying to be an accountant?"

"I want to do work I like. I like numbers."

"Okay, so then you'll work for free. Money doesn't matter?"

"No, I didn't say that," Chrissie retorted. "I want to make a decent living. But I don't want to hate what I do."

"I agree," Jason said. "My work is important to me as well."

"But so is money, right?" Chrissie lifted a roll from the basket, tore off a chunk and daintily slipped it between her lips.

"Of course, it is. Life is a competition, Chrissie. I like competition. I pay attention to details. It's why I'm a decent student. Money is one measure of a person's success."

"That sounds awfully unsavory."

"No, it's not. It's just one measure. There are others."

"Like?"

"Well, there's success with family. Friends. Charitable work. Things like that."

"So, what does a successful family mean?"

"It means having a wonderful wife who I love and who shares the same values I have, like in parenting and relationships. Are you available?"

Chrissie's perfectly manicured brows scrunched together. Her face flushed with embarrassment. Her head moved backward an inch or two as a quizzical grin spread over her lips. "Did you just ask me to marry you?"

What the hell are you doing? He asked himself silently.

Jason had no clue where that question originated. He had wondered about her social life. And asked himself why she was not with someone. It had been on his mind, but he'd shoved into the dark cubbies of his mind because he was not going to pursue her. But, nonetheless, the question had been tossed out there like a live grenade.

Jason smiled and played as nonchalant as he could. "I don't know, did I?"

He locked his gaze onto hers, refusing to release it. His question had shocked her and appeared to knock her off balance.

"It sure sounded that way," Chrissie said finally.

"Do you want children?"

"Jason!"

"It's just a question."

Jason chastised himself again silently. *What the hell?*

Chrissie grabbed her wine and gulped down a large swallow.

Uh-oh! Jason suddenly became filled with anxiety. It was time to put a stop to this!

Chrissie waved her hand in front of her face. "We've just met, Jason. I didn't think I was going to have to decide my whole future tonight."

"You don't have to," Jason began hesitantly. "I like you, Chrissie. I do. But I don't think it's a good idea for us to be involved. Especially since your father is going to be my preceptor. I agreed to take you to dinner and I always live up to my obligations. I think you should know that up front."

"You are direct, aren't you?"

"And you're not?"

Chrissie shrugged and smiled. "I guess so."

"I'm just trying to be honest here."

"Then what was with the marriage proposal and asking about children?" Chrissie's voice increased a few decibels. A woman at the next table glanced in their direction.

"I honestly don't know," Jason replied. "Just making conversation."

"You like me. Admit it! I can see it in your eyes. Admit it!"

Jason had been leaning forward, keeping his voice low as the volume of Chrissie's had pitched higher. Now, he sat back as if trying to avoid being hit by her words.

"Go on Mister Honesty," she persisted, "Tell me."

"Chrissie," Jason countered. "Thomas is your father. If we dated, do you realize the spot that would put me in?"

"What's that?"

"I'm going to be his extern in the spring. And I'm on a date with his daughter. What would happen if he found out? He scuttled Manny, didn't he?"

"He doesn't need to know. My personal life is mine, not his."

"Don't you live at home with him?"

"Yes."

"What happens when I show up at the door to pick you up for a date like I did tonight?"

"We'll figure it out?"

Jason met her determined gaze. Chrissie's wide brown eyes possessed the gravitational pull of a pair of miniature planets. Jason could not or would not look away. God, she was gorgeous!

"So, you're going to let this be the only date between us because Thomas Pettigrew is my father?"

℞

Jason cleared his throat and tried to match her granite gaze with one of his own. As he did, he remembered his feelings before and after the interview.

Jason had experienced a lifetime's worth of angst over the interview with Thomas. Once he'd been told he acquired one of the coveted slots, he'd been swarmed with relief and joy. But just as quickly that personal celebration had been replaced by equal measures of concern. After Chrissie had revealed to him in The Colonial's parking lot that Thomas was her father, Jason's anxiety level took on the proportions of an exploding supernova. His goal with the externship was to succeed, make a great grade and put the experience on his resume for recruiters to see and drool over. Passing through the meat grinder of Thomas Pettigrew's externship was like being awarded the Medal of Honor in battle, it ensured the recipient lifelong respect. All Jason wanted was for it to earn him a good job, a lifetime of good earnings and respect from his peers and family. The last thing he needed to do now was piss off Pettigrew before he even set foot in the pharmacy as a student.

In the forty-eight hours before calling Chrissie to ask her out, he finally decided he would take her out, spend a few hours with her and then be done with her. It would be better that way. Less complicated. He needed to focus on school and the externships.

But in those same forty-eight hours, he'd found his thoughts focused on her. He practiced what he would say and the first few comments he would make in the mirror while brushing his teeth or in the car while driving. His thoughts became consumed by the forthcoming

call. He found himself becoming anxious like he did before a big test…
or a big first "date".

On Wednesday, the day of the call, he glanced at his Casio every
so often as he counted down the hours to his self-imposed deadline.
When he rang her, she sounded genuinely pleased to hear his voice.
There was no game-playing or teasing as she had done during his interview. They spoke for ten minutes. Chrissie was witty and shy at the
same time. Her voice held a sexy, come-hither quality with minute
amounts of huskiness Jason found enticing. She said she was glad that
her information helped him get the externship.

"I'll pick you up at five-thirty," he said finally.

"Call me before you leave and we'll make arrangements," Chrissie
had replied.

Jason offered a half-hearted protest. "For the record, I don't like doing it this way. I like to pick up the woman." In reality, he was relieved.

"Trust me it will be better my way. Just call me."

Of course, it hadn't been scheduled as a traditional pick-up at her
front door. In the two days between the phone call and their date, Jason
had fretted about how the pickup would go. He was a traditional man.
Since this was going to be a one-time event, he shouldn't care where
they met. But in his mind, the man always picked up his date. But
Chrissie eased his worries, taking the burden from his mind. She still
lived with her parents. According to Chrissie, Thomas Pettigrew was a
strict task master about mixing work and pleasure. So, her date with
Jason had to stay a secret. Chrissie insisted that they meet somewhere
besides her front door. And as it turned out, his worry was unfounded
because he had been able to pick her up honestly.

In the four days since the Monday interview, Jason's attitude had
performed a complete three-hundred-and-sixty-degree turn. Before the
mid-week phone call, he was adamant that he would not see her again.

Then he'd called her and asked about Friday. After he'd hung up, he kept picturing her on the other end of the phone and he replayed the conversation over in his head. He began to bandy about the what-ifs of a dating scenario. He hadn't even gone out with her and he was anxious to spend more time with her, to get to know her better, to kiss those soft lips.

But Jason slept on it and decided that he needed to follow his head, not his heart. It would be better not to pursue a relationship right now. No, he decided. This was not a good time.

$$R_x$$

Jason's eyes remained locked on her as he dipped his head slightly to deliver his final judgment. "Chrissie, in another place or time maybe. But it's not a good idea. This externship is too important."

His words hung between them. She met his gaze as her eyes communicated the maelstrom of emotions swirling within her. He was rejecting her. She looked away, trying to steel herself. She had never been turned down by a man. Of course, she had never actually put herself out there like she had with Jason Rodgers on Monday. Most people knew her to be a vivacious extrovert with a playful streak. But never had she asked a man on a date.

Well, actually, it had been blackmail...or date mail. She'd simply negotiated her way into an evening with Jason Rodgers. She knew she should have been prepared for only a single evening scenario. That is, after all, what she'd negotiated.

In her original plan, Chrissie was going to meet Jason at Keller's Food and Drug parking lot, a grocery store on Warwick Boulevard across from John Radcliffe University. But only a few hours before their date, Chrissie learned that her mother had made plans to spend the evening with a good friend named Agatha. Whenever her mother and Agatha got together, they sipped wine and gossiped until late into the night. And since her father was working at The Colonial, Chrissie would be at home alone all evening. So she called Jason and told him the coast would be clear for him to pick her up at her house. She texted him the address.

At the store, he'd worn a blue business suit that hung well on his athletic frame. It was easy for a man to look good when he knew he was going on an interview. She'd been mildly curious about what Jason would wear to their dinner engagement. He did not disappoint. He wore a pair of light blue jeans; tan slip-ons loafers; his starched button downed shirt glowed against his dark blue blazer and tan skin. He looked like a model in a men's magazine.

When she requested that they meet at the grocery store, Jason had seemed a little perturbed by the request. But he reluctantly agreed because of the circumstances, though she sensed he was relieved. He didn't strike her as a man who liked keeping secrets. Evidently based on the comments he'd just made he liked to put it all out there. But in the end, he was able to stride to her front door and ring the bell. Chrissie was still getting ready when she heard the bell. She texted him that the door was open and that he should let himself in.

Though she'd only known him for five days and spoken to him twice, Chrissie felt strongly attracted to him. It could not be denied. The other men she'd dated somehow seemed like boys compared to Jason Rodgers. He was handsome. He was about to become a pharmacist, so he had to have something of substance between those cute ears. And, apparently, he was driven. He wanted this externship badly enough that he traded a fancy, expensive dinner for the words that had become his ticket in. Finally, she liked the way he teased her. At the pharmacy, he was nervous and pre-occupied. But tonight, he also engaged in a teasing banter about her looks, keeping her off balance and in anticipation.

What the hell did D-D-F-G mean?

There was something different about him. He was a strong man with a dash of vulnerability. She did not sense he was the controlling type. But he was in control and seemed to know who he was. There was a frankness and a sincerity about him that made her want to draw close. She'd seen it the first time she'd laid eyes on him in the pharmacy. He was being honest with her about not wanting a relationship. Right now, he was out of reach. And that made her want him even more. She decided she needed a change of tactics.

"Are you a good kisser?" She asked.

Jason scoffed then grinned. "I do alright."

"I want one kiss," she said, knowing this newest surge of brazenness was fueled by desperation but she was nonetheless surprised by it.

"Now?"

"No, at the end of the night."

"That wasn't part of our deal," Jason countered.

"I'm amending our deal."

"And if I say 'no'?"

Chrissie pursed her lips, pretending to think.

"Then I might have to tell my father how you came up with the answer to his question. I'm sure he'd be less than pleased."

She watched Jason's chocolate eyes widened like two lens apertures trying to absorb the information and their ramifications. She saw the gears of his mind grinding away inside his skull, trying to determine if her threat was serious. Anger flashed in them. Then they narrowed. "You wouldn't?" he hissed.

"Wouldn't I?"

"That's not fair.

"Life's not fair," she countered.

℞

Jason paused then shook his head in the short, slow sideways movement of a man who found himself in a no-win situation, somewhat like a criminal being asked to flip on one of his bosses. He sawed off a piece of steak, placed it in his mouth and chomped.

"Son of a bitch," he whispered.

He sliced off another hunk of his steak and devoured the cube of meat. In the last ten minutes, Jason had watched the expression on Chrissie's face morph, revealing a multitude of conflicting emotions.

Before he'd delivered the bombshell that this would be their one and only date, Chrissie's eyes possessed the glowing expectancy normally scene on a first date: one of hope and intrigue. Engaged and curious, she had been completely engrossed in his words. She seemed to want to be nowhere else. He had found himself caught up in the moment as well. Drawn in by her alluring features: her earnest and penetrating gaze, the slight blush of her cheeks and the crinkle at the corner of her eyes when she smiled. All of it captivated him.

Then, it was as if she had reached into his soul and pulled out the questions about marriage and children. The words were not his. *Or were they?*

Then Jason had over corrected, blurting out his decision that this would be their only evening together. He had wanted to save it for the end of the night and slip away so he couldn't see the aftermath of his choice. The flash of hurt in her eyes told him he'd struck her in a place in which no man had ever ventured. It didn't last long however, evaporating quickly. Chrissie was a strong, resilient woman. But his candor had stung.

In the last few minutes, she had regained that resolute feminine swagger. She'd shrugged off his rejection as if it were simply a heavy rucksack to be tossed aside. Though Jason guessed it was a wound that would not be forgotten. As women often did, Chrissie changed the conversation, topic and tone of the evening with a simple question, leaving a man stymied. This question was about a kiss. Now, he was off balance. As she responded to his explanation and countered with her own, her self-assurance once again surfaced and was revealed by the expression on her face.

He'd surmised that she wasn't used to men in life standing up for and stating what they wanted, especially when it involved the word, "no". Potential suitors and former boyfriends had catered to her every whim. As she had indicated earlier, it was probably why they were no longer in her life. She'd grown bored of the constant fawning. She needed a man who knew what he wanted...and went after it.

Tonight, Jason had shed the desperation he'd demonstrated at the interview. Desperate men often agreed to anything to get what they wanted. Tonight, Jason was demonstrating he was his own man, had his own ideas and pursued them. It was not a facade, not a false strategy. It was simply who he was. He sensed that Chrissie liked and admired his honesty even if she didn't like *what* he was saying. And Jason sensed she was stimulated by the challenge it represented.

"I don't know you very well, Chrissie," he replied as evenly as he could, taking careful measure of the tone in his words. "But I don't get the impression that you would stoop that low. You know if you force me to go out with you under these circumstances, I will resent it. And that would not be a good way to start a relationship."

She scrunched her lips into a circle as if they had been cinched by a drawstring. Pushing out a quick breath through her nose , she reached for her wine, sipped it, and placed the glass back down. Moving a piece of broccoli around on her plate, her eyes met his. "One date is not acceptable," she demanded. She hesitated then asked, "Are you going to kiss me tonight?"

"You know if the roles were reversed and I were acting the way you were, I could be accused of being a stalker or harassing you."

Chrissie smiled. "The roles aren't reversed. They are what they are. So, are you going to kiss me?"

Jason closed his eyes and rubbed his forehead with two fingers. Drawing in a long breath, he said, "One kiss. And that's it."

"Great," Chrissie said, a wide grin spreading across her face.

The waitress appeared once more. "Did you save room for dessert?"

Jason didn't think that it could, but her smile widened. He could tell it was forced, difficult. "Absolutely!" Chrissie beamed.

And Jason also knew that beneath her seemingly renewed enthusiasm stretched a firm bedrock of unyielding determination.

$$R_X$$

"I checked out the website," Victor declared from behind the wheel of the rented Taurus. "This place is for heavy hitters. The student is going to drop at least two bills on dinner just for two of them."

"Yeah," Simon replied. "And we're stuck eating this shit."

They had tailed the pharmacy student named Jason Rodgers from his parent's house in York County to a quiet, tree-lined street in midtown Newport News. They were familiar with the address since they knew where Thomas Pettigrew lived and had watched the pharmacist there many times. There Rodgers picked up Christine Pettigrew for their clandestine date. Clandestine, that is, to Thomas, the overprotective father.

Now, they surveilled the restaurant the couple had entered from the parking area of a handful of boutiques housed in structures of Colonial design called Village Shoppes. The parking area was situated across Governor's Pointe Drive with a perfect view of the restaurant.

The couple was inside enjoying a sumptuous meal while Victor and Simon sat in the rented vehicle, eating fast food burgers out of a wrinkled paper bag. Victor kept the car engine and the air conditioning on full blast. Nonetheless, they both managed to become damp with perspiration.

The tech geeks at Langley had worked their magic on the pharmacy student's phone and had recorded his conversations. Victor and Simon quickly learned that Christine Pettigrew had somehow managed to convince the petrified student to take her on a date. The call had taken place this past Wednesday. It had been short. Christine had intimated that she had given Rodgers some advice that helped land an externship later in the school year.

"I bet you this is going to end badly for the pharmacy student. What's his name again?" Victor said.

"Rodgers. Jason Rodgers. And how do you mean?"

"He's on a date with the daughter. Rodgers said he was not comfortable keeping secrets. The Old Man has no idea Rodgers is out with her. Thomas doesn't strike me as a man who would take kindly to one of his students slipping his daughter the old…" Victor stopped and grinned at his partner with a lascivious smile.

"Define end badly?"

"They will not be able to keep the secret. The Old Man will find out and his externship will be over before it begins."

Simon thought for a moment. 'I'll take that bet. Pettigrew will never know."

"You're on. How much?"

"A Jackson."

"Okay, done!" Simon chuckled. "And don't get any thoughts, Vic. Don't you dare intercede so that Pettigrew finds out."

Victor lifted his nose. "I'm insulted. I would never…"

"Yeah, you would," Simon interrupted. "Keep it fair. Here they come."

The two men watched the young man and woman exit the restaurant. Their body language and the distance between them signaled that something untoward had transpired between them during dinner.

Simon lifted the field glasses to his eyes. "Don't look good. The relationship could be over before it ever started." Simon lowered the glasses then said, "If it doesn't work out, you still owe me. Because then Pettigrew won't ever find out."

℞

Jason pulled into the drive beside Chrissie's Volkswagen Golf and left the car running. He'd wondered how he would have handled matters if the date had gone better and they had returned later in the evening after her father returned home. As it was, that was not a concern. His watch told him it was fifteen minutes after eight. The Colonial would be close in forty-five minutes. "Thanks again for helping me with the interview. I do really appreciate it."

"No problem," she said stiffly.

Chrissie's body language and the frustrated tone in her voice announced that she still was still unaccepting and frustrated by his decision.

After dessert, Jason had paid the bill, escorted his date through the door and retrieved the car. Again, he was a perfect gentleman opening the door for her. The ride back had been tense and filled with long periods of silence. Jason had asked her questions about her internship at the accounting firm and her plans after graduation, trying to move her mind off the fact that he'd spurned her. Chrissie's answers had been polite but monosyllabic.

"I'm sorry we didn't meet under different circumstances," Jason said.

"The circumstances are what that are," Chrissie countered. "Walk me to my door?"

Jason's hesitated then said, "Sure."

He alighted from the car and circled to open her door. Chrissie had fished her keys from her bag. She stood quickly Jason could not get out of the way fast enough and bumped into him awkwardly. Her scent filled his nostrils. An ached developed in his gut.

"Sorry," he said as they stood in the cramped space between the cars. "I hope you had a good time."

Chrissie cocked her head and peered into his eyes. He saw a combination of rigid determination coated with a steely veneer of resilience that failed miserably at hiding the hurt. "It was okay," she said.

If only the circumstances had been different. Who knows… maybe after I finish my externship."

Chrissie scoffed as Jason trained his gaze on her. "That's next spring…eight months from now. I will have moved on."

A stab of guilt sliced through him. *She's pissed.*

Chrissie closed the car door and moved to slide past him.

"I still owe you something," he said, touching her arm. "That kiss?"

Chrissie pressed her soft lips into a tight line and gently moved her arm out of reach. "Keep it."

She pushed passed him and marched to the front door. Unlocking it, she disappeared inside. The door closed with a firm, final thunk.

"Fuck," he hissed to himself.

℞

"Fuck," Chrissie spat as she stood in the foyer.

Chrissie stood frozen on the tile wanting to move to the window in the living room to catch a glimpse of him as he left. But she would be damned if she would give him the satisfaction of letting him see such weakness.

During dinner, his declaration that tonight would be their first and last evening together had stung. But Chrissie had deflected it and focused on changing tactics in order to find another way allowing him into her world. She'd brought up him kissing her because it was the only thing she could think of. She had wanted to feel his lips pressed against hers. She'd pretended to savor the strawberry shortcake during dessert, making small talk and at the same time regretting the demand that he kiss her.

It had made her look desperate and that made her even more angry. On the drive back, Chrissie regretted saying it and her anger festered and quickly redirected itself at Jason Rodgers. He'd tried to engage her with small talk. But with each mile that passed, her disgust mounted. She would just get away from him as fast as she could, she'd decided.

As they tunneled through the canopy of tree limbs on Hidden Boulevard, she fought back tears. She had put herself out there. And she'd been spurned. The rejection hurt. She didn't like it. And she decided then and there she would never do it again.

As he pulled onto her street, she steeled herself. The lamp beside the front door glowed white in the darkness. Her thoughts turned to her father. She had threatened Jason with exposure. She'd threatened to tell her father how Jason had come up with the perfect answer. For a moment, she gave the notion serious consideration. But as Jason's Honda bumped into the driveway; Chrissie just as quickly trashed the idea.

It would not be fair or right. She had made a deal with Jason. She'd given him his answer and he'd bought her dinner. They'd both fulfilled their ends of the deal Though she was hurt and disappointed, it was not in her nature to sabotage Jason's externship. Some women, even women she knew, could be vindictive when spurned. Chrissie was not like them.

She stood in the foyer, shook her head and tried to shrug off the evening. Jason wanted the spot badly. He'd done everything she'd asked him to do. He just didn't want to pursue *her*. As she stood behind the closed door, Chrissie silently kicked herself for not asking for more and for assuming one date with her would result in a second.

Damn! she whispered. She paused then thought:

What would that kiss have been like?

PHARMACY PHACT:

The average debt for graduating pharmacy students in 2020 is $179, 514. This is a four percent increase over 2019 and has risen fourteen percent since 2016.

American Association of Colleges of Pharmacy

Assuming the average debt with a ten-year repayment term at a 7% interest rate, the newly graduated pharmacist would owe $2080 per month.

NerdWallet, Student *Debt Continues to Rise for New Pharmacists*, September 3, 2020, Ryan Lane

CHAPTER 11

The sunlight knifed through a gap in the curtains, stabbing at Jason's closed eyes. A bright orange glow penetrated his eyelids creating a dull pain. Or was it the two gin and tonic's he'd had last night?

Dinner last night?

He swung the covers off his body, climbed out of bed and padded into the hallway bathroom, showered, and brushed his teeth. All the while his mind flamed with snippets of his evening with her. He remembered her sensual, natural beauty carried like the subject of an oil on canvas painting by one of the European masters; the flawless skin; the bright, intelligent eyes aglow with anticipation holding his gaze. Chrissie was one of those women who looked you directly in the eye without pretense or deception. She told you the truth and expected the same in return. Her simple beauty was only accentuated by her resolute sincerity.

After finishing in the bathroom, he shed his pajama pants and tee-shirt and tossed them in the closet hamper. He donned a pair of athletic shorts, a fresh tee shirt and slid on a pair of flipflops that were slick from years of use. Grabbing his phone from the nightstand he walked without haste to the kitchen. During dinner--before his embarrassing overreaction--they'd conversed amicably, comfortably. There had been no tension, especially on Chrissie's end. He sensed profound contentment and delight to be sitting there with him. Her eyes and body language communicated everything to him now even the morning after. The way she leaned in as she spoke, how she studied him, and seemingly hung on his every word, communicated to him how she truly felt about him. Jason had not realized it at the time, or perhaps that realization had been blunted by his preoccupation with ending their relationship before it began. In fact, the message flooded him now.

The other women he'd dated recently had all seemed to be self-absorbed. There was a narcissistic quality about them requiring they be the center of attention, the conversation had to revolve around them all the time. Not that there had been that many. Three or four women in the last two years. They had resulted in a few dates and one overnight tryst several months ago with a student he'd met at a bar that Jason still regretted.

He poured a bowl of cereal and sat at the breakfast bar chomping away at the milk-soaked flakes. Diverting his thoughts from Chrissie, he considered briefly what he should do today. His first externship would not start for another week. Now that he'd sewn up The Colonial spot, he had seven days to himself and his mind was now free of that worry. He would ponder the forthcoming rotations in both hospitals and retail pharmacies later. At the moment, his only concern was how to occupy himself for the next seven days.

There were a few things he needed to do. The dirt-caked Honda desperately needed water, soap and a sponge. The oil needed changing. And it needed an alignment. He would get those things done tomorrow or the day after, he told himself. There was a book or two he'd wanted to read by Robert Ludlum, the spymaster. Of course, there was always the beach. The summer heat wave had subsided somewhat but still blazed. He could pack a cooler with some beers, call a couple of his buddies from high school and they could shoot the shit in the hot breeze and girl watch until the sun went down.

He needed to earn some cash before school started, especially to pay for the car repairs. One of his friend's father owned a landscaping business and was always in need of help. He had called last week asking if Jason was available but Jason had begged off saying the time wasn't right. The money was good, and he paid Jason under the table.

Jason picked up his phone and dialed the number. Jim, the landscaper, picked up right away. When Jason told him he was free, the man jumped at the offer. Jim told him that he had a big project scheduled for the day after tomorrow that would require at least four days of work. Jason told him he'd be there. Jim said he'd text him the address and to be there at nine sharp two days from now.

Pleased with the promise of extra cash, Jason promised himself to have the car maintenance completed tomorrow. He'd charge it on his credit card and put the landscaping money in his checking account to pay the bill when it arrived.

So now his week was filled up with work and errands. That left today. Jason ultimately decided he wanted to spend the day alone. He needed time to decompress and relax. He carried the cereal bowl to the sink, rinsed it out and placed it in the dishwasher. His parents were both at work, so he cleaned up the few remaining breakfast dishes, wiped down the counter and took out the trash. There was a load of laundry in the dryer. Jason placed it in a basket and carried it to the living room.

Flipping on the television for some distraction, he proceeded to fold the towels. He always did it wrong. His mother had a way of folding them in tight rectangles that fit perfectly into the linen closet. Jason could never duplicate the result, but he gave it his best shot nonetheless.

As he muddled through folding the bath towels, beach towels, hand towels and face cloths, the television showed a movie Jason loved;

The American President starring Michael Douglas and Annette Bening. The movie was almost over, but Jason knew the plot by heart.

President Andrew Shepherd, a widower, meets Sydney Ellen Wade, a lobbyist, and wants to date her. With an election looming and against the advice of his senior advisers, the couple embark on a public romance that costs the President in the polls. When politics comes between them, they have a huge fight and Wade ends their relationship.

The president reconsiders his political stance and makes a heartfelt confession at a press conference. Now on the screen, Douglas and Bening are in the oval office about to rekindle their love affair.

That evening the president is about to give his State of the Union address, he finally gives Wade the roses he'd been trying to give her throughout the movie.

As the ending credits rolled, Jason said out loud, "If only it were that easy."

Deciding on the beach, he packed a cooler with a six pack of Miller Lite longnecks, a zippered koozie in the shape of a beer bottle with some kind of redneck slogan on it, two tuna sandwiches and two small bags of Doritos. He stuffed Ludlum's Scarlatti Inheritance, a tube of sunscreen and two poorly folded beach towels into his tattered but reliable bookbag. Then he changed into a pair of swim trunks. In the garage, he retrieved a rusted beach chair and placed it in the back seat of the car along with the cooler and bookbag.

He drove south along Warwick Boulevard and cranked the radio to a pop radio station playing hits from yesterday and today. The first was "I want you to want me," by Cheap Trick.

I want you to want me

I need you to need me

I'd love you to love me

I'm begging you to beg me

I want you to want me

I need you to need me

I'd love you to love me

Jason smiled. "How appropriate," he said aloud, thinking about Chrissie.

When things were good in his life, especially romantically, Jason tended to focus on the upbeat tempos of the music. But when his love life struggled--and there were two instances--he tended to focus on the words...the messages the artists were trying to convey. He'd also noticed that there were a lot of songs out there about failed love. People loved to listen to other people's miseries.

The next tune was "Let's Stay Together," by Al Green:

Oh baby

Let's, let's stay together ('gether)

Lovin' you whether, whether

Times are good or bad, happy or sad

Oh, oh, oh, oh, yeah

Whether times are good or bad, happy or sad

Jason changed the channel, flipping it to AM and talk radio. Some DJ was railing against some bullshit going on in Washington...blah, blah, blah.

That was better, Jason thought.

He saw the Peninsula War Memorial Museum to his right, then the YMCA. He eased the Honda onto the ramp towards the James River Bridge. His mind flashed a shot of Chrissie sitting beside him in the passenger seat last night, moving her caramel silken hair behind her ear as she laughed at one of his stupid jokes.

As he crested the overpass, he saw the James River Bridge looming in the distance. Something inside him wanted to forget the beach and retrace their steps to the restaurant last night. He fought the urge and turned right at the light and into the Huntington beach area.

His mood began to foul now. The thought of this woman would not leave him. Frustrated, he grabbed the cooler, book bag and chair and slammed the Honda door shut. Something rattled inside the door like a piece had come loose. It pinballed to the bottom of the door cavity.

Fuck!

Ignoring it, he walked down to the beach and set up his chair with the cooler beside it serving as a makeshift table. It was the weekend so he imagined that the beach would be crowded soon. For now, only about ten or twelve people, mostly in pairs, dotted the rough sand. Across the road, the Windsor Towers loomed and beyond that, Jason knew, was the Penrose Gatling Shipyard. Pulling out a longneck, he slugged half of the bottle down in one pull. Jason reclined the chair, pulled off his t-shirt and lay back, allowing the warm rays to penetrate his skin. The thick humid air washed over him. Sunscreen could wait a while. He laid back, placed a towel over his eyes and tried to forget and relax.

Descending through various levels of consciousness, the heat and his frustration eventually faded into a semi-comatose oblivion.

Later, Jason awoke, blinking against the bright summer day. He checked his phone and saw that he'd been asleep for forty-five minutes. Pressing a finger against his pectoral muscle near his nipple, the skin blanched then instantly returned to a rosy hue.

Shit. He was sunburned. Grabbing the sunscreen from his bag, he began slathering it on. He was going to pay for this, he told himself. After he had covered all his exposed skin with a thick layer of sunblock, Jason slugged down the rest of the beer which now held only a hint of coldness.

He placed the sunglasses over his eyes and scanned the beach. The area had become crowded while he dozed and roasted. The lifeguard stand was now occupied by a male red-swimsuit-clad, white-nosed guard not much younger than Jason. Beachgoers crowded onto the sand; the noise level had increased. Kids screeched and splashed in the water as adults supervised and chatted. Two jet skis carved through the waters of the James. The wind had kicked up off the river and the whoosh of cars speeding onto and off the bridge created a constant low drone.

Jason spied a couple not much older than him twenty-five feet to his right and halfway to the water. The woman, a natural blonde with an hourglass figure and wearing a white two-piece suit and large round sunglasses faced her husband or boyfriend. Her skin was bronzed and smooth. Her hair was pulled back in a tight ponytail. The man loomed a few inches taller than her with wide shoulders and equally sun-darkened skin with a build that suggested he worked out but was not a fanatic. They walked in Jason's direction hand-in-hand up the beach toward the parking area, angling slightly toward him. They would pass fifteen feet away. He studied them, moving his eyes but not his head from behind the shades. Jason felt invisible.

"I love you, honey," he heard the woman say as they drew even with Jason's chair.

The man stopped and faced her. The woman rose on her tiptoes, closed her eyes and kissed him briefly but with the deep emotion of a woman in love. The man's left hand moved to caress the side of her face. The ring finger was bare.

Jason's mind shifted back to last night in the parking lot. He saw Chrissie's face, pained and sullen, as she declined his offer for a kiss. A kiss she had requested. Jason's heart gave a sideways lurch. A sudden feeling of want enveloped him as the couple disappeared behind him.

His cell phone chimed. He did not recognize the caller's phone number. Jason answered and was greeted by a familiar voice that he could not quite place.

"Jason?" The voice asked.

"Yeah, who's this?"

"It's Ernie. Ernie Harrison. From the Rotary."

Jason hesitated for a second. "Yeah, Mr. Harrison, how are you?"

"Fine. Just fine," came the reply. "It's been a few months since the trip to Ecuador. We haven't seen you since the trip."

"Ah…I wasn't sure it was appropriate considering what happened."

"You did the right thing, son. No worries. We'd really like to have you come by one of the meetings soon."

Jason said he would try and explained that his rotations would keep him busy for the next eight months.

"No problem," Harrison said. "Hey, I was calling for another reason."

"What's that?"

"I received a visit from a gentleman who said he was gathering some background information on you. Said he was a recruiter…a headhunter."

"Really?"

"Yeah, he said his company was evaluating you for a position. Are you applying for jobs once you graduate?"

"Uh…I haven't quite started that process yet."

"Well, I guess they start early trying to entice the cream of the crop. I gave you glowing reviews. I even told him about what you did down in Central America. He was impressed." Harrison's voice hesitated then resumed speaking in a more tentative tone. "Thing is, he didn't strike me as the corporate type."

"Well, thanks…I guess."

"No problem. Just wanted to give you a heads up. It was great talking with you. Please let me know when you can make a meeting."

Jason thanked the Rotarian again, slightly confused by the call. He shrugged it off, telling himself that maybe the big pharmacy chains did their homework early on candidates. He placed his phone in the back pocket of his book bag and scanned the James River and the beach once more.

The bronzed couple were now back on their blankets, laying on their butts and propped on their elbows. A mother and a young child had taken one of the few remaining empty spots about ten feet from him. The woman looked to be in her mid-thirties with a decent, pale body that had precious little time for sun. The boy appeared to be about ten. Mom looked in his direction and smiled. Jason smiled back.

He finished the second Miller and deposited the empty bottle back in the cooler with a glassy clank. Two minutes later, his cell phone rang once more. The caller ID indicated it was Jake Taylor, a friend from high school. They had not seen each other for nearly six months because of college commitments.

Jake and Jason had played varsity baseball at Menchville High for two seasons. Jake played second base and could turn a double play better than anyone in the District. Jason haunted third base. Jake had played ball for James Madison and graduated four years ago with a degree in Biology. He was currently in medical school at Vanderbilt and scheduled to graduate this coming spring. They got together as often as their schedules allowed, which was once or twice a year during breaks.

Jason clicked on. "What's up?"

"What's goin' on man?" Jake countered.

"How's Vandy?"

"Getting ready to start my last year. They say it's a bitch. How 'bout you? You ready to fill all my prescriptions?"

Jason scoffed. "Yeah, you've got the perfect handwriting to be a doctor. It looks it was scribbled by a drunken chicken. You still in town?"

"Naw," Jake replied. "In Nashville. Living in a house with three other med students."

"When's your first break?"

"Don't know yet."

"Let me know," Jason said. "We need to grab a couple of brewskis."

"Sounds good. Hey, I was calling 'cuz I've got news."

"Yeah?"

"I proposed to Sally," Jake declared as if he was bragging about having just climbed Mount Everest.

"No shit. Did you have to hold her at gun point?"

Jake and Sally had met at Vanderbilt and been dating all through med school. She was also a med student. Jason had met her several times when they had returned to Virginia.

"Funny man," Jake countered. "You were eighty-ninth on my list to call. There were a couple of no answers, so I moved you up to eight-one."

Jason laughed. He saw movement to his right once more. With the phone still glued to his ear, he the couple heading back down the beach toward the water arm-in-arm this time, laughing and joking and sipping from insulated drink carriers.

"You still there, buddy?"

"Yeah...yeah, I'm here. Someone was talking to me. That's great news, Jake. I wish you two nothing but the best. You set a date yet?"

"No. I just asked her two nights ago. We'll probably have an engagement party back in Newport News at my folk's place. I'll keep you posted."

"Sounds good."

"How 'bout you?" Jake asked.

"What about me?"

"You seeing anybody?"

Jason cleared his throat. "Nothing serious."

"Don't worry," Jake said. "I'll happen. And if it doesn't, you're going to be a pharmacist. You can always drug them."

Jason chuckled with a feigned enthusiasm. "Give Sally my best." He severed the connection and placed the phone in the bookbag.

The young, beautiful couple was now in the water, standing knee deep with their arms around each other's waists.

Jason watched them for another moment. A yearning swelled in him as he watched the couple in love. He was missing that in his life. Then a revelation swamped him like a swollen storm surge.

"You fucking idiot," Jason said out loud.

The mother and the boy heard his outburst. She cast him a disparaging stare and appeared ready to berate him. The ten-year-old had the shocked, raised-eyebrow look children get when they hear a bad word.

"Sorry," he said, gathering up his things. "I just remembered I forgot to do something important."

℞

Jason stormed into the kitchen and located a bottle of aloe in the refrigerator that had probably been there for two years. He marched to the bathroom and removed the t-shirt. He regarded himself in the mirror, he assessed the damage. His chest had begun to take on the rosy crimson of a boiled lobster. The lower half of his face, the section not covered by the towel, was also burned. It looked as if he held the startled expression of an albino raccoon.

He squeezed out a large dollop of aloe into his palm, rubbed his hands together and gently smoothed it over his skin. After getting over the initial burst of pain, he worked the lotion over his arms. The memory of his evening with Chrissie returned to him…again.

For most of it, her presence created a warm, tranquil sensation like the gentle wash of warm Caribbean water. It had been present for the first part of their… "date", at least. But Jason had ignored it, or least had failed to appreciate it for what it was. That comfortable easiness with her had been blunted by Jason's I-have-a-plan-and-I'm-sticking-to-it attitude. The externship and the fact that she was Thomas Pettigrew's daughter had scared him. His head had been so far up his future, he failed to see his potential future sitting in front of him.

If he was honest with himself, Jason knew he longed for a relationship. But the women he'd met in the past two years did not seem to hold a candle to Chrissie. *What if he and Chrissie were meant to be together? What if she was the one?*

His attitude had clouded his ability to be receptive to Chrissie's overtures. She genuinely liked him. And he was attracted to her. There had been a connection there for both of them. But he had been too worried about the externship to give over to it. The question had formed at some point in the last twenty-four hours, initially laying hidden just below the surface of his consciousness. But now it nagged at him openly, tearing at the fabric of his soul.

What if Chrissie was the one?

Jason poured out more aloe and worked it into the skin of his thighs and shins, wincing as he did.

He'd only known her for a week. They'd only talked during his interview for a few minutes, on the phone for another ten and then for an hour or two at dinner last night. He barely knew the woman. But the attraction was there. And it was a strong one.

Hearing the songs on the radio, seeing the lovey-dovey couple at the beach and hearing the happiness in Jake's voice all reminded Jason of one vital human craving. He wanted to be with someone. He wanted to feel that same connection Jake did. In fact, he'd kind of stopped looking for it after the last two failed dates...they couldn't even be called relationships. He'd just concluded that maybe his romantic life was doomed to be a complicated, jumbled mess.

Was it him? Was he the problem?

He squeezed out one more large mound of cream in his hands and slathered it over his abdomen and chest.

He hadn't felt sorry for himself. He was tired of all the dating bullshit. So, he'd decided to take a break from worrying about it and focus on his school and career. Then provenance, or God, or the cosmos had thrown Christine Pettigrew before him like the swirling beacon of a lighthouse piercing his darkened romantic life.

His mother always told him opportunities appear when you're not looking for them. *Was this one of them? Was Chrissie his opportunity for true love? Would his externship really matter in the long run, if he didn't end up with someone he'd loved in his life? Would he ever be happy?*

Would he have to earn this relationship like the American President despite the public perception? Would he have to run the gauntlet of Thomas Pettigrew in order to be with a woman who loved him? Was Christine Pettigrew that woman?

It would be easier to just forget the whole thing, Jason told himself. *Just stick to the plan and get through the externship and school.* Worry about your love life later.

But once again his mind returned to that relaxed contentment and stimulating challenge he'd experienced with Chrissie. The first hour or so of conversation before he'd been scared into telling her there would be no second date had been genuine. He found himself wanting to be with her again. And then the question reared again, refusing to be ignored.

Was she the one?

Jason washed his hands and went back into his bedroom. He shed his swim trunks and t-shirt to the laundry basket and fished out a fresh pair of jeans and a Polo t-shirt from his dresser. Sliding his feet into a pair of leather slip-ons, he grabbed his wallet and phone and headed for the door.

PHARMACY PHACT:

As of July 2020, there are one hundred and forty-one accredited schools of pharmacy in the United States.

American Association of Colleges of Pharmacy

CHAPTER 12

Chrissie woke later than normal on Saturday and ate a quick breakfast of toasted English muffins with raspberry jam, two pieces of microwaved bacon and a cup of coffee. Eleanor, her mother, was sitting at the table drinking coffee and reading the newspaper. Last night when she arrived home, her mother was still not home from her evening with Agatha. Her tired face held the ravages of the wine and lack of sleep. Her father was still at the store. Chrissie had been relieved; she hadn't the strength to face anyone. Her only goal: to be alone and crawl into bed. So, Chrissie had locked herself in her room and did just that.

Eleanor bade her daughter a good morning as Chrissie nibbled at her food and sipped her coffee. Her father was already back at The Colonial. Earlier from the bedroom, Chrissie had heard him talking to Eleanor in the kitchen. Then she heard the front door open and close as he left. He always arrived an hour before the store opened. Thomas had still been at work when she left for her date, or rather her non-date and now he had departed for work once more.

Apparently when she realized that Chrissie was not going to offer any information about last night's activities, Eleanor asked in a soft, inquisitive voice, "So how was your evening?"

"Okay," Chrissie replied flatly.

"What's his name?"

Eleanor knew she'd had a date. She hadn't asked Chrissie, she just knew. She always knew. It was the sixth sense that came with motherhood.

Chrissie didn't want to discuss it. But she also didn't want to be rude. She was just being a mother. "I'll tell you later, Mom. I'm late for work." She got up from the table and placed the mostly uneaten breakfast in the sink. She kissed her mother on the cheek and headed back to her room to get ready.

"Work? It's Saturday."

"It's a casual day. I can get there when I get there. I'm going to be an accountant. There are going to be plenty of working Saturdays and days with long hours."

She excused herself and showered, then dressed for work in a simple but stylish outfit; a form-fitting, sleeveless striped Adriatic blue silk blouse over a pair of hip-hugging jeans and white tennis shoes. To finish off the ensemble she draped a ten-inch faux pearl necklace around her neck. Not totally casual, but she wanted to feel good about herself today.

As she drove across town to City Center, she tried to put the events of the previous evening out of her mind. She'd gone to bed angry and, at the same time, sad. Fatigued from the pent-up anxiety in anticipation of the dinner, then angry and frustrated afterward, her body needed sleep. Nonetheless, it had still taken her a fitful hour to finally nod off.

Those sixty minutes had been filled with what-ifs and I-should-have-saids. She wondered if there was someone else Jason was interested in, a girlfriend or a budding romance yet-to-be that precluded him from committing to a second or third date with her; perhaps a relationship he did not want to admit to. Or maybe he was gay, she thought. That would be a waste of a decent looking man, she thought. But something told her he did not play for the other team.

Chrissie smirked and chuckled to herself a moment before she stomped on the brakes. The car in front of her had stopped short. She had almost missed the glowing taillights. Her Volkswagen's bumper stopped inches from the other car as her heart nearly jumped out of her chest.

As she waited at the light avoiding the eyes of the driver glaring through the rearview mirror, Chrissie's heart thumped inside her ribcage. She took several long breaths and tried to slow her heart rate.

In the end all the pondering and guessing did her no good, she just ended up in the same place: frustrated and angry. Chrissie concluded that if Jason Rodgers wasn't ready to date her--or anyone-- there was nothing she was going to be able to do about it. But the unfulfilled desire in her belly still lurked; the course not taken had an firm hold on her.

She found a parking spot in the garage, walked to the inside elevator and pressed the button for the fifth floor of the PNC building. At her cubicle, she dropped her bag and her briefcase onto the desk as Claudette Person appeared.

Claudette was one of the other interns at the firm, a tall, gorgeous black woman with perfect ebony skin and piercing brown eyes. They had been hired the same day and had shared some classes at Tech last year. They'd become fast friends and decided to try for internships at the same firm. They'd actually interviewed together with the managing partner, Beatrice the Beast. And wowed her.

"So how did it go?" Claudette asked. In a moment of weakness, Chrissie had confided to Claudette about her date mail scheme involving Jason Rodgers over lunch on the Tuesday following Jason's interview. Chrissie had confessed how excited she was about the possibilities. The roll of Chrissie's eyes followed by the rapid fluttering of her lids told Claudette the news was not good.

"I'm so sorry," Claudette said. "I've got to go. Got a meeting with my CPA's client in three minutes. Let's meet for lunch and you can tell me everything?"

"Sure. Sounds great, CP," Chrissie replied.

℞

The morning had evaporated. She'd arrived shortly after ten-thirty and placed her cell phone on silent, then buried it at the bottom of her bag. No one was going to disturb her today. Her work would be her singular focus this morning. And Chrissie immersed herself in it for almost two hours. A few minutes after noon, Beatrice "The Beast" had piled work on the new intern. Her jowly cheeks and thinning blonde hair resembled that of an old man's, and she had enough bracelets on each wrist to sink an ocean liner. Yes, Chrissie learned, Beatrice Collins was the same Collins of Casper, White and Collins. The firm had eighteen partners, but Chrissie had been assigned to the woman who'd started the firm more than twenty-five years ago. One of the more experienced interns, Aiden Twomey, who'd been with CWC for more than six months, had named her Beatrice the Beast--behind her back, of course. She expected everyone to live, breathe and crap accounting, interns included.

"There's no better way to learn the job than jumping in the deep end," she had said at the orientation.

It was a Saturday at the end of August. In her orientation earlier in the week, it been made clear to her and all the new interns that CWC was the busiest accounting firm south of Richmond. This was their slow season. But they still had enough work to keep the staff grinding away six days a week. During busy season which would start in January with the advent of taxes, they could expect to work seven days a week until the end of April, and perhaps beyond.

"Welcome to the world of public accounting," the slender, bookish Human Resources and Recruiting woman declared.

A goodly portion of junior accountants, secretarial staff and interns had come in early in the hopes of getting their tasks completed so they might be able to enjoy the rest of the weekend. Beatrice the Beast appeared to be the only partner present. Between the orientation packet Chrissie was expected to read and the spreadsheets and bookkeeping duties, Chrissie had had her eyes glued to a computer screen since she'd arrived.

"I'm heading out to grab a bite. How about keeping me company," Aiden said, leaning over the wall of her cubicle.

The tone of his voice and the imploring nature of his gaze told Chrissie he was interested in more than a sandwich. This was the last thing she needed or wanted today.

"Ah, actually," Chrissie replied. "I'm supposed to be having lunch with Claudette."

The sunlight slanted through a large picture window onto the spacious common area and captured the gray flecks in his sapphire blue eyes. His thick blonde hair capped a round, cherubic face. He was on the plump side but not unpleasing to the eye.

"She's welcome too," Aiden offered. "The Southern Belle across the street has great sandwiches."

Chrissie saw Claudette approaching from behind Aiden. Aiden saw Chrissie's eye registering her closing in. He turned.

"Hey, Claudette,'" he said. "Join us for lunch." He held up an American Express card. "It's on the firm."

Claudette and Chrissie exchanged glances and with no excuses readily available, they shrugged in agreement. Chrissie grabbed her purse and the two women followed Aiden through the glass doors. They rode the elevator to the lobby and exited the carriage.

Out of the corner of her eye, Chrissie noticed a large bouquet of mixed flowers being held by a man whose face was hidden behind them. She caught a fleeting glimpse of his face partially hidden behind the flowers and a pair of mirrored sunglasses. As she, Aiden and Claudette debarked from the elevator, the man entered the neighboring car.

$$R_x$$

Jason lifted the massive mixed arrangement of flowers he'd purchased at Keller's Food and Drug higher as he stepped onto the elevator. The skin of his lower face felt like it had been seared by a blow torch. The cloth of his shirt scraped his chest, irritating it and creating a large dose of discomfort.

A gaggle of people were exiting the carriage when the doors of the one in front of which he was standing slid open. He couldn't tell how many there were in the group because he was trying his best to hide behind the flowers. His half-burned face looked ridiculous and he wanted to find Chrissie with as few people seeing him as possible. The pair of sunglasses he'd donned managed to cover a good portion of the unburned area. Despite hiding his face, his ears still registered the animated, jovial conversation.

Jason stepped aboard the carriage. The doors slid closed and the chatter disappeared like a midnight whisper. He hesitated for a moment, regarded the flowers then recalled how he'd managed to arrive at this place and time.

His goal--to avoid becoming entangled in any kind of love affair with Chrissie--had crumbled on Huntington beach like a sandcastle in a swelling tide. The previous evening he'd actually been proud of the fact that he had managed not to succumb to the dark power of temptation. But this morning, the combination of songs on the radio, the phone call from Jake, the sight of the young couple obviously in love and, to some degree, the fact that on this specific occasion he had chosen to be alone, had battered and weakened his shaky resolve. These incidents had coalesced like a perfect storm on this hot Saturday to spotlight the folly of his thinking. Such were the vagaries of a lonely heart.

As he raced home from the beach, he chided himself for not understanding or recognizing his situation. He could be so oblivious to certain signs because, sometimes, he had an all-consuming singular focus. The words "idiot" and "jackass" spilled from his lips every minute during the drive home.

He had pushed the Honda north along Warwick Boulevard to the Hilton Village district and Main Street across from the Village Community Theater. There he hung a right and passed the Main Street Library, dipping beneath the railroad underpass. The light was green as he hit Jefferson Avenue, so he continued along Main and it eventually carried him to the Hampton city line. There, Main turned into Todds Lane. Traffic was light on this Saturday, so Jason risked pushing the accelerator closer to the floorboard. The Honda's anemic engine wheezed and strained into another gear. When Jason turned north once more at Big Bethel Road and the Assembly of God church, he stopped kicking himself. And he began to formulate a plan.

Chrissie had mentioned at some point during the evening that she was working today. Jason considered calling her to make sure she was there. But he nixed that notion. He wanted to surprise her. No, he needed to surprise her.

He would show up at her new firm unannounced and take her to lunch. Then he would apologize for being hard-headed and explain that he hadn't stop thinking about her since dropping her off last night. *I made a mistake*, he would explain. Over lunch, he would ask her out again.

As he crossed into the Tabb section of York County, he had almost finished devising his strategy and practicing his first few opening lines. But Jason did not want to show up empty-handed. He had spurned her. It wouldn't be right to show up without some kind of peace offering, something to show her he wanted to make it right.

He'd pulled into the driveway and strode to the front door. As soon as he entered the house, he pulled up a number and dialed. Flowers, he thought. Everyone woman liked flowers. So, he rang Keller's Food and Drug, navigated the voice menu and was finally connected with the floral department. After placing an order for a bright, cheerful mixed bouquet, the young lady who sounded like she was twelve told him to come by in about thirty minutes. The pre-teen sounding woman had been dreadfully wrong. When Jason arrived, he was disgusted to see that there were no less than four customers queued at the floral counter. For some reason, several shoppers had decided, today of all days, to order flowers. He stepped into the queue and waited impatiently as a middle-aged woman pelted the floral clerk with questions about what assortment would look best together and the prices. To the consternation of the rest of the queue, she instructed the clerk to assemble an arrangement then quickly changed her mind. She did this three times.

Jason busied himself with a search on his phone. Chrissie had mentioned the name of her new firm. The web told him that Casper, White and Collins was in the PNC building in City Center. Fifth floor.

After twenty-five minutes, Jason reached the exasperated floral clerk and learned that his arrangement was not ready. Ten minutes after that, he departed Keller's, bouquet in hand. He practically ran to the car.

In the elevator now, he pushed out a long breath and punched the number five on the panel. The ascent began.

$$R_x$$

"How much you think he spent on them?" Victor asked Simon, pushing a lungful of acrid smoke into the cabin of the Taurus.

Simon had followed Jason Rodgers to Huntington a hundred yards north of where the James River Bridge begin its nearly five-mile span over the murky brown waters of the historic river. It was on these same waters more than four centuries earlier, the Susan Constant, Godspeed and Discovery, carrying one hundred and five future colonists and thirty-nine crew, made landfall at Jamestown.

Simon tailed Rodgers's Honda into the parking area and then parked on a higher plateau near the tennis courts behind the YMCA. He watched and waited, working his crossword and occasionally twirling his expensive pen as the pharmacy student planted himself under the sun for a little more than an hour with a cooler. It appeared Simon was in for a long day of watching a twenty-something sun himself while getting drunk.

About an hour after settling into his beach chair, Rodgers took a phone call that lasted no more than a few minutes. Twenty minutes after that, Rodgers suddenly packed up his stuff and practically ran back to his car and raced to his parent home in lower York County.

As he disappeared into the house, Simon had called the tech geeks in Washington to get a transcript of the phone calls Rodgers had received on the beach. The second call seemed innocuous enough. Some friend named Jake had called to inform Rodgers he was getting married. After some jocular teasing, the call ended.

But the first call concerned Simon. A Rotarian named Harrison had called to inform Rodgers that someone had been asking questions about the pharmacy student. Simon did not know who had interviewed the Rotarian. But he was certain the man was an asset of the CIA. Fortunately, Rodgers did not appear overly concerned.

Fifteen minutes after Rodgers pushed through the front door, the techie at Langley called to tell Simon that Rodgers had just called a grocery store to ask about ordering flowers.

"Why the hell are we wasting company assets on a pharmacy student who orders flowers?" The technician demanded.

"How the hell do I know," Simon barked in return. "Just do your job and feed me the intel. Got it?"

The tech hung up on Simon. Simon didn't give two shits. Then he smiled to himself. Rodgers left the beach in a rush. Then he ordered flowers. It all made perfect sense. He was having seconds thoughts about Christine Pettigrew.

"Shit," he had exclaimed out loud to himself in the car, which sat parked a hundred yards away from the Rodgers residence. Last night, it seemed Rodgers had followed through on his promise to ditch the bitch. But today, it appeared he was reneging on that promise.

Simon whispered four simple words as he dialed Victor, "Son of a bitch."

Victor clicked on to the call after three rings.

"What do you have?" the slim agent asked.

"Nothing's going on here," Victor replied. He was sitting outside The Colonial in a second rental, a Ford Edge. "Just another boring-ass day at the pharmacy."

"There's been a development."

"Oh yeah?"

"I'm sitting outside Christine Pettigrew's work. Rodgers just entered the building."

"Really?"

"Really." Simon sighed and paused. "He was carrying flowers."

He'd been ready to collect on his wager with Victor. If the Old Man never found out about the relationship, Victor would owe him twenty dollars. And it looked like he was going to collect today because Rodgers had given the Pettigrew woman the heave-ho after one night. But today's developments signaled something new was brewing and there was still a chance that Thomas Pettigrew might find out.

Victor coughed out a deep, smoke-addled laugh through the phone. "I have your twenty right here. I'll be putting that back in my pocket right now. The Vic still lives."

R̲x

Jason departed the carriage and turned right. He walked thirty feet. Behind a large, curved reception desk, a matronly woman sat wearing make-up that appeared to have been applied in layers. The scent of her perfume seemed to bellow from the air conditioning vents. She eyed the bouquet of flowers in their plastic cone and greeted him with a pleasant but curt, "May I help you?"

"I'm looking for Christine Pettigrew."

"Just a moment."

The receptionist picked up a handset and punched a button. As she did this, Jason regarded the expansive space. The entire floor spread out before him. There were no walls or corridors, only a sea of endless cubicles. The tops of heads were angled down studying computer screens behind chest-high dividers. The accounting firm of Casper, White and Collins appeared to occupy the entire fifth floor of the PNC building.

The soft buzz of ringing phones mingled with the hum of unintelligible voices engaged in indistinct conversation. Workers clad in casual business attire walked about with file folders and leather portfolios clutched in hand. Busy for a Saturday, he thought. Jason scanned the tops of heads trying to locate Chrissie's silken chestnut hair, perhaps with her head cocked to one side nestling the handset of a phone between her ear and her shoulder, scribbling notes. Nothing.

His search was interrupted by the muted, intermittent hum of the receptionist's phone. She picked up the receiver, spoke her name into it, and listened for a moment. Covering the mouthpiece with her hand, she looked up at Jason.

"I'm sorry she just left for lunch."

"Any idea where she went?"

The woman spoke once more into the phone and asked.

"No," the receptionist said. "But I'm told that they were staying in the area because they were going to walk." She motioned with her head to the bouquet. "Would you like to leave those with me. I'll see she gets them."

Jason declined, thanked the woman and headed for the elevator with the bouquet clutched in his fist.

℞

Chrissie, Claudette and Aiden sat at a table looking onto Town Center Drive and a partial view of the massive, circular reflecting pond and its eleven fountains.

"The pimento cheese sandwich is killer," Aiden declared.

The Southern Belle had been a breakfast and lunch staple for more than two decades in Newport News. Its humble beginnings as a sandwich and hot dog shop on nearby Thimble Shoals Boulevard, equipped with only a microwave, hot plate and a crock pot, began a storied existence that locals craved. Now, the quaint dining area was quickly becoming filled with bankers, insurance agents, lawyers and a few mothers making a quick getaway for lunch before hurrying back to pick up kids from Hampton Roads Academy, Peninsula Catholic or any number of public schools.

The waitress brought water and the trio placed drink orders. When she departed, Aiden asked, "So how have your first few days been?"

Both Claudette and Chrissie answered with a generic, non-committal, "Okay."

"Claudette, how's your accountant? It's Kevin Selden, correct?"

Claudette nodded. "Yes, he seems nice enough. Very charming."

Aiden allowed a grin to slowly creep over his lips. He leaned in over the table and whispered his next utterance. "Be careful. He's a real lady's man--"

"He's married," Claudette explained.

"Oh, we're all well aware of that," Aiden replied. "But that doesn't stop him from having a few dalliances on the side. Rumor has it that he was reprimanded by the partners about seven months ago for an inappropriate relationship with an intern. She ended up leaving the firm." He made air quotes and said, "for personal reasons."

Claudette moved her gaze to Chrissie. "Just what I need. An undersexed supervisor. How the hell is he going to resist all this," she said moving her hands from head to waist like a game show hostess.

Chrissie laughed as Aiden winked, turning his attention to Chrissie.

"So, Chrissie," Aiden began. "How are you liking the Beast?"

Chrissie chuckled. "Already up to my eyeballs in work."

It was Aiden's turn to smile. "Don't worry. It only goes downhill from there. She was my accountant when I first started. The more work she gives you, the more she likes you."

"Marvelous," Chrissie replied. "Then she must love me."

"If you need any help, just let me know," Aiden said conspiratorially over another narrow-eyed smile. "I can put a good word in for you."

Chrissie and Claudette exchanged a brief look. Claudette rolled her eyes in a manner that said, "All guys are pigs".

The waitress reappeared. "Are we ready?"

They each quickly perused the one-page laminated menu and placed their orders. When she moved off, Claudette's cell phone chimed a Destiny's Child tune, "Dangerously in Love."

"I've got to take this," she said, excusing herself. "It's Kevin."

"Do you want me to order for you?" Aiden asked.

Claudette stood, blinked in exasperation. "Thanks, Aiden. Yeah, I'll have the pimento, " she sighed, removed her earring and clicked on the call.

"Hi Kevin," she said loudly as she headed for the door.

℞

Jason exited the building onto the sidewalk in front of the PNC Building on Town Center Drive. The faint sound of falling water hissed from his left. The fountains of the five-acre reflecting pool in City Center jetted high into the air. The sound was amplified by the combination of nearly a dozen jets. The warm summer breeze carried the gentle mist that both refreshed and annoyed Jason. The sun had climbed to its zenith in the sky. Its hot rays reminded Jason that the skin on his face was still raw. *Should have worn a hat,* he thought.

The City Center district of Newport News sat sandwiched between Interstate 64 and Jefferson Avenue in the Oyster Point Business Park and was home to a plethora of boutiques, restaurants, cafes, specialty shops and businesses, a movie theater, and a major hotel chain. Apartments and townhomes in the Center allowed for upscale living without the chore of managing a lawn. The area also hosted holiday festivities, weekly summertime concerts and farmer's markets. Jason had visited the area many times and was familiar with its layout.

His problem was there were more than a dozen restaurants within walking distance. The entire Oyster Point district in which City Center dwelled sported even more eateries and a brewing company. Jason could only go on the information he had been given. If Chrissie and her lunchmates were walking, they would probably not stray too far from the PNC building. Depending on which restaurant they chose, he might still see them walking. They probably only had an hour at most, and all of their choices were within walking distance.

Deciding on a methodical approach, he would walk to the farthest restaurant in the immediate area and work his way back to the PNC building. The City Center area was bounded by Canon Boulevard to the east and Thimble Shoals Boulevard, which dissected the industrial Park to the south and the majority of the business park, to the north and west.

He turned toward the fountains and made his way across Town Center Drive angling toward the outdoor shopping mall where most of the restaurants were. A glass door squealed open as Jason hit the middle of the street. A tall, long-legged, and strikingly attractive black woman exited the Southern Belle with a cell phone pressed to her ear. She talked rapidly and confidently into the device.

A lawyer, Jason thought.

He glanced toward the door of the Southern Belle for a glimpse inside. But the door closed too quickly. He then shot a look into the large window. But the shadow and reflections from the street made any view inside impossible.

I'll check it on the way back, he told himself. His first stop would be the Brazilian Grill right next to the Marriott. *Then I'll work backward.*

℞

Claudette returned to the table as their lunches were being laid before them.

"Everything okay?" Chrissie asked.

"No," Claudette huffed. "Kevin needs me to meet with him and a client so I can get up to speed on their business and accounting practices. It starts in ten minutes."

"And he's just telling you now?" Chrissie asked.

Claudette frowned and nodded. "Sorry," she said. She flagged down the waitress and asked for a plastic box to take her sandwich with her. "I'll catch up with you two later."

After retrieving her to-go box, the tall, slender black woman sauntered her hour-glass figure to the door zigzagging through the tables with the elan of a model.

"Welcome to the world of public accounting," Aiden said watching Claudette exit and lifting half of his Reuben off the plate. Just before he bit into it, he asked Chrissie, "What makes you want to be an accountant?"

℞

The Brazilian Grill held no luck for Jason. He'd entered and made quick work of its dining area. The place was nearly empty. The early lunch crowds had not decided on South American cuisine. Next, Jason made his way south crossing Fountain Way to have a gander in the windows of the coffee shop, Aromas. A quick glance through the glass also showed no sign of Chrissie.

Past the currently closed cinema, Jason entered the Travinia Italian Kitchen and Wine Bar with its décor of stone and wood. He circled and, again, found nothing.

Shit!

He pushed out a frustrated sigh as he exited the Italian eatery. He scratched his chin and regarded the bouquet in his hand which now felt like a twenty-pound weight. Reconsidering his decision to find her, Jason pondered whether to let the matter wither on the vine, find a trash receptacle for the flowers and head back to the parking garage.

Why were women always so damned frustrating for him?

℞

"Boyfriend?" Aiden asked gently, trying to sound innocuous and innocent.

He had skillfully navigated the direction and tenor of the conversation since sitting down. After Claudette had been called back to the office for her impromptu with the lecherous Kevin Selden and his new client, Aiden seemed a little more at ease now that he was alone with her. Chrissie usually had an ability to judge people's intentions. The way Aiden had looked at her from day one had communicated an unspoken interest in more than work matters.

Aiden Twomey defined the word preppy. His smooth, flawless skin and swell of wavy hair artfully combed to one side, along with his colorfully knotted, bright pink Windsor tie, navy suitcoat, khaki trousers and docksiders screamed that he'd graduated from Choate or Phillips Exeter Academy. Obviously, no day of the week was a casual day for him. His round Rubenesque face, cobalt, intelligent eyes, and a physique edging on the thick side that suggested a childhood comprised of books, puzzles and matters of the mind. *This guy was not an athlete*, Chrissie thought.

In the last ten minutes, he'd managed to inquire as to why she'd chosen accounting, what she thought of Tech; he had graduated from Old Dominion in Norfolk and was waiting for a permanent position at CWC to open up. He was also currently waiting on the results of his CPA exam. In the same short time, he'd also managed to let Chrissie know that he'd broken up with his girlfriend of eight months four months ago and was currently unencumbered by a relationship.

"No, I don't," Chrissie answered. She did not want to lie. But she also needed to set him straight. "But I'm currently not looking for one either."

Aiden nibbled on a French fry. "I see," he said. "Any particular reason?"

Chrissie's response was borrowed from Jason's playbook. "I know I'm going to be working long hours. And I won't have much time for a love life."

"Well, when you decide you're ready for romance. Let me know. I know a guy." A slow but pleasant smile spread across his face as a playful glint shimmered in his eyes.

"You know a guy?" Chrissie asked with a friendly smirk.

Aiden nodded.

"That guy wouldn't happen to be you now, would it?"

"Naw," he replied. "It wouldn't be fair."

"Fair? Fair to who?"

"You?"

"Me? Why's that?"

"I'm way too much man for you," he explained, leaning back in his chair and spreading his arms. "Better for us to start off as co-workers so I can evaluate whether or not you can handle my manhood."

Chrissie narrowed her eye and screwed up her lips, staring at him with astonishment.

Aiden's jaw dropped open, instantly realizing the lewd way in which his words had been interpreted.

"Ah..." he muttered. "What I meant was...my manliness."

"Manliness? Really?" Chrissie grinned, pressing her advantage and not allowing him time to dig himself out of his sexist hole. "You want to try again?"

"Virility?"

Chrissie laughed loudly, unable to suppress the sound. Several nearby patrons glanced in their direction.

Aiden shrugged. "I'm out of words."

"That's good," Chrissie replied, glancing at her watch. "Let's get out of here."

Aiden raised his glass of iced tea. "Here's to long hours at the office."

Chrissie raised her and touched it to his. "To Beatrice the Beast... and my new friend, Manhood!"

$$\text{R}_\text{X}$$

With a renewed sense of purpose and having shed his momentary bout of self-pity, Jason completed his circuit of City Center. He'd circled back, having had no success in any of the restaurants along the way. He'd surveilled Salsa's, Vedeat, and Hayashi Japanese Steakhouse, with similar, empty results. The only restaurants he'd not yet searched were the Southern Belle and the Cove which sat overlooking the reflecting pool and the fountains diametrically opposite the Marriott.

He turned the corner leaving Merchant's Way and found himself back on Town Center Drive. The Southern Belle was only fifty yards ahead. Jason strode toward it with purpose, still clutching the now sagging bouquet.

He marched ten steps toward the door of the Southern Belle when it opened abruptly. Two people exited, a man and a woman, gliding across the sidewalk and into the street. The woman was on the left facing away from Jason. She was talking animatedly with a plump, young man in a dark suit and a bright pink tie who struggled to keep pace with the woman's determined stride.

By the tilt of her head and the easy glide of her steps, Jason recognized Chrissie. The pair walked and talked as they crossed the boulevard. Chrissie chatted freely as the young man struggled to pull even and still managed to be listening attentively. His face held the crimson, rosy hue of self-consciousness. But his smile never dimmed and the look in his eyes told Jason he was smitten with her.

Who wouldn't be?

As this last notion entered his thoughts, Jason felt a stab of cold regret. Chrissie was a gorgeous woman. She would not want for suitors. *Had he blown his one and only chance?*

Jason swiveled his torso and took three steps along a path to intersect them. But the pair walked fast, and he himself felt a sudden spasm of self-consciousness. He stood on the curb, frozen, watching Chrissie and her lunch companion disappearing beyond the tinted glass of the PNC building.

Anchored to the sidewalk, he stood transfixed for several moments. Jason pushed out an exasperated sigh and spotted a community trash receptacle nearby. A second later the bouquet of mixed flowers found itself rammed, blossoms-down, into the pile of garbage. He fumed, angry with himself at such an emotional, unplanned attempt. And more importantly, that the rash, unplanned gambit had failed.

Jason remained on the curb for a few minutes, unable to bring himself to move. The white sunlight burned the skin of his head and neck, irritating the already fried patches. Ignoring the mounting sting, he prayed that Chrissie would re-appear at the entrance, race across the street back to the restaurant because she'd left something behind. Then he could intercept her and have a few private moments with her. Paralyzed by the hope she might comeback, but, at the same time, wanting to flee the scene, Jason stood statue-like on the sunbaked sidewalk.

Finally, he came to grips with the fact that she would not reappear again until she left at the end of her day and, not knowing when that would be, Jason stepped off the curb and into the street. Heading for the parking garage, Jason shook his head in disgust.

℞

Before settling into her cubicle to resume chipping away at the mountain of work and files on her desk, Chrissie walked to the large window looking out over Town Center Drive. From the fifth floor, she gazed down on the street glowing under the soaring Virginia sun. She glimpsed a man walking across the street toward her building. It was difficult to tell, but she swore it was Jason.

She leaned closer to the glass for a better look at the man. But he'd disappeared onto to the sidewalk near the foot of the building. Popping a stick of gum into her mouth, she lowered herself into her chair and stared at the desktop screen of her computer. Maybe, it was just her mind hoping it was him. Chrissie recalled the previous evening with Jason...and the four days leading up to it.

She had been filled with excitement and anticipation in the days leading up to dinner. After Jason had left The Colonial that Monday morning after meeting with her father, she'd practically floated around the pharmacy until her shift ended.

That evening she kept her phone at her side, hoping he'd call, and not wanting to miss it. She busied herself by doing laundry and laying out several potential outfits for her first few day at Collins, White and Casper. Having killed an hour, she then pulled out a box of pasta and a package of hamburger which she sautéed with olive oil and onions in a saucepan, then poured in sauce from a jar. She broiled some buttered slices of bread sprinkled with garlic in the oven to make poor man's Texas Toast. She poured a glass of red from an already open bottle. With her father still at the store and Eleanor off to her bridge night, Chrissie sat alone at her parent's kitchen table; eating slowly, savoring the spaghetti and Pinot Noir and imagining Jason seated across from her, reliving her meeting with him that morning and replaying their conversation in her head.

After dinner that same day in a shameless display of cocksureness, she combed through her closet looking for an outfit to wear for their dinner. Of course, at the time, she didn't know when that would occur. Nonetheless, she had stood before the mirror, placing outfits in front of her image and evaluating their appropriateness. She had settled on her favorite summer ensemble: the floral print white summer dress and the ankle strap heels. Chrissie had hung the dress on her closet door and let it stay there until their date.

With nothing left to do and still no call, she filled out her internship questionnaire for the firm. Finally, she watched a few shows on television and climbed into bed.

Tuesday had been more of the same. A long day at work, her final day at The Colonial. Her father had ordered a cake and punch to celebrate her last day. He'd given her five hundred dollars and a sweet card and told her to buy some nice work outfits. That night, again she supped with her mother and spent alone time in the evening. Still, Jason hadn't called.

She remembered thinking this was not like her. She'd given her number out a few times in her life, but never had she pined for a phone call like this. *But she had to admit she was more invested in this call because she was the one who initiated contact, and the rejection stung.* Had she not done that, had she not reached out to him, they would have passed like two strangers on a subway platform getting on different trains, never to cross paths again. Of course, it was possible they would have met if Jason had landed one of her father's rotations. But that was never a foregone conclusion.

Jason was too nervous and distracted by the interview to even give her a second look that morning. *But he had noticed her?* He had admitted as much last night. Chrissie cringed at the memory of trolling for a compliment from him and flushed with embarrassment now. That was something else she had never done.

Why had she acted like that? What was it about him that made her act this way? She couldn't quite put her finger on it, but there was something very different about Jason Rodgers. She felt more comfortable around him. She'd recognized it from the moment she'd seen him.

During dinner, he had made an off-hand comment about marriage and children, but then performed the perfect pirouette, or as they called it in politics—spin control--changing course about another date. *There wouldn't be one!*

Her recollection was abruptly interrupted by the pained knowledge that when all was said and done, she had been rejected. Jason Rodgers had done something no other man in her life had ever done. He'd turned her down. He was afraid to get involved with her because of who her father was...and the control he held over Jason's future. A sudden, deep regret filled her.

It had all ended before it ever began.

℞

A week later, Jason began his first externship at a large retail pharmacy in Hampton. The workload was incredibly fast-paced and hectic. The phones rang constantly while the bell of drive-thru dinged with similar frequency, signaling that a car had pulled up. Then in a maddening acting of impatience, the driver would push the call button before anyone had a chance to react.

A perpetual line of patients stood queued at the inside counter. Jason was thrown into the suck and expected to keep up despite having little experience with the computer system or its layout. The harried pharmacist, a young, short Asian woman with sharp, black eyes and short-cropped hair, scurried about trying to enter prescriptions into the computer, fill them, then check them and have them ready within minutes for steely-eyed, impatient, fire-breathing patients.

Only one other person was with them in the pharmacy department, a technician, a large black woman who spoke in a slow Southern drawl and moved even slower. She seemed to be unaffected by the constant flow of prescriptions, nor did she feel the apparent pressure to get them done. Though, Jason learned quickly, she had no time to fill prescriptions because she was constantly ringing the register inside before scampering as quickly as she could to the drive thru.

This was his first real, bitter taste of what it was like in retail pharmacy. Over the course of the last five days, the two pharmacists Jason had worked with, the Asian woman and a short rotund white male, had explained the demands they were expected to meet albeit with too few bodies. They were expected to call patients to recruit shots and get refills so they could meet their prescription goals all while filling hundreds of prescriptions, not receive any customer complaints and—most importantly—not make any mistakes.

He noticed on many occasions that they were so busy dealing with pick-ups or questions or just trying to get prescriptions out that the phone went unanswered. There just weren't enough bodies or hours to handle all the tasks.

The young Asian pharmacist told him that she spent many nights lying in bed unable to sleep wondering how many medication errors she'd made during a particular shift.

After that long first week, Jason returned home around seven in the evening on Friday, exhausted and hungry. He craved food and wanted something fast and did not want to wait until he got home. He stopped at a sub shop on Warwick Boulevard, ordered a large tuna and a soda. He choked down two large bites in the car along with a couple of swallows of cola before heading back to his parent's place.

As he passed Keller's Food and Drug, the sudden urge for a beer hit him. He was about to miss the turn-in of the parking lot. This second craving and last second change of mind caused him to jerk the wheel right. His balding tires squealed. The car listed left. He barely managed to slide the Civic into the parking area.

The careless maneuver placed his car on the left side of the entrance and directly in the path of another vehicle exiting onto Warwick. Jason stabbed the brake pedal, squealing the tires again. The opposing vehicle did the same. Jason saw the driver's head and torso lurch forward as the car skidded to a stop a foot from Jason's bumper.

The driver's eyes widened in surprise then instantly flashed with anger. He could see it was a woman. But the angle of the sunlight obscured most of her face. The woman threw up her hands and laid on the horn, blasting her annoyance for a good three seconds. Jason held up his hands in front of his face in a gesture trying to communicate an apology.

Unsatisfied, the woman immediately whipped open the door and hurriedly climbed out. She slammed her door and marched around the front, squeezing between the grills of the two vehicles. Then Jason recognized the car. A Volkswagen Golf. He then watched in shock and awe as Chrissie marched toward his window.

Her eyes popped when she recognized him.

$$R_x$$

"What the hell do you think you're doing?" Chrissie barked. "You almost hit me!" Her words were slightly muffled over the hum of the rattling air conditioner and through the closed window.

Jason pressed the button and the window descended. "Sorry," he said.

"What the hell is wrong with your face?"

Jason's sunburn had melted into a bronze tan on the lower half of his face. The upper half was still lily white. "Fell asleep with a towel on my face on the beach," he explained. He thought about confessing the remainder of his activities that day but decided against it.

A car pulled in behind Chrissie's Golf trying to exit the lot. Another was trying to enter the parking lot from behind Jason. Both cars honked simultaneously.

"Be more careful," she chided him.

More toots of car horns. Chrissie held up her hand impatiently.

Jason said, "I haven't eaten dinner yet. Follow me to Steve's Steakhouse and we'll grab a bite. My treat."

Chrissie spied the grinder on the seat. Its wrapper open and a couple of bites missing. Several cars on the street were now backed up behind Jason's car also waiting to pass or enter the grocery store's lot. They continued to voice their displeasure with their horns.

"Looks like you already have dinner."

"I'll save that for later. Come on," he begged. "Just dinner. An hour then you are free again."

"What if I already have plans?"

"You don't."

More blasts of multiple horns chimed longer and louder like an out-of-tune orchestra. "And how do you know that?"

"Because your first reaction was to say yes."

Chrissie looked over the Honda's roof, thinking.

"Or I won't move!" Jason added.

The driver of the car behind Chrissie's Volkswagen alighted irritated as the blaring intensified. He started to march toward them when Jason called out, "We're leaving. We're leaving," he said, waving him away with an arm through the window.

Chrissie scrunched up her lips then said, "Okay. Meet me there."

"You better show," Jason replied.

℞

They sat at a comfortable, leather-upholstered booth along the far wall of a dining area the size of a tennis court. The booths and tables were not the high-end variety, much like the restaurant's clientele and the mom-and-pop owners. They were the hard-working bourgeoisie of a middle-class town of shipyard workers, tradesmen and front-line breadwinners who sought decent food at decent prices.

Steve's Steakhouse occupied a half-acre lot of land on the southwest corner of one of the busiest intersections in Newport News: Middle Ground Boulevard and Jefferson Avenue, one of two main thoroughfares travelling the entire length of the twenty-five-mile stretch of Newport News.

The walls of the foyer were lined with framed photographs of Steve and his wife, hosting important events and serving local celebrities and politicians from decades of serving meals. Jason ate here as often as he could. It was the type of place where you showed up in jeans or shorts without feeling underdressed.

They waitress took their orders and reappeared with an iced tea for Chrissie and a beer for Jason. He took a long pull on the ice-cold longneck.

"I needed that," he said, lifting the glass. "This is what I was trying to get at Keller's. I made up my mind almost too late. I nearly missed the turn."

"Yeah. And you nearly plowed into me."

"Sorry about that."

"We're you following me?"

"What? No. Why did you ask me that?"

"Never mind," Chrissie said, sipping her tea.

"You think I'm following you?"

"No, I was just asking."

"Why?"

"Because I thought I saw you last week in City Center."

Jason's felt the expression on his face spilling forth his secret. He pretended to think. "Ah, yeah I was in City Center last week sometime."

"When did you think you saw me?"

"It was last Saturday. I was at my internship at CWC."

"Where was I?"

"I had just come back from lunch and was looking out the window onto the street. We're five floors up. So, I didn't get a good look, but it could have been you."

"I see," Jason replied, studying his beer. Then he slugged another gulp.

"Long day," Chrissie asked, eyeing the half-empty bottle.

"Long week," he countered. "I started my first rotation at Murray's in Hampton." Murray's was a regional chain with forty stores up and down the East Coast. "They're known for their brutal working conditions. And they proved it. What were you doing at your internship on a Saturday? Don't accountants get the weekends off?" Jason knew she had been scheduled to work but wanted to deflect the subject away from her sighting of him.

"Not there. They do a lot of public accounting and they're very busy. They usually take Sundays off...and we work at least a half day on Saturdays. They push the envelope with their staff. But I hear that a good recommendation from them means a lot to potential employers. Who knows, maybe they'll hire me one day."

"So, you understand, then?"

"Understand what?"

"Understand why I was hesitant to get involved."

"Maybe. Yes...and no," she admitted.

Their dinners arrived. They ate in silence for a few minutes. Chrissie nibbled on a Caesar salad while Jason devoured a large cheeseburger and fries.

"Have some," he offered, spinning the side of the plate holding the fries toward her.

She eyed him for a moment, then grabbed one off his plate. "Thanks."

"No problem," he replied. "Have as many as you like."

Jason ordered a second beer. He turned the conversation to less controversial issues like sports, music and family histories. Jason told him about his sister, Katherine, who lived in Fort Myers, Florida.

"Why is she in Florida?"

"She married a doctor. Katherine's a nurse. Or, at least, she was. She worked in the ICU at Sentara Norfolk General. Hubby was a resident there. They fell in love. When his residency was done, he proposed and moved them down there. She doesn't practice nursing anymore. They have three kids under seven. She's the ultimate soccer mom."

Chrissie nodded and smiled. "What kind of doctor is he?"

"He's an internist with a subspecialty in geriatrics. What about you? Any brothers or sisters?"

Chrissie shook her head as she poached another fry from his plate. "No, my mom always said they broke the mold when I was born. I think they tried. She had a couple of miscarriages after I was born. But she doesn't talk about it. Plus, Daddy has always been consumed with his work."

Jason raised his beer. "Well, your mom's right they did pretty good on their first try."

Chrissie grinned. "Thanks."

The waitress offered them dessert. They both begged off. On the way out the door, Jason paid the bill at the register and left a generous tip. He walked Chrissie to her car which was parked three spots away from the Honda.

"Thanks for dinner," she said.

"No problem. Glad I almost ran into you." He flashed her a wide grin. The sun had dipped below the tree line, but an orange-reddish hue still painted the flat clouds.

Chrissie's rich, liquid eyes appeared almost a sienna red in the vanishing light. They were wide and intelligent and, once again, seemed to draw him in. A long moment yawned between them as they held each other's gazes with unspoken thoughts.

"I guess I better go," she said turning. "Thanks again."

Jason reached out and touched her arm, stopping her. "Can I make a confession?"

Chrissie appeared slightly nonplussed by his question. "I don't know, can you?"

"I was at City Center last week. Last Saturday."

"So you are following me?"

"No," he countered. "Running into you today was just a coincidence. I was at my externship in Hampton until I drove home. I was there all week. I don't have time to follow you."

"So, were you following me last Saturday?"

"No. I came there to find you."

"You did?"

Jason nodded. "I actually bought some flowers and came to your office. But they said you were at lunch. So, I walked around to all the restaurants looking for you."

"And you didn't find me?"

"No. Well, yes, I did. I saw you coming out of the Southern Belle with a guy. Preppy-looking, chubby-faced. You were walking across the street. I had just turned the corner and was heading there when you came out."

Chrissie smiled and nodded. "Really?" She asked with an intrigued lilt in her voice.

"Who was the guy?"

"Jealous?"

"No, just curious"

Chrissie glanced at her shoes, recalling the time and place of the lunch. "That's Aiden. He's another intern." Then a thought occurred to her. "You could have called. Unless you deleted my number from your phone."

"I thought about it. But I wanted it to be a surprise." Jason had stepped closer as he uttered those words. He hesitated with his next statement, looking at her high heel ankle boots and the hems of her tight jeans that stopped just above the boot. "I...um...made a mistake," he confessed.

"Yeah, what kind?"

Jason peered into her magnetic caramel eyes. "I want to see you. I want to get to know you. I like you. And I don't want to let my externship at The Colonial or your father to get in the way of that."

"Really?" Chrissie moved her head away a few inches as she absorbed the news.

Jason nodded. "I was overly worried...kind of overwhelmed, too. I guess."

Jason opened his mouth to say something else, but Chrissie had recovered and stepped into his space. She placed her warm lips on his and pressed them there for a long moment.

"Wow," Jason said as they separated. "I was just hoping to get a second date."

"That was the kiss I asked you for and then denied you."

Jason smiled. "Well, I hope there are more of those to come."

"Call me," Chrissie said, getting in the Golf.

"Let's do something tonight," he persisted.

"I'd love to. But I have plans with a girlfriend and I have some work to get done for tomorrow morning."

PHARMACY PHACT:

There were 321,700 pharmacists in the United States in 2019. And those positions are expected to decline to 311,200 by 2029.

Occupational Outlook Handbook, U.S. Bureau of Labor

CHAPTER 13

Over the next two weeks, they saw each other four times. Twice for lunch and twice for dinner, these meals were less extravagant than their first at the Vintage Tavern. Because Chrissie was not alone at home on these occasions, they met at various places to begin their dates like parking lots at John Radcliffe University or the grocery store. Their first lunch occurred three days after their chance encounter in the Keller Food and Drug parking lot. It was at a place called Asian Grill, a small Chinese restaurant nestled in the center of a strip of shops up the road from Keller's Food and Drug. It was a twelve-table affair and had earned a reputation as one of the best in the 757-area code. Their third date and second lunch, two days after date number two, happened at Plaza Azteca on Jefferson Avenue and their fourth rendezvous was at a burger joint near Patrick Henry Mall.

With each date they learned a little more about each other. The strong attraction they held for each other deepened quickly. Chrissie quizzed Jason about pharmacy school and his soon-to-be profession. Jason was impressed by what she already knew about it. Since she had worked as a technician at The Colonial, her knowledge was not surprising. It was obvious Thomas had discussed with Chrissie many issues regarding his future career. And Chrissie had retained and understood a great deal.

Jason asked her about accounting and Virginia Tech. She said the Blacksburg campus was wonderful and her professors were first rate. As an only child, she didn't like being so far away from her mother and father, but she enjoyed the freedom.

He also interrogated her about her father and what he could expect from his externship even though it was still months in the future. Chrissie outlined for him a sketch of the man and the pharmacist.

Thomas Pettigrew was a perfectionist and a demanding boss. He cared about his patients and put their well-being and safety above all else. He expected his technicians to use their heads and not just perform tasks like preprogrammed automatons. He constantly educated, taught and counseled them, squeezing every ounce of performance from them. If they didn't show improvement, they were counseled. If after the counseling, they still did not adapt, they were let go. If they were habitually late or called out sick frequently, they were let go. He'd fired four in the last two years, she told him.

"Wow," Jason whispered.

"Many pharmacy technicians are not always dedicated to the profession. Like any profession, you have your high performers, your middle mousers and your slackers. He wants to know that his technicians are learning and growing. It's hard to find good help with what some of the chains pay these people. Some make only a little more than cashiers at grocery stores. And they're handling patient's medications. My father pays better because he can. But the chains are really cheap."

After their lunches or dinners, they would drive around the large finger of land known as the Peninsula, surrounded on three sides by different rivers: the James, Elizabeth and York. Or they would go and sit by the water at Huntington Beach and chat and cuddle in the warm late summer breeze.

Jason learned that Christine Pettigrew was a hard-working, extremely intelligent woman. She could crunch numbers with speed and accuracy. She had not lied when she'd told him she was a "numbers' girl." Once during their third date, they were discussing math and the subject of Pi, the ratio of a circle's circumference to its diameter, had come up. If you divided the circumference by the diameter, it always returned the same number and it was an endless, non-repeating decimal...3.14159...and so on.

Chrissie told him that she had memorized the decimal portion of it out to one hundred places. Incredulous, Jason tested her. He pulled up pi on his phone and punched it in. Chrissie recited it. She spilled out the numbers like she was reciting a long ago learned prayer that had been burned into her DNA.

Jason stopped her after thirty-five places. "Okay, okay...I give. That's very impressive."

On their fourth date as they sat eating burgers at Red Robin, they discussed the recent past and the future.

"Have you had fun these last two weeks? Jason asked.

"Yes, I have," Chrissie replied. "Have you?"

Jason nodded. "Very much so. I guess we'll keep seeing each other?"

"What is this, the two-week free trial period is over and now I have to give you my credit card number?"

Jason chuckled. "No, I just wanted to make sure you were still interested."

When they weren't together, they talked by phone in the evenings three or four times a week. Their conversations lasted hours, discussing their days, what their jobs were like, who they liked working with and who they didn't.

Chrissie would tell Jason about interesting firms that Collins, White and Casper had retained as clients. Jason would share interesting encounters in the pharmacy from dying patients who couldn't afford their medications to the difficult, drug-addicted pains-in-the-asses trying to weasel early refills of opiates or sleeping pills from the pharmacist. On the weekends, Chrissie was always free on Saturday evenings and Sundays, but Jason had to pull shifts every other weekend since he was externing in mostly retail settings. But they would make time to see each other when neither had to work the next day. Their dates lasted into the wee morning hours. At the end of each date, they would sit in Jason's old Honda, making out. Kissing eventually led to fondling. They parked wherever they could find a secluded spot, steaming up the windows well past midnight. Jason would then drive her back to her car and go home, hot, bothered and frustrated.

Chrissie said it would be a good idea not to see each other during the week if they were going to have such late nights. She worked ten- to eleven-hour days at the firm. And Jason, she said, needed to be sharp, when filling prescriptions. Jason agreed.

Six weeks in, with Jason about to start his second rotation at a hospital, their relationship continued to hurtle along. Their carnal desire gained speed like an express locomotive going downhill in high gear. Their dates had progressed past steaming up the windows of the Honda or the Volkswagen.

One night in the cramped backseat of his Honda, Chrissie brought the runaway train to a screeching halt. They lay together, kissing and fondling. They groaned and moaned in anticipatory ecstasy. Her blouse and bra had been shed. Her jeans were unbuckled and open. Jason's clothes were in a similar state. Their hands groped and fondled warm, sweaty skin. Chrissie had brought him to the edge of completion, nibbling on his ear and gently caressing him. Jason began to pull off her jeans. His hand slipped into her panties. Chrissie arched her back and moaned soft and low, running her hands through his thick hair.

"Oh, Jason," she sighed.

"Chrissie, I want you," Jason whispered as he began to push his jeans past his hips.

"I want you, too."

Then without warning, Chrissie stiffened. She placed her hands against his bare chest and gently pushed him away.

Jason stopped, gawking at her wondering what he'd done. "What's wrong?"

"I can't. Not here."

"What? Why?"

Her large eyes peered into his. She was ready for him. He could see it, taste it.

"I don't want to do this here," she said.

Jason sat back, his breathing heavy and rapid. "Geez, Chrissie, you're killing me here."

They slowly dressed in the back seat in an awkward silence. Each slipped from the back to the front seat. He started the car and drove in a frustrated manner, gunning the engine on starts and braking hard for the stops. He pulled into the spot next to her white Volkswagen Golf so that she was beside the driver's door.

"You're mad!" She said anxiously.

Jason sighed. "No, Chrissie, I'm not mad."

"You seem mad."

"I'm frustrated. We get together. Then we get all hot and bothered then I have to take you home. Hell, it's not even home. I take you back to a parking lot and your car!"

Chrissie smiled. "So, you want me?"

Jason chuckled and shook his head. He shot her a wide grin. "Yes, Very badly." He placed his hand on his crotch. His erection threatened to poke a hole through his jeans. "So does my buddy here."

Chrissie leaned over and placed her hand between his legs. "My goodness," she said. "He sure does. We're going to have to do something about that."

"We don't have anywhere to go to be alone. We can't go to your house because you don't want your father knowing that I'm dating you...And I guess I don't either."

"Believe me, you don't want him to know…not yet."

"I'm still living with my parents until I graduate, so it's awkward to go there."

"Jason, I don't want our first time to be in the backseat of a car like we're in high school or something. I want it to be...special."

"I do to," Jason agreed. "But we better think of something fast 'cause my balls are turning from blue to purple."

"Oh Jason. Bless you heart!"

Jason smiled tensely and shook his head. "Oh no. Don't say that. I know what that means. That's Southern for 'You poor bastard'!"

Chrissie brought her hand to her mouth and began to giggle. Jason's statement about the color of his testicles had been delivered with extreme seriousness through a tight-lipped scowl. Her giggle grew in intensity morphing into a chortle then an all-out full-throated laugh. She howled. Finally, the comical aspect of his predicament loosened the edges of his frustration and torment. The corners of his lips lifted into a grin. As Chrissie sucked in another lungful of air allowing her to continue her laughing fit, Jason joined in and they laughed until they cried.

When they could sustain it no longer, they fell into a happy silence, catching their breath and wiping away joyful tears. Chrissie leaned over the center console hugged him. She whispered in his ear, "I'm sorry, baby. I want to so bad." Her words brimmed with love and desire.

He kissed her hard and long. Then he pulled back and said, "I'm going to get us a hotel room. We'll have a nice dinner then go back to our room and I'm going to screw your lights out!"

She smiled. Then a measure of concern spread over her features. "You can't afford that, you're not working. You still haven't paid off the credit card charge for the dinner at Vintage Tavern."

"I don't care. I can't afford not to," Jason scoffed, glancing down at the bulge in his pants.

℞

Chrissie regarded Jason in the dim light spilling into the cab from a streetlamp. Incredibly handsome and vulnerable, he was a sorry sight. His eyes were filled with desire and frustration. It was the ultimate compliment that he wanted her so desperately. But she was not going to compromise. She had seen this coming. They had no place to go for privacy...intimacy, except the backseat of a rusting Honda.

This budding relationship held mountains of promise. He was not like the other boys she'd dated. She'd had many potential suitors. But only a handful had ever been allowed to darken her father's doorstep for an official date. Of those, she had not felt any kind of true connection. They were either too self-centered, lacked ambition or were intimidated by her wit and playfulness. Jason Rodgers was a different kind of man. He was smart, funny and motivated. And most definitely not intimidated.

That fact that he'd initially balked at a second date and then had changed his mind and had the guts to reverse course was extremely endearing and the ultimate compliment.

Her first time with Jason Rodgers was going to be something she--and he--would remember for the rest of their lives. She was going to fall in love with him. She was already halfway there.

Jason had been paying for all their dates. As the man, he expected nothing less from himself, he'd told her. He'd figure out a way to pay it off somehow. He'd picked up some extra cash with the landscaping job a few weeks back. He could work on the weekends, spreading mulch and cutting grass for Jim the landscaper.

Chrissie had offered to pay. She was working and getting paid after all. His externships were unpaid help for the pharmacies in which he toiled. Chrissie felt bad that he was going into debt for them to see each other. She vowed then and there that would stop for a while. There were plenty of things to do that cost little or nothing. She would figure out what they were.

But first, she decided, they were going to get that hotel room. She was going to give herself over to Jason Rodgers. And make it a night he would never forget.

"Okay," Chrissie said. "We can get a hotel room. You make the arrangements. But I'm going to pay for it. I'm getting paid. You're not."

Jason opened his mouth to protest.

"I won't take no for answer." She unbuttoned her blouse and lowered the cups of her bra, flashing her breasts. "If you refuse me, you won't see these ever again. Understood?"

Jason's gazed whipped between her eyes and her chest. "Whatever you say, ma'am."

She leaned over and kissed him again and moved his hand to her still exposed breasts. "And since I'm paying, you better perform well, sailor. I expect nothing but the best."

PHARMACY PHACT:

[Pharmacy dates back to the beginning of man's presence on Earth.] Paleopharmacological studies attest to the use of medicinal plants during prehistoric times.

Ellis, Linda (2000). *Archaeological Method and Theory: An Encyclopedia.* Taylor & Francis: pp 443-448. ISBN 978-0-8153-1305-2

CHAPTER 14

One week later on Friday, Jason met Chrissie in the parking lot of the Hilton Garden Inn in Newport News, near the York County line. They drove separately and parked beside each other. Chrissie hopped out of her Golf and into the passenger side of Jason's Honda.

"Let's check in, first," she instructed.

"Did you bring a suitcase?"

She nodded. "It's in the car. I'll get it after dinner."

Jason and Chrissie had concocted their alibis for the night. Jason was having a night of poker and drinking with the guys. Since they would be drinking, he was going to stay over. He would be back the next morning, he told his mother. And, yes, they had a designated driver. His father rattled his newspaper as Jason passed and said, "Be safe. Have a good time." He hesitated a beat then added, "What's her name?"

Jason smiled, thought about lying and said, "Christine."

"Are you packing protection? You need a job before you make me a grandfather!'"

"Good night, Pop," Jason said as he closed the door.

Chrissie, on the other hand, told her parents that she was going to a birthday party in Norfolk at The Main for one of her co-workers at the firms' Norfolk office. "Have fun, dear," her mother, Eleanor said.

Thomas Pettigrew gave her a peck on the forehead. "When do we get to meet this guy?"

Chrissie hedged and replied, "As soon as I find a good one, I'll let you know."

"Make sure he treats you right," he called after her as she closed the door.

They walked the thirty yards to the hotel hand-in-hand. Chrissie wore a loose white V-neck sweater and pair of skintight black slacks. Her black open-toed, three-inch pumps clicked smartly as they crossed the pavement. A pair of pearl earrings hung from her petite ears and a matching choker circled her neck. Her hair sashayed from side to side as she walked, bouncing playfully with each step.

Jason wore a blue button-down oxford, a pair of neatly pressed khakis and brown deck shoes.

It was the first week of October and the evening air had begun to take on a chill. He took her hand in his and squeezed gently.

"You look amazing. D-D-F-G, as a matter of fact."

"Thank you! Look you spiffy yourself. You gonna tell me what that means?"

"Eventually," he answered beaming.

Chrissie shook her head and smiled.

After they checked in, they returned to the car. They drove a few miles to The Vineyards Trattoria in the Kiln Creek section of Newport News. Set in a quaint, shaded strip mall with quick service and exquisite wines, Jason thought it a romantic way to begin their evening.

He pulled out her chair as they were seated. He placed his nose into her hair and breathed in a long breath. "Wow, that's a new perfume. I love it."

Chrissie's face lit up as the waiter appeared with a basket of gnocchi and water.

One hour and a bottle of chianti later, stuffed and sated, the check was placed between them. Chrissie scooped it up as Jason reached for his wallet.

"This whole evening's on me, darling."

"We agreed you would pay for the hotel," Jason replied a little too loudly. A diner at the next table gave a quick glance. Jason nodded at him quietly and turned back to Chrissie.

"I know," Chrissie said evenly. "But I thought about it. This night is my treat." She leaned over and whispered through an expectant grin. "Remember I expect to get my money's worth later."

"Thank you for dinner, baby."

"You're welcome. Let's go."

Jason raced back to the hotel. He slowed at each stop sign but rolled through them rather than coming to a full stop. Then he gunned the gas, causing Chrissie to say, "Easy Jason, I'm not going anywhere."

Jason slowed reluctantly. Five minutes later, they were in the Hilton parking lot again. Chrissie retrieved her overnight bag from the Golf and Jason pulled his suitcase from his back seat. Another few minutes later, they rolled their suitcases along the carpeted hallway to the room on the third floor.

Jason placed the key card against the pad on the door. The light turned green and the door clicked open. The room was comfortable and well-furnished and had all the typical features of a standard hotel room. A queen-sized bed sat in the middle of the room flanked on either side by nightstands and facing a large flat screen television that would not be used this evening.

Jason strode to the window and spread the thick drapes. "Not much of a view unless you like looking at the Farm Fresh."

Chrissie walked past him and quickly closed them, "You're not going to need to be seeing anything out there tonight!"

She turned to him, stood on her tiptoes and gave him a long kiss. When she pulled back, he moved his hand along her side and to the swell of her breast.

"Not so fast."

"What do you want me to do?"

"I want you to stay right there. Don't take anything off, just relax for a minute while I get ready."

"Get ready?"

"Yeah. I have to get ready. You want me to look beautiful for you, right?"

"You already are."

"Well, I do declare, Mister Jason," Chrissie replied in her best Scarlett O'Hara voice, "that you just gave me a compliment." She fluttered her eyelids and pretended to wave a fan on her face.

"You should have been an actress."

Chrissie smiled, kissed him hard on the lips once more and disappeared into the bathroom with her overnight bag. Jason had anticipated this moment as well. He moved to his suitcase and removed three tall fat candles. He placed one on the credenza beside the television and one on each nightstand. Digging a lighter from his bag, he lit each candle and the turned off the lights, smiling at his romantic handiwork. The soft flickering candlelight created a golden, amber glow. Finally, Jason removed a single long stem rose from the pouch of his bag and placed it on one of the nightstands beside the candle. He retrieved a bottle of cologne from the suitcase, sprayed two squirts in his hands and patted them over his cheeks and neck.

℞

"Looks like your boy," Victor chided Simon through his cell phone, "is finally getting some tonight."

"Are they at the hotel?"

"Yep. You owe me twenty bucks."

With little else to do but babysit the couple, Victor and Simon had wagered that Jason Rodgers would finally have his way with Pettigrew's daughter. It was not so much "if" but "where." Simon had said that they would not be able to resist each other and it would happen in one of their vehicles. Victor had predicted, correctly as it appeared, they would do it in a bed, perhaps a parent's bed while they were away. Neither man would have guessed they would hire a hotel room.

They were monitoring Christine Pettigrew, her father and all the employees at The Colonial. Since Jason Rodgers would be his student in six months, they were also tracking his movements along with the other externs who had earned spots with Pettigrew. None of the other students Pettigrew had precepted showed anything other than what they expected from twenty-somethings in college.

Jason Rodgers, as they were learning each day, was a principled and determined man. He was something else altogether. A force to be watched...and possibly dealt with.

℞

Jason planted himself in the comfortable side chair and tried to relax. But the nerves in his gut performed an electric dance of anticipation. He drummed his fingers on the arm of the chair and tapped his shoe on the carpet.

"How much longer?"

"Just another minute," Chrissie called from behind the bathroom door.

Thirty seconds later, it swung open and a sterile white light cut through the room, obscuring the candlelight. Jason heard the light switch click and the bathroom light went dark. Two clicks of her shoes on the tiled floor and Chrissie appeared from the bathroom, stepping into the bedroom with the long, silky stride of a lingerie model.

Jason's eyes widened in boyish adoration as if the teenage crush from a girly magazine had just materialized before his eyes. Instinctively, he rose to his feet. Chrissie strode to him as if floating. Jason stepped in her direction, meeting her between the television credenza and the queen-sized bed.

"Oh my God, Chrissie," he whispered as his eyes soaked in the sight of her.

At dinner, Jason had marveled at his good fortune to be seen around town with such a beautiful woman. Chrissie, as always, was the complete package; well-dressed, composed and witty. He didn't think it possible, but the few minutes she'd spent in the bathroom had transformed her into an alluring siren with a come-hither gaze and plenty of exposed, soft, supple skin. She had somehow managed to make her hair appear different, more sensual than it was only minutes ago. Her caramel eyes invited him to make love to her. Her perfect skin glowed, begging him to touch it. No words could adequately describe what he felt and saw at this moment.

Jason placed his hand along the side of her face, pushing a lock of hair behind her ear, releasing a burst of alluring fragrance that filled his nostrils. His thumb caressed her cheek just above the jaw in slow, gentle arcs at the edge of her moist, round lips. He wanted to kiss her then and there, to take her now on the bed. But he resisted the impulse, he wanted to admire her and burn this image into his memory.

He moved back one step. "Let me look at you," he said.

He tore his eyes away from hers and permitted his gaze to descend past the cute nose and moist, pillowy lips to the smooth curve of her neck, sliding along the gentle slope of her throat to the swell of her creamy breasts. The black lacy brassiere cradled them, squeezing them into a deep, long cleavage into which Jason wanted to disappear. The lacy fabric allowed a dark, gauzy hint of the skin and nipples beneath. Only moments ago, as she strode toward him, these perfectly proportioned, teardrop mounds swayed and undulated in unison with each stride.

As his eyes wandered over her flat mid-section and her belly button, the fingers of each hand moved over the contours of her hourglass torso, coming together where the waist narrowed and then meandering outward as they approached her hips and meeting the fabric of her matching panties. Unable to stop himself, Jason allowed his fingers to continue past, proceeding along the profile of her well-toned thighs. He allowed the tip of his thumb to slip under the hem of the panty, tantalizingly close to her womanhood. Her long, athletic legs struck a model's pose. Her petite feet still wore the black, sexy pumps she'd been wearing at dinner.

Chrissie grabbed both of his hands in hers and held them out wide. "You like?"

"Wow," he replied in a breathless, awe-struck tone. "You are a vision."

"I like what you've done with the atmosphere." She whispered gazing around the room. She elevated on her tiptoes again and pressed her lips against his. Their tongues explored, thrusting and withdrawing in the tantalizing dance of foreplay. She wrapped her arms around his neck as he squeezed her hard, near-naked body into his. His firmness swelled and announced itself. His hands gently clasped her torso; his thumbs found the swell of her breasts through the brassiere and stroked slowly.

She pulled back. "Make love to me Jason." Her breathy whispered words were those of an angel. Jason pressed his hips into her. Chrissie matched it. Then she took him by the hand and led him around to the side of the bed. Chrissie sat and scooted fully onto the mattress. She laid back, peered up at Jason with wide bedroom eyes and patted the bed beside her.

Jason raced around to the opposite side, quickly shedding his jacket and unbuttoning his shirt. Now bare-chested, he crawled over the mattress to her. He dug his face into her neck and hair, nuzzling his way back to her lips. They kissed again losing themselves in a chasm of want. Their hands explored each other's bodies until they each brimmed with anticipation and expectation.

Jason pulled back and looked at her. "There's one more thing," he said, "before we make love."

"What?" Chrissie asked breathlessly.

"Close your eyes."

Chrissie compiled.

Jason whispered, "A little more foreplay..."

Jason reached across her, pressing his bare chest against her heaving torso. He retrieved the single rose and brought the plump, perfect flower to her lips, touching it to her nose. Chrissie sucked in a long breath of fragrance.

With the rose in his right hand, Jason moved his left arm under Chrissie's head and said, "Give me your hand."

Chrissie moved her left hand to Jason's. He closed his fingers around her left wrist, holding it firmly. He gently pinned her right arm to the bed with his body and now held her free hand in his. "Just so you don't try to getaway."

With her eyes still closed, she lifted her head trying to find his lips. "Never," she sighed.

Jason placed the flower back on her lips, sliding it along her cheek. Then across her forehead and down the bridge of her nose, over her lips once more and to the edge of her chin. Chrissie raised her chin, anticipating where it would go next, willing it to find a target.

"I can't stand this," she begged.

"Just a few more seconds," he replied as he moved the pedals down along her throat to the top of her chest at the collarbone. He hesitated there and kissed her cheek. Chrissie rotated her head and found his lips.

Jason said, "I'm going to let go of your arm. Move onto your side so I can take off your bra."

Chrissie rolled toward him. He placed the rose on her shoulder and moved his right hand around to her back. With one quick flick, the brassiere clasp snapped open. "Wow," she said impressed as she rolled onto her back again. "Do that often?"

"I get lucky once in a while." He helped her out of her bra, picked up the rose and placed it between her breasts. For the next two minutes, he moved it expertly over her body as Chrissie writhed and squirmed beside him.

Finally, she could stand it no longer. Struggling free from Jason's loose grasp, she slipped out from under him. In a minute, she had helped him out his trousers and underwear. Chrissie shed her panties and shoes. In the glow of flickering candlelight, they lay legs entwined, hands and fingers exploring every inch of skin. Suddenly, Chrissie stopped and rolled atop him as she pushed herself to a kneeling position. She gazed down at him as a wicked, mischievous smile spread across her face.

"What?" he said.

"Before you make love to me, I want something."

"Okay. What?"

"Tell me what it means," she demanded.

"Tell you what 'what' means?"

"You know, D-D-F-G. You said it was a compliment."

"Oh, it is," he replied with a smirk.

Chrissie puffed up her chest slightly. "If you're going to have me tonight, you will tell me."

An impish smile curved up one side of his face. "Let me think about it," he countered. His face taking on a serious moue. A moment of confused hesitation and a flash of doubt flickered over her features.

"You wouldn't?" She dared.

"I ain't stupid." Jason elevated his hips with a quick thrust, tossed Chrissie to one side and back onto the bed. She squealed in surprise. This time, Jason assumed the dominate position, poised and ready, over her. He lowered his head inches from hers, drinking in her scent. He kissed her softly and long on the lips then moved his mouth to her ear. He gently clamped the lobe gently between his teeth and flicked it with his tongue. Chrissie moaned, arching her back. Her hand reached for him, finding his firmness.

Jason maneuvered closer to her as Chrissie guided him to the edge of an all-encompassing bliss.

"It means...You're Drop-Dead-Fucking-Gorgeous!" He groaned, plunging inside her and becoming swallowed by the ecstasy.

CHAPTER 15

Their relationship played out swimmingly over the next few months. They managed to keep their dating a secret with well-planned dates away from Newport News. They spent time in Norfolk, Williamsburg and on the Southside of Hampton Roads in Virginia Beach and Chesapeake. Only the one time on their first date had Jason picked Chrissie up at her front door.

Jason continued with his string of pharmacy rotations at various sites around the area while Chrissie ground away long hours at the accounting firm. However, one late afternoon in mid-November, their secret relationship was nearly obliterated by a nearly fateful left-hand turn.

Chrissie and Jason had returned home from an afternoon romping around Colonial Williamsburg. Chrissie needed some make-up and asked Jason to stop at the mall on Jefferson Avenue. They entered through the north doors and strolled and chatted toward the large up-scale department store where she always purchased her cosmetics.

"I don't like that we're not going to be able to spend family time together at Christmas," she said forlornly.

"I know. But it will only be for this year. Best not to upset the apple cart, especially around the holidays."

Chrissie frowned. "I guess."

"We'll have our own private Christmas."

"They suspect I'm seeing someone. Daddy mentioned it that night we spent at the hotel. And he's asked a couple more times."

"Mine did too. They're not as dumb as they look. Since we're not telling your folks, I haven't said anything to mine either. But they know somethings going on." Jason failed to mention that he had told his father her name the night of their hotel stay.

"Mom and Dad have both said something several times in the last month. I don't like keeping the secret, Jason."

"I don't either. But it's just until springtime. Once my rotation with your father is over, we tell him. We'll tell my parents, too. You know how your father would react."

"I guess," Chrissie repeated.

They strolled passed a shoe store towards the Macy's wing where Chrissie planned on making her purchases. They began to turn right down the large wide colonnade when Jason stopped short, spotting a kiosk with sports memorabilia.

"I want to take a look over there. Do you want me to catch up with you?"

"Naw," Chrissie replied. "I'll come with you. But be quick about it."

They strolled to the kiosk filled with photos of all kinds of sports heroes, logoed hats and shirts along with all kinds of cups, glasses and other sundries emblazoned with team logos.

The kiosk possessed a small footprint but was floor-to-ceiling and filled with goods on all four sides. Jason perused the collection of Red Sox hats and shirts and an autographed action photo of David Ortiz. Chrissie meandered to the opposite side of the small kiosk, checking out the supply of Virginia Tech shirts.

"Well, well, well, if it isn't my future student!"

Jason's heart nearly stopped when he heard the words and the voice delivering them. He'd only spoken to Thomas Pettigrew during his interview back in August. But he could never forget the formidable and authoritative timbre of that voice.

"Ah…"

Thomas Pettigrew waited for words from Jason…any words. Jason stood perplexed and dumfounded.

"You do remember me? Thomas. Thomas Pettigrew. The Colonial Pharmacy," he stated, extending a large beefy hand.

"Ah…yeah. I mean, 'yes'. I'm sorry. Forgive me, Mr. Pettigrew." Jason replied, adding extra emphasis to his name. He dared not look around for Chrissie. "I'm sorry. Forgive me. You surprised me. Doing some shopping?"

Pettigrew nodded. "Just window shopping. Killing sometime while Eleanor tries on some dresses."

"Eleanor?"

"My wife, she's in Macy's right now."

Jason could not resist and he glanced quickly to his right, looking for Chrissie. He did not see her. And he did not know if she heard her father's voice or if she had any idea what was happening.

℞

Chrissie heard Jason speaking to someone. At first, she didn't understand what he was saying. Then she recognized her father's voice coming from around the corner of the small kiosk. The size of the kiosk seemed to shrink with each passing second.

She froze. Her father had somehow snuck up on Jason.

Had he seen her?

Had he seen them…together?

Chrissie slipped to her left and peeked with one eye around the corner of the kiosk. Jason was angled with his back to her talking to her father who she could not see. But his words were clear and distinct.

"…she's in Macy's right now."

Chrissie thought about stepping forward and interrupting the conversation. She could pretend that Jason and she did not know each and feign an initial meeting. Or she could just step up and place her arm around Jason, thus telling her father everything. Though she wanted to, she also did not want to go against Jason's wishes.

Instead, she stood stock still, listening.

Her father was asking Jason a question. "Are you a big sports fan!"

"Yessir. Big Red Sox and Patriots fan."

Chrissie could see the right side of her father's body. He had crossed his arms in front of him. His massive left hand rested on his right bicep. She could see his right shoulder but that was all. If her father took one step to his right or leaned farther in, he would see her.

"I'm particular to the Redskins myself."

She watched as the visible portion of her father's body disappeared.

"Let's see if they have any 'Skins stuff."

Jason glanced her way. His eyes widened and his eyebrows hiked higher.

There were gaps in the merchandise hanging on the stall of the kiosk allowing one to see through to the opposite side. Chrissie saw her father's torso moving slowly toward her end of the kiosk apparently perusing the merchandise. She moved around towards Jason on the opposite side, moving in the opposite direction but in concert with her father.

She looked toward Jason. He was out of sight now and moving around to the other side of the kiosk along with her father, still engaging him in conversation.

"'Skins have had it tough lately," she heard Jason say.

"Yeah, ever since Gibbs left," her father replied. "They have not done well. They need a quarterback."

Chrissie discarded any thoughts of confronting her father and darted to her left and away from the kiosk. She aimed straight for Macy's department store. As she did, she removed her mobile, tapped the screen several times and initiated a call.

$$R_x$$

Jason watched Pettigrew slowly scanning the sports merchandise as he tried to focus on his words.

"Would you like that?" Pettigrew's question pulled Jason from his distraction.

"I'm sorry, sir," he replied as his phone chirped.

"I said I am acquainted with our Congressman from this district. I was fortunate enough to be invited to speak before the Subcommittee on Health in Washington as part of a panel discussing reform. I played golf with him once. I can get tickets to the Redskins owner's box. Would you be interested?"

His phone chirped louder. "Most definitely, sir." He removed the phone, checked the screen and announced, "Excuse me, I need to take this."

Pettigrew nodded as Jason clicked onto the call and moved out of earshot. "Hello there," he said sotto voce as his heart thumped in his chest.

"Hi there, darling. Are you having fun?"

"Did he see you?" Jason whispered.

"I don't think so. I stayed out of sight. I'm walking towards Macy's. Extricate yourself and meet me there."

"Be careful," Jason replied, glancing over his shoulder at Chrissie's father. "He said your mother is in Macy's!"

"What?!"

Oh Chrissie! What are you doing here! Jason heard a woman's voice coming faintly over the line.

"Okay, Stacy," Jason heard Chrissie say loudly on her end. "I see my mother. I'll call you in a few."

The call ended abruptly.

℞

"Mom," Chrissie replied, placing the phone in her purse. "What are you doing here?"

"Just trying on dresses," Eleanor Pettigrew replied, holding up a bag full of clothing.

"It looks like you did more than try them on."

"Did you see your father, honey?"

"Is he here? I must have missed him."

"He said he'd be waiting right outside."

"Nope, didn't see him."

Eleanor glanced at her watch. "I'll have dinner ready at six. Why don't you bring the mystery man over so your father and I can meet him?"

Chrissie smiled and lied. "Sorry, mom. He's working."

℞

"I'd love the chance to see the 'Skins play," Jason said as he returned to the kiosk.

"I'll see if I can make that happen," Pettigrew replied. He checked his watch. "I better go find the missus before she spends so much I have to close the store. Good seeing you again, son."

"You, too, sir."

Pettigrew smiled and said, "*Considera aegrum totum.*" He then spun and walked toward Macy's.

$$\text{R}_\text{x}$$

Chrissie's phone rang. She clicked on.

"He's on his way to you," Jason's voice announced softly. "I'll meet you at the south entrance in ten minutes."

"There's my girl," Thomas declared, wrapping an arm around his daughter's shoulder. "I just saw one of my future students, Jason Rodgers. He came in for an interview this past summer. He's scheduled for a rotation with me in April."

"Oh really," Chrissie replied. "You've had so many, Daddy. I can't remember them all."

"We will see you for dinner?"

"Yeah, I'll be there." Chrissie kissed her parent's cheeks in turn, told them she still needed to buy make-up and departed. Having lost the desire to shop, Chrissie entered Macy's, marched right through the store and exited to the outside. She found Jason with his car idling near the south entrance.

"That was interesting," Chrissie declared as she slid into the passenger's side.

"Yeah," Jason replied. "I need to change my underwear."

As Jason pulled from the curb, they sighed simultaneously then burst into a prolonged episode of relieved laughter.

CHAPTER 16

Sɪx Mᴏɴᴛʜs Lᴀᴛᴇʀ

The Colonial's pharmacy department--abuzz with activity--to the untrained eye looked like a discordant jumble of uncoordinated sounds and movement. Four phone lines blinked with callers waiting to speak with the pharmacist on-duty, probably patients or doctor's offices, no doubt wanting to ask a question, address an issue or call-in new prescriptions. Small countertop printers hummed, ejecting prescription labels that would find their way onto amber vials stuffed with pills or capsules. Larger under-the-counter laser jets dispensed massive quantities of paper prescription receipts and information leaflets that accompanied each prescription. A fax machine chimed as an incoming fax was about to fall into the output tray. Amidst it all, two blue-coated technicians scurried back and forth between the drug bays and the prescription bench fetching stock bottles like harried squirrels gathering nuts.

Intermittently, the sound of tablets or multi-colored capsules splashed onto specialized counting trays and was immediately followed by rapid strokes of the metal spatulas scratching across hard plastic and depositing the medications into an open hinged cylindrical chamber on the left side of the tray. When the appropriate number of pills had been counted, a flick of a finger snapped the chamber shut. The excess pills were returned to the stock bottle, then an amber vial was positioned against the small opening at the end of the chamber, the tray and the chamber were lifted, and the pills were transferred to the vial. The correct-sized cap was twisted on and a label affixed. When all the prescriptions for an order were finished, the stock bottle, the vial and the paperwork were placed in a small basket and slid to pharmacist's computer station for final approval.

Once there, Pettigrew or Kyle Griffin, The Colonial's staff pharmacist, would review the technician's work by removing the cap and inspecting the pills, ensuring the contents matched the image on the computer screen. The pharmacist would then read the label to ensure that the correct patient and directions had been entered. With everything reviewed and satisfied it was correct, the vials were placed in a prescription bag, the bag receipt was stapled to it and the bag was set in the appropriate alphabetically labeled tray to await pick-up by an impatient, drug-seeking public. This procedure was repeated hundreds of times at The Colonial and millions of times in retail pharmacies across the country every day.

Jason stood transfixed, watching the scene as the cacophony of sound enveloped him; the rustle of clothing; the clack spatulas; the rattle of pills onto trays and the quick, abbreviated but efficient communications between the technicians and pharmacist working in a well-choreographed dance and, of course, the constant ringing of the telephone with its quick, muted rings or sharp beeps reminding someone, anyone that a caller was waiting on hold demanding attention.

The listing stack of the finalized baskets grew steadily alongside the pharmacist's station. Today's pharmacist was Thomas Pettigrew. His ear was pressed to a telephone handset, one of six phones spread throughout the department. His opposite hand, his left, held a second handset with another caller. Their cords stretched from the base on the face of a thin wall between two drug bays, oscillated vertically as he moved to and fro along the pharmacy counter arguing with the person on the other end about some kind of charge for some drug he had not received from the wholesaler. He was simultaneously making hand signals and mouthing silent words to his pair of technicians.

From the second call, Jason learned that Pettigrew's attorney was apparently begging him to increase his liability coverage for the business in case he was sued. Pettigrew rushed the lawyer off the phone and returned to bitching about his messed-up delivery. Jason sensed things like insurance didn't matter much to Pettigrew. The aging pharmacist mumbled an expletive about lawyers and insurance companies.

Today, a Monday, was busy with activity in much the same fashion as the day Jason had interviewed with Pettigrew six months earlier. A pair of cashiers, two middle-aged matrons, dispensed finished prescriptions and rang up sundries and health and beauty aids for the patients as they chatted about families, doctor or dentist visits, local or national politics. Jason had arrived ten minutes ago and waited patiently for Pettigrew to end his call and to give him his first set of instructions. He had been on the phone or talking to patients since Jason's arrival.

While he waited, Jason scanned the expansive square footage of the sales floor fronting the pharmacy department. He had been surprised and mesmerized by the aspect of the place when he arrived for his externship interview more than six months ago. But he'd been so pre-occupied by his pending meeting with Pettigrew, his surroundings had been a nervous blur viewed through a haze of anticipation and anxiety. Only now did the full retro aura of the place hit him.

With the interview months behind him, Jason absorbed the quaint Fifties feel of the apothecary. It was a split-level affair. The lower level a step above the sales floor was roamed by the cashiers in a narrow space between a waist-high counter on which sat two registers on either end, standing like guardian sentinels. The salespeople were framed by a backdrop of goods shelved behind the counter, unavailable just for the taking like their sales floor counterparts. These specialized items had to be asked for and, often, the patient was counseled by the pharmacist before they were dispensed: products like condoms, morning-after pills, diabetic testing supplies and nicotine patches or gum.

On the upper level lay the prescription department proper fronted by the same shoulder-high wall serving as the backdrop for the cashiers and towering over the registers. It was topped by a thin ledge and backed by a one-foot horizontal ribbon of frosted glass. A four-foot gap bisected the wall and was equipped with two steps allowing pharmacy employees to gain access to the pharmacy itself.

To left of the walkway, on the ledge in front of the frosted glass, rested a hodgepodge of antique pharmacy memorabilia: stout, porcelain pharmacy bottles inscribed with Latin words like Lactucarium, Paeonia Albiflora, and Pro Dolore; mortars and pestles manufactured out of various materials; ceramic, marble and brass. To the right of the gap rested two thick tomes covered in parched, yellowed leather, peeling and faded, with equally yellowed pages, *The United States Dispensatory* and the *United States Pharmacopeia*. A third tome, leaning against the glass with its front dust jacket facing out, a more modern, bound title lay: *An Illustrated History of Pharmacy.*

Extending down a few feet from the ceiling, a facade of robin's egg blue hung above the frosted glass, creating a six-foot gap through which the pharmacy and its inhabitants could be viewed by customers and patients. The word *Prescriptions* was spelled out in a handsome, gold cursive. Just below the fancy façade, the heads and shoulders of the pharmacist and technicians circulated about with hurried purpose against the backdrop of bays and shelves brimming with medication stock bottles of all sizes, shapes and colors. It was a mysterious and forbidden expanse filled with elixirs, ointments, salves and medicaments in all forms and sizes.

From within the elevated department, Jason gazed out over the sales floor aglow with morning sunlight. The slow turn of the ancient ceiling fans dangling from the yellowed ceiling tiles mesmerized him, temporarily blocking out all sound and motion. His day had finally arrived. The sought-after externship had been attained and the moments of truth which would extend over the next six weeks were upon him. But now as he waited for Pettigrew, Jason's thoughts transported him through a slideshow of images and remembrances from the last months: back to the previous August as he sat sweating in his Honda, worried and anxious about his interview. He had completed six externships at various locations in Hampton Roads. Four were retail pharmacies and two were at local hospitals.

At each retail rotation, he'd experienced pharmacy in all its glory and encumbrances. He'd witnessed his soon-to-be contemporaries dispensing pain-relieving and disease-alleviating pills along with wise advice on the best way to use them. He witnessed the grateful, patient customers who allowed the pharmacy teams enough time to fill their orders safely. He spoke with patients struggling with cancer and the fear it evoked or any other number devastating conditions. He'd experienced the angst and frustration created by those obnoxious patrons who, for whatever reason, had decided to take out the frustration of their miserable existences on the harried and overworked pharmacists and technicians. He'd watched pharmacists having to send their help home while dozens of prescriptions still needed filling because the corporate bean counters—men and women who had probably never filled a prescription in their lives, nor held a patient's health and safety at the end of a spatula—had decided the bottom line had to be preserved. Thus, the pharmacists and Jason were left to fend for themselves. And if Jason had not been present, the pharmacist would have been alone. As a student extern, he was free help.

The last thirty weeks had been crammed with new experiences and each was eye-opening. Each pharmacist had imparted on him select nuggets about the practice of pharmacy. And Jason was grateful for all they had done for him.

But, the next six weeks at The Colonial, Jason hoped, would be an experience he would never forget—nor regret. His gut tingled with expectation. Then, of course, there was his relationship with Chrissie and the eventuality that they would have to reveal it to Thomas. The tingling in Jason's belly roiled with gastric acid, generating a mild wave of nausea.

His recollections and musings were abruptly interrupted. One of the technicians brushed past him into a bay. Jason glimpsed her nametag. "Sarah". She retrieved a huge bottle of water pills and moved back toward the counter. Stopping, she turned and peered into his eyes.

"You know the Old Man," Sarah said softly in a lilting English accent, cocking her head in Pettigrew's direction, "is going to be awhile. You could be a dear and help. No need to be shy around here, luv. Besides, I think he'll be impressed if you jump in without him asking." Her inflection leant a kind, inviting quality to her message. She smiled at him like a mother who was suggesting a child perform a household chore. But in the definitive and commanding way only a mother can produce, her tone left no doubt as to what she expected. Sarah's dirty blonde hair, parted in the middle, hung like a curtain to her shoulders. Her serious brown eyes and the dark roots of her locks told Jason she was not a natural blonde. The pale, slender face was not altogether unpleasing to look at.

"Where do you want me to start?" Jason replied softly.

"He's going to be on the phone with this billing mix-up. We have three doctor's offices waiting to call in prescriptions. Start there."

Jason dropped his leather briefcase and draped his jacket over it in a corner and strode to one end of the counter where no activity had been taking place. He retrieved a pen from a cylindrical holder on the counter and a blank prescription pad. He clicked the pen so the nib appeared and moved it to the pad. Then he retrieved the handset from the base and pressed the button beside one of the blinking lines.

"Colonial Pharmacy, this Jason. Can I help you?"

"Yeah," the frustrated woman's voice spat on the other end. "What the hell is taking you all so long. I've been holding for five minutes."

Jason apologized. "What can I do for you?"

"I need to call in a prescription for Dr. Hackett's patient."

"Go ahead," Jason instructed.

With royal impatience and in a rapid-fire fusillade, the woman rattled off the patient's name and date of birth, the name of the drug and strength in milligrams, the quantity, instructions, number of refills, the doctor's name and the office phone number. The woman was a pro. She'd probably called in thousands of prescriptions in her career and her frustration combined with the hectic nature of her own day caused her to shoot the instructions at him. Because Jason had spent the last six months at externships at other pharmacies, he had performed this task dozens of times. It was one he was becoming more comfortable with and would at some point eventually become expertly proficient. Today, he still struggled to keep up.

He transcribed the prescription using the abbreviations he'd learned and memorized in his pharmacy practice class and previous phone calls from previous externships. The nurse wanted to hang up. But Jason made her wait while he repeated the prescription back to her. When he was finished, the woman quipped, "You got it, hon!".

"Just need your name," Jason added.

She spat it at him then disconnected without another word.

Technically, a pharmacist should do this or at least be listening in on the call since Jason was not a graduate or licensed. But he had taken the office numbers and if Thomas Pettigrew had questions, he could call them back. Jason knew he'd taken the prescriptions correctly.

Jason tore the new prescription off the pad and placed it on the counter. He punched the next line and repeated this process until all the lines were clear. The final tally: seven new prescriptions.

He strode to Pettigrew's station. Thomas was still engaged in the animated conversation as Jason approached. "Where do you want these?" Jason mouthed.

Pettigrew's eyebrows arched in surprise and relief. He pointed to a spot beside the computer terminal. Jason placed them there and stepped in front of his gruffy mentor. The computer dispensing system The Colonial used was one that Jason had seen before; the pharmacy he'd externed at two stints earlier used the same one.

Without thinking, Jason motioned with his hand for Pettigrew to make room. Pettigrew retreated a step and Jason moved in front of the terminal. He picked up the first prescription and began typing it into the computer. Ten minutes later, he'd completed the other six.

Jason cracked a slight smile when he heard silence from Pettigrew who'd stopped fussing at the man on the phone. Jason felt the Old Man's eyes on him.

"I don't have time for this," Pettigrew barked finally. "I'll call you back later." He slammed the handset onto the base hanging on the bay wall.

Without another word, Pettigrew moved his leaning tower of prescription baskets over a few feet and began checking them. Jason watched the seasoned, grizzled druggist check the filled prescription vials with speed and confidence. Working methodically, he read the paper prescriptions, compared it to what had been typed on the label: patient name, drug name, strength, instructions and physician. Then Pettigrew opened the vial and compared the pills or capsules to the description listed on the label...and utilizing his twenty-something years of experience...to make sure it was all correct.

As a pharmacist, Pettigrew's job was to check each prescription and ensure that it matched the doctor's instructions exactly. Jason had learned in the last six months that pharmacists had mere seconds to enter prescriptions, check for allergies or drug interactions, bill the insurance accurately and ensure, in just a few seconds more, that the pills and everything about the prescription was perfect.

It was high pressure job just as Thomas Pettigrew had told him during his interview. Jason had learned this fact quickly at his other rotations. If the pharmacy staff could not enter, fill and check quickly, things rapidly went to shit. The prescriptions began to pile up and the patients starting bitching. Then, in order to catch up, the pharmacy staff began to rush. It was easy to become distracted and make mistakes even if you stayed abreast of the volume. If you got behind, the chances of a mistake occurring multiplied greatly.

"You gonna watch me all day? What do you think this is a peep show?" Pettigrew bellowed.

Sarah and the other technician whose name Jason did not know snickered as they cast sideways glances in his direction. Jason realized he had been swallowed up in Pettigrew's checking process. The Old Man continued to check, whittling away at the mountain of prescription baskets before him. Not once had he glanced in Jason's direction. Yet, he knew Jason had been staring at him and--without skipping a beat--had chastised him for slowing down. Jason wondered how much of the good will he'd earned by jumping in to help and been torched by his rookie lapse.

"No sir," Jason replied, turning back to his terminal...Pettigrew's terminal...and continued punching in orders.

For two solid hours, Pettigrew, the pharmacist, Jason, the student extern, and the two technicians cut into the backlog of prescriptions like strip miners carving away a mountain. Pettigrew turned to Jason without pretense or preamble as they finished up the last of them.

"You made four mistakes that we had to correct. Those all could have left the store and resulted in medication errors. Take a few minutes. Grab something to eat. The next rush will start again when the doctor's offices return from lunch." Without allowing Jason a chance to reply, Pettigrew spun and walked toward the back hallway and his office.

Jason's entire body sagged, deflating like a balloon. He had been proud of his work. He'd kept up with these seasoned pros and with very little direction. Yes, Pettigrew had tossed four prescriptions at him over the two hours for corrections. All in all, Jason thought he'd done well. But Thomas Pettigrew had only pointed out his mistakes.

"Oh wait! There's one other thing," Pettigrew added, snapping his fingers, turning and addressing his newest extern just before he reached the doorway. He appeared to have no inclination that his critique of Jason's first day was having a devastating effect on his newest student. If he was aware of it, he made no show of it. Pettigrew reached for a basket. In it was a prescription vial with pills, a bag receipt and the hard copy prescription. "This is mistake number five!"

Pettigrew held up the small tray. "This prescription was dropped off earlier. You put it into the computer. I want you to look at the patient's profile and tell me what you see. I just remembered this patient is waiting in the store for this prescription. Do it now before going to lunch!"

Jason accepted the basket and walked to Pettigrew's computer terminal. While Pettigrew watched and waited, he typed in the patient's name and date of birth. The history of the patient's prescriptions for the last few months filled the screen. He compared the hardcopy prescription to what he had put into the computer, studying each element with extreme care. There had to be a mistake, he told himself, otherwise the Old Man would not be making a stink about it.

After two long minutes, Jason proclaimed, "This is a prescription for digoxin 0.25mg daily. I put the prescription in, and it matches what the doctor wrote exactly,"

"It does match what the doc wrote."

"So, what's the issue," Jason replied, challenging his preceptor.

"Would you feel comfortable dispensing this to the patient?"

Jason hesitated, checked the information on the hardcopy and the prescription label, then replied with a tentative, "Absolutely."

"Take a look at the patient's medical history and demographics."

Jason turned to the computer again and studied it for a moment, then asked, "Where do I find that?" Though he was familiar with the computer program, he was not completely proficient.

Pettigrew inched beside him and grabbed the mouse. He moved the arrowed cursor to a tab labelled, "Medical History". He clicked on it. Jason saw two conditions load onto the screen: liver failure, renal failure.

"How old is he?" Pettigrew asked.

Jason knew where to find that information. He clicked on the demographics tab. The patient was nearly eighty years old.

"Digoxin is not used as much as it used to be. But we do see patients on it...like this gentleman. What can you tell me about digoxin and how the body metabolizes it?" Pettigrew demanded.

Digoxin or digitalis is a naturally produced compound found in the foxglove plant and had been used medically for a century. An ionotropic agent, it increases the force of cardiac contractions in congestive heart failure patients but can also slow the heart rate. Its dosage must be carefully regulated and kept within in a narrow range. High levels can cause a plethora of dangerous side effects which need to be dealt with immediately when observed.

Jason did not hesitate with his response. "Digoxin is well-absorbed from the GI tract with a bioavailability of seventy to eighty percent."

Bioavailability was the percentage of a dose of drug that will actually be absorbed into the blood stream in order to give the desired effect.

"What can affect the bioavailability from the gut?"

"It's hydrolyzed by the acidic environment of the stomach or by intestinal bacteria. So, antibiotics which can kill the bugs in the gut can cause a higher dose to be absorbed or doses of antacids which neutralize the stomach acid can cause more of the drug to be absorbed."

"Very good. I asked you how the body metabolizes it once it's in the blood stream?"

"Most of the dose is excreted unchanged by the kidneys."

"How about the liver?"

"A small fraction is metabolized by the hepatic means...eight to ten percent."

"So, check his medical history once again."

Jason clicked on the medical history tab once more. Liver failure. Kidney failure. His heart sank like an anvil dropped into the ocean.

"So, what do you think now?" Pettigrew asked, holding the prescription bottle and rattling the pills inside.

Jason re-checked the medical history. He saw that the man had been on the lower dose of digoxin and taking it every other day. For some reason, the doctor, a different prescriber from previous prescriptions, had prescribed double the dose and wanted the elderly man to take it every day instead of every other day.

"This prescription doubled the dose and had him taking it every day instead of every other day. That's four times the dose he's been on!

So, if you were the pharmacist responsible for this prescription what would you do?"

Jason cleared his throat and swallowed. "Call to clarify the dosage and direction?"

A bemused grin spread across Pettigrew's face. "Correct," he said. Sarcasm dripped from his words. "Wait here."

Jason watched him descend the two steps to the lower prescription area and call the old man over. Pettigrew calmly explained that the prescription the man had carried to them was different from his previous fills. When Pettigrew asked the patient if the new doctor had said he was going to increase his dose, the patient said he'd been told nothing.

"We're going to call and clarify with the office just to be sure. Are you out of your pills?"

The patient indicated that he still had some left. Pettigrew explained that they would call him as soon as they had an answer and he should continue taking his pills as he had been until told otherwise.

Pettigrew returned to the upper level and handed the vial and the basket to Jason. "One more question. What are the symptoms of digoxin toxicity?"

Jason, again, was ready with a textbook answer. "Fatigue, malaise, confusion, delirium, irregular heartbeat such as PVCs...and visual disturbances." PVC's are premature ventricular contractions of the heart.

"What kind of visual disturbances?"

"A yellow or green halo effect."

"You seem to know your stuff, Jason. Now, you need to learn how to put that knowledge to good effect. Question. Did you check the patient's profile as you were entering this prescription into the computer?"

Jason felt like a child being reprimanded and responded in a weak, timid voice. "There was no time. We were busy."

Pettigrew shot him a chastising smile. "That's not an excuse. You must make time. That man's life is in your...our hands! Not only can you not make mistakes; you also have to make sure the doctor hasn't made any!"

Jason peered into his eyes for a heartbeat. Then simply nodded.

"What do you think would have happened if we filled this prescription and the patient took it every day at the doubled dose?"

Jason sucked in a lungful of air and let it out. "He would have gone into dig toxicity."

Pettigrew nodded. "Most definitely. And with his advanced years and renal failure, his levels would have gone through the roof. The electrolyte imbalances and arrhythmias would have probably killed him."

Jason could only nod.

"One more thing. You see the handwriting on this man's prescription, how neat and proper it is?"

"Yes."

"Compare that to the signature."

The prescription had been carefully written whereas the signature was scrawled and messy.

"Two different people?"

"Yep. The nurse probably filled out the prescription and the doc signed it without realizing the change."

"Get the doctor's office on the phone. I want to speak to the doctor about it."

Jason called the office and placed the nurse on hold. Pettigrew picked up. Jason listened to Pettigrew calmly explain the situation to the nurse. He was not accusatory in tone, but simply stated the facts. She said she would get with the doctor and call back.

"You want to bet that they change this back to his earlier dosage?"

"No sir."

"Always check the patient profile when filling. And really look at it," Pettigrew chided once again. "Look for any changes in therapies that might not make sense. Don't let that happen again! Now go get some lunch!" Pettigrew marched back in the direction of his office once more.

Jason suddenly felt drained. His reserves of adrenaline were exhausted. He was grateful to have a few minutes to sit down and recover.

To add to his rapidly disintegrating day, Jason had forgotten to pack something to eat. He checked his pockets. He had three dollars and some change. Not even enough to get a sub sandwich from the place a few doors away in the shopping center.

"Here," Sarah said, noticing his dilemma. She held out half a tuna sandwich.

"No thanks, I'm fine," Jason said.

"Yeah, right. I've seen that look a thousand times. You're not the first extern we've had you know." She grabbed his hand and placed the half-sandwich in it. "Sodas are over there."

Jason stepped down from the pharmacy and walked to the soda machine. He let out a long cleansing sigh. As he slipped dollar bills into the machine, he thought about Chrissie.

PHARMACY PHACT:

Medicinal herbs were discovered in the Shanidar Cave (Iraq), and remains of areca nut in the Spirit Cave (Nevada). These findings suggest medicines were used by Neanderthals during prehistoric times.

Sneader, Walter (2005-10-31). Drug Discovery: A History. John Wiley & Sons. ISBN 978-0-4700-1552-0

CHAPTER 17

Sunday evening, the night before Jason's externship at The Colonial, they spent the evening together like a warrior preparing to leave his betrothed on the eve of battle. Chrissie's excitement over the start of his highly anticipated rotation at The Colonial had grown steadily with each passing day, but Jason had become increasingly nervous over the last week. Edgy and quick to temper, he had snapped twice at Chrissie during what was supposed to be a quiet evening together. Chrissie ended up leaving early. Feeling badly, he called her on her way home and apologized. His anxiety had been fertilized by concern that the moment Thomas Pettigrew laid eyes on him the Old Man would know that Jason and Chrissie were dating. He felt like the facts were etched into his face like an epitaph on a granite tombstone. Chrissie, to her credit, was understanding and unfazed.

After he'd called her to apologize, Jason lay awake late into the night imagining how Pettigrew would call him out in front of the staff and tear into him with one of his patented but calmly delivered, vitriol-filled tirades. Over the six months they'd spent together, Chrissie had told Jason about her father, his protectiveness and his need for the truth. Unknowingly, she'd fed into Jason's fears. Jason was convinced that Pettigrew would make his existence so miserable for the next six weeks that Jason would perform poorly and fail this externship, ending any chance for a promising career and a future with Chrissie. There would be no way Pettigrew would endorse a relationship with a pharmacy student who hadn't stood up to one of his externships.

Jason felt as if the balance of his entire professional future hinged on his performance over the next six weeks.

But in the first few minutes at the store as Jason watched the commotion and the frenzied activity at the prescription bench, he knew that Chrissie and any relationship she was involved in was the farthest thing from Pettigrew's mind. He relaxed and let out a long breath, not realizing he'd been holding it. Jason understood that working in a busy pharmacy--and they all were busy these days or they went out of business--required total focus and concentration. Being immersed in such an environment required nothing less. A crack in concentration or focus on the pharmacist's part, at a crucial time, could lead to a drug error and patient injury or death.

With Christine no longer working at The Colonial, her internship work at the accounting firm was now her primary concern. Her father had hired another young woman, a technician/billing clerk to replace her. Chrissie was so busy with her co-op job she spent extraordinarily little time now at the pharmacy. And for that, Jason was extremely grateful. If they had ever worked together or been there at the same time, Jason was certain Thomas Pettigrew would deduce instantly from the way they spoke to each other and exchanged glances that his student had been making time with his little girl.

In the last six months, Jason and Chrissie dated regularly, seeing each other multiple times each week. After their passionate night at the hotel, their relationship blossomed like a rose in spring. There had been no more talk of whether they would continue to see each other. They were a couple, bound together and inseparable. And though it had not been spoken aloud, Jason knew they were both in love.

A month earlier and ahead of schedule, Jason had introduced Chrissie to his parents over a quiet dinner of roast chicken, grilled asparagus and Caesar salads prepared by Jason's mother. Afterward over coffee and dessert, they played Hearts, nibbled on cookies and sipped coffee. Chrissie teamed with Jason's father and they trounced Jason and his mother easily in four games before calling it a night. After Jason had walked her to her car and returned to the house, they had expressed their enthusiastic approval.

Jason and Chrissie had discussed when it would be best to let her father know about the love affair. Chrissie had suggested that they tell him immediately after his six weeks of externship at The Colonial were over. Jason balked and said that he wanted to wait until he'd received his final grade and evaluation which would take at least a week.

"I can't wait for them to meet you. My parents have been asking when they are going to meet the new mystery man. It can't come soon enough. They're going to love you," she said.

"We'll see," Jason countered nervously.

PHARMACY PHACT:

The Greek physician, Pedanius Dioscoridies wrote a five-volume book entitled, *De Materia Medica* listing over 600 plants used for medicinal purposes. It formed the basis for many medieval texts. The knowledge contained therein was further developed by middle eastern scientists during the Islamic Golden Age.

Sneader, Walter, (2005-10-31) *Drug Discovery: A History* John Wiley & Sons ISBN 978-0-4700-1552-0

CHAPTER 18

Victor and Simon sat beneath a large square umbrella at a shaded table in the outdoor patio of the Saltine restaurant, the first-floor eatery in the Norfolk Hilton. The late morning spring sunshine sliced sharply between the buildings along Main Street as a chilly breeze buffeted pedestrians scurrying past and rattled the white canopies overhead. Victor, the diminutive, bowling ball of a man sipped strong dark coffee from a mug with one hand as a small cigarillo rested between the first and second fingers of the other. His dark, moist eyes whipped back and forth with paranoia, studying the faces of each passerby.

His compatriot, Simon, the bowling pin to Victor's circular physique, was tall and slender. He had dressed in a manner that combated the weather: two shirts and a heavy blazer to ward off the cold Virginia spring air. The ubiquitous gold-rimmed, blue-tinted Maui Jim's sat perched on a nose that mirrored his build, appearing more like a beak than a nose. The shades hid green, sterile eyes. His teeming locks reflected a golden cast in the morning glow and flitted in the gusty air. A drink befitting him rested on the teak tabletop: a tall, slim glass of a clear carbonated liquid rimmed with a lemon and lime. His Mont

Blanc pen, which when he was not scribbling or doodling, was twirled deftly in one hand, had been left back at the apartment in Newport News. In its place, he allowed his deft fingers to slowly rotate the drinking vessel on the table as beads of condensation slipped down the circular glass, forming a small puddle at the base.

Normally, the drive from Newport News to Norfolk took thirty minutes. Today, there had been a wreck on the Hampton Roads Bridge Tunnel on the Peninsula side which had closed one lane and backed up traffic for a mile. Victor feared they would be late for their appointment with their handler. But as it turned out, their handler had texted saying he was delayed as well and would meet them at 11:30am.

Simon and Victor shared the safe house rented by the Agency behind the shopping center in which The Colonial was located. Less than half a mile as the crow flies, it provided proximity and immediacy. Thinking it best to stay close to the pharmacy since Pettigrew spent most of his waking hours there, their time was divided between the house and the various parking lots in and around the pharmacy, observing and recording the comings and goings of employees and patients with great monotony. Their eight months on site had, for the most part, consisted of boring and uneventful observations followed by monotonous monitoring of the audio recordings of trivial conversations.

Months ago, they had managed to insert the listening devices in a carefully planned operation that had taken three weeks of preparation. Using a device provided by the Office of Science and Technology geeks in DC, they jammed the electronic signal coming from the server in Thomas's office. This caused the internet, Wi-Fi, landlines, fax machine and computers to become non-functional. In a busy pharmacy, this was tantamount to an emergency. They were also careful not to disrupt the cellular service to any of the cell phones lest they be unable to call for assistance.

When Pettigrew did call for service, the call had been intercepted by a call cloaking software loaded on their shared laptop and routed to Simon who, wearing a headset, then promised a quick turnaround time. Victor showed up wearing a stolen uniform from the service provider. While in the store, he managed to place several other listening devices in the building including in Thomas Pettigrew's office.

So far, the sole source of moderate excitement in this incredibly tedious operation had been the appearance of Jason Rodgers, the pharmacy student, who had been coerced into a date by Christine, Pettigrew's comely daughter, in exchange for the key phrase that had floored the Old Man. The two spies had secretly watched their relationship heat up quickly and the pharmacy extern was now schtupping the boss's daughter on a regular basis. They had splurged on a hotel room months ago to consummate the relationship. Since then, they used Jason's house on occasion when his parents were away and several times, they had rented a room at a cheap but reputable motel near City Center.

The whole soap opera-styled drama had added some juicy intrigue to their otherwise banal days. *Would Pettigrew find out? Would the young couple confess their hidden relationship to her father? And, if so, when? And what would be the pharmacist's reaction when confronted with this information?*

Victor and Simon knew something was about to change. The fact that they were sitting here now waiting for their handler signaled that a serious turn in their assignment was in the offing. Maybe, just maybe, they could get back in the game and earn another juicy assignment after the disaster in Bologna.

Simon glanced at the Citizen's Chronograph on his left wrist. "He should be here any minute."

"What do you think this means? Victor grunted in his husky, gravelly voice.

Simon did not have time to respond. A gentleman dressed in a gray business suit of medium quality and dark wingtips and carrying a hard-sided briefcase approached. He appeared to be in his late forties. His dark hair, moustache and goatee flecked with silver and gray lent him the appearance of a tired academic rather than an intrepid spy.

"Gentlemen," the spook said without preamble, taking the unoccupied chair.

Both Victor and Simon made imperceptible nods toward the new man. The waiter approached. The handler ordered an iced tea. When the waiter had departed, the handler reached into the pocket of his suitcoat and removed a thin disk that resembled a quarter. He placed it on the table.

"Is that really necessary, Carl," Victor asked.

Carl studied Victor for a beat, appearing pained and irritated. "Victor, you have no idea what this operation is about or how vital it is. So do not question matters outside your sphere of influence. With everything that happened in Italy, consider yourselves lucky not to be shoveling shit in some third world country." Carl picked up the coin-like device and tapped it twice on the wooden table and glanced around the open-air space. "Now that's it's activated, we may begin," he said softly.

He had just activated a miniature electronic jamming device which dispersed a jamming signal fifty feet in all directions. Anyone attempting to capture their conversation by electronic means would be greeted with only white noise.

"If this mission is so important," Simon asked. "Why are we on it? It feels like a banishment."

Carl chuckled more to himself. "Believe me, gentlemen. If I had any other operatives I could use, I would have. But your fuck-up happened at a time when we are thin on available agents. The seventh floor was pushing to boot you after the fiasco in Bologna. I was the only person standing between you, an Italian prison or the end of your careers with the agency." Carl swung his head, first toward Victor, then Simon and held each man's gaze for a long, uncomfortable moment.

"Did you drive down from DC just for this meet?" Victor inquired, changing the topic.

Carl regarded him with a flash of irritation. "Yes, but I think I'll take in some sights while I'm here. Driving back tomorrow."

"Check out the Chrysler Museum and the MacArthur Memorial. They're close," Simon said.

"Thanks, Simon, I'll do that. Let's get down to business." Without pausing, the spymaster continued his lecture in a conversational tone an octave above a whisper. "And since we are operating on American soil, it is vital that this op not be compromised in anyway. So, no matter what you think, Victor, we will take all precautions necessary." Carl motioned with his head to the disc on the table.

Victor's face registered the rebuke. "Point taken," Victor said. "Why are we here? Why have we been watching a goddamned pharmacy with no strategic importance for the last eight months?"

The waiter returned with Carl's iced tea. The spy ripped open two packets of artificial sweetener, poured them into the glass and stirred. He glanced over his shoulder to make sure the waiter had moved out of earshot. Satisfied, he turned to look at Victor, then Simon.

"It's time to let you in on some of the operational details. The Colonial Pharmacy has been targeted for an upcoming op. Your reports and observations have been thorough and detailed. The senior staff on the seventh floor have decided to proceed. As you know, we need to know everything about everyone that works there. We have asked you to gather extensive intel. The information you have provided about Thomas Pettigrew and his employees, his daughter, and the students he teaches as externs has been comprehensive and in-depth. It pains me to say it but, 'Great job'."

"We aim to please," Simon joked, flashing a sardonic grin.

Carl did not react and continued as if he had not heard Simon. "We are going to be making an offer to purchase The Colonial Pharmacy from Thomas Pettigrew in the coming months..."

"For what purpose," Victor asked, confused. "What good can owning," Victor leaned closer to Carl, "a pharmacy do for the Agency?"

"This area, Hampton Roads, has been a staging ground for infiltrators from subversive elements in the Middle East wishing to establish sleeper cells inside our borders. This area is populated with thousands of military personnel and is only three hours from DC. We have solid intel confirming this. The Director wants us to ferret them out."

"Why isn't the FBI working on this?" Simon demanded. "This is their domain."

"They are. But with all their backlogged cases the FBI is investigating drug trafficking, financial crimes and the hunt for any lone gunmen ready to shoot up schools and shopping malls, the Director is convinced not enough is being done and that the Bureau does not have the manpower. With budget cuts, they are having to allocate most of their resources to higher priority targets. The Director feels this threat is not being given enough attention. In fact, as far as we can tell, only one or two agents are tasked to it. And he is also afraid that the intel will not be completely shared with the Agency if and when they gather enough evidence. So, we will send in agents to take over The Colonial and set up shop to conduct our own investigation without the knowledge of the Bureau."

"Again, why a pharmacy?" Victor repeated.

"Because no one will think to look at a pharmacy. It will help maintain the secrecy of the operation. Again, we are not supposed to be doing this within our borders. It's the perfect cover."

"How can we ensure Pettigrew will sell?"

"He will not have a choice. We will develop a plan that will make selling his only option."

"What is the plan?"

"In due time. We will need your input."

Victor and Simon exchanged a satisfied glance. They had just been told they had a future with this operation.

"When is this purchase supposed to take place?" Simon asked, sipping his drink.

"No time frame yet. That is temporarily on hold. The Agency has set up a dummy corporation and already funded it. The money is sitting in multiple accounts waiting to be dispersed. However, there is a small glitch which will delay implementation."

"Glitch?"

"Jason Rodgers."

Victor and Simon exchanged confused looks. Each acknowledging silently what the other was thinking. It fell to Victor to ask the obvious. "Jason Rodgers? He's the extern currently at The Colonial. What the hell kind of risk does he pose? He'll only be there for six weeks."

"That's right," Carl replied. He retrieved a folded paper from the interior breast pocket of his suit. He opened it. "But the background investigation and canvass on Rodgers indicates that he poses a risk. Covert interviews with neighbors, professors, the fellow students and Rotarians he traveled with to Ecuador indicates that he is prone to stick his nose in places that don't smell right." Carl read from the document, "…his natural curiosity and sense of justice could get in the way—"

"How the hell does a pharmacy student stick his nose somewhere it doesn't belong in Ecuador?" Simon interjected.

Carl sighed and peered at Simon like he was an irritating five-year-old asking a series of endlessly inane questions. He shook his head and explained. "Rodgers was on a trip with one of the local Rotary clubs."

Over the next thirty minutes, Carl, the spymaster, explained that last May, Rodgers hooked up with a member of a local Rotary club in Newport News that had partnered with Bridges to Prosperity, a non-profit that travels to poverty-stricken areas to build foot bridges and provide inhabitants improved access to food, water and healthcare.

"Our interviewer," he continued, "tracked down the Rotarian, a man named Ernie Harrison, and was able to get some scoop on our man, Rodgers. They went to a small village several miles west of the town of Riobamba in the Andean Highland. The mountainous terrain made it almost impossible for the villagers to find food or basic health-care without trekking nearly fifteen miles into a valley and back up a mountain.

"The plan was for the twenty-person group to go down and build a rope and wood foot bridge. They had been on-site for about a week when Rodgers spotted one of the villagers getting rough with a woman. As it turned out, she was the man's wife. Rodgers stepped in.

"Rodgers's actions insulted and embarrassed the man. An argument ensued; tempers flared. The man's brother was a member of a gang running cocaine down from Colombia. The local police were called. Luckily, one of the Rotarians on the trip was a Peruvian who was able to calm the situation down.

"So," Carl said, completing his lecture. "If Rodgers has the balls to step in and nearly get himself killed by the brother of a Columbian drug runner, he'll have no problem stepping in if he gets a whiff of something amiss at The Colonial. Therefore, we will wait until his externship is over and he is gone. Then we will implement the plan and force Pettigrew to sell."

PHARMACY PHACT:

It is estimated that 5.8 billion prescriptions were filled in the United States in 2018.

Medicine Use and Spending in the U.S.,
May 09, 2019, The IQVIA Institute

CHAPTER 19

The first week of Jason's externship had been nothing short of disastrous. Other than the fact that he jumped in on that first day to help, everything he did afterward was not up to Thomas Pettigrew's rigorous standards. Pettigrew, who was in the store every day that week whether he was filling prescriptions or not, took a keen interest in every aspect of Jason's training and existence.

Pharmacy students working in pharmacies are basically pharmacists-in-training. They are groomed to perform the duties that would consume the remainder of their careers: data entry of new prescriptions, retrieving pills from the shelf, counting, pouring, licking and sticking, as it were. They rang registers, assisted patients looking for over-the-counter items, answered endless phone calls. They were also given the scut work every pharmacist hated and was too busy to handle, like calling to obtain incoming transferred prescriptions from competing pharmacies, talking to insurance companies about prior authorizations and invalid account numbers and calling patients about problems with their prescription orders. Jason was also expected to handle clinical duties like calling patients about improving their drug therapy, making sure they were taking their medications and educating them, with the pharmacist's assistance, about the drug regimens. The only thing they were not allowed to do was provide the final check on a prescription. That task always fell to the licensed pharmacist on duty.

Thomas Pettigrew piled these duties on Jason's plate in heaping portions. Just as Jason completed one task, Pettigrew spooned out three more. When he asked him to call an insurance company about a problem, he hounded Jason about why it was taking so long. Then he would follow it up by asking why the data entry on the six prescriptions at his terminal were not done yet when Jason had spent the last ten minutes on the phone at Pettigrew's behest. For the entirety of the first five days, Jason scrambled around the department trying to get five things done at once and not doing any of them particularly well. He remained in a perpetual state of agitated panic.

In order to catch up, Jason would hastily enter prescriptions and, in that haste, would make mistakes. Mistakes for which Pettigrew lambasted him. Each time Pettigrew called him out, he felt his face filling with blood and frustration, embarrassed and humiliated while the technicians, Gloria and Sarah, shared knowing glances and avoided Jason's eyes. Then Pettigrew would demand one more task from Jason, and say, "I want this done before I get back!" He would spin on his heel and disappear into his office.

Several times that first week after barking out an order, Pettigrew would announce to Jason over his shoulder, "And don't forget to check the damned patient profile!" This, of course, referred to the episode with the elderly man with renal failure who, according to Pettigrew, Jason had nearly killed by filling a prescription correctly according to the doctor's instructions, yet had failed to notice that the increase in dosage and directions would have harmed the patient. That same day earlier in the week, the doctor's office had called back and changed his heart medicine prescription back to the original dosage as Pettigrew had predicted.

Blasted ceaselessly each day, Jason would let out a sigh and walk back to his computer terminal like a man going to the gallows. For the five days that initial week, Jason was drained and frustrated. On Friday, Kyle Griffin, Pettigrew's staff pharmacist, was on duty. After Pettigrew had chided Jason again for one more of a million things, Griffin approached Jason at the computer. Pettigrew had retreated to his office to take a phone call.

"How you doing?" Griffin asked.

"I'm quivering with excitement at being here," Jason spat back sarcastically.

Griffin laughed. "Keep that sense of humor, Jason. You're going to need it, especially in this industry. If you are going to work retail for one of the big chains after your graduate, what you're going through now will seem like a day at the spa by comparison."

Kyle Griffin appeared to Jason to be in his mid-thirties. Below average in height, he appeared to be a dwarf compared to Pettigrew. His indigo blue eyes, square jaw and rigid posture possessed a granite constitution. Jason guessed that Pettigrew and Kyle had gone to battle a few times. Kyle did not look like the type that would shrink from a fight.

"Kyle, I can't see things being much worse than they are right now. Has anyone ever complained to the school about him and his behavior?"

"Yep. And they did not get a good evaluation or grade from the Old Man. Thomas Pettigrew is highly regarded by the faculties of the four pharmacy schools in Virginia. You don't want to complain. It may not seem like it now. But he's doing you a big favor."

"How long have you been drinking the Kool-Aid?"

"I've been here for three years. And I've worked for the large chains, Walgreens, CVS, Wal-Mart. If you think this is stressful, try filling three times the prescriptions we do with half the help. You think Thomas is a bear, try dealing with a drug-seeking patient whose been out of their meds for two days and their insurance won't pay for it. You haven't seen nasty until you can't get their prescriptions filled in less than thirty minutes because the drive-thru has you backed up and the patients are cussing at you. This is nothing."

"So I'm supposed to grin and bear it?"

"Jason, you're going to have to learn how to manage expectations now and in the future."

"What the hell does that mean?"

"Weren't your previous externships at chain stores?"

"Most of them, yeah, but the pharmacists didn't throw this amount of crap at me."

"No because they were so busy trying to get their jobs done, they didn't have time to think too much about you, right? Think! How busy were they? They tossed all the scut work at you, trying to keep you busy...and out of the way. The only way you're going to survive in this business is to start managing expectations. Figure out what you need to do to get the most important work done first. Prioritize! And don't let people push you around, including the patients... and him." Griffin hefted a thumb in the direction of Pettigrew's office. "First and foremost, put patient safety first."

CHAPTER 20

Jason arrived home later that night, frustrated and overwhelmed. He sulked at the dinner table playing with his warmed-over food thinking about his first horrible week. For the first hour, he replayed every day, every incident over in his head, trying to figure out how he could have handled any of them differently. *How could he have done better? How could he have met Thomas's expectations?* It was too much to pack into an eight-hour day. Pharmacists normally worked twelve-hour shifts. Thomas was expecting him to get all that work done in only eight, expecting perfection to boot…and riding him hard when he wasn't.

His cell phone vibrated on the table. It was Chrissie. They had spoken only once this week because she was also slammed with her internship.

"So how was your first week?" She asked.

Jason scoffed. "A disaster."

"Really? What happened? I haven't been home yet. Did he find out about us?"

"I wish it were that simple. No, your father is a monster."

"We talked about that, Jason. I told you what to expect."

In fact, Chrissie had seen her father handle many externs. He was a brutal task master. The first week was always the hardest, she'd told him. A lot of students can't handle him. One or two ended up dropping out after the first week every year. As a matter of fact, one quit earlier in the school year, only to be replaced by someone lower on the list."

"I don't know if I can do this."

"Wow," Chrissie said, amazement brimming in her tone. "That's the first time I've ever heard you express any kind of doubt about your ability to do anything. And we've been dating for eight months now."

Neither of them said anything. A long silence filled the line. Finally, Jason changed the subject.

"How was your day?"

"Long. I'll be here for another two hours or so. It's tax season so the partners and the accountants have me doing anything and everything."

"You've been putting in a lot of hours."

"Eighty or so. Once April 15 comes and goes, it'll be better."

"You still sound so fresh," Jason observed.

"I'm exhausted, Jase. I need to see you. How about a quiet night at your parent's place? I'll bring dinner."

"That sounds good. My folks are going away for the weekend."

"Well, well, bless your heart," she exclaimed in her Scarlett O'Hara voice. "I do declare. What are we going to do with ourselves?"

"I'm beat too," Jason declared. "I promise I'll be in a better mood to-morrow...and with more energy...much more." His meaning was clear.

"That sounds appetizing. Okay, let's shoot for six. I have to work some more tomorrow. Even though it's Saturday, it's got to be done. You up for Chinese?"

PHARMACY PHACT:

The revenue of U.S.Pharmacies and drug stores in 2019 was estimated to be $312.6 billion and is projected to reach a value of $318.9 billion by 2020.

Statista.com, November 26, 2020

CHAPTER 21

The next day, Saturday, Chrissie descended on the Rodgers's residence with an Oriental feast from Asian Grill. Open boxes of egg foo young, General Tsao's Chicken and pork fried rice lay spread over the coffee table with a bottle of white wine, which was now half-full along with two plastic bottles of water. The last remnants of what had once been heaping servings lay amidst puddles of duck and soy sauces as if a ravenous storm had swept over the plates, leaving destruction in its wake.

"That was delish," he said with a contented sigh.

Jason sat back on the sofa and put his feet on the coffee table, pushing aside the wine bottle and his plate. He tossed his paper napkin toward the maelstrom of food. It missed, dropping to the floor.

"Yes, it was," Chrissie agreed, laying her head on his shoulder and placing her hand on his chest.

Chrissie arrived late, twenty minutes past six. She had been stuck at the office because one of the accountants needed her to run some copies for a Monday presentation. They said little during the meal, both eating like they had not seen food in a month, scarfing down mounds of rice in heaping spoonsful. They stabbed at the balls of General Tsao's chicken and egg foo young as if they might jump off the plate.

Sated now, they cuddled in an easy silence. The television was on but muted. The national news flickered on the screen and one of the talking heads, serious and tanned, was explaining the latest tragedy they so loved to cover.

"Are you feeling better tonight?" Chrissie asked. "You sounded desperate last night."

"Last night, I was. But I got a decent night's sleep. I was exhausted and miserable. Things always look better in the morning."

"You said, 'I don't know if I can do this'. Do you still feel that way?"

"I didn't realize how much of a..."

Jason hesitated. He had temporarily forgotten that the man he was about to slander was still Chrissie's flesh and blood. Chrissie rose and peered into Jason's eyes.

"What?"

"Nothing."

"What were you going to say?"

"It doesn't matter."

"Jason," Chrissie said. "I love my father very much. And I have seen how he acts around the students. I appreciate that you don't want to criticize him, especially to me. I'm a big girl. I can handle it. Say it!"

Jason cocked his head to one side as if to say "Okay, you asked for it." He cleared his throat. "I didn't realize what a bastard he was to his externs."

Chrissie smiled and kissed him. "I've seen him act that way for years. You want some advice?"

"Yeah," Jason said. Then rethinking his answer, he blurted. "No. No. As much as your advice would help, I don't want it."

"You don't? I know him better than anyone."

"I know but I'm going to figure this out myself."

"You are feeling better." She kissed him again. "So, what's your plan?"

"I thought about that. I have a plan for your father."

"I was talking about me."

He nuzzled her neck and nibbled on her ear. Chrissie groaned. "I can't describe it in words. My folks won't be home until tomorrow," he whispered. "Let's use their bed."

An hour and a half later, they both lay naked and sweating. "Oh, my darling," Chrissie sighed. "If I could bottle that feeling."

Jason stroked her hair. "Remember, you can't do that without me."

Chrissie kissed him and stroked his chest with her hand. Then she laid her head back on his heaving chest. "Oh, I forgot to mention. Daddy knows about us!"

CHAPTER 22

Jason shot out from under Chrissie and the covers like they were on fire. "What!? How?! How did this happen?"

Chrissie began to offer an explanation, but Jason cut her off by restating the same question, "How did this happen?" He started to pace around his parent's bed still completely naked. He took the Lord's name in vain at least seven times. He threw several "shits" and "son-of-a-bitches" in for good measure. On his fourth circuit around the bed, he ran his hands through his mangled hair.

Finally, he stopped and faced her. "Well? How?"

Chrissie's face was a mask of concern. "I guess one of my father's friends saw us out one night about three days ago. He stopped by the pharmacy after you had gone and said he saw us kissing. The guy knows you and knows your father."

Jason grabbed his head with both hands. "Aw, shit! Not now. Not after the week I had." He sank onto his knees and buried his face in the rumpled comforter.

"Wait," Jason said, lifting his angst-filled eyes. "How did you find out he knows?"

"Daddy told my Mom and she said something to me."

"Is he mad at you?"

"I'm sure he's not happy. But I can handle him."

Jason glared up at her like a distraught child who'd been caught with his hand in the money jar. "What am I going to do?"

"We'll figure it out."

"Wait," Jason blurted. "You knew the whole time. Ever since you came over. You knew and you didn't say anything?"

Chrissie sighed and smiled with resignation. "I knew how you'd react. I didn't want the news to spoil our evening…and I wanted you to do what you just did to me."

Jason shook his head as she delivered these statements. "What am I going to do?"

"Let's talk again in the morning and come up with a plan. Everything looks better in the daylight." Chrissie pulled back the covers and climbed out of the bed. She gathered up her scattered clothing and dressed.

"That's easy for you to say. You're his daughter. He *has* to love you. I'm just a student screw-up whose fucking the preceptor's daughter."

Chrissie walked around the bed and embraced him. She stood on her tiptoes to kiss him. "Go take a shower then get some sleep. I'll call you tomorrow."

Jason escorted her to the door through the darkened house. She kissed him once more. As he closed the door behind her, Chrissie could hear Jason whimpering. "This is a disaster."

℞

The next day, Sunday, Jason had fixed himself a strong cup of coffee. He figured he would need it. Unable to even think about eating breakfast, he forced himself to sit outside on his parent's deck and sip the hot liquid.

A glorious, golden spring morning had blossomed over the Virginia peninsula. The sun floated in a crystalline blue sky amidst large, pillowy clouds. A cool breeze sifted through the pines and oaks behind the house. It was a beautiful day for golf or a stroll at the beach or on the water fishing. As he drank the coffee, Jason, however, enjoyed neither the sunny weather nor the promise of leisure pursuits.

Jason had, in fact, taken Chrissie's advice and run a hot shower and gone to bed. But, as expected, sleep did not come. He simply replayed Chrissie's words and their implication over in his mind. The thoughts and worries tumbled in his brain like a cement mixer loaded with bricks.

And this morning, his mind was—and had been—occupied by one singular, seemingly disastrous obsession. Thomas Pettigrew, his preceptor, had been told by an eyewitness that Jason and Chrissie were dating. At the very least, they'd been spotted kissing in public. Thomas Pettigrew would easily deduce the rest.

He couldn't understand how, though. He was certain they had been discreet. They had promised to keep their displays of affection private and out of the public eye. They'd dated for eight months now; Jason tried to replay every hand hold or kiss since their first.

Of course, their first kiss had been in public and unplanned outside Steve's Steakhouse after Jason had literally almost run into her at the grocery store. That had been a three second kiss. And if that had been the cause, they would have heard about it long ago. He tried, but he could not relive every touch or loving peck since last August. Nonetheless, he was confident they'd been careful. *So how had they been discovered?*

Jason recalled their close call in the Patrick Henry Mall when a last-second course change had nearly obliterated the plan for secrecy.

But it was too late now, the milk had been spilt. He had to get his shit together for the next five weeks of his rotation at The Colonial. And that Herculean task was now complicated by one question: how was he going to deal with Thomas and the fallout from the outing of their relationship?

He took another sip when his phone chimed and vibrated on the small deck table. It was Chrissie.

"Did you get any sleep?"

"What do you think?"

"That's what I thought," she replied.

"Have you spoken with him?"

Chrissie hesitated. "No, I've been avoiding him. They're at church this morning. When do your parents get home?"

"They spent the weekend in Charlottesville at a winery. They'll probably be home early afternoon."

She sighed then said, "Let's have breakfast."

"I'm not very hungry."

"It'll do you good to get out. We can talk about what to do. I'll come to you and we'll eat up there. See you in thirty."

℞

Nearly ninety-minutes later, they sat a small outside table at the Water Street Grille in Yorktown overlooking the York River and the shadow of the Coleman Bridge. It was approaching noon, so they ordered a light lunch of fish tacos, salads and iced tea. The breeze rippled the water of the river and the golden sunlight created millions of diamond-like twinkles on the tiny waves.

Chrissie had just returned from the ladies' room and found Jason still in a heavy funk, looking out over the river but not really seeing it.

"This meal will make you feel better," she said, leaning down to kiss him before taking her seat.

"How can you sound so certain?"

She shrugged. "Woman's intuition."

As she said this, their server appeared with two Caesar salads. She placed the plates before them. On Jason's salad, a small envelope lay over a napkin draped on the salad.

"What's this?"

Jason picked it up and opened it. Inside was a small white card on which had been written one word in Chrissie's perfect script: "Gotcha".

Jason lifted his eyes and saw Chrissie grinning like a schoolgirl who'd just aced an exam. His forehead and eyebrows contorted into a confused maze of wrinkles momentarily then relaxed.

He let out an exasperated but relieved sigh. "Are you kidding me right now?"

Her smile widened. "Nope. Hook, line and sinker," she beamed.

"You've never pranked me before."

"That's what's made it so perfect...."

Jason shook his head slowly as an easy grin spread across his mouth. "So, he doesn't know?"

Chrissie shook her head. "He knows nothing."

Jason lifted his fork and jabbed it into the crisp, dressing-coated lettuce. "Girl, I owe you," he said.

Chrissie undid two buttons of her blouse, revealing cleavage. "I'll make it up to you."

PHARMACY PHACT:

There are approximately 88,000 pharmacies in the United States. Forty-three percent of those represent the twenty-five top chain stores, employing about 149,000 pharmacists.

"U.S. National Pharmacy Market Summary",
OneKey by IQVIA, July 2019

CHAPTER 23

Student externs worked eight-hour shifts. But a retail pharmacist's shift encompassed twelve grueling hours, sometimes more. The student's start time depended on the pharmacy. Pettigrew had asked Jason to arrive every day at ten in the morning and work until six-thirty with thirty minutes for lunch.

On Monday of the second week, Jason showed up at The Colonial at fifteen minutes before nine. The front door was locked. He could see Thomas's silhouette moving around the pharmacy in the half-light created the by the morning sun filtering through the tinted windows. Jason pounded on the glass of the door rattling its frame, flexing the plexiglass pane.

Jason cupped his hand over his eyes and placed it to the glass. Pettigrew looked up surprised and irritated at the racket. Fifteen seconds passed before the tall, aging pharmacist made his way to the front entrance. As he waited, Jason wondered if Chrissie would have tried to prank him again by telling him that his father didn't know about their relationship when he actually did. He didn't think so. Chrissie could be a prankster, but she wasn't mean.

"What in bloody hell are you doing, Jason? You're going to wake the dead. You're not due in for another hour and a half."

Jason could see by the lack of concerned expression on the man's face that he did not know about their relationship. The cloud under which Jason had been existing for the previous thirty-six hours dissipated instantly.

"I'm starting my day now." Jason, instilled with renewed confidence, marched passed the stunned Pettigrew who was still holding the door open into the store.

"Why?"

Jason called out over his shoulder. "Because there's work to be done!"

Pettigrew let the hydraulic spring slowly close the door, then flipped on the lights. In the pharmacy, Jason booted up one of the terminals while Thomas checked some of the prescriptions he'd filled earlier. Jason printed off three reports and picked them out of the receiving tray on the printer under the counter. He placed the reports beside the printer and started to work on some of the unfilled prescriptions in the queue of the program.

For thirty minutes, he worked quickly retrieving stock bottles, counting out the pills and dispatching the filled vials toward Pettigrew' station. Then he went to where Pettigrew had lain several hard copy prescriptions left over from last night.

"What are you doing with those?" Pettigrew demanded.

"They aren't going to fill themselves, Thomas. I'm going to enter them into the computer."

"Why are you here so early?" Pettigrew demanded.

"Eight hours is not enough time for me to get my work done. So, I'm coming in early to get a jump on it. Don't worry, I don't plan on leaving early. I'm staying until six-thirty and later if necessary."

"I didn't ask you to do that."

"I'm going to do what it takes."

Pettigrew's reaction flashed a combination of impressed surprise and a quizzical frown.

"Something wrong?" Jason asked.

"No," Pettigrew replied.

"Good, I also printed three reports for you. You should be calling your patients and trying to switch them to 90-day prescriptions. I've printed off all the patients who are on certain blood pressure medications and other maintenance medications. Studies have shown 90-day fills provide better compliance. I'll contact the doctors to the get the switch approved then call the patients. Also, any patients who have a diagnosis of diabetes in the system should be taking cholesterol medications, a statin. So, I've printed all those that aren't on one and will contact the doctor to get one started. They may also need prophylactic baby aspirin. So, I'll make those calls as well."

Pettigrew stared at Jason like he'd grown three heads.

"A pharmacist should do what it takes, correct?"

Pettigrew stuttered. "Ah, yeah. That's right."

"Oh, and by the way," Jason continued. "When I make a mistake, I expect to be treated with respect and not like some two-bit moron. I'll give you two hundred percent. Don't ever speak to me the way you spoke to me last week. Understood?"

Jason's heart raced, rattling like a kettle drum against the inside of his ribcage. Rivulets of sweat trickled down his neck and back. He forced a smile, he didn't feel, and said, "You need to get to work and get those prescriptions checked. We open in ten minutes."

Pettigrew's eye's widened with a flare of anger coating his expression, but then dissolved quickly into utter bemusement.

Unable to look at his preceptor any longer, Jason moved into the back hallway to deposit his coat on one of the hooks in the hallway and placed his briefcase on the floor beneath it. As he lifted the coat to the hook, he saw his hand shaking like a patient with Parkinson's. He braced himself against the wall and tried to suck air into his lungs. But it was like his airway had closed off. His head began to swim. He took small quick breaths until the sensation passed.

What the hell did I just do? he thought.

Thirty seconds later, he summoned the courage to re-enter the pharmacy department. Pettigrew had busied himself with the mountain of prescriptions that needed verification. Jason walked to his computer terminal and was going to enter prescriptions when the phone rang.

Thank God!

He answered the call and took the refill from the patient and hung up. The phone rang once more. Jason snapped up the receiver like it would disappear if he didn't answer it. It was a patient asking questions about his prescriptions and how many refills he had. It took Jason three minutes to answer his questions. By then, Sarah, the technician with the smooth English accent had arrived. She spoke with Thomas for a minute, then dove into her work. Within fifteen minutes of opening, the task of filling prescriptions dominated everything.

Jason threw himself into the work. He did not want to think about the consequences of the verbal rebuke he'd levied on his preceptor. Pettigrew held Jason's future in his hands. At least, he held the keys to which doors would be opened for him. Before long Pettigrew and Jason were engrossed in their duties, communicating about prescription issues and getting prescriptions filled and into the will call rack. Gradually, Jason's angst subsided because his mind had become consumed with the job at hand.

At six-forty-five, fifteen minutes after his scheduled end time, Pettigrew turned to Jason.

"You can go now."

"There's still stuff to do."

"Gloria and I can handle it. Go home before I change my mind." Gloria had relieved Sarah in the early afternoon.

Jason levied a long look at the Old Man, retrieved his coat and scurried out. In the car, his anxiety returned. But it was much less than before. *Had Pettigrew told him to go because he was irritated?* He detected no hint of anger or frustration in his voice. The uncertainty left him uneasy. Pettigrew had not shown anger or frustration. He was a master at delivering his messages without emotion. The story of the late female student who'd been ordered by Pettigrew to leave and not return flashed in his mind. He didn't tell me to leave and not return, Jason reasoned finally. But he still could. That consequence always lurked in the dark future. He drove home wondering what Chrissie's reaction would be to the news he'd told off her father.

CHAPTER 24

"You did what?" Chrissie asked.

Jason cocked his head to one side for an instant. "I told him off."

"What exactly did you say?"

"I told him he had no right to speak to me the way he did last week, and I wasn't going to stand for it anymore."

It was Chrissie's turn to cock her head. She studied for a few seconds. "You're trying to get me back, aren't you?"

Jason shook his head. "No."

"What did he say?"

"Not much. After we both got over the shock, we got to work."

They were seated inside Schooner's Restaurant, having a bite and a beer. Jason explained that he'd showed up ninety minutes before he was scheduled and dove into the work, printed reports, filled prescriptions and suggested three areas where they could contact patients to enhance their therapies.

"Oh yeah. And I told him he needed to get to work filling prescriptions."

Chrissie's eyes widened. "You have a death wish! That's quite the reversal for someone who last week said he wasn't sure he could do this."

Jason shook his head. He couldn't tell if her comment was a statement or a question. "I just figured that if I was going to fail, I was going down fighting."

"You told me you had a plan. This was your plan? To go in there and tell him off?"

"No, that just happened. It wasn't planned, " Jason answered. "I took a page out of your playbook, though."

"Mine?"

"Yep." Jason nodded then smiled.

Jason explained how impressed he was at the way she was handling the mountains of work being thrown at her. She put in the hours and kept at it until it was done. Then she would come in the next day and do the same thing. No complaining.

"I was so afraid of failing, I forgot to stand up for myself. And do what it takes," he said, grinning at her. "Thanks."

She leaned over the table and gave him a kiss. "That's my Jason."

"What's done is done," he continued, sipping a Corona. "I've accepted my fate. If your father is going to nail me to the cross and fail me because I gave him a piece of my mind, so be it."

Jason had mulled over everything in the few hours since leaving The Colonial, pondering if what he'd done was correct and professional.

Sure, he'd told Pettigrew that he did not want to be treated the way he'd been treated. But Jason remembered his words. He had not cussed or been emotional. He'd delivered his rebuke in a professional, even tone that left no doubt about the sincerity of his statement. He was also sure that some nervousness had infected his tone. All in all, he was okay with what he'd said.

He had made a conscious effort to make sure he'd get the work done by coming in early. It was a personal vow to bust his rump for the next five weeks, working as hard as he could to complete every assignment no matter how long it took. He'd felt good about it when he'd shown up at opening. But he was still trying to explain to himself where his words of reproach to Pettigrew had come from. As he'd told Chrissie, he had not planned them.

The best he could figure, Jason assumed that it was his inability to allow injustices to go unpunished or, at the very least, unchallenged. He had done nothing to warrant Pettigrew's harsh and bitter critiques last week. Sure, he'd made a few mistakes, but what student doesn't? Jason always tried his hardest to meet expectations. He expected more from himself than anyone else did. And he didn't appreciate Pettigrew's tongue lashings. As Kyle Griffin had told him, he needed to manage expectations. He wasn't sure what that meant at the time. He'd finally figured it out. He needed to manage how other people dealt with him. It meant not tolerating intimidating behavior from anyone: patients or the mullah of medications, Thomas Pettigrew.

Jason leveled a firm gaze at Chrissie. "You know Chrissie, you work sixty or seventy hours a week at your internship. I noticed that. You bust your butt. I told myself I needed to do the same thing. So, I went in early today to make sure I could complete all the tasks. And you know what? I did. I got everything done, I wasn't rushing to fill prescriptions because I knew I had other duties to attend to. And I'm going to do it every day. If he flunks me, he flunks me. But I will not cower to your father. I deserve respect, too."

Chrissie nodded solemnly. She went to him and kissed him gently on the lips once more.

"Have you talked to him today?" Jason asked, glancing at his watch. It was close to nine. Pettigrew would be closing The Colonial about now.

"Not yet. But I rarely get to communicate with him on days he's filling prescriptions." Chrissie sipped her iced tea and grinned. "This should make my introduction of you as my boyfriend very interesting."

"Oh yeah, and then there's that," Jason deadpanned.

CHAPTER 25

Jason showed up the next morning one hour and thirty minutes before opening with a steaming Styrofoam cup of coffee and an egg sandwich. He did not see Pettigrew's car, a large silver sedan he'd not yet identified, in the parking lot. The store front was dark. He wanted to see how early the Old Man arrived each morning. He nibbled at his breakfast and sipped the coffee as he waited.

Today, his anxiety had mounted as it did every morning along the drive to The Colonial. Chrissie had texted him after she got home last night. Evidently, she'd tried to ask her father about his day, hoping she could mine a nugget of information from him. He simply had kissed her on the forehead and said, "It was a normal day." She'd passed this information along to Jason. It had done nothing to clarify his current standing with Pettigrew or ease his angst about any repercussions he might face. Jason continued to take solace in the fact that Pettigrew had not expelled him on the spot like he'd done with the student last year who had been late.

Pettigrew arrived sixteen minutes after Jason did, an hour and fifteen minutes before opening. Jason watched as he exited his car, which he could now see was a Buick. The tall druggist walked toward the store oblivious to Jason's presence. Jason alighted from his Honda and caught up to him as he reached the front door.

"Good Morning, Mr. Pettigrew!"

The pharmacist spun surprised by the unexpectedly cheerful nature of the greeting. His brow furrowed in confusion.

"What the hell--"

"There's work to be done. Let's get to it."

Pettigrew recovered and pulled out his key chain. Then he replied with a single word. "Jason."

Pettigrew turned to the door, keys in hand. He struggled to find the right one. Finally, the lock yielded, and Pettigrew held the door. Jason noticed the Old Man's eyes boring into him as he passed. When his back was to Pettigrew, he smiled to himself, imagining the questions pinballing around in his head. It felt good.

This morning Jason had one goal: let Pettigrew know that as far as he was concerned yesterday was behind them. It was a lie, of course. It was the thousand-pound gorilla perched on Jason's shoulders.

Jason led Pettigrew to the pharmacy department through the gap in the wall and up the pair of steps. He scanned the counter and booted up a terminal. Mondays in pharmacy were usually the busiest day of the week. Today was Tuesday, so the pile of prescriptions waiting to be filled in the computer's queue and paper prescriptions still on the counter was smaller, but impressive, nonetheless. Pettigrew followed a few feet behind and veered to his computer.

After a minute, Thomas Pettigrew spoke. "I'd like to talk to you, Jason." His normally deep voice boomed like God speaking to Moses from on high.

Jason turned his head at the sound of Pettigrew's deep baritone and waited.

What judgment was about to passed?

Pettigrew took a few moments to finish typing a prescription into the computer. When he was done, he pivoted slowly like a prosecutor about to confront a hostile witness. Pettigrew's eyes met Jason's with unwavering stoicism. Jason wanted to look away. Instead, he held his gaze. He could not read Pettigrew's intent.

"Yes sir."

Thomas glanced at his watch. "We only have about an hour before we open. I'll make this quick." Jason's swallowed.

"I like your idea about calling the patients about cholesterol and aspirin treatments. I want to hold off on the thirty to ninety-day conversions for one simple reason. If we fill a ninety-day prescription, we lose two fills. Every time a patient gets a monthly refill, we earn a dispensing fee and a miniscule profit from the insurance payment. If we only fill their prescription once every three months, the dispensing fee does not change, we lose two dispensing fees and two more instances of profit. So, I want to hold off..."

"But studies show that patient compliance is better when they fill every three months. Which means more prescriptions filled in the long run."

Pettigrew held up his massive, long-fingered hands. "I know. I understand. That's a position that the large chains take. And I'm sure they told you all that in your previous externships. They can afford to take that stance. As an independent, we must fight for every dollar. And we will. The thirty to ninety-day conversion is being pushed by the large chains to improve compliance. We can improve compliance without switching to ninety days. If we can improve compliance on the thirty-day prescriptions, we can also improve the bottom line. That's where I want you to focus your efforts."

Pettigrew reached onto the counter and picked up his own computer report. He held it up and shook it. "This is a compliance report.

It shows patients who are not picking up their prescriptions regularly. There are a hundred names on it. I want you to call these folks and explain to them why it's vital they pick up their blood pressure and cholesterol medications. We have a delivery service. We charge a small fee for deliveries. We can use that to improve compliance and make some money. I want you to push it. Can you do that for me?" Pettigrew placed a heavy, but gentle hand on Jason's shoulder.

Jason peered up at this living monument of a man. The simple gesture of placing his hand on Jason's shoulder, its formidable weight and the gentle squeeze of the fingers communicated a myriad of positive messages.

Pettigrew's words about the non-compliance issue were spoken with sincerity and conviction. The fact that he was discussing the salient points with Jason told him that Pettigrew had considered his points and had given them honest consideration. In fact, he had accepted two of them, the cholesterol medications and the aspirin therapies. But Pettigrew was also a businessman. Even though the ninety-day conversions were an important point, doing so would cut into his bottom line. Yet, Pettigrew had offered Jason a compromise. Improve compliance without converting to ninety days.

It was a peace offering. And it was more than that. It was an acknowledgment that Jason's suggestions held merit. However, there was one thing it was not: an apology. Jason realized Thomas Pettigrew was not a man who apologized. The words "I'm sorry" never passed his lips. The fact that he'd reached out and put a comforting hand on his shoulder were stronger and more effective than any verbal expression of regret.

Jason's croaked. "Yes. I'll do my best."

Pettigrew's lips curved into a semi-smile but for only an instant. "I know you will."

Jason swallowed hard as Pettigrew's gaze hardened. Then he glanced at his watch and repeated the words Jason had said to him twenty-four hours earlier. "Now, you better get to work because we have prescriptions to fill."

PHARMACY PHACT:

There are over 20,000 prescription medications approved for marketing in the United States.

FDA Fact Sheet, November 2020

CHAPTER 26

For the rest of that Tuesday of the second week, Jason worked liked he'd never worked before. He had always been a hard worker, going above and beyond in his jobs waiting tables and cutting lawns in high school. But at The Colonial, this day and for the days that lay ahead, he worked with an intensity and abandon he never knew he possessed.

Jason pushed himself to the limits of his ability. He entered prescriptions into the dispensing system's database, generated labels, filled the prescriptions and slid them to Pettigrew for a final check with more efficiency, working with both Sarah and Gloria. As a team, they pushed out a seemingly endless number of prescriptions. Pettigrew found no glaring errors. However, he did ask Jason to re-type a few labels, not because they were wrong, but because Pettigrew wanted them to read differently and more effectively for the patient. Pettigrew's attitude and tone were no longer that of a petulant dictator. He was congenial, less confrontational, and his words took on more of a professorial tone.

When Pettigrew offered feedback, Jason saw and understood what his preceptor was trying to accomplish. One label had been written in very technical terms. Jason had used the word "subcutaneously". Pettigrew asked Jason to change it to "under the skin."

"Every prescription's directions need to be written at a sixth-grade level," he advised. "So, all patients understand."

Later in the afternoon, Pettigrew allowed Jason to call his list of patients to discuss new therapies for cholesterol medications and preventative aspirin regimens. Jason then followed up those calls with faxes to the doctors asking them to initiate said therapies.

He wasn't able to get through the whole list, but he put a sizeable dent in it. Next, Jason turned to calling patients requiring refills for maintenance medications for diabetes, blood pressure and thyroid. He focused especially on those overdue for refills. He was able to get thirteen prescriptions refilled that otherwise might not have been filled that day. Seven patients allowed the driver at The Colonial to bring them their drugs for a nominal fee.

When he wasn't filling prescriptions, Jason logged narcotic prescriptions into the thick three-ring binder, tracking the quantity on hand of each medication down to the pill. He performed cycle counts on the general inventory, checking the accuracy of on-hand inventories against those in the computer. When those duties were complete and he had a few spare moments, he would go out onto the sales floor to front and face the over-the-counter products.

At six-thirty, Thomas once again told Jason he could retire for the evening. Jason started for the hallway to get his jacket. After two steps, he stopped and addressed Pettigrew.

"I think I'll stay," he declared.

Gloria who, at that moment, was counting pills stopped and turned to study at Jason then she looked to Pettigrew. Pettigrew surveyed her with a crooked smile. Gloria smiled back and turned her attention once again to her counting. Three quick squeaks of the spatula scratched across the counting tray.

"And why would that be?" Pettigrew asked without looking at Jason.

Jason shrugged. "I'm training to be a pharmacist," he replied. "No time like the present to start experiencing the long shifts."

"You sure?"

"Yep."

Pettigrew gave a half-nod, again, without turning. "Gloria and I have the bench under control. You can start sorting that box of drugs in the corner. Time to send back outdates."

Pettigrew gave him a quick tutorial, delivered with the speed of an estate auctioneer. Jason, now accustomed to his method of delivering instructions like a verbal tsunami, managed to absorb most of it. He counted bottles of expired stock bottles, entered them into the reverse distributor website and packaged them up to be picked up by the FedEx driver in the morning. He did this until nine in the evening: closing time.

Five minutes after nine, the three of them, Pettigrew, Jason and Gloria, exited the store and stepped off the curb into the near-empty parking lot. Gloria peeled off toward her car and bid the men a good night as Jason and Pettigrew continued on.

Jason arrived at his Honda and fished his keys from his pocket. Pettigrew's Buick Enclave sat two spots farther away.

"Mr. Rodgers," Pettigrew bellowed in that rumbling, rich nature that would always cause a momentary sensation of panic to course through him.

"Yes sir?"

"Good work today."

Because of the dim lighting from the lot's sodium lamps, the angle of the light and his unruly silver hair created dark shadows. Jason could not see Pettigrew's whole face, only one eye and the top part of the nose. His entire mouth was engulfed in darkness. Jason thought he saw, for a flickering instant, a reluctant, but genuine smile materialize, only to disappear like a breath of smoke carried away by the evening breeze.

Jason nodded slightly. "Thank you, sir."

CHAPTER 27

For the next five weeks, Jason worked twelve hours shifts alongside both Thomas and Kyle Griffin, the staff pharmacist, doing what pharmacists did. He learned the nuances of billing claims to the various pharmacy insurances. They allowed him to check prescriptions as if he were on duty and responsible for the final product, though they would always give one final check before the prescriptions were bagged and hung in will call. Their names were on the label as the pharmacist of record after all.

They kept a running tally on a slip of paper of how many errors Pettigrew and Griffin had found after Jason checked each prescription. Knowing the numbers were being tallied allowed Jason the ability to experience the vast responsibility resting on a pharmacist's shoulders.

He watched with rapt fascination how Pettigrew and Griffin handled the exasperatingly difficult patients. For the most part, Jason learned that these pains-in-the-ass patients were usually on addictive medications such as alprazolam and lorazepam for anxiety, sleep medications like zolpidem and temazepam and, of course, pain medications like hydrocodone and oxycodone. Unfortunately, Jason had too many opportunities to witness such encounters. These types of encounters happened all too frequently for pharmacists and technicians.

He witnessed the interaction between Griffin and an irate patient who was being refused her zolpidem, the generic version of the sleeping pill, Ambien.

"I need my pills. I have to have them," the middle-aged woman demanded.

"Mrs. Turner," Griffin said in an even but firm tone. "You picked up those pills two weeks ago. You should still have two weeks' worth of pills left. Our policy is to not fill controlled substances more than two days early."

"I'm going out of town," Mrs. Turner said.

Griffin shot Jason a quick look and without allowing the patient to see his face, rolled his eyes. Jason knew that was the go-to excuse for why a patient needed an addictive drug early.

"When are you leaving?" he asked.

"Tomorrow."

"How long are you going for?"

Mrs. Turner responded, apparently without thinking about her answer. "A week."

Griffin replied instantly. "So, you have plenty of pills to get you through your trip. We can fill them again on the twenty-third."

"I don't know why I have so much trouble with you people," she mumbled before turning to leave.

"Why are these patients such trouble?" Jason asked Kyle Griffin later.

The pharmacist explained to Jason the low down on the addiction crisis in Newport News, the state and the country. "They are so much trouble because they are addicted. Addiction causes them to act that way. It's their body's physical and psychological dependence dictating their behavior."

"So, you're saying that kind of behavior is okay?"

"I didn't say that!"

"Why don't the docs stop prescribing them?" Jason asked.

"That's one hundred-thousand-dollar question, isn't it? But it's also more than that. Why don't we just turn them away and not fill the prescription?"

"They'll just go somewhere else to get it filled?"

Griffin nodded. "That's right. And the docs are in the same position we are. If they don't fill it, the patient will find another doc who will. It's all driven by money and profit. A lot of these docs are evaluated by the patients for the service and treatment they receive. The large healthcare organizations expect exemplary customer satisfaction. Just like the big chains pharmacies. If a doc or a dentist refuses to fill a prescription, they might get a complaint or lose them as a patient. So, they write the prescriptions, and we fill them."

"What if the correct thing to do is not to write for it or fill it," Jason said.

Kyle shrugged. "How do we know?"

"What do you mean? Know what?"

"When a patient comes into doc's office and they say they're in pain or stressed. How do they really know? We can't see the pain. We can't see stress. It's very subjective. The doc can only assume they're in pain because of a condition they've diagnosed, like a broken arm or after surgery, or the way they're acting."

"But why are patients being kept on these medications for so long. For example, I checked Mrs. Turner's profile. She's been on zolpidem, a potent hypnotic for sleep, for almost two years. The literature says it should be used only for short term treatment. How can a doc justify continuing to write for it?"

"And how can we justify continuing to fill it?" Griffin asked. "Are we not just as guilty? Why don't we turn her away?"

"Well how about calling the doc to discuss it?"

"I have," Griffin responded, "at least three times. The doc says she needs it."

"Yeah, but she's obviously addicted to it now. Maybe she needed it in the beginning. But it should have been stopped."

"Perhaps you're right. Mrs. Turner came to us from Walgreens across the street. I spoke with the pharmacist over there when she transferred her prescriptions here. She told me that Turner was seeing three different docs for four different medications. They finally refused to fill her prescriptions because the PMP showed she was doctor and pharmacy shopping. They called her on it, and she came across the street to us. You know what the PMP is?"

"The Prescription Monitoring Program. We learned about it in Pharmacy Law," Jason replied. "All states now have database to which healthcare providers can refer to see where, when and how often a patient is filling controlled medications from which pharmacies and from which doctors. It was an invaluable tool in curbing the overuse of controlled medications."

In the eighties and nineties, pill mills popped up all over the country when Oxycontin was being touted by the manufacturer, Purdue Pharma, as the addiction-free alternative for pain management. Some greedy and less-than-moral doctors were writing prescriptions for opioids in an assembly-line type operation. They did not rigorously evaluate patients and many simply took cash payment in exchange for a written prescription which could then be carried to a pharmacy to be filled. At that time, there was no way for a pharmacist or doctor to know if a patient was filling multiple prescriptions for addictive substances from multiple doctors and/or pharmacies. Many "patients" were selling the pills on the street. Pharmacies were also complicit by filling the prescriptions.

"So, we continued the problem by taking her on as a patient?" Jason said, referring once again to Mrs. Turner.

"No, Jason. Thomas sat her down and told her that if she was going to get her prescriptions here, she was going to have to start seeing only one doctor. And she was going to have to use only this pharmacy. She balked and said she didn't have to. So, Thomas told her she could go on her merry way.

"She left then came back four days later to fill her zolpidem. Since then, she has, according to the PMP anyway, only been filling here and only sees one physician, Dr. Swenson. So, I'd say she's doing better than she was before. Is she still addicted? No question. But she's not doctor or pharmacy shopping. We know that because we can see her prescriptions on the PMP."

"But," Jason persisted, "she just tried to get her refill early even though she had two weeks left. She's still trying to get over on us?"

"Maybe?" Griffin paused. "I don't know why she wanted it filled early. It's common with these types of patients. But at least now we can be vigilant in the fight." Then a question formed in Griffin's eyes. "Do you know how long it takes to become addicted to a controlled substance?"

"A month?" Jason guessed.

Griffin shook his head. "I have a neighbor who had shoulder surgery. He was given a prescription for oxycodone. He took it for three consecutive days. He happens to be a firefighter. He was concerned about how much he was taking. So, he stopped taking them and started experiencing withdrawal symptoms. Three days!"

"Wow." Jason mouthed the word.

"It can vary from patient to patient depending on the drug and the medication. But it happens quickly. Addiction is a problem that has been with man since the dawn of time. Alcohol, opium, tobacco. It's everywhere."

"So, what do we do?"

"You figure that out and you'll be rich and famous."

CHAPTER 28

Two weeks later, Jason and Thomas strolled to their cars at the end of a long day like the weary combatants they were. Jason had been working twelve-hour shifts alongside Pettigrew and Kyle Griffin for his last eleven shifts at The Colonial.

"You've been working many more hours than any student I've ever had, Jason," Pettigrew said evenly.

"Just getting ready for the real world."

"You want to work in retail?"

"Yes sir."

"Why?"

"It's exciting. Sure, the hours are long. But I enjoy the patient contact."

"What about jobs? Have you had any interviews?"

"We have a job fair at the school on the Saturday after I finish the externship. I've also been contacted by two of the pharmacies where I had rotations before Christmas."

Pettigrew nodded. "I'm impressed with your work ethic and your dedication. You've asked a lot of great questions. I think you'll make a fine pharmacist."

"Thank you, Mr. Pettigrew."

"Please call me Thomas."

Jason almost stopped short but caught himself. "Okay...Thomas," he said weakly.

Jason had been told by all the previous externs he'd contacted that had worked at The Colonial that Thomas Pettigrew was to be called "Mr. Pettigrew."

"And I guess someday, I'll be calling you Dr. Rodgers what with the PharmD being the entry level degree now."

"I guess so."

"Any way, I want you to take the day off tomorrow. I appreciate all the long hours, but the school would have my head if they knew you were working so much. You're required to put in forty hours. I'll let you work four twelve hour shifts a week as long as you don't tell the school. Take one day off a week plus every other weekend. Tomorrow okay?"

"Yes sir. Thank you, sir."

"I'm sure you have a girlfriend that would like to see you, eh?"

Jason swallowed hard. "Uh, yeah...I...do."

"What's her name?"

CHAPTER 29

"Her name?" Jason stuttered.

"She does have a name, doesn't she?"

"Of...course," Jason paused, buying time. *Oh shit! He thought. What do I do?*

Suddenly and for some unexplained reason, the letters he'd recited to Chrissie came to him. *D-D-F-G! D-D-F-G!* The last thing he needed in his mind now was his carnal relations with Chrissie.

"Did you forget her name?"

"Dee," he muttered. "Her name's Dee."

"That short for something?"

"Ah...No."

They arrived at Pettigrew's Enclave. "Well tell her that I appreciate all the hours you've put in. I hope it hasn't been too much of an inconvenience for either of you. You know my daughter's studying to be an accountant. I haven't seen much her lately. She's working ungodly hours like her father. She's an intern at Collins, White and Casper." Jason sensed that Pettigrew wanted to say more. But no more information was forthcoming.

"Really? She sounds terribly busy?" Jason searched Pettigrew's eye for any hint that he might know. He found none.

"She is. I think you met her when I interviewed you for the externship."

"I did? Really?"

"Yep," Pettigrew said as he pressed the unlock button on his key fob. "Anyway. I'll see you on Wednesday."

"Yes sir...Mr. Pett...Thomas."

℞

During the final week of his externship, Jason experienced one more aspect of a pharmacist's responsibility to his patient. A sixtyish woman named Lula Johnson had run out of her Premarin tablets. She needed a refill. However, her refills had all been used. It was past six o'clock in the evening. The doctor's office was closed, and she said she'd been out of pills for three days.

Thomas returned to the pharmacy department taking the two steps in one giant long-legged stride and asked Jason a question. "As a pharmacist what do you do now?"

"We wait for the doctor to call us back?"

"That's one option," Pettigrew replied.

"But she's out of her pills and should have known she was out of refills," Jason argued.

"I agree. But she didn't. And you'll find in our profession a lot of patients don't pay attention to such details."

So, what are you going to do?" Jason asked.

"Lula is a loyal customer. She's been filling with me for many years. So, I know she's not going anywhere else to get her prescriptions filled. And this type of thing does not happen often with her. As a matter of fact, I can't remember the last time it did. So, I'm going to give her two pills at no charge. We'll subtract them from her next fill when the doctor calls in the new prescription. And I've bought a little goodwill with her. Keeps them loyal."

"Okay," Jason said tentatively.

"It is within the pharmacist's scope to forward some tablets called an emergency supply for vital medications like blood pressure and diabetes medications, or in this case, estrogen. We just can't do it over and over. So, after these two pills, I'm not going to give her anymore without a new 'scrip. It's up to your professional judgment and is done on a patient-by-patient and case-by-case basis."

Jason nodded.

Pettigrew continued. "If she were a habitual offender and constantly asking for emergency supplies, I might say no and give her a lecture about being proactive. And we never give out emergency supplies for controlled substances of any kind, ever."

"Got it. What if the doctor doesn't call in a new prescription?"

"I won't give her any more pills. Then it's going to be up to Lula Johnson to call her doctor and give them a little reminder. We can't let patients completely abdicate responsibility for their own healthcare. Too many patients do, leaving it all up to the doctors and pharmacists."

"I've noticed over the last six weeks that this whole industry seems to cater to the whims of these patients. What I mean is a lot of these patients ask for the world. And then they get upset when we can't or won't give it to them."

Pettigrew nodded in a knowing way. "That's very observant, Jason. Of course, being in business of any kind, we want to meet the needs of the patients or customers. But this is a pharmacy, a healthcare discipline, so we must follow laws and protocols. Our payment structure is determined by the insurance companies and what they will reimburse, not by our own pricing schedules. In the retail pharmacy setting, the culture of getting it fast and cheap has been advanced by the big chains. They have kissed these patient's asses for too long. You sure you want to go work for a big retail chain?"

"What else is there? I don't really want to do hospital pharmacy. Are you suggesting I shouldn't go into retail?"

"No, that's not it at all. I just want you to know what you are getting into. Every segment of the pharmacy industry has its issues. But all in all, it's a very rewarding profession. If you go work for a large chain, you will be working long hours with not enough staff and be asked to do more and more with less and less. But you must remember who you serve. Sometimes the patients can be surly and overdemanding, especially when they call in complaints to your corporate offices. Those corporate yokels only care about one thing, the bottom line."

"I'll keep that in mind," Jason said sotto voce.

A comfortable silence passed between the teacher and student. Pettigrew finished up a prescription on his screen.

A sudden feeling of nostalgia set in. He realized that for all the hard work and extra hours he'd put in over the last six weeks, he was going to miss this place. Pettigrew, though a task master, had softened his demeanor and they'd experienced five weeks of quality student-teacher interaction. Thomas had not sacrificed his principles. He continued to demand excellence. Hell, he expected perfection.

And the gruff old teacher and druggist had taught Jason some valuable lessons. In his other externships, they'd taught him the nuts and bolts of the profession, the day-to-day activities. The Colonial's externship had done that, too. But Pettigrew had gone beyond that. He'd tried to instill in Jason a sense that he needed to look beyond the day-to-day and understand that he was serving something greater than himself. Jason understood now why Thomas Pettigrew's externship had become so coveted by so many pharmacy students.

A growing sense of emotion swelled within Jason. He wasn't sure if it was borne of the fact that Pettigrew had been hard on him like a demanding father, teaching valuable lessons that the son would not appreciate until years later. Or if it came from the knowledge that in short order, Pettigrew would learn that Jason had been seeing and sleeping with his daughter.

"Thomas," Jason began. "Thank you for everything. You've taught me a lot in the last six weeks."

"You're welcome, Jason." He winked at his pupil. "Not bad for the Old Man, eh?"

Jason's face must have registered his surprise for he saw Pettigrew's reaction. "You know about that?"

"Of course, I know. Believe me, I've been called much worse."

Jason smiled and looked away.

"Anyway, I don't often hear that kind of gratitude from my externs. Usually, they are out the door so fast flames are shooting out of their arses. You will be a great pharmacist. Don't lose your sense of duty and hard work. I hope we get to work together again."

Pettigrew grinned. It was the first time he remembered seeing a genuine smile adorn his face.

"Maybe we'll see each other again real soon."

Pettigrew's forehead crinkled and a pinch of confusion flickered across his face. "Maybe."

PHARMACY PHACT:

Pharmacists consistently rank in the top four of most trusted professionals.

Drug Topics, January 2020

CHAPTER 30

On Friday of that final week, Gloria and Sarah were both on duty during the middle of the day, overlapping for a few hours. Kyle Griffin manned the bench. Thomas had the day off and was not expected in. He had informed Jason that he would be submitting his grade to the school on Monday. Jason had gently pressed him for a clue as to what the grade might be. Pettigrew had said, "You'll just to have to wait and see."

At two o'clock during the day's lull between the lunch and evening rushes, Sarah brought out a small cake while Gloria retrieved a gift-wrapped box and a few paper plates, a carafe of coffee, and some plastic cutlery.

"Congrats," Gloria said. "You survived the Old Man."

"You stood up to him, too," Kyle Griffin said. "Thomas told me that you let him know in no uncertain terms that you would not continue to be spoken to disrespectfully. He was impressed with your backbone. You did it. You took my advice."

"Thanks," Jason said as Sarah cut the cake and served slices and coffee.

Gloria handed Jason the thin, narrow gift box. "We got you something. Just to say best of luck." She nudged Jason's elbow. "We don't normally do this for externs. But we thought it was appropriate."

Jason accepted the box and gazed with appreciation into the eyes of each of them in turn. "I...I don't know what to say. Thank you so much."

"Well open it, luv," Sarah said in her lilted English accent.

Jason tore off the wrapping and lifted the lid. Inside, nestled in white foam was a sleek black pen and a gleaming new counting spatula. He lifted them out and saw that his name had been inscribed on the wooden handle of the spatula.

Griffin said, "Every pharmacist needs a good pen and a spatula. You will be reducing prescriptions to writing and counting pills for a good many years to come." Griffin pumped Jason's hand several times. "Best of luck. Even Thomas chipped in. You really made an impression on the Old Man."

Sarah and Gloria each hugged him. They choked down a few bites of cake and sips of coffee before the next wave of customers arrived and the phone began its non-stop chirping. A swell of pride and satisfaction washed over him.

Griffin allowed Jason to leave at six-thirty. As he neared his car, he saw her. Chrissie leaned with her backside on the hood of her Volkswagen Golf, wearing a pair of tight, hip-hugging jeans, a white, soft cotton sweater, white tennis shoes and a come-hither smile.

"What are you doing here?" Jason said, scanning the parking area. A sudden self-consciousness consumed him. "What if someone sees you?"

"My father's on a trip to Richmond. Something about some new pharmacy legislation he was asked to consult on. He'll be back tomorrow."

Nevertheless, Jason's eyes continued to scan the parking lot.

"Relax," she said. "He's not going to find out."

"What about the people inside the pharmacy? What if they see us?"

"No one will say anything. Besides it's only a matter of time before we tell him, anyway, right? You'll get your evaluation in about a week."

"Yeah."

Chrissie straightened and strode to him. She pressed a full, lingering kiss on his lips. At first, Jason remained stiff, not responding not only because they were in public, but because they were fifty yards from the pharmacy. But Chrissie did not relent. Gradually, he yielded to the firm pressure of her lips on his and her breasts pressing against his chest. Then he flung his arms around her and lost himself for a few wonderful moments.

When she pulled back, she peered into his eyes. "I'm taking you to a nice quiet dinner followed by a movie and then..." The look in her eyes turned expectantly amorous. "Who knows?"

Jason smiled. "I like the sound of that."

"Follow me in your car."

CHAPTER 31

"What's this young man's name?" Pettigrew asked.

"I told you," Chrissie replied with a wide smile. "You'll meet him in just a few minutes."

"Look at that smile," Thomas remarked. His eyes held a slightly different cast. It was something Chrissie had never seen before and she could not interpret it's meaning. "I've never seen you like this before."

Over the past months, it seemed Thomas had asked his daughter a hundred times about the man she had been seeing. Despite his constant inquiries, Chrissie had not yielded a scintilla of information to him. Of course, if she had their secret would have been revealed. Every now and then, she had experienced mild bouts of anxiety since she and Jason had started dating. She had only once let Jason know about her concerns. That first time, she had explained how her father might react. She had seen the concern and apprehension in Jason's eyes. She'd told herself he had been anxious enough for the both of them. So, she promised herself she would not bring it up again.

Her own anxiety had also swelled during Jason's six weeks at The Colonial. Once his tenure began, it dawned on her that the outcome of

Jason's externship would have an enormous impact on her father's ultimate opinion of Jason. If Jason had, like many other externs, performed poorly or caved to her father's intense pressure, her father would have a lesser opinion of her new love. So, Chrissie had asked Jason on every occasion they were together how things were going.

Chrissie was a doer, not a worrier. There wasn't a problem she'd ever faced that she couldn't overcome without an appropriate amount of work or research. But when Jason had told her that he'd confronted Thomas about his behavior during the second week of his stint and demanded to be treated with respect, Chrissie had been initially overcome by an ominous sense of dread. Her mind brimmed with concern. But, it was an issue over which she had no control. It was about and between the two of them. The outcome of their interactions and Jason's performance at The Colonial would cast a lingering influence over her relationship with Jason, good or bad. In fact, if he failed or quit, it might end it. Questions had abounded. *Would her father take well to the rebuke? Would he punish Jason for calling him out?*

Chrissie had never asked Thomas about any of his externs in the past. So, it took an enormous amount of willpower not to inquire about how this one student was doing for fear it would telegraph the fact there was something between them. Her angst eased in the days following Jason's rebuke. Jason had dug in, worked long hours and seemed to be excelling. Though those assessments came from Jason, she trusted his judgment. Jason had also told her that her father had warmed to him, though he'd never apologized for his intransigent and rude behavior. He was a difficult and demanding teacher. She had witnessed many dressing-downs in her time at the store. Jason didn't need to explain to her how the one-sided interactions had played out. Chrissie had witnessed every variation. They numbered in the hundreds. And Thomas made no apologies for them. It was his way of toughening up students and preparing them for the real pharmacy world. The fact that her father had changed his demeanor toward Jason was evidence enough that he'd taken the hint.

"This is not like you honey," Pettigrew persisted. "You've always told us about your boyfriends in the past. It's been at least six months since you've started dating him. What's the big secret?"

Chrissie retorted with a one-line shot across Thomas's bow. "Because you've always been hard on my boyfriends, asking the GPA and their life's ambitions, never letting them get comfortable. They've always felt like they were on the hot seat. I'm not letting you do that to this one! Promise me you won't do that!"

"I'll do my best, honey," Thomas said in as soothing a manner as he could muster. He pulled her into long bear hug. But, Chrissie knew how he would respond.

They stood in the small hallway leading from foyer where the large oil-on-canvas portrait of her mother and father hung. Thomas had commissioned it a three years ago. She rested her head on her father's chest.

They separated and Chrissie peered into her father's cold blue eyes looking for a sign that he was lying. Eleanor passed them on her way into the dining room to finish laying out the silverware. She completed the last place setting and was returning to the kitchen. Eleanor made eye contact with Chrissie as she returned and passed by father and daughter. Eleanor winked at her and grinned. Chrissie had confided in her two weeks ago that she had been dating one of her father's externs. Snippets of that conversation returned to her now.

Her mother had expressed, once more, concern about her lack of information. Chrissie swore her to secrecy. Over an hour, she'd laid out the how and when the relationship began.

"What do you think Daddy will do?" Chrissie asked.

Eleanor knew her husband better than anyone. His moods, his like and dislikes. He could be blustery and overbearing at times, spouting opinions to anyone and everyone within earshot. Eleanor always dealt with him in an even-tempered, patient manner. She was the calm before, during, and after his tumultuous storms. She modulated his reactions by how and when she presented him with various pieces of information. She could predict how Thomas would react to just about any given scenario.

But when Chrissie posed the question to her. She hesitated, wrinkled her brow and filled her lungs with air. Then she let it out slowly. "You know, sweetie. I have no idea."

"Marvelous," Chrissie had replied.

"Do you want me to say something to him to feel him out? To prepare him?"

"No, mother!" Chrissie shouted. "You promised. Jason wants to wait until his externship is over."

"Okay, okay. I won't say a word. Just remember. Your father loves you and he wants you to be happy."

Chrissie pushed out a sigh of relief. "He has a weird way of showing it."

"But then again," Eleanor added. "He also doesn't like surprises."

"Shit," she'd muttered.

The reverie of that conversation fourteen days earlier shattered like a dropped Christmas ornament when the doorbell rang.

"I'll get it," Thomas said.

PHARMACY PHACT:

The Centers for Medicare and Medicaid Services estimates retail prescription drug expenditures in the United States came to $355 billion in 2018. Estimates for 2019 and 2020 are $345.7 billion and $358.7 billion respectively.

CHAPTER 32

Jason had just rung the bell. As he waited for the large door on the Colonial-styled home to open, he held a bottle of non-alcoholic red wine—in essence grape juice--in his right hand and a bouquet of flowers in his left. Jason had boasted that he would bring wine to his first meeting as Chrissie's newly announced beau. But she quickly nixed that notion and had warned him a month ago that Thomas Pettigrew was a strict Southern Baptist and forbade alcohol in his home. From beyond the door, a low, muffled voice, Thomas's voice, announced, "I'll get it."

The bottle felt like a ship's anchor in his hand.

In the last eight months, he had experienced three episodes of extreme anxiety. All of them related to his future. The third and, hopefully, final moment, one that he'd anticipated, dreaded, fretted over and wanted behind him, was now upon him.

The first episode had been that stiflingly hot Monday morning eight months previous. Jason had thought he would never again be as nervous as he had been that day. That morning his words and actions, he thought, were so crucial it could determine the trajectory of the rest of his life. The second occurred less than eight weeks ago. He'd arrived at The Colonial for his first day as Pettigrew's newest student. His stress level had pegged higher because the day he'd hoped for and worried about had arrived. He worried about how he would respond to the tyrant's expectations. That would have been enough to match Jason's anxiety from eight months earlier. But to add to it, Jason held knowledge that Thomas Pettigrew did not. Information that could destroy Jason's externship and his future. Pettigrew's beloved daughter and only child, his princess Christine, was embroiled in a torrid, passionate love affair with a lowly extern. Jason was that man. Tonight was the night Pettigrew would come to know all that Jason knew. If anxiety were measured in distance, at that moment, Jason's would be streaking past Jupiter.

So here he was. Darkening the doorstep of an especially important and influential man in Jason's chosen profession. And Jason was about to drop a ten-megaton warhead on him in his own home.

He'd arrived ten minutes ago; parked on the street two houses down. The orange orb had just fallen behind the tree line. It would be dark soon. For some reason, he did not want to announce his arrival. He did not want the sound of his rattling engine, a flash of movement through the drapes or the sound of his car door closing alerting Thomas that Chrissie's mysterious beau had arrived. He did not want him venturing to the window for a peak and spy Jason Rodgers, The Colonial's former extern, sauntering up the path with a bottle and flowers. He did not want Thomas Pettigrew to have the ability to formulate a response or, even worse, a non-response before the door opened. He guessed he just wanted to maintain some modicum of control.

Muted footfalls from inside the house moved closer. Jason circled the wine and flowers behind his back. The latch clicked. The knob turned. The door swung silently open.

Jason peered into the eyes of his former preceptor and forced his best smile.

"Hi Thomas. How are you?"

CHAPTER 33

"Jason? What are you doing he..."

In his chest, Jason's heart had been dancing a wild and erratic beat and seemed to stop as he watched Pettigrew's normally stoic, arrogant countenance morph. The expressions on it seemed to pass through a range of emotions like clouds passing overhead. Then the Old Man's forehead crinkled while the normally focused blue eyes clouded with uncertainty, then, finally, fogged over with an icy hardness.

Jason opened his mouth to speak. Like his interview almost a year earlier, Jason wasn't sure what words would spew forth. Luckily, the awkwardness and uncertainty of the moment was interrupted by a flash of movement from behind Pettigrew.

Chrissie bounded into the small foyer, brushing past her father. She wrapped her arms around Jason's neck in an overly dramatic public display and planted a deep, loving kiss on his mouth. Jason while still holding the faux-wine and the flowers slowly, tentatively wrapped his arms around Chrissie. His eyes, however, remained open, watching Thomas Pettigrew's reaction fulminate from a simmer to full, roiling boil.

Chrissie squeezed as much passion out of the embrace and kiss with her newly introduced beau as she could. Her head moved exaggeratedly as did her hands through his thick hair. His eyes wide and his jaw slack, Pettigrew's expression was that of a driver peering at a car wreck happening in slow motion. A wreck involving his daughter.

After the seemingly interminable kiss ended, Chrissie pulled back and clasped Jason's right wrist. She turned to her father. "Daddy, I believe you know Jason."

"Mr. Pettigrew," Jason said, afraid to use his first name as he'd become accustomed.

The Old Man could think of nothing else than to grunt, "Jason."

Pettigrew eyes whipsawed slowly back and forth between Chrissie and Jason.

Chrissie said to no one in particular, "Mom's made a wonderful steak dinner. I'm starved."

She tugged on Jason's wrist and lead him past Pettigrew who remained anchored to the floor. Chrissie planted a soft kiss on her father's cheek. As Jason moved by him, he angled his shoulders making sure not to touch the six-four mountain of a seething flesh.

℞

After the tense, awkward interval between the front door bomb blast and being seated for dinner, Chrissie had introduced Jason to her mother who said, "I've heard quite a lot of good things about you, Jason."

Jason said, "Well, I'm sure Chrissie has exaggerated."

Eleanor, feeling the massive tension, talked incessantly as she relieved Jason of the bottle and flowers. She described the meal they were about to experience and how she'd spent all day shopping and preparing. Out of Thomas's view, she poured Jason two inches of real wine from an open bottle on the kitchen counter and stuffed it into his hand. Jason was about to protest when she smiled at him and said, "Trust me, you're going to need it."

"But Chrissie told me no alcohol…"

Eleanor patted his arm. "Just this once will be alright. Just don't say anything to my husband."

Then Chrissie's mother called out to Thomas. "Thomas, darling, be a dear and open the bottle Jason so kindly brought with him. We'll have that with dinner tonight."

This caused Jason to crack a half-smile while in the hall leading to the dining room Thomas cocked his head in Eleanor's direction. The anger silently fumed behind his eyes, reaching new levels of intensity.

"Let's not waste any time," Eleanor declared. "Let's eat."

Eleanor Pettigrew had, indeed, prepared a wonderful supper of Chateaubriand, roasted asparagus and a platter of baked stuffed potatoes. They flanked three sides of the polished oak dining table on which an assortment of steaming platters and bowls were arranged; Thomas at the head, Eleanor dined at the opposite end and Jason and Chrissie sat beside each other on Thomas's right side. A matching oak buffet stood against the right-hand wall beneath an ornately framed mirror.

Jason sneaked a glance toward Thomas who was now shooting daggers at his wife. He cleared his throat and said, "I guess I'm the only one who's been in the dark about you dating one of my externs. Eh, Chrissie?"

"Relax. Jason and I thought it would be best to not say anything to you so as not to influence his grade with the externship. She just found out. I just told mother two weeks ago. It was better that you not know." She flashed a perfect, angelic smile. "Surprise!"

Pettigrew harrumphed then said, "And exactly how long has this tryst been going on?"

"It's not a tryst..."

Eleanor interrupted Chrissie. "Everything's ready. Let's eat and you and Jason can tell your father everything."

Thomas Pettigrew poured Jason's faux wine, he'd purchased at Total Wine, as a vinegary frown played out over his lips.

Jason shot Chrissie a confused glance. She had warned Jason that her father was devote Southern Baptist and forbade alcohol of any kind in his home or presence.

"I hope bringing the grape juice was okay," Jason asked.

Thomas interrupted. "Did my daughter tell you that I forbid alcohol in my household, Jason?"

"Uh...yes sir, she did. But she also said you have wine on special occasions. Chrissie said Eleanor gave her approval."

Thomas glanced up at Eleanor. "Et tu, Brute?" He shot his wife another dagger with his eyes. "So, you're wondering about the wine my wife gave you earlier?" He continued, addressing the question to Jason.

Jason nodded.

"Chrissie is correct. We adhere to strict Southern Baptist doctrine in this house. We serve no hard liquors and no beer. They are tools of the devil and cause men and women to do evil things. It promotes promiscuity and other sinful deeds.

"However, wine is appropriate for certain occasions. Of course, our savior turned water into wine. He drank it at the last supper. We do not keep it in the house as a rule. I purchased a bottle especially for this night...to meet...you." The word "you" hung over the table like an ominous accusation. Then Thomas finished his thought. "But since you were thoughtful enough to bring grape juice, we'll drink this.

"I give you credit, you're a smart man," Thomas continued. "Bringing your own because if I had had the chance, I might have slipped some strychnine in the stuff I bought."

"Thomas!" Eleanor chided.

This was followed by a sharp, "Daddy!" from Chrissie like she was speaking to a puppy who had just soiled the carpet.

"I'm glad you didn't," Jason replied with a smirk. "I'd hate to see it go to waste."

Immediately, Chrissie nudged Jason with her elbow. And Jason realized he'd stepped in it.

"Are you a drinker, young man?" Thomas demanded.

Chrissie snapped her head around to see an expression of dread on Jason's face. Her concerned, irritated moue melted away at his reply. "In moderation, sir."

Thomas continued pouring and allowed the tone of his comment to waft away. He then said, "I expect you to adhere to my rules when you are in my house. Is that clear?"

"Crystal."

Thomas finished filling everyone's glasses with an inch or two of the virgin crimson liquid, nothing more. They passed the platters around and everyone spooned out portions, the clink of silverware on ceramic filled the dining room. Jason had given the house a quick once-over on his way to the door.

The two-story, brick Colonial with a small brick stairway leading to the front door did not boast wealth or poverty. It was entrenched firmly in the middle class, a staple in the working-class city of Newport News. The first floor consisted of several boxy rooms with no open living spaces, a true throwback to Revolutionary times. It was decently decorated and furnished with no signs of extravagance. The only item that caught Jason's attention was the six-foot portrait of Thomas and Eleanor hanging in the small foyer.

"Let's pray," Thomas said. They all held hands as Thomas recited a quick, clipped blessing.

As they dug tentatively into their meals, Thomas began the dreaded inquiry for which Jason and Chrissie had been bracing themselves for nearly ten months.

"So, Jason, how is it that you came to interject yourself into my daughter's life?"

"Thomas, be nice," Eleanor chided.

Jason drained half of the juice in his glass. "Well…"

"Daddy, I…"

Thomas cut his daughter off. "I am speaking with Jason."

"What was the question again?"

"How long? How long has…this…" Pettigrew lifted an upturned palm and gestured toward Jason then Chrissie. "How long has this been going on?"

"Uh…we've been dating since August," Jason replied.

"August?"

Thomas cut into a strip of the braised, roasted tenderloin, shredding it into three pieces. He stabbed at one and stuffed it into his mouth. He chewed multiple times, drank another healthy gulp of faux-wine and swallowed. He dragged the cloth napkin across his lips. The whole time Eleanor, Jason and Chrissie could see the gears turning behind the betrayed eyes. "It's almost May. So, you have been sneaking around for eight months?"

"Yes, sir. I mean I wouldn't call it sneaking around. We just didn't tell you," Jason confirmed, recalling their near-outing at the mall. "And to be honest. It's been almost ten months."

Thomas jabbed his fork into an asparagus spear and lifted the whole piece into the air and chomped off the tapered end.

"Thomas," Eleanor began, "how many times have I told you to cut the asparagus. We are polite, civilized people. Where are your manners?"

Pettigrew's gaze cut through his wife. He did not reply verbally. Instead, a withering gaze communicated his disdain for her comment... and everything else he had seen and heard so far this evening. But Eleanor's words still held sway. He placed the half-piece of the vegetable back on the plate and chopped it into two sections. As he did this and then moved to attack the pieces, he spoke to Jason again. "If I recall," he began. "After your first two days at The Colonial, you gave me a tongue-lashing about respect and how you wanted to be treated. Did you not?"

"That was different," Jason said.

Pettigrew pointed the business end of his knife at his former extern. "No. No, it's not! Respect young man goes both ways."

"Thomas, sir, with all due respect. My life...my private life and... Chrissie's is none of your business. What I do...and who I do it with outside of pharmacy is none of your concern."

Jason was not hungry. His appetite had deserted him hours before the appointed dinner hour. Nonetheless, he made his best show of nonchalance and sliced into the beef and placed a cube in his mouth, chewing slowly. As he sipped his juice, he managed a glance down the table. Eleanor and Chrissie's eyes were riveted on him. Their expressions brimming with leaden concern and electric anticipation.

Chrissie tried to break the tension. "It's my fault. I asked Jason out to dinner during his interview."

Thomas studied his daughter then spoke, a new thought occurring to him. "Was it your idea to keep me in the dark until after I submitted his grade for the externship, Chrissie, my dear?"

Jason replied before Chrissie could. "No sir, it was my idea. I wanted a true evaluation of my externship from you. Not one clouded by the knowledge that I was involved with Chrissie. I believe I am entitled to a fair evaluation, am I not?" Jason demanded, flipping the focus back toward the head of the table.

Thomas chopped off another piece of meat and grunted an unintelligible reply.

Thomas leaned toward Chrissie as he looked in Jason's direction. "At least, give me the satisfaction of knowing that you are using appropriate birth control with my daughter."

Jason had just brought the water glass to his lips and was drinking when Thomas launched that verbal missile. He choked and coughed, then wiped water from his chin.

"Daddy!?" Chrissie admonished.

Eleanor's eyes spewed invisible laser beams at her husband as Thomas lowered his eyes and studied his plate of mangled tenderloin.

Hesitating only a moment, Jason produced a wide grin. "Well, Thomas," he began. "I'm still a virgin. My penis was cut off in a freak motorcycle accident when I was twelve years old. I'm afraid you don't have to worry about any unwanted grandchildren." Jason's grin widened into an ear-to-ear smile as he finished sipping his water.

Thomas stopped eating and glared at Jason. His eyes wide with confusion, concern and sympathy for the apparent gruesome loss. The sentiment evaporated when Pettigrew spied Jason's slowly spreading, shit-eating grin. After thirty seconds and with great reluctance, Thomas's frown slid into a half-smile and a one snort chuckle.

Chrissie and Eleanor tried to stifle their own laughter but failed. Jason continued beaming as Chrissie and Eleanor burst into full belly laughs while Thomas simply could no longer suppress an unabashed expression and an I-don't-believe-this-shit grin.

Everyone ate in silence for several minutes as the smiles took a minute to fade. The only sound was the intermittent clinking of silverware.

Finally, Thomas spoke, signaling the discussion and interrogation about Chrissie's formerly secret relationship with Jason had entered a new phase.

"You may have lost your penis, but not your balls! Pass the potatoes, please."

CHAPTER 34

After dinner, they partook of strawberry shortcake dripping with whipped cream and cups of steaming coffee. In the hopes of keeping the conversation away from his and Chrissie's relationship, Jason posed questions to Thomas about the status of things at The Colonial. He inquired about the programs he had initiated: starting patients on statins and the compliance phone calls.

"They are doing quite well, Jason," Thomas admitted. "I have seen a five percent increase in business from them." Thomas lifted his coffee cup in salute.

"And how is your new extern doing?"

"He just started. So, we will see. And how is *your* new externship going?"

"It's also only been a week." Jason let out a silent breath, beginning to feel the tension slipping from his body. The electric tautness that had hung in the air like a black storm cloud throughout the early part of the evening had eased. The skies hadn't turned sunny yet but, maybe, the blustery winds were letting up.

"You're working at a compounding pharmacy, correct?"

Jason nodded. "Yes sir. It's very intimidating. A lot of preparations I'm not familiar with."

"I see. And how did your interviews go?"

Jason had attended a career fair at his pharmacy school in Richmond one Saturday during his time at The Colonial. He had interviewed with several large pharmacy chains. "They were all impressed that I was externing at The Colonial. Your reputation is quite impressive."

"Any job offers?"

"Not yet," Jason admitted. "They wanted to see what my evaluation from you was. Thank you for the glowing comments."

Jason had received his grade. An "A" minus. But Thomas had lavished some wonderful and unexpected comments about Jason in his personal observations. Comments he apparently had difficulty expressing verbally. Jason wondered if Pettigrew would still be as generous if he were given the chance to re-write those comments and re-consider Jason's grade after learning what he'd learned tonight. His answer came straight away.

"You're welcome. You deserved them." Thomas hesitated. His tone taking a more serious timbre. "You better live up to them. Because I know where to find you now."

Jason hefted a forkful of the shortcake to his lips and smiled. "I will try."

When the evening ended, Chrissie walked Jason to his car. They shared a long kiss as Jason leaned on the front fender and wrapped his arms around her waist. "That went fairly well," she said.

"After he got over the shock, maybe. I think he' still pissed though."

"He will come around. He's got no choice. I think he's already started," Chrissie said. "I'll work on him. He doesn't like surprises. We'll have you over for dinner again, next week." Chrissie kissed him again. "Where the hell did you come up with the motorcycle thing?"

Jason shrugged. "It just came to me. Needed to lighten the mood."

"You certainly did that. He won't admit it, Jason. But I think he likes that you're not intimidated by him. I think he respects you for it."

"I hope so. Because if he doesn't, he's going to make our lives—my life--very difficult."

"It'll be fine," she said. "I know that's what I love about you...your sense of humor."

Jason cast a surprised look at her in the dim, suffused light from the moon and distant streetlamps. "Did you just say 'love'? Are you in love with me, Christine Pettigrew?"

The wide inviting way her eyes studied him supplied him with an answer. Her dark caramel eyes swam with emotion. "Maybe," she replied.

℞

Three weeks later, Jason dined with Chrissie and her parents for the fourth time. Dinners two and three were simple affairs as was this evening's fare. They dined simply on hamburgers and hot dogs Thomas had grilled out back along with potato salad, sodas and iced tea.

Thomas inquired about Jason's job prospects. "Have you had any job offers yet?"

"Well," Jason replied. "I have. Walgreens, Drug-Rite and Keller's Food and Drug have offered me positions with their companies. Of course, all that depends on my passing the Boards. I'm still waiting to hear from others."

Jason had seen a remarkable change in Thomas's attitude towards him and his relationship with Chrissie. He had stopped talking about being kept in the dark and was now asking questions about his job prospects.

Jason had two weeks left in his last rotation at the compounding pharmacy. That would be followed by his graduation ceremony a week later. Then Jason would be free for the summer. He would spend six to eight hours a day cramming all the knowledge he'd acquired in the last four years of pharmacy school back into his brain with the help of a prep course so it would be readily retrievable at a moment's notice. His board exam was scheduled for the middle of July. If he was lucky, he would get the results before the end of July and become a licensed pharmacist.

"Walgreens, eh?"

"Yes sir."

"You know there's a Walgreens right across the street from The Colonial?"

"I do," Jason said.

"Did they say where they'll put you? It would be extremely awkward for you to work for my competition and be dating my daughter. Don't you agree?"

"No sir, they have not discussed with me where I would work. And, yes, I can see how it would look." Jason had, in fact, considered the awkwardness of such an arrangement. He wasn't sure how Walgreens would perceive it. And Jason wasn't sure if he should divulge such information to them. In the final analysis, it was none of their business.

"Can I offer you some advice on which jobs to seriously consider?"

Jason shrugged. Over the last weeks, Thomas Pettigrew had warmed to the notion of Jason and Chrissie's relationship. He was now offering Jason unsolicited professional advice. "You're not just trying to make sure I don't work across the street from you, are you?"

"No, Jason. I just want to impart some of my twenty years of experience."

"Sure. Shoot."

"Great," Thomas replied. "We won't spoil our evening with such details tonight. Let's enjoy each other's company. Come by the store tomorrow after you finish at the compounding pharmacy and we'll talk. Okay?"

Jason hesitated not sure he'd heard Thomas correctly. "I'll be there," Jason said. He cast a glance at Chrissie who winked, smiled and blew him a quick kiss.

CHAPTER 35

The next evening, Jason appeared at The Colonial at fifteen minutes to seven. He had completed his shift at the compounding pharmacy forty-five minutes earlier. Thomas waved him back into the pharmacy. Jason greeted the cashier, the delivery driver, and Gloria, who happened to be working tonight. It was late spring, traditionally a slower time for pharmacies. The cough, cold and flu season were months in the past. But allergies and other ailments still supplied steady business. The next flu season was three months away.

Thomas led him into the same office where Jason had first met with him for his interview and in which he'd first met Chrissie. Thomas pointed to the uncomfortable metal chair across from the dented metal desk. Today, he sat in a much more relaxed state than he did all those months ago.

Thomas offered him coffee, pointing to a new machine. Piles of reports and papers had been moved to make room for it. Jason accepted. "Do you have decaf?"

Thomas popped a K-cup into the machine and made two cups. When they were finished brewing, he pointed to the powdered creamer and sweeteners. Jason added some of each to his mug.

"So, are you leaning toward any particular company at the moment?" Thomas asked.

"I can't say that I am. In the last twenty-four hours, I've received two more offers from CVS and from Wal-Mart."

"Impressive," Thomas said, bunching his lips together. "That's five offers. What are you going to do?"

"I'm not sure what to do," Jason admitted. "I did externships with CVS and Walgreens. Their offers aren't as attractive as Drug-Rite's or Wal-Mart's. Keller's is not close when it comes to salary."

"There's more to it than just money. The pharmacy industry is changing rapidly. You never know what's going to happen in the next few years. There will be a lot of consolidation. Salaries are great right now. Pharmacists are in a good negotiating position. There's a shortage. You can demand pretty much any salary you desire. But that will change eventually. It always does."

"Consolidation?"

"Companies will buy other companies. You start out working for one and could end up working for another. It's inevitable."

"What would you do if you were me?"

"Don't accept their first offer. If they're offering you something, they are willing to pay more. Especially if you have received a great evaluation from me. Use that to your advantage."

"But I don't know how much I should ask for?"

"Ask for twenty percent more than they're offering and don't settle for anything less than ten percent above their initial offer."

Jason furrowed his brow with concern. "My father said pretty much the same thing."

"He's a smart man. Don't worry. You are in the driver's seat. They need good pharmacists."

"If you say so. What else do I need to think about?"

"How much help are they offering you."

"Help with what?"

"Technician help. Ask them how many tech hours they have at the stores where they want to place you."

"Really?"

"Especially if they're cheap with hours. Pharmacists are useless without good technician help. You also might want to consider going to a company that does not have a drive thru. Unfortunately, that is the current trend. They are going to be the death of a good pharmacy practice. Trust me," Thomas said.

Thomas had opined on several occasions about the growing number of pharmacies using drive-thru windows and how speaking through thick, bullet-proof glass was de-personalizing the profession.

"I don't know what to do," Jason said.

"Or you could work for an independent pharmacy. They usually don't have issues with help because they set their own technician hours, not some bean counter in a corporate office hundreds of miles away."

"They don't pay as well though, do they?"

"That's true. They can't compete with the chains in terms of salary. But they can offer a better learning experience for a young pharmacist."

"I hadn't considered an independent. I don't know any independents looking for a pharmacist."

"I do," Pettigrew said as a slow smile spread beneath his intense blue eyes.

PHARMACY PHACT:

There are 21,767 independent retail pharmacies in the United States in 2018, down from 22,478 in 2014.

Drug Store News, *Independent Pharmacies Fight Back*, Mark Hamstra, March 24 ,2020

CHAPTER 36

"So how was your meeting? Did he help you make a decision?" Chrissie asked.

"He did."

"So, who are you going to work for?"

Jason was on his cell phone in his Honda while Chrissie sat in her own car in the parking lot of a salon waiting for her hair appointment.

"Your father had a lot of good advice. He told me which companies to watch out for and which might be good for a new pharmacist."

"So, which one?"

"Actually, it's an independent that's looking for a pharmacist. It'll be a great learning opportunity. Though the money won't be as good as the chains."

"Okay?" Chrissie said.

Jason did not speak. He smiled into the phone. After ten seconds, she got it. "You're kidding, right? This is some kind of twisted joke?"

"No, Chrissie. It isn't."

"But he has a staff pharmacist. Kyle Griffin."

"Your father kept it quiet. But evidently, Kyle is going to take a job at a hospital. He's given four weeks' notice. So, he said he wanted me to come work for him."

℞

Simon's spindly frame barely dented the threadbare cushions on the sofa in the small flat behind The Colonial while Victor, the short, plump, balding fireplug of a man careened around the tiny kitchen preparing a bachelor's dinner of frozen pizza, chips and dip and sodas.

Though he was smaller and skinnier that Victor, Simon nonetheless grabbed a thick hunk of flab around his mid-section. They had been on this assignment now for almost a year. Neither he nor Victor liked to cook. So, their meals consisted of fast food or, on the few occasions when they did venture into a grocery store, they simply stockpiled frozen meals or steaks which they seared on the rusting gas grill on the back deck. Simon promised himself that he would start exercising again tomorrow. He'd start with a daily run and try to cut back on the junk food.

Victor often volunteered his marginal culinary expertise for meal preparation, a discipline that entailed setting the timer on the microwave or the oven. At first, Simon thought it was because Victor liked to cook...if that's what one could call it. But he learned a few months ago it was because he wanted to get out of listening to the endless string of banal conversations between Thomas and Eleanor Pettigrew, his daughter, Christine, and her boyfriend, Jason Rodgers.

They had been meeting with their handler Carl once a month and trading secure emails every two weeks with reports containing the colorless details of a middle-aged pharmacy owner, his wife, daughter, and their employees, including the pharmacy students.

Both spies were excited that this phase of their excruciatingly mundane tour of duty was apparently almost over. Jason Rodgers had completed his externship at The Colonial. Thomas Pettigrew had given the student Rodgers an extremely complimentary evaluation and an A minus for his six weeks of work at the pharmacy.

In the last two months, Simon and Victor had been caught up in the family drama that had played out and come to a head a few weeks ago. They added spice to the monotony by placing wagers on the outcome of various aspects of their subject's lives. *Would Thomas take a certain route home from the store? Would the latest extern quit before their six weeks were up? Would Chrissie and Jason finally end up together?* And on and on the wagering went.

Many months ago, when Christine and Jason were on their first date, they had wagered on whether Thomas would find out about them before they were ready to announce their relationship. It had been their longest running bet, nearly ten months.

And Thomas had not found out. Though there had been a close call or two. Simon collected his winnings from Victor two weeks ago.

They had bet on what Thomas Pettigrew's reaction would be to the news that Jason Rodgers was banging his only daughter. Simon had guessed that the Old Man would blow a gasket, forbid them to see each other and throw Rodgers out of the house. Victor had guessed that Pettigrew would eventually succumb and grudgingly bless the relationship. Yesterday, Simon had finally handed over a crumpled twenty-dollar bill to his co-worker/roommate. In essence, they had been trading the same crumpled twenty back and forth for months.

While Victor toiled in the kitchen and with the air reeking of cooking pizza crust, Simon listened to the latest conversation between the two lovers, twirling his Mont Blanc pen in his right hand. They had placed another bet on which job Rodgers would take. He leaned in and cocked an ear to listen.

"He's about to tell her what job he took," Simon announced over his shoulder.

Every second of every conversation of the major players at The Colonial had been and would continue to be recorded through the electronic wiretaps that had been illegally placed on their cellphones and landlines. So far, they had recorded over a hundred hours of conversations. The listening device placed in Pettigrew's office had stopped working a few days ago. Its tiny lithium battery had probably gone dead. Either that or Thomas Pettigrew had found it and discarded it not knowing what it was. They had placed the devices under the guise of working for The Colonial's internet provider. If they were to replace it, that would require a different plan. Either way, they currently had no ears in his office right now.

The devices in the pharmacy proper still functioned. They had heard Pettigrew invite the pharmacy extern into his office. To which Victor chided Simon, "I told you we needed to get in there."

An open laptop sat on the scratched, distressed coffee table. The activated computer program displayed a voice print analysis meter active on the screen. A thin green line danced, oscillating on the graph with each utterance as Chrissie and Jason's voices were recorded.

Victor had pulled the pizza from the oven and--not satisfied--quickly slid it back in, wiped his hands on a dish towel desperately needing to experience soap, and moved as fast as his portly frame would allow to the living room. He leaned on the back of the sofa as the Pettigrew's daughter questioned Rodgers.

So who are you going to work for?

Your father had a lot of good advice. He told me which companies to watch out for and which might be good for a new pharmacist.

So which one?

It's an independent that's looking for a pharmacist. It'll be a great learning opportunity. Thought the money won't be as good as the chains.

"Goddamnit," Simon seethed. "He's not taking any of those jobs. He's going with an independent."

"Shut up," Victor chided his partner. "They're still talking. You can get your money back on another bet." They had both been wrong.

Chrissie continued.

Okay?

Seconds elapsed. *You're kidding, right? This is some kind of twisted joke?*

No, Chrissie. It isn't.

But he has a staff pharmacist. Kyle Griffin?

Your father kept it quiet. But evidently, Kyle is going to take a job at a hospital. He's given four weeks' notice. So, he said he wanted me to come work for him.

"Holy shit," Victor spat. "He's taking a job at The Colonial."

"How the hell did we miss the fact that Griffin had resigned?" Simon's pen stopped spinning in hand.

"I told you. We need to replace that bug in Pettigrew's office," Simon said. "Carl's gonna want to hear this...immediately."

PHARMACY PHACT:

Each year between 7,000 and 9,000 people die due to
a medication error.

Medication and Dispensing Errors,
StatPearl, November 2020

CHAPTER 37

Chrissie glanced at her watch. She was going to be late to her appointment. Her eyes widened. Then they narrowed as the ramifications hit home. "Are you sure you want to work for him?"

"Why not?'

"Because...it's him…my father…the 'Old Man'. He can be a bear."

"I've seen what it's like at the competitors. They are driven hard and put up wet. There's very little help and they are always cutting hours. It's not good for a new pharmacist. Chains are a meat grinder to work for. There are layers and layers of bureaucratic bullshit to go through. Your father is the one who signs the checks. He can't pay me as much. But I have a plan. The only debt I have right now is my student loans. I'm going to put as much money as I can toward that. And I'll keep driving this clunker until it stops running."

Jason had reviewed his loan statements just the other day. Six months after graduation, he would have to begin paying on his student debt. Between his undergraduate education at John Radcliffe University and the pharmacy degree from Virginia Commonwealth

University in Richmond, he had amassed a debt of more than one hundred and ninety thousand dollars.

"Wow," was all Chrissie could manage.

"It'll be fine. Your father and I have grown to respect each other."

"So, when is Kyle leaving?" Chrissie thought about how much had changed in the few weeks Jason had spent at The Colonial and since completing his rotation.

"Four weeks. Apparently as soon as Kyle told your father he said the first person he thought of was me."

"Wow, that's saying something." Chrissie paused then said. "But you're not a pharmacist yet. You still haven't passed your pharmacy test."

"Not a problem. Your father said he'd pick up some extra shifts and he'd call a relief labor service to find a fill-in pharmacist until I pass. I called the Board of Pharmacy asking how long it would take for the results to come back. I was told they're having computer issues. It could take weeks."

"You better pass!"

"I will. Guess I should hang up and hit the books."

℞

The next afternoon, Simon and Victor met Carl in the glass-and-steel walled lobby of the Norfolk Hilton hotel on Main Street once more. The spymaster from Washington appeared through the main entrance and spotted his two-man team fidgeting like fathers about to confess they had a bastard child. Simon had the laptop case slung over one shoulder and was holding it firmly against his side.

"What the hell's so important that I had to drive down from Langley to meet you?"

Carl walked toward the outdoor eatery expecting them to follow. Victor stopped him. Carl turned and threw his hands up as if to say, "What the hell?"

"Follow us," Victor ordered.

The trio stepped to the bank of elevators at the rear of the lobby and escorted their supervisor to a corner suite on the eighteenth floor with a panoramic view of the Norfolk Waterside District, the Elizabeth river and Portsmouth on the far bank.

Yesterday, Simon had been the one to make the call and deliver the news that Carl would need to drive down from Langley to Norfolk. After Carl had launched into a profanity-laced tirade which caused Simon to place the call on his secure cell phone on speaker so Victor could participate in the tongue lashing. Exactly seventeen seconds after it began, Carl, spent and out of breath, simply said, "This better be good!"

"It's not good," Simon declared. "But you need to hear it."

Simon explained that they had evidence that he needed to hear right away, and it could not be sent electronically. Carl threatened both men with careers cleaning toilets at Langley if they were wasting his time.

"This better be good," Carl barked in a low, menacing voice, repeating his exact words from twenty-four hours earlier.

Without a word, Simon unpacked the laptop and placed it on the desk beside the television credenza. The three men hunched over the screen as it booted up. Simon then slipped the thumb drive into the port and clicked on the single file it held...an audio file.

"This is a conversation between Jason Rodgers and Christine Pettigrew last night. They're talking about a conversation Rodgers had with Thomas Pettigrew an hour earlier. Listen."

Simon pressed the triangular play icon.

As Jason and Christine's words slipped from the laptop's speaker, Carl's expression turned from one of profound irritation directed at his operatives to one of perplexed shock and frustration.

"Shit," he seethed when the recording ended. "This changes everything."

"He's not a pharmacist yet. He still needs to pass his exam," Victor explained.

"When is the test?"

"Evidently in July. He'll get the results by the end of July or August," Simon explained

"Sit tight," Carl said. "We have to neutralize Jason Rodgers. I'll get back to you."

Simon brought his hand to his mouth and cleared his throat into his curled hand. "One other thing."

Carl spun and raised an eyebrow.

Simon looked to Victor for a dose of courage. "We are tired of babysitting Jason Rodgers and Thomas Pettigrew. We want in on the operation when it goes down."

Carl's eyes narrowed, then his stone-like expression softened. One side of his mouth elevated into a half-smirk. He scratched his nose with the tip of his forefinger. "Okay. This is a shit assignment. I'll grant you that. You've served your penance. I'll see what I can do."

CHAPTER 38

Jason walked arm-in-arm with Chrissie along the glass-enclosed elevated walkway spanning North Fifth Street and connecting the Greater Richmond Convention Center with the second level of the parking deck. The sun glowed like a giant circular jewel in a pristine cloudless sky. It was the second Saturday in May. Graduation Day.

Chrissie had graduated from Virginia Tech the previous Saturday. Jason and his parents had followed the Pettigrew's to Blacksburg on the Friday prior and stayed in a hotel to support Chrissie in the successful completion of her degree.

This morning, a warm, gentle breeze whipped between downtown Richmond's towering edifices. The young couple led Jason's parents, Edward and Evelyn Rodgers, and Thomas and Eleanor Pettigrew. Jason wished his brother, Peter, could be here. But he was currently deployed in the Middle East with the Marine Corps. Peter had spoken with Jason via videoconferencing two days ago. Peter congratulated his younger brother on his upcoming ceremony. He told Jason and their parents that he was scheduled to undertake a mission the following day and would be unavailable for about a week. This news caused great anxiety for everyone especially Evelyn. Peter was her first born. As a Force Recon sniper, Peter was always being sent on dangerous missions about which he could not divulge any information.

The families had met for the first time over dinner at the Rodgers's home ten days earlier before Chrissie's ceremony to celebrate the graduation of their children. They'd spent a quiet, somewhat tense evening discussing their children and their ten-month relationship over chicken pot pie, corn, salad and soft drinks.

Edward Rodgers, a barrel-chested man who was deaf in his right ear, possessed the physique of a longshoreman yielding to the slow advance of years with a well-developed beer gut. A plump, slightly oversized head with a ruddy-complected face sat perched between a pair of powerful shoulders. Normally a heavy drinker and smoker, he had placed all the beer and liquor out of view as a courtesy to Thomas Pettigrew, but only after a great deal of bitching and moaning to his wife, Jason's mother.

He managed to keep his frustration in check for the evening but blurted after their guests had left, "This will be the only time I hide my drink from anyone."

That night, the six had sat around the modest dining room table with Edward, the man of the house, at the head. Evelyn had made sure that Thomas sat on Edward's left because of the deafness in his right ear, the result of a grenade going off near his head during his time in the Middle East and the first Gulf War. He'd suffered only the hearing loss and a few lacerations as he ducked behind a Humvee with a second to spare.

The main topic of discussion was Thomas's job offer to Jason. Edward bragged about his youngest son and stated that Jason was a very responsible, hard-working man. He complimented Thomas and Eleanor on what a lovely daughter they had raised, causing Chrissie to blush. Thomas even managed to begrudgingly compliment Jason on how hard he worked and was looking forward to having him as his staff pharmacist.

The fact that Jason and Chrissie had kept their relationship a secret from Thomas and Eleanor came up early in the evening. Thomas allowed himself a brief smile and admitted that he was managing to get past the romantic cloak and dagger.

Edward grinned like the cat that had swallowed the proverbial canary when he learned that Thomas had been brought into the loop only in the last four weeks. Though it was never spoken aloud, it appeared that the fact he'd known about Chrissie and Jason longer than Thomas brought him enormous satisfaction. For the most part, the conversation was convivial but dotted with periods of silence in which the six struggled to find topics to discuss.

Thomas discussed pharmacy and the deplorable state of healthcare in general, while Edward railed about labor cuts at the shipyard despite the company pulling in billions from Navy contracts. Eleanor and Evelyn managed to find common ground in a sidebar about their children, their career choices and what a beautiful couple they made. After two and half hours and some dessert, the Pettigrews departed, leaving Jason and Chrissie and his parents to spend the rest of the evening together.

Now, the six of them crossed the breezeway into the convention center. They rode the escalator to the first level. Hundreds of graduates dressed in black and tan gowns milled about along with their families and guests in the L-shaped glass-walled lobby, circling the perimeter. Jason's sister, Katherine, and her doctor husband appeared through the crowd. With tears in her eyes, she hugged her brother tightly.

Sunlight streamed through the glass, filling the space with another level of anticipation. Exhibit hall walls had been removed to create one gigantic space. The din of excitement and conversation was frequently punctuated by excited squeals and shouts of friends and fellow students greeting each other.

Inside the vast space of the graduation hall, a wide stage of risers had been prepared with seats for dignitaries and school administration. Row upon row of chairs had been lined up, stretching from one wall to the other as a wide gap cut through the center for the walk of the graduates. Elegant draperies and bunting lined the room and the various flags hung from stand poles along the dais: The Stars and Stripes, the Virginia state flag with its deep blue field and the circular logo with the words "Sic Semper Tyrannus" encircling it, the flag of Richmond city, and the banner of Virginia Commonwealth University.

An overhead announcement encouraged family members to take their places as the graduates were escorted to another, private area to prepare for their ceremony.

Four long hours later, Jason Rodgers had graduated. As they gathered back in the glass-enclosed lobby of the convention center, Jason hugged Chrissie, his mother and father, and shook hands with Thomas and Eleanor.

Thomas looked him square in the eye and said, "Let's hope you pass the Board exam. I won't pay a relief pharmacist for another three months while you wait to re-take the exam."

℞

The next day, Sunday, the phone on the coffee table of the small apartment in Newport News gave a shrill, intermittent ring. Simon sat on the sofa reading a dog-eared paperback copy of Robert Ludlum's The Scarlatti Inheritance. It was the same novel Jason had been reading on the beach the day he'd decided to try and win her back. He had made a mental note to read it, but only had gotten around to it in the last few days.

He regarded the ringing device like it was an irritating shrew. After four ear-penetrating rings, he lifted the cordless handset from the cradle.

"Hello."

"Put this call into secure mode." Carl's curt voice caused him to sit upright.

Simon reached over to the base and depressed a red button. The button illuminated indicating the call was now being encrypted.

"Okay, we're good," Simon said.

"What's the latest?"

"Well, our boy graduated yesterday."

"He's not our boy," Carl corrected.

Simon let the comment fall away. "He's going to work at The Colonial twenty hours a week as a graduate intern while he spends the rest of his time studying to pass his test," Simon said.

By this time, Victor had emerged from the bathroom while re-buckling his trousers. The fan, working overtime, hummed behind him.

He spoke to Simon sotto voce. "Ask him what the plan is…?"

Simon nodded and motioned for him to be quiet. "So are we going to neutralize him before he even takes his test? We can make it so that Pettigrew refuses to hire him. Perhaps we can arrange for Rodgers to have an affair with someone. Some photos and phone calls could be arranged. Once that is made known to Pettigrew, he will most certainly refuse to hire him."

"That's not a bad idea," Victor observed. "But it would require us to get a female operative into place in Newport News.

"What about framing Rodgers for stealing money or drugs? That too would give Pettigrew plenty of reason to send him packing."

Victor, understanding what Simon was suggesting to Carl, offered an idea. "We could have a car accident…a very bad car accident. He could land in the hospital for months…or worse."

Simon nodded. "Victor recommends a car accident."

"Enough, gentlemen," Carl interrupted. "Remember, the ultimate goal of this operation is to get Thomas Pettigrew to sell The Colonial. We need to make sure that he is motivated to sell the business to our front company. The plan is to put Pettigrew into an extremely dire financial dilemma. Then we swoop in and save the day."

"And how do we do that?"

"Those details are being worked out. It is important that Rodgers pass his exam and become a licensed pharmacist. He must then become employed by The Colonial. When the time is right, Rodgers will be the catalyst that causes the financial disaster required to persuade Pettigrew to sell. It will need to be ugly. But, then again, you two do ugly very well. We'll work out the details later."

Simon smiled to Victor then said to Carl, "So that means we're back in the game?"

Carl chuckled. "Yeah, you're back in the game. Don't fuck it up!

PHARMACY PHACT:

It is estimated that at least 1.5 million people are harmed by errors involving prescription medication each year. The report adds that this figure is likely an underestimate.

Institute of Medicine, 2007, *Preventing Medication Errors*, Washington D.C.: The National Academies Press

CHAPTER 39

On a steamy summer morning on the second Tuesday of July, Jason walked into the testing center in Hampton in a strip mall on Hampton Roads Center Parkway at precisely nine-thirty, exactly thirty minutes before his scheduled testing appointment. The indifferent clerk did not meet his gaze while retrieving and confirming his reservation. After proffering two forms of identification, his driver's license and a passport which had been stamped only once for his relief mission to Ecuador, he then slid his Authorization To Test, or ATT, across the desk. The clerk verified his name on the ATT was an exact match to his driver's license and passport.

Jason then surrendered his phone and wristwatch and was asked to empty his pockets. His change, car keys and a scrap of paper with the address to the exam center were placed in a Ziplock bag on which his name was scribbled in black marker and placed in a bin under the desk.

For the next six hours, Jason sat before a computer screen and answered two hundred and fifty questions related to the practice of pharmacy. Two-thirds of the questions dealt with Safe and Effective Pharmacotherapy and Health Outcomes, while the remainder covered the Safe and Accurate Preparation, Compounding, Dispensing and Administration of Medications and provision of Health Care Products.

After a break for lunch, he returned to the testing center. The second exam for Jason's licensure for the State of Virginia required that he pass the pharmacy law exam. This test consisted of one hundred and fifty questions related to both Federal and Virginia pharmacy law. After two more hours, Jason exited the building into a stifling summer breeze feeling exhausted, relieved and exhilarated.

All that remained now was the waiting, he told himself.

He drove from the testing center back to his parent's house and changed clothes. He went to the refrigerator and retrieved a Miller Lite just as his father entered the kitchen. When he asked how his test had gone, Jason simply replied, "I'm glad it's over."

"I'm sure you did fine," his father said.

"Thanks, Pop," Jason replied, taking a long pull on the beer.

"Will you be home for dinner?"

"Sorry, I have plans with Chrissie tonight. We're celebrating."

"No problem son," came the reply.

Fathers and sons often clashed at Jason's age. At least, that's what he and some of his buddies had talked about. And Jason and his father were no different. One of the things Jason did appreciate about his old man was the fact that he never pushed him to change plans or be with family. He seemed to know how to let Jason make his own decisions and live his own life.

"She's a nice girl," his father continued. "I like her...a lot."

"So, do I."

His father grinned. "I hope so. I can't say the same for her old man. He seems like a pompous ass! What's with this no alcohol thing?"

"Thomas is a devout Southern Baptist. He does not drink except on special occasions and only wine. He takes some getting used to. He's a very strong personality, incredibly well-respected in the profession and is often consulted about legislation from the politicians in Richmond."

"That's tell me everything I need to know," Edward Rodgers said. "Are you sure you want to work for someone like him? You yourself said you're taking a pay cut to work for an independent pharmacy." This wasn't first time the senior Rodgers had broached the topic of money with his son.

Jason sucked more beer from his long neck and aimed his words in the direction of his father's left ear. "I can't take a pay cut because I haven't even worked as a pharmacist yet. No matter what I make, it will be a massive increase over what I make now. I've thought it through. I will learn a lot from him. I'm not going to change my mind, Pop!"

His father raised both hands in a defensive gesture. "Okay, okay. I won't bring it up again. The next time we get together with Thomas and Eleanor, just so you are prepared, I will be having a drink. Maybe three."

℞

"My treat tonight," Chrissie declared.

"You might regret that statement tonight because I'm famished. I've done nothing but study and work for the last six weeks." He eyed the menu. "That surf and turf doesn't stand a chance.

"I know," she complained. "I feel neglected. You're going to make that up to me."

The 99 Main Restaurant sat in the shade of tall maples on Main Street, forty feet from the intersection with Warwick Boulevard in the Hilton Village of Newport News. Hilton Village had been established nearly one hundred years ago to provide affordable housing for employees of Penrose Gatling Shipyard during World War One, The Great War, and was placed on the National Register of Historic Places in 1969. The narrow, tree-lined streets set just off the James River provided an idyllic setting to raise families. Over the years, its reputation grew. Local politicians knew participation in the annual parade was a must and sought votes from the Hilton electorate or risked losing their seats. Hilton had even been home to one William Styron as a child. His Pulitzer prize for *The Confessions of Nat Turner* was one of several prestigious awards bestowed upon the Newport News native

"Oh really," Jason said with a smile. "I can't wait to hear how."

99 Main had been one of the go-to places for years for the residents of the area and the Peninsula. The quaint two-room dining area with soft-lighting, old-fashioned decor and friendly waiters and bartenders who would converse with patrons about local gossip and politics.

"Well, you're going to take me away for a week."

"Sounds good. I could use some time away. I'm going to have to check with your father to get the time off."

"Already done," Chrissie bragged. "I spoke with him last night. We leave on Saturday."

The waitress offered a warm smile, greeted them and said, "What can we get you tonight?"

℞

"Where are we headed?" Jason asked.

"I want it to be a surprise," Chrissie replied. "Just get on 95 and head south."

Chrissie had arranged everything. But she refused to give Jason any details. Jason pointed the Honda west along Route 58 toward Emporia. This long, undulating stretch of pavement would connect them with Interstate 95 and points south. He settled in for a perhaps long but enjoyable ride. He did not have to worry about prescriptions or job offers or test results. For the next few hours, Jason could drive, enjoy talking with his love and give his overtaxed mind a well-deserved break.

In Emporia, Jason took the on-ramp for I-95 South and depressed the accelerator until the engine strained at seventy miles per hour. As the old Honda rattled and vibrated, they listened to music and discussed Chrissie's future at Casper, White and Collins and Jason's future with The Colonial.

"At least tell me how long we have to drive?" He asked after an hour on the interstate.

"About eight hours," Chrissie replied.

Jason performed some quick calculations. "That put us in South Carolina somewhere."

Chrissie smirked and shook her head. "You think you're so smart. That's all you get."

℞

South Forest Beach Drive on Hilton Head Island meandered through thick trees as it paralleled the Atlantic Ocean. Jason had always wanted to visit this resort area. He and Chrissie had talked about it a few times in the last few months. It was not as stark and over-commercialized as he'd imagined. The planners had maintained the natural beauty of the island with strictly enforced building codes.

All business enterprises were set back off the tree-lined boulevards and hidden amidst thick expanses of oaks, palmettoes, loblolly pines and wax myrtles. Hanging from many species of trees, especially the oaks, was the ever present, rootless Spanish Moss, soaking up moisture from the humid atmosphere. With ordinances not allowing any structure to be erected higher than six stories and banning large gawdy signs, the city planners had kept the quaint, forested flavor. The island possessed all the routine and luxurious amenities of more starkly developed areas. But the businesses, restaurants and shopping were all camouflaged in an idyllic atmosphere that reminded him of Williamsburg back home in Virginia.

"Here we are," Chrissie said. "Turn left here."

Jason pulled into Ocean Oak Resort, a Hilton Grand Vacations property. They rolled their bags into the foyer and were checked in by a pleasant black woman. Ten minutes later, Jason slid the key card across the pad to the door of an apartment on the fifth floor and pushed it open.

"Nice digs," he said. "Do your parents own this?"

"No. It's a time share. One of my father's colleagues in the House of Delegates in Richmond owns it. He owed my father a favor. So here we are."

"I might get used to being around your father."

They toured the suite, impressed by its elegance and simplicity. The small foyer opened into a modern, well-equipped kitchen with clean, stainless steel appliances. A granite countertop breakfast bar protruded from the north wall. They slipped around it to the dining room and into a spacious living area with a comfy sleeper sofa. A massive, mounted flat screen TV covered most of the opposite wall. The master bedroom sported a king-sized bed and a tiled master bath with a full tub, a separate walk-in shower, and a lighted mirror. Backtracking, they explored a second bedroom off the foyer with two queen-sized beds and another wall-mounted screen along with its own private bath.

They clasped hands and kissed. Jason gently pushed her onto one of the beds.

"Oh no, not yet," Chrissie said, standing back up. "There's more to see."

They returned to the living area and slid open the thick, heavy glass door leading to a balcony overlooking a quadrangle nestled between three buildings creating an expansive U-shaped common area expert-ly landscaped with lush plants, tall oaks, Palmetto trees and verdant Bermuda grass with shaded, meandering walkways, promising more fun and relaxation farther along.

Directly below them, various lawn games like ladder ball, corn-hole and a large black and white outdoor chess set lay scattered on the lawn. Gaggles of adults engaged in relaxed conversations while holding libations, and children darted about playing the games and squealing. Music from unseen speakers played at a pleasing volume pumping out energetic, toe-tapping tunes, energizing the carefree party atmosphere.

Beyond the gaming area, a rectangular fenced pool area with a per-gola-covered hot tub was ringed by perfectly aligned pool chairs in use by swim-suited guests. Beyond this first pool lay a covered bar and grille with a waitress hustling between packed tables. Beyond this, an-other more elaborate and tropically shaped pool beckoned with curved walls and jets sprouting water intermittently in parabolic arcs from the deck. Two more waiters scurried back and forth delivering food and drink to guests frolicking in the water and soaking in the golden rays of summer.

Beyond this second pool stretched a hundred yards of American Beachgrass and Cord Grass, then the vast blue-green waters of the Atlantic Ocean which could be accessed by a sandy walkway. The low sweeping hum of the surging and receding surf wafted in the warm air as a salty wind stroked their faces.

"You planned all this?"

Chrissie smiled and nodded. "We're here for three days, then we're driving north to Myrtle Beach for another three days at a place called the Sands. Then we head home."

"Let's make the best of it," Jason said. "I need some down time after all that studying. And I know what I want to do first."

He took her by the hand and led her back into the suite to the large king-sized bed in the master bedroom. He drew her to him and kissed her hard. Then, slowly, he pulled the gauzy blouse over her head and removed her jeans. When she was completely naked, he picked her up and placed her on the bed.

For the next two hours, they made love three times.

CHAPTER 40

"What do you have for me?" Carl asked over the secure landline in the living area.

Simon held the handset to his ear and explained while Victor listened in on a second line in the kitchen.

"First, there has been no other major activity with our package. He is currently out of town with the daughter. They are taking a holiday in Hilton Head," Simon explained.

"In order for Operation Pill Crusher to be effective," Simon explained, "there must be a significant threat to the existence of The Colonial. It can't be any half-assed bullshit. Thomas Pettigrew must realize he must sell or lose the business. I want *extreme* financial discomfort."

Officially, their operation had no codename. Over the last forty-eight hours, Victor and Simon had come up with Pill Crusher as they debated various options for grinding The Colonial financially beneath a devastating heel of misfortune.

"What options have you come up with?"

"As requested," Victor chimed in, "we have developed four potential scenarios."

"Yes," Simon added. "First, we could create a physical disaster of some sort. Perhaps there could be some devastating destruction to the building he occupies. A fire or significant water damage. We could put him out of business for several months. This would mean that he would be unable to fill prescriptions for an extended period. His patients would go elsewhere to fill their prescriptions and he would be in a severe bind."

Carl was not impressed. He had specifically asked his agents to come up with a plan that involved Jason Rodgers, eliminating the young pharmacist from the business. But Carl let them decided not to remind them of that…for the moment.

"That would most likely create a financial crisis for him," Carl began. "He would need cash to maintain his lifestyle and rebuild the business. Then we could come in and offer him the money to rebuild in exchange for ownership in the business. Does he have casualty insurance on the property?"

"Yes," Victor said, clearing his throat.

"Income replacement insurance?"

"Yes," Simon replied. "But this option also puts Jason Rodgers out of work. Pettigrew will not be able to afford to keep him employed. He will have to seek employment elsewhere."

"Maybe," Carl questioned. "How much income replacement insurance does he have?"

"Two million dollars, in addition to the property and casualty insurance on the building and inventory," Victor added.

They heard the muted clicks of Carl's fingers rapidly punching keys on a computer.

"Then he has no motivation to sell?" Carl explained. "And as far as Jason Rodgers is concerned, you must remember that he is involved with the daughter. Pettigrew is going to do whatever he can to keep him employed. There's a strong personal motivation."

"Then there's that," Simon said, glancing at Victor and mouthing the words, "I told you!"

"Also," Carl added. "If we create a situation where his patients go elsewhere, then we are pushing business away. There's no guarantee he--or we--will be able to get them back. In the end, we want to take over The Colonial as a viable business."

"True, but he might be able to have a grand re-opening and lure that business back. Pettigrew is a well-known and vital part of the community," Victor chimed in. The scenario they were currently discussing had been suggested by Victor. Simon sensed he was clinging to it like a drowning man to a life ring.

"And what about Rodgers?" Carl continued. "The goal is to get him out of the pharmacy. If Pettigrew re-opens, even if he were to sell to us, he might want to hire Rodgers back. He might even make that part of the deal. This option is not an attractive one. We need something more definitive that will get rid of Rodgers permanently. What's next?"

Victor turned pages in a notebook spread before him on the kitchen counter. For a long moment, the only sound was the rustle of paper. "Okay, the second option might work better. The common denominator is a financial one, correct? We must create a scenario where Pettigrew has no other option but to sell because he needs cash."

"Go on."

"We create a health scenario for Pettigrew or his family, most likely his wife. Perhaps something along the lines of what we did with that South American dictator a few years back.

Victor referred to a clandestine operation in which they poisoned the food of one Cesar Garcia. Garcia's administration had been blocking the sale of oil rights to three American companies, holding the American administration hostage. The Agency had been propping up Garcia's opponent and sabotaging Garcia's administration with scandals and economic crises. They had had little success in getting the insurgents and opposition leaders to make enough headway because they ended up being lured away by large sums of cash, by threats…or they ended up dead.

With a rigged election rapidly approaching, it was decided that a more aggressive approach was needed. A double agent inside the Casa Rosada, the Argentinian White House, placed an undetectable poison into Garcia's breakfast two weeks before election day. The dictator ended up severely ill and, in the end, died ten days later, just four days before the voters went to the polls. With Garcia gone, his opponent won the election and was now the country's leader. The contracts with the American oil companies were ratified three months after election day.

"Why not just use it on Rodgers?" Simon asked. "That gets rid of him. Then we can figure out another way to put Pettigrew in financial jeopardy."

Carl put that notion immediately to rest. "No, Rodgers is as healthy as a horse. A sudden death could trigger questions. We don't need a murder investigation surrounding The Colonial before we take it over. It would create scrutiny we do not want. A murder investigation could put his business in danger. Again, we don't want the business to go away."

Carl continued to think out loud through the phone, returning to sabotaging the wife's health. "If the wife is the target, she can't die. We would need her to become extremely sick. Something that would drain his financial resources," Carl added. "Garcia died and that served our purposes. If she died, he would probably get life insurance money. Does he carry life insurance on her?"

"Yes," Victor said. "Five hundred thou."

"There's your answer. He gets richer if she dies. I don't like this option either. We could attempt to make her ill. She's not a spring chicken. But, again, that holds no guarantees. If she gets ill, she could die. If that happens, we can't control how Pettigrew will react. He might become despondent and no longer take care of the business. Remember we need a viable business.

"Or she might stay ill long enough to drain all her husband's resources. That would possibly put him in a position where he would need to sell. But that could take years. We've already spent too much time on this operation. There are too many variables. Making her sick is not the answer."

"What if Pettigrew were to die?" Simon asked.

Carl thought a moment, then asked a question. "What does Pettigrew's will say about the disposition of the business if he were to die?"

In the last weeks, Simon and Victor had scoured City Hall records regarding all of Pettigrew's and The Colonial's assets. At Carl's direction, they had coordinated with the Technology branch of the service. The professionals whom Pettigrew had hired to manage his personal wealth and his pharmacy enterprises had had their computer networks hacked. The insurance agent, lawyers, estate planners and financial advisors had unknowingly yielded a windfall of information. Every aspect of Thomas Pettigrew's personal and professional life had been placed under the microscopic examination of the nerds and accountants at Langley and the pair of spies living as roommates in Newport News.

Simon leafed through his notes and found a highlighted section in a copy of Pettigrew's will that had been sent by secure email from

Langley and obtained from his attorney's files. "The business would pass to the daughter, Christine."

There was a prolonged silence on Carl's end of the phone. "You there, boss?" Victor asked.

"Yeah," Carl replied. "Just thinking it through." Carl the spymaster hadn't risen through the ranks to his current position without having the ability to think through scenarios with lightning speed. The fact that he was pondering gave Victor and Simon hope that they'd found a possible solution. Victor produced a cheesy grin and gave Simon a thumb's up.

The Carl spoke. "No, it won't work. The fact that the daughter is not a pharmacist would mean that she would probably need to dispose of the pharmacy after Pettigrew's death. In fact, it would almost be guaranteed. However, Thomas Pettigrew is The Colonial. The man is the business.

"My father was a sick man, "Carl continued. Immediately, the pair of spies in Newport News looked at each other and rolled their eyes in unison. Carl was about to regale them with a long-drawn-out story. Simon laid his head on the back of the tattered sofa and closed his eyes. Victor pulled up a kitchen stool. It groaned under his weight.

Carl went on to explain that his father had several severe medical conditions. Having been a lifelong smoker, he suffered three heart attacks and advanced lung disease. These conditions required that he take a mountain of medications every day for his heart, his blood pressure and to be able to breathe. When his chronic obstructive pulmonary disease flared, he often needed antibiotics and steroids to breathe, along with inhalers.

"The point being," Carl continued, "was that my father got to know his pharmacist quite well. The pharmacist eventually decided to seek employment elsewhere. My father was so trusting of his druggist, he transferred all his prescriptions to the new pharmacy."

Victor, always the brave soul, asked. "Is there a point here, boss?"

They heard an exasperated sigh-hiss over the line. "The point is that most patients buy the pharmacist if their prescription insurance gives them a choice. They go to with person they trust to fill the prescriptions."

"Now, if The Colonial had no competition and it were out in the middle of nowhere, killing Pettigrew might work. We could come in, snatch it up from the daughter and not worry about losing business. Customers like their convenience, too. But the Colonial sits right across the street from a Walgreens. If Pettigrew dies, we lose the trust factor and patients will go somewhere else. You follow? This business needs to stay viable."

Victor and Simon remained silent.

Carl locked that option away. "No. We do not kill Pettigrew. I hope your fourth option works. You guys are not blowing my skirt up. And remember, these scenarios are supposed to include getting rid of Jason Rodgers!"

"Well," Simon said, "This last option will most likely work. However, loss of life *will* be required."

Over the next thirty minutes, Victor and Simon explained the fourth and final option.

"Are you there?" Victor asked.

Carl had listened, interjecting a few questions. Finally, he remained silent. "Okay, this sounds like it will work. Start making plans. I don't like the fact that it will take more time, but it's the best option I've heard so far. Make it happen about nine months after Jason Rodgers becomes a licensed pharmacist of The Colonial. I'll pass along the news to the suits on the seventh floor."

CHAPTER 41

After their afternoon and evening of lovemaking, Chrissie was wide-awake and energized like the mechanical rabbit of the television battery commercials. She hopped out of bed and quickly dressed. Jason, half-comatose, required at least four bouts of shaking and nudging from Chrissie before he managed to drag himself out of bed. Thirty minutes later, he had showered and dressed. They drove to the closest grocery store and stocked up with three days' worth of food and drink.

Returning to their suite, they sat on the balcony and watched the gauzy daylight give way to a brilliant, star-speckled night. Chrissie sipped white wine while Jason guzzled beer. After several hours of talking, they went to bed well after midnight, this time to sleep.

The next morning, they woke around noon. Jason crawled out of bed and made his signature breakfast dish, an omelet bulging with chopped ham, sausage and bacon along with diced bell peppers, onions and an assortment of cheeses. He served it all with toasted English muffins and spiced Bloody Mary's.

When they'd finished eating, they walked down to the ocean and rented an umbrella and chairs from the lifeguard. They spent the rest of the day on the hard-packed sand, sunbathing, and people watching.

Since their breakfast had been lunch, they took dinner at the outdoor bar and grille. When the sun faded, they returned to the room, plopped themselves on chairs on the balcony and, once again, watched the last vestiges of sunlight melt into darkness.

They repeated this ritual for the next two days, the sole difference being that Chrissie made healthier, less cardiac-risky fare. On the fourth morning, they packed up their leftover food and their belongings and drove north to North Myrtle Beach. They checked into the Sands Resort on the ocean front around one and found an older, but still adequate, suite with an ocean view looking down over an open-air bar called Ocean Annie's with its open-air bandstand and dance floor.

They shopped, buying a few inexpensive items their meager budgets would allow like t-shirts and hats. Then they sunbathed some more. In the evenings, they danced to the live music at Ocean Annie's in front of the outdoor stage and partied with all the other inebriated guests.

On the afternoon of their last day in Myrtle Beach, Chrissie shared news with Jason. "I've decided to hold off on taking the CPA exam," she declared.

"Really? Change of heart about accounting?"

"No. The firm offered me a permanent position. And I accepted. In six months, they said they'll pay for my prep course and also pay for the test. I'll take it this time next year." She cocked her head and grinned with pride.

"That's awesome, honey," Jason beamed. "I'm so proud of you!"

That night, Chrissie took Jason on a late-night stroll along the shore where the water met the sand. They walked hand-in-hand a good distance in comfortable silence. Then Chrissie stopped and faced him.

By the dim light from the ocean front resorts and the few scattered spotlights, he peered into her liquid, brown eyes. She held his gaze with an intense but gentle one of her own. The way she gazed upon him in the dim light had a pleasing and electric power over him. He had never seen this look in her eyes. It was deeper and seemed to reach directly into his soul. In the moonlight her skin glowed. She wore her bikini top under a see-through beach blouse and a pair of cut-off jeans. Gauzy wisps of hair floated in front of her face in the stiff breeze.

He could not resist reaching out and caressing her cheek with his hand. He pulled her in. They kissed passionately.

"I bought you a present," she said, pulling away slightly but keeping her head tucked in his neck.

Always prepared with a jocular reply, he said, "Really? Is it X-rated?"

"No, silly boy! Close your eyes," she instructed.

Jason did. Her soft fingers wrapped around his wrist and brought his arm up before him. She turned his palm toward the star-kissed sky and placed something smooth and hard into it. Chrissie moved in closer and put her mouth near his ear. She whispered, "I love you, Jason Rodgers."

Jason opened his eyes. The object was smooth, dense, and plump. He turned his body, allowing the moonlight to shine upon it.

"It's a heart," he whispered.

"That's right," Chrissie replied. "A polished stone painted red."

Jason brought it closer to his face. It was indeed dense and had been polished into the shape of a perfect heart. In the darkness it looked more gray than red, with swirled striations of liquid brush strokes appearing beneath the varnish, as if frozen in place.

"It's beautiful," he whispered. "Just like you."

"I love you, Jason" Her lips were on his again and he closed his eyes once more, losing himself in the moment. Chrissie had finally said aloud what Jason already knew.

It was the best kiss of his life.

CHAPTER 42

On Thursday, August 1st, Jason's mother retrieved a stack of envelopes and solicitations from the mailbox. She leafed through bills, catalogs, and advertisements. The last item was an official looking letter on which was stamped the seal of the state of Virginia Department of Health Professions addressed to her son. She immediately called Jason at work at The Colonial.

"I think it's about your exam," she said with anticipation.

With Thomas Pettigrew's permission, Jason rushed home and retrieved the letter. He returned to work with the unopened letter folded in half in his lab coat pocket.

"Well, what does it say?" Pettigrew demanded.

Jason hesitated. "I haven't opened it yet. If you don't mind, Thomas. I'd like to wait for Chrissie."

Thomas rolled his eyes. "You have great patience, Jason. If it wasn't my daughter..." His voice trailed off.

That night Chrissie and Jason dined at Chrissie's house with Thomas and Eleanor over pot roast, steamed carrots, salad, and potatoes. Thomas had called a pharmacist friend who agreed to cover the last few hours of Thomas's shift at the pharmacy. Jason's parents had been invited and Edward Rodgers and his wife joined them in a hastily prepared celebration. Jason laid the letter on the oak buffet behind him. "I'll open this later," he said.

Once again, Edward managed to survive the evening without any alcohol and engaged in a casual conversation with Thomas, although several times he asked for softly spoken comments or questions to be repeated. After dinner, Eleanor brought out a large chocolate sheet cake. The icing inscription read Congratulations Jason.

She hefted the large knife in the air. "I think it's time," she said, nodding toward the unopened letter. "I hope you passed."

Jason reached back and grabbed the letter. Slipping his forefinger under the glued flap, he sliced it open. The letter was folded in thirds and was written on a heavy bonded paper. Jason unfurled it and the Seal of Virginia Department of Health had been embossed at the top.

He read the text of the letter silently as his eyes moved back and forth over the page. When he was done, he placed the letter on the table. His eyes darkened and the smile on his face flattened to a frown.

"Jason," Chrissie asked. "What does it say?"

Tears welled in his eyes. He shook his head slowly. "I guess I should have opened it privately. I'm sorry."

All four parents exchanged concerned, uneasy looks. Jason handed the letter to Chrissie and buried his head in his hands. The knife in Eleanor's hand slowly moved lower. Her grin evaporated.

Chrissie read the letter, a look of agony on her face.

"...It is with great pleasure that we inform you that you passed both the NAPLEX portion and the law portion of the pharmacy exam."

Jason's head and shoulders began to shake as Chrissie read. A low almost sinister cackle emanated through his hands. He lifted his head revealing a wide, satisfied grin. "Gotcha!"

Everyone let out a collective sigh of relief followed by shaking heads and cacophony of guffaws and laughter. Jason howled with delight as Chrissie slapped his shoulder. "Jerk," she said with a grin. Then she planted a kiss on his mouth.

After the excitement died down, Edward, who sat opposite Jason, lifted his water glass in salute. "Well done, son." Jason clicked his own glass on his father's. Thomas followed suit and then everyone held their water glasses aloft. "To The Colonial's newest pharmacist."

After dinner when they were alone, Edward leaned in and whispered to Jason. "We'll have a proper drink later."

PHARMACY PHACT:

Dispensing errors are a problem on a national level; at a rate of 4 errors per day in a pharmacy filling 250 prescriptions daily. This would result in an estimated 51.5 million errors occurring during 3 billion prescriptions each year.

National Observational Study of Prescription Dispensing Accuracy and Safety in 50 Pharmacies; J AM Pharm Assoc 2003:43:191-200

CHAPTER 43

Jason's first day working as a registered pharmacist began the following Monday, August 19th. At 8am, he appeared at The Colonial with his freshly starched white lab coat draped over his arm and the two gifts he'd been given by the staff of The Colonial: his personally engraved pharmacy spatula with the oak handle and his personal pen. Thomas met him and handed him a set of keys on a large key ring and walked him around the store.

Since graduating in May and now having passed his state licensing exam, Jason was now a Doctor of Pharmacy (also known as a PharmD) and a licensed pharmacist in the Commonwealth of Virginia. His career had been on the launch pad. Now, the ignition sequence had counted down to zero and he was lifting off. An electric sense of fear and excitement gripped him.

He'd laid awake most of the night filled with an equal measure of anticipation. He managed a few intermittent hours of sleep. When he wasn't sleeping, he tried to envision how his first day as a pharmacist would go. Jason woke thirty minutes before the alarm went off.

He showered, shaved and dressed in record time. As he peered at himself in the mirror and pushed the knot of his red power tie tightly into the collar of his white, starched Oxford cloth shirt, he glanced at the brilliant red, heart-shaped stone laying in the small coin dish on his dresser. No bigger than a quarter, it was a rich, Valentine crimson and three-dimensionally plump, the two top circular lobes tapered to a sharp point.

Nothing more than a rock, paint, and varnish, it represented everything Chrissie felt about him. The Heart Stone and what it represented filled him with a profound joy, especially on this most milestone morning.

As he pulled into a spot in the parking lot, his phone flared with a text message from Chrissie. She had an early meeting. But she had managed to send a tender note of encouragement along with those three magical words.

"Are you paying attention, Jason?" Pettigrew barked. His question yanked Jason back to the present.

"Ah, yeah," he replied. "Just a little nervous."

"You'll do fine," Pettigrew said robotically, "Each key has been labelled as to its purpose. But the two that you will use most often are the one to the front door and the one for the closing gate for the pharmacy department itself."

Pettigrew had shown him several times over the past weeks how to activate and deactivate the pharmacy alarm. The console was mounted on the wall beside the front door. But the Old Man demonstrated it for him once more for good measure.

In the days since Jason had learned he had passed the exam, Thomas Pettigrew had called off the contract pharmacists who had been covering some of the open shifts. Kyle Griffin, now a hospital pharmacist in Williamsburg, filled in a weekend shift here and there to give Thomas some time to himself, and had been informed that Jason was now a full-fledged druggist. Griffin had texted Jason a congratulatory message as well.

"You know what to do. I've shown you everything there is to know about running a shift here. Make sure you count down the registers every night and make the deposit across the street at Langley Federal Credit Union. If you have any questions, call me."

Pettigrew exited the store without any fanfare. Jason peered up at the pharmacy department now. He'd lain eyes on it many times in the last months. He was familiar with its layout like he was in his own bedroom, where various items and paperwork were stored; invoices, both for controlled drugs and non-controlled; daily prescription reports required by the state board of pharmacy; and lists of convenient phone numbers. Jason even knew where the silent alarm button was located under the counter near the pharmacist's terminal. He had come to know every inch of this department.

But now, at this moment, though its dimensions had not changed, not even by a fraction of an inch, the place appeared vastly larger and significantly more intimidating. Though he'd worked many shifts at The Colonial, this was the first in which every prescription, every decision and all the incumbent responsibilities that came along with them rested squarely on his shoulders. Every question that a technician or a patient had would be directed to him. They would expect answers quickly and decisively. Any problem or issue they brought through the front door would end up in his lap. Jason had witnessed other pharmacists, including Thomas and Kyle, handle the responsibilities with the assured confidence of men who'd done it thousands of times. But until he'd actually stepped into their licensed shoes, he had not been able to comprehend the stresses and enormous responsibilities they encompassed. He felt like Atlas holding up the world. He hoped he was ready.

His first day was an eventful conglomeration of incidents and decisions that stressed Jason greatly. Most of the day, they had just been plain busy. Jason, now burdened with the awesome task of making sure every prescription that crossed before him was perfect, took his time checking and re-checking each one. This caused him to fall behind. The piles of baskets grew higher as the minutes ticked by.

Jason realized he had literally only a few seconds to check each prescription for accuracy, ensuring that the drug, strength, directions, quantities and physician were depicted accurately on the label. Then he had to open each vial to make sure the tablets or capsules matched the descriptions of the pills. He performed this task hundreds of times that day. Many times, after he'd released a prescription, he'd wanted to double check it. The bottles and pills melded into on endless collage of images lasting only a moment before his eyes, then they were gone and another one appeared in its place.

He learned quickly it was easy to lose focus and several times Jason caught his mind wandering to other issues like phone calls that needed to be made to doctor's offices, or patient's taking addictive medications such as narcotics or anxiolytics who stalked and paced the sales floor looking like predators who would pounce any moment if the desired narcotics were not delivered forthwith.

Though the workload was nothing Jason hadn't experienced before, now that he was "The Man," everything moved so much faster. Issues and responsibilities assaulted him. At one point, Jason commented to Sarah, "Holy crap, this pace is incredible."

Sarah laughed. "You've seen this before. This is nothing. Wait until cough and cold and flu season hits."

Jason knew she was right. Prescription volumes increased. Patients came in demanding flu shots and didn't want to wait more than a few minutes for them. He'd been able to give shots during his externships since he'd received training in his third year of pharmacy school. As a student, he had been able to lighten the pharmacist's workload slightly with this ability.

But today, the real fun began with the late afternoon rush. The hours between 3 and 7 in the afternoon when folks who were heading home from work would stop by to pick up prescriptions that were supposed to have been phoned in by doctor's offices or refills they'd called in earlier. Many were tired, irritable, and therefore impatient. Some unleashed their frustration on the pharmacy staff.

He spent several agonizing minutes speaking with two customers who were displeased with the co-pays their insurance companies expected them to pay. "I've never had to pay one hundred and fifty dollars before. Why is it so high now?"

Jason shrugged. "I don't know ma'am. That's a question for your insurance company." This was a comment he'd heard Thomas and Kyle speak many times. And he was right. He was only the messenger.

"So, you mean I can't get my pills now?"

"No, you can get your pills. But you have to pay one hundred and fifty dollars."

"Forget it," the first lady said, storming off.

The existence of insurance companies and the expectations they garnered seemed to instill in patients the thought that they couldn't get their medications if the insurance company didn't pay for it or expected the patient to pay a huge co-pay. When this occurred, many patients chose to not get their medications or sought other alternatives. Insurance companies ruled not only the pharmacy world, but all of healthcare.

The second patient was also unhappy that they were not paying for her prescription anymore. They wanted her to change to another drug.

"But the doctor prescribed that medication. I know that one works. What am I supposed to do?"

Over the months watching his mentor, Jason quickly learned to just tell the truth. "You can get the original medication. But you'll have to pay the full cash price. Or we can ask the doctor to change it to the drug the insurance will pay for."

"How much is my medication without insurance?"

"Three hundred and twenty dollars."

"How much is it for the generic?"

"That is for the generic."

The man just shook his head and grumbled something inaudible. Then he said with a sigh, "Call the doctor."

His first real challenge, though, arrived in the form of a small, feisty elderly woman named Hilda Donovan. An aged retiree, Jason wasn't quite sure what the source of her irascibility was. Filled with piss and vinegar and a septuagenarian with a short-temper and a penchant for foul language, Donovan thought The Colonial was her own personal dispensary and its pharmacists and technicians her own personal healthcare staff. She didn't care how many prescriptions had been dropped off before she'd arrived or what other matters were ongoing. Hers were the only issues that mattered and the only one that should matter to The Colonial. And she wanted her prescriptions filled in less than ten minutes. A feat which was nearly impossible and equally unsafe to accomplish. But none of that mattered to Hilda Donovan.

That was the essence of great customer service, Jason had been told many times. Make each patient think they are the most important person in the world. It was a dogma that was true for any business. However, in the world of pharmacy with its extensive laws and regulations and ever-increasing volume of prescriptions, it was nearly impossible to accomplish. The advent of newer technologies and higher prescription volumes was pushing the pharmacist farther away from the patients they served.

Jason had encountered Donovan twice before. Once when he was an extern and again about six weeks ago as a paid intern awaiting his Board exam results. On each occasion, he'd observed Thomas and then Kyle handling her with kid gloves. She paced about the sales floor glaring up at the staff wondering what kind of incompetent imbeciles they had to be to take so long to simply count pills and put them in a bottle.

Donovan also insisted that her prescriptions be filled with the brand name drugs and always complained about the co-pays because her insurance company made her pay more because she had not opted for the generic versions. She was not a compliant patient and often ran out of her pills, thus creating an emergency in her mind which resulted in her to having to wait for her refills while they were being filled. Today, she approached the counter, slammed her palm down and insisted on speaking to the pharmacist. The new pharmacist.

On the two previous occasions, Jason had witnessed her tirades. And Jason had watched as the technicians or cashiers immediately summoned Thomas or Kyle Griffin to deal with her. Today, Jason's gut clenched as Sarah, the English accented technician called out to him.

"Oh, Jason hon, Mrs. Donovan would like a word." Sarah stepped back into the pharmacy and leaned close. She whispered, "She sees a new body and smells blood in the water."

Jason descended the two steps to the lower level of the pharmacy department.

"Who are you? Where's Thomas? Where's Kyle?" The words hissed from her mouth.

"I'm Jason. I've taken Mr. Griffin's place!"

"That'll be the day! How old are you, boy? Are you even shavin' yet?" The word "boy" was uttered like a profanity.

"What can I do for you, Mrs. Donovan?"

"I've been waiting," She made an exaggerated motion of twisting her wrist so she could read the small feminine watch on her liver-spotted wrist. "...for fifteen minutes. Why is my prescription not ready yet?"

Jason had been occupied with the evening rush. He'd been sidetracked from filling several prescriptions because he'd had three consecutive phone calls, two from patients requesting information about illnesses and possible over-the-counter treatments and one from a dentist calling in four prescriptions for a patient who was having oral surgery in the morning. Sarah had been filling and stacking baskets of orders at Jason's terminal waiting for him to give them a final check before placing them in the will call bin. He'd seen Mrs. Donovan's prescription, remembered that it was in the stack to check but had lost track of it.

"Let me see what's going on," Jason said, his voice trailing off.

"If Thomas were here," she goaded him. "I'd have been home twenty minutes ago."

Jason ascended the two steps into the elevated pharmacy department and glanced toward Sarah whose eyes belied her concern and disdain for the old bitty.

"Where is her prescription?" Jason didn't need to tell her any of the details since Donovan was speaking so loudly everyone in the store including the customers roaming the isles had looked toward the sound of her voice.

Sarah lifted a plastic basket with gray-tinted hard copy, a stock bottle of Premarin and a label that had been printed but not applied to a prescription vial.

"Can you count it out real quick, please?"

"No," Sarah whispered, sliding the basket before him.

Jason's head whipped in Sarah's direction. "What? Why?"

"This stock bottle is expired."

Jason let out a low audible groan. "Really?" He lifted the stock bottle which was no bigger than a small bottle of Tylenol and read the lot number and expiration date. The pills had expired a month earlier.

Shit!

The pharmacy staff scoured the shelves every month looking for expired product. Evidently, this one had been missed.

"What's...taking...so...fucking...long?" Donovan's voice was louder and more toxic than before.

"We can order more but they won't be in until tomorrow afternoon," Sarah said in a low voice.

Jason leaned toward Sarah and said in a barely audible voice, "I'll give you a hundred dollars if you'll tell her."

Sarah smiled and patted Jason on the shoulder. "Sorry, boss. That's why you get the big bucks now."

Jason pushed out a long, slow breath, angling it up so it moved his bangs. He smiled at Gloria and said, "Remind me to have a will drawn up as soon as possible."

He descended the two steps and stood across the counter from the small irate woman who seemed ready to pounce. Her once perceived frailness had been replaced by a seething anger and an apparent willingness to lash out.

"Mrs. Donovan, we have a slight problem."

"No, you have a problem, young man. And it's not small."

"The pills we have in stock have expired. I have to order more. They will..."

"What the hell kinda place you running here? How the hell can you have expired drugs on the shelf?"

He kicked himself. He should have just said they didn't have the drug in stock.

Jason made her an offer. "We can order them and have them delivered to your house tomorrow. Okay?"

"No, it's not okay. I need my pills; I haven't had them for 4 days. I need my pills!"

Jason moved his hands in a gesture of futility and shrugged. "That's the best I can do."

She moved her pained gaze up and down the course of his torso like he was a rotting piece of meat hanging from a hook.

"I can put you on our courtesy refill service. That way this doesn't happen again. You shouldn't wait until you run out of pills to call in the refills."

"You're an ass," the woman spat. She spun as quickly as her spindly seventy-year-old legs would allow and shuffled down the center aisle. When she had disappeared outside and the door had closed behind her, Jason smiled and said loud enough for everyone to hear, "Another satisfied customer!"

℞

"So how was your first day as a pharmacist, dear?" Jason's mother, Evelyn, inquired as he trudged through the front door.

Simple fatigue did not begin to describe Jason's physical and mental state. Exhaustion did not fit the bill either. His all-encompassing weariness felt like a heavy shroud draped over his shoulders. His bones and muscles ached. But more importantly, his depleted mind had never been taxed in this manner. This enervated condition was the result of a three-pronged attack over the previous thirteen hours. His extremely depleted state was the combination of intense physical, intellectual, and mental fatigue.

Jason had been a student and therefore studying for the better part of the last eight years, four as an undergraduate at John Radcliffe University where he maintained a perfect four-point zero GPA, along with four more post-graduate years at the MCV in Richmond to train in pharmacy. His grades slipped slightly during pharmacy school but were still in the top five percent of his class. He had been utilizing his mind, filling it with medical and pharmacological data for those last forty-eight months. It was a well-exercised muscle that had been whipped into shape by rigorous academic pursuits and demanding professors.

But the cerebral and psychological beating he'd experienced today was akin to a fifteen round heavy weight bout in which the two combatants waged a relentless war of body blows and head shots. His opponent was the pharmacy public who paraded before him constantly with mountains of prescriptions that should have been ready for pickup five minutes after they'd been received. The patients and their slips of paper, electronic requests and phone calls pounded Jason and the pharmacy staff in periodic but relentless waves over the course of the twelve-hour day. Jason ducked and weaved and managed to land a few retaliatory punches of his own. All-in-all, he was still standing but had lost in a unanimous decision.

"It was long," Jason replied in a weary voice like the defeated warrior he was.

"Are you hungry? Do you want me to make you a sandwich?"

Jason shook his head. His mouth was too tired to chew and his body too weary to digest. "No. I'm going to bed."

As he plodded down the hallway toward his room, he anticipated the moment his head would sink slowly onto the cool, silky pillow where he would drift into a long, rejuvenating slumber; recharging his mental batteries for the next fight that would resume tomorrow.

Jason slipped out of his clothes, letting them lay in a heap where they fell. Padding into the bathroom in his skivvies, he ran the toothbrush over his teeth in slow, tired strokes. From the faucet, he gathered a pool of cool water into his cupped hands and rinsed his mouth. He repeated the process and splashed it onto his face, then toweled off. Back in his bedroom, he pulled back the covers, which tonight felt like they had been weaved with lead and iron then crawled beneath them. He closed his eyes and waited to descend into a deep, replenishing sleep.

The cool, fresh bedsheets enveloped him in a cocoon of relaxation. The pillow cradled his throbbing head and aching neck. He lay there for several minutes. But sleep did not come. He rolled onto his side and splayed his legs as if frozen in a running stride and breathed in long, slow breaths, hugging one of the pillows close to his chest. After several more minutes, unconsciousness still felt like a train that had left the station, one he desperately wanted to catch but was out of reach.

Jason tossed again, rolling onto his opposite side. His eyes found the red numerals of the bedside clock. It was just after ten. He'd laid down nearly ten minutes ago. That's when the images assaulted him.

They flashed before his mind's eye in rapid fire strobes, revisiting him in static scenes and snippets of conversation: the afternoon lines of patients queued at one end of the pharmacy cash register waiting impatiently to pick up and pay for their drugs; the customer who expressed indignation that he was not allowed to pick-up a pseudoephedrine containing medication because he'd exceeded the legal limit; the woman bitching about the price of her medication; the man with prescriptions for tramadol and oxycodone who had to have the medications filled in ten minutes and hollering at Jason from down below when he was told that they would need at least thirty. Then, of course, there was the angry elderly woman who'd called him an ass because the

Premarin stock was expired and had to be re-ordered; falling behind because he was trying to take great care in checking his prescriptions and the frustrated looks of barely concealed contempt from throngs of waiting patients. Then there were the endless phone calls from doctor's offices; the prescriptions requiring prior authorizations from the insurance companies and the faxes that needed to be sent because of them and the steady hiss of paper flowing into the output trays of the fax machine and the prescription printer.

Then some of the prescriptions he'd filled made their appearance like Philip Marley's ghost. They were ghosts of prescription errors yet to come. Of course, Jason could not remember all the prescriptions he'd filled and checked today. The end-of-day computer report had tallied the final number: three hundred and eighty. The drug names and dosages in milligrams flowed before him in an endless stream; some in mountainous waves, some in a steady dribble. But came they did...a never ceasing flow. Some of the prescriptions and their fills were burned into his memory because the patients had showed some sign of frustration with a loud sigh or an agitated shake of the head. These situations angered Jason. He'd learned today better than all the days previous because he was now a pharmacist and that retail pharmacy--or at least their patients--expected their prescriptions with the speed of a fast-food restaurant.

Just before the dinner hour when most folks returned from work, The Colonial's sales floor appeared to be a gathering place for the entire city's sick and medicated populace. Jason, already backlogged with prescriptions, had to pick up his pace, checking faster and faster to get the finished medication vials down to the registers all the while being interrupted by Gloria with questions or comments or patients in store with questions about a cough and cold medication or what to use for hemorrhoids or the patient on the phone who wanted to tell Jason her whole life story when all she needed to know was if her medication was ready.

He remembered the diminutive Asian pharmacist whose name escaped him. During his first rotation many months ago, she explained how she often laid awake at night wondering how many mistakes she'd made.

That same question now reared it self before Jason.

As he lay in bed, the frustration-filled snapshots assaulted Jason for the better part of an hour.

Then he finally admonished himself. It was over. Let it go! At that point, he'd allowed himself to uncork the fatigued annoyance welling in him and it seeped from him. Then with his mind freed, unable and unwilling to tolerate any more abuse, his brain finally shut down and allowed him to close his eyes and fall into a fitful sleep.

PHARMACY PHACT:

As many as 12% of drug prescriptions sent electroni-cally to pharmacies contain errors, a rate that matches handwritten orders, researchers said.

www.bloomberg.com/news/articles/2011-06-29/
errors-occur-in-12-of-electronic-drug-
prescriptions-matching-handwritten

CHAPTER 44

Over the next few weeks and months, Jason started the slow and lengthy process of becoming more effective and efficient in his practice of pharmacy. Each day he was presented with new challenges and opportunities to understand the pharmacist's role in the community and how to fill that role. He filled prescriptions for young mothers with sick children, middle-aged men for their blood pressure and cholesterol medications, cancer patients who were scared out of their wits about what the future held. He dealt with elderly patients who were becoming feebler and needed guidance from their pharmacist. He dealt with patients taking pain medications in all phases of their addiction cycle.

A great number of patients had been taking painkillers and at the current time were so dependent on their medications it was hard to tell if they truly needed the pills to treat pain or if they had just become so physically and psychologically dependent, they couldn't function without them. And it seemed every day he was being verbally accosted by frustrated patients that "had to have" their sleeping pills or anti-anxiety meds even though they were early in their refill cycle.

Each day he was assaulted by two or three more patients trying get over on him because he was a new face and a young one at that. Thomas had warned him that these patients would "appear" like vampires when the sun goes down. Their goal was to see if the new guy would cower to their threats and cave, thus giving them their medications early.

Thomas had warned him, "I better not find out your filling addictive medications early. If they are early say 'no'. Otherwise, you will be opening Pandora's Box and they will never relent. I will back you up, Jason. Give it a few months and they will realize that the threats won't work."

In the few months he'd been practicing, he'd already heard a myriad of excuses as to why patients had to have refills early: I'm going out of town; I lost my pills; I had friends over last night and someone stole them; I accidentally dropped them into the toilet; you didn't give me the correct number of pills in the last prescription...and on and on it went.

This last excuse always prompted an immediate investigation to determine if they had, in fact, shorted a patient. They would be forced to check the on-hand counts of his Schedule Two medications like oxycodone or hydrocodone or lesser addictive medications like lorazepam or zolpidem. Schedule Two medications were a step below illegal drugs in addictiveness like heroin or cocaine. They were usually pain medications like oxycodone or hydrocodone but included drugs for attention deficit such as dextroamphetamine or methylphenidate.

Jason had been taught--and he always practiced--the procedure of double counting the quantity of a controlled substance going into the patient's vial and then back counting the remainder left in the stock bottle to ensure it matched the on-hand quantity in the computer. It helped to ensure that the correct amount was always dispensed but it also greatly slowed down the filling process.

Pharmacy law required that the "oxys," "hydros," or the "dextros" be accounted for down to the pill. And at the end of every month, he or Thomas had to count every Schedule Two medication on hand and reconcile those counts to what the computer stated. And after each investigation, he would invariably have to inform the patient that their counts were spot on and that they had dispensed the correct number of pills.

After a particularly bad week with numerous irate patients, Jason turned to Gloria, the technician and asked, "Is this what my career is going to be like for the next twenty-five years?"

Gloria chuckled and replied, "No, all these frequent flyers see that there is a new pharmacist in the store. So, they figure they can try all their stories out on the new guy. They've all tried these on Kyle and Thomas in past years and they know they can't get away with that behavior. My advice to you is to stand your ground. When you see suspicious behavior, call them on it. Don't be rude. Don't accuse them. Just present them with the facts and say I'm not going to fill your prescription. In fact, because you're here early, I'm going to call your physician. When they see that you're not going to budge, they'll stop. It's the nature of addiction."

"How long will it take?"

Gloria confirmed what Thomas had told him earlier. "A few months. I've been in this business for fifteen years. Trust me, it happens every time a new pharmacist starts in a pharmacy whether that pharmacist is a veteran or a rookie."

"I never knew there were so many drug seekers."

"Believe it. They're sick people. I mean, their addicted. It changes the way people act."

"That may be true. But they're still pains-in-the-asses to deal with."

Then there were the patients Jason came to understand and respect who were not trouble, just troubled and truly sick. They were the patients fighting for their lives every day. Patients with growing cancers and HIV who needed medications simply to stay alive or be comfortable.

One patient named Janet was battling lung cancer and required constant therapy for breathing medications from inhalers and nebulizer solutions and antibiotics just so she could take a half-meaningful breath. She too took pain medications, but she never worried the staff about her refills and was always pleasant. A forty year, two-pack-a-day smoker whose condition had progressed to stage four, she'd never been able to quit smoking and still smoked to this day. She too was battling addiction, albeit a different form. All her treatment options had been exhausted, even the experimental ones. She'd come to terms that her smoking and her cancer were going to kill her, and she'd told the doctors it was time to stop fighting and accept her fate. Jason learned all this one afternoon in a candid, sincere moment as they talked about her antibiotics while his prescriptions piled up. As usual, Jason had a ton of work before him. But he lost himself in this tender moment with a woman facing her own mortality. She seemed to be dealing with it with grace and honor.

Everything else could wait, Jason told himself, just for this moment.

She always came to the pharmacy herself to pick up prescriptions and was always cheerful to the pharmacy staff. Janet and Jason had struck up a sort of professional friendship. She always shuffled slowly to the counter with her nasal cannula in her nostrils and the tubing wrapped around her ears and toting a backpack with an oxygen generator in it.

Knowing her condition and her prognosis, Jason always took extra time to come down the two steps to spend a few minutes talking with her. She bragged about her grandchildren and her kids and asked Jason about his life and his girlfriend.

"Have a nice day, Janet," Jason would say.

"I will. You, too, Jason. Thanks for taking good care of me," she would reply.

He would watch her shuffle slowly and with great difficulty to the door as if her legs were filled with cement and wonder if each visit would be her last. A sharp stab of mourning and grief jabbed at him. It was Janet and his interactions with her that made him understand why he wanted to be a pharmacist. He, like most of his colleagues, wanted to make a difference in people's lives. If the medications Jason dispensed to her eased her suffering even slightly, it was all worth it. More importantly, if time and kindness made her life more tolerable, Jason would dispense those in large quantities.

As the months passed, Jason became more confident in his role. He began to recognize the patients before they reached the counter and often would call out their names as the approached. He quickly learned that by remembering their names he gave the impression that they were important. And, of course, they were, even if all he knew about them was their name and the medications they took.

Sometimes, he even was able to pull a patient aside and offer suggestions on how they could improve their medication therapies. Discontinue this or try that. Of course, they would need to check with their physician, he'd tell them. Soon his confidence soared, and Jason felt a good number of his patients were coming to respect him. He remembered an adage one of his professors had recited to his class one day. Jason had jotted it down. And it has stayed with him: *People do not care how much you know until they know how much you care.* There was still a lot to learn, of that he was certain. Jason was filled with facts, figures, side effects, dosages and ideas. But in order to get his patients to listen to him, he had to listen and show them he was concerned about them. Unfortunately, time and patience were two things his profession currently lacked. He felt as if he was beginning to turn a corner. It was a long, winding curve. But he was a pharmacist now.

Gradually, as Gloria had predicted, Jason and the often-difficult patients reached a state of detente. They knew not to challenge him on early refill issues because he would not budge. Jason knew that if he addressed their prescriptions as promptly as possible, they gave him little push back. Above all, he'd learned that if he was honest and straight forward with all his patients and did not pretend to offer time frames or services he could not deliver, there were fewer and fewer conflicts.

Eventually, even the pain-in-the-ass narcotic-addicted patients settled down and did not make his life as difficult as they had in the first months. They were still a constant thorn in his side, but he was learning to deal with the irritation and sting of their barbs and insults. Though it was difficult, he was learning not to take them personally. He knew it would be a long, arduous process. But it would come with time. He had a responsibility as their pharmacist to them. In many instances, his job was to deliver medications to patients safely and as quickly as time and workload allowed. In other instances, his service to his patients was to withhold their medications. Even if it meant incurring their wrath.

One afternoon, he'd met a pleasant older woman named Ada Mae Renforth. She was in her seventies with a full head of perfectly coifed white hair, a round wrinkled face and sharp blue eyes. Ada Mae was a plump woman who always dressed as if she were on her way to church. A widow who still drove her husband's white Cadillac everywhere, she spoke about her dear Chester every chance she got with infinite affection and wistful longing.

Ada Mae had had two heart attacks in the last five years and had been prescribed two medications for this condition, Coumadin, a blood thinner that reduced the chance of a clot developing in one of her cardiac arteries but also presented the increased risk of bleeding and diltiazem, a calcium channel blocker to control blood pressure and regulate her heart rhythm.

Jason had also developed a kinship with Ada Mae. It seemed that all the older ladies liked the young pharmacist, all except Hilda Donovan.

"Be careful there, hon," Sarah the other technician with the British accent said one day. "There's a lot of cougars out there."

Jason simply shook his head with a wry grin and descended the steps to counsel Ada Mae.

CHAPTER 45

The first time it happened, Jason had been a licensed pharmacist for no more than three weeks. The incidents usually started the same way, with the words that stop a pharmacist's heart like a bullet ripping through his chest.

"My medication is not right!"

Those words spilled from the lips of a small, bookish man standing at the register and looking like he wanted to extract a pound of flesh from someone. He glared at the cashier and rammed the large medicine vial onto the counter with a sharp plastic crack. Jason looked up immediately. His heart seized in his chest and his throat felt like it was going to close. Three other waiters stood nearby, heard the comment and the sound of the prescription vial slamming the countertop. Their heads whipped in the direction of the commotion, anticipating what would happen next.

Jason swallowed hard and descended the two steps. "What's wrong?" He asked.

"I picked these up last week. I just opened the bottle today. The pills are supposed to be blue, but these are yellow."

"Okay, let me take a look." Jason tried to keep his hand from shaking as he lifted and rotated the vial to read the label.

Most pharmacies provide a description of the pills contained in the vial on the label affixed to it. In most cases, the print is so small, patients never notice it. But as Jason reviewed the label, his eyes became riveted on the microprint. The label did read that the capsules should be light blue with a set of markings on them. The pills in the bottle were, in fact, yellow, and the markings were not what they should be.

The second thing he noticed on the label was the initials of the filling pharmacist. In equally tiny print, the letters "JR" were printed in a corner of the label. Jason had been the pharmacist on duty when this medication had been filled. He was the responsible party.

"Let me see what's going on," Jason explained in a weak voice.

He brought the offending vial back up to the prescription department. Sometimes, it was possible for the tablets or capsules to look different but consist of the same medication. This usually happened when a different drug manufacturer had been used to fill the prescription. Jason hoped to God that was the case now.

Forgetting everything else that was going on in the department, including the waiters who were gawking at the man standing at the counter, Jason pulled up on his computer screen a drug identification software program which allowed him to enter the shape, color and markings of a capsule or tablet and would then tell him what medication was contained within.

A minute later, Jason had his answer. He began to shake with fear. The medication had been filled incorrectly.

"It's wrong," he whispered to Sarah who was standing beside him now. "What do I do now?"

℞

It was every pharmacist's worst nightmare. Jason, frozen with fear, felt the moisture leaving his throat.

"We need to fix it," Sarah said.

"Would you print another label and fill the correct pills, please," Jason asked.

Sarah moved off to do just that.

This was not something anyone had discussed with Jason in any of his training. Medication errors were not routinely discussed in school... and Jason had not been exposed to any in his externships. He wanted to call Thomas to ask him what to do. But the man was staring at him and was expecting a resolution immediately. He decided to handle it and then he would call Thomas.

Sarah returned with the corrected pills. Jason inspected them and made sure they were correct this time.

Unsure of what to say, Jason decided to be honest. "These pills were not correct, Mr. Anderson. I have corrected them. Here are the right ones."

"How did this happen, young man?" His voice holding more than a hint of anger.

"Uh..." Jason hesitated. He wanted to say, "I'm human. We make mistakes." But he held his tongue. Thinking quickly, he replied, "I'm going to have to investigate that."

"I want to know why these were filled wrongly."

"I will take this to Thomas."

"See that he gets back with me."

Mr. Anderson departed with his pills. Jason ascended the steps back to the department, still shaking but feeling like he'd just escaped a near-death experience.

℞

"Who was the patient?" Thomas asked.

Jason had gone back to work, filling the prescriptions for the wait-ers. But he was completely distracted and terrified. Going forward that afternoon, Jason checked each prescription with a renewed intensity and checked and re-checked each one at least four times. This slowed him down even more as the prescriptions backed up.

A flood of mixed emotions: anger at the patient for not under-standing; anger at himself for not catching the error; frustration that he was in an environment that demanded perfection and yet pelted him with distractions; and finally, fear at the potential consequences. At one point, he wanted to close the doors and go home.

"Charles Anderson," Jason replied, trying to keep the emotion out of his voice and failing.

"Relax, Jason," Thomas said evenly. "Every pharmacist will make mistakes in his career. It's inevitable. Just be glad Mr. Anderson was aware enough and smart enough to know the pills looked different. Some patients don't pay attention. The mistakes I worry about are the ones that we don't hear about."

"Did he take any of the pills?"

In the emotionally charged minutes after finding out about the error, Jason had not thought to ask if the patient had taken any. "I didn't ask."

"Do you still have the bottle he brought back?"

"Yes."

"Count the pills."

"Hold on." Jason did. The label indicated there should be thirty capsules in the bottle. There were exactly thirty of the wrong medica-tion in the prescription vial.

"No," he reported to Thomas. "There's still thirty in the vial."

A gush of relief filled him.

"Okay, no problem. If he'd taken them, we would have to call the doctor and let them know. That could result in us having to foot the bill for a doctor's visit for the patient. What pills were given and what should they have been?"

"They should have been Uribel. But we filled it with Ursodiol."

Uribel treated the pain, discomfort, and the frequent urge to urinate caused by a urinary tract infection or a urinary procedure. Ursodil is a bile acid used to dissolve gallstones, prevent gallstones from forming and to treat certain types of liver disease. And Jason noticed that they were sitting next to each other on the pharmacy shelf.

"Jason, I know you're upset. We will have to look into how it happened. But you have to let it go and continue to fill. We're human. The first mistake for a pharmacist is one you'll never forget. Use this to motivate you."

"This is going to bother me for a while."

"Good. That tells me you care."

That night at home, it took Jason hours to fall asleep. Again, he was pounded by the images of the day, especially of the smug, holier-than-thou look on Charles Anderson's face as he confronted Jason about the faulty prescription. And once again, Jason's mind rolled through the Rolodex of emotions and feelings the error had ignited.

He felt a profound sense of embarrassment at having not been perfect. The inevitable questions reared themselves:

What could he have done differently to prevent the error?

How had the error occurred?

Jason did not even remember checking the prescription. It had been filled a week earlier. Luckily, Anderson had not even opened the bottle until that morning, seven days later.

The computer recorded everything that had occurred in filling the prescription, including who had performed each step. Gloria had filled the medication that day and Jason had obviously checked it. He was the only pharmacist on duty. His name was on the prescription vial. He was responsible for everything that left the pharmacy. Jason promised himself he would ask Gloria if she remembered what happened the next time he saw her.

But how had it happened? How had he allowed it to get past him? It had been one of hundreds of prescriptions that had been filled that day.

Jason knew in his short time as a pharmacist that he caught or corrected mistakes every day; mistakes by technicians inputting medications incorrectly whether it was an incorrect dosage form, an incorrect strength, or mistyped directions. Jason had seen that the number of errors created by one of the technicians depended on their level of training or experience. Gloria was a more seasoned technician and made fewer errors than Sarah did. There were mistakes by doctors or their office staff who sent over prescriptions or left them on the voicemail. Mistakes of varying degrees and severity.

Had Jason been interrupted as he was checking this one prescription? Had a patient asked him a question? Had he received a phone call? Had Gloria or someone else engaged him in conversation about a television show or politics at just the wrong moment?

Or had he simply been human and had a mental lapse at the crucial moment when he was verifying the prescription?

During the course of a long day, occasionally he found his mind wandering; thinking of Chrissie or a conversation they'd had. *Had he thought about a bill he needed to pay? Or had he been thinking about one of fifty customers who'd bitched or complained?*

These distractions taken alone were nothing of significance. But when combined with the process of checking a prescription, they represented crucial causes for drug errors. A stray thought, a misplaced comment or an interruption could, at the inopportune moment, cause a pharmacist to miss a mistake on the endless conveyor belt of prescriptions placed before him or her.

Jason toiled twelve hours a day. He often found his mind wandering over the course of the twelve hours. He was, after all, only human. No one, he decided, could maintain absolute focus for twelve straight hours. It was impossible. And yet, he was expected to be perfect. The juxtaposition of perfection and the long, arduous hours he worked angered him. *How had the profession of pharmacy placed its pharmacists in such precarious situations?*

Jason thought about his colleagues in the profession. Over the weeks he'd been practicing, Jason had spoken to a few of his fellow graduates who now toiled in the chain pharmacy segment of the profession. They had told him about the deplorable work conditions; the lack of technician help because labor budgets had been cut to the breaking point; they told him about the incessant interruptions from patients and customers in-store and at the drive-thru; the non-stop incoming phone calls from patients (sometimes the same patient would call three or four times about their prescription) and doctors; the hundreds of phone calls they were expected to make every week to drive prescription volumes; the lack of consistent lunch breaks; the constant standing; having to work in ten or twenty immunizations every day and more during flu season; having to verify prescriptions from other stores. And in the end when the invariable errors occurred, their district and corporate leaders placed the blame squarely on the shoulders of the pharmacist.

One friend of Jason's, working for the largest chain in the country, told him that when he complained to his boss about the working conditions, he was told to "shut up or be replaced." Another told him that she had made a drug error because she was verifying a large number of prescriptions that had been left over from the previous day. She was having to rush to get caught up and inadvertently allowed an ear drop to be substituted for an eye drop. The technician had entered the prescription into the computer, but the pharmacist had been interrupted three times while trying to check it and missed the mistake. The error was reported the same day, so the pharmacist had a fresh recollection about what had happened. A rarity in pharmacy. When filling out her drug error report, the pharmacist included all these details, but was later told to remove the comments about the workload.

"I guess the corporate lawyers don't want any blame placed on the company and the work environment," she told Jason. "They take no responsibility for the work environment they have created. It's all on our shoulders!"

The fact that his colleagues were experiencing worse conditions than him both mollified Jason and, at the same time, filled him with great concern. He realized that he had it better than most. The Colonial was an independent and Thomas Pettigrew had hired more help than the chains allowed. The proverbial buck stopped with him. If there was a labor issue, he alone could instantly rectify it. The chains were stacked with layers of management concerned with only one thing: the bottom line.

In order to be profitable, they still had to push through large numbers of prescriptions. He was glad that he had chosen to work for Thomas despite taking a lower salary than his colleagues. But he also worried that he had entered a profession that was being squeezed by the corporate lawyers, bean counters and insurance companies into a dangerous workplace for the pharmacists, technicians, and the patients they served.

After wrestling with the error and its possible causes but never really coming up with any answers other than the fact that mistakes happen, Jason managed to slide the incident into one of the dark cub-byholes of his brain. Stored for the time being, Jason's mind--battered and weary--managed to quiet itself for now.

Just before drifting off to sleep, he promised himself one thing: he would do everything in his power to avoid distractions when filling prescriptions and to avoid mistakes. He would use this to make himself a better pharmacist.

CHAPTER 46

Despite the medication error or, possibly because of it, Jason grew as a pharmacist. The mistake shocked him; scared the shit out of him and drilled home the importance of accuracy.

After investigating the medication error of Charles Anderson's prescription, Thomas had asked Jason to come in on his day off to go over his findings. In less than an hour, Thomas had shared the results with his new pharmacist.

An inspection of the electronic logs, reporting who had performed what task during that prescription fill showed that Gloria had performed the data entry, entering the information from the paper prescription into the computer. Then Jason verified that everything had been entered correctly. At that point, Gloria then pulled the medication from the shelf and counted the pills.

During this part of the process, Thomas referred to The Colonial's camera system. It was a remarkably simple system consisting of two cameras: one covering the pharmacy and another the sales floor. Thomas had only installed it because his insurance company had demanded it in case of a robbery. Thomas had never had a problem with internal theft by store employees. If he ever suspected drug diversion by an employee, he would have immediately installed hidden pinhole cameras. As it was, this current system would be replaced at some point in the next year or two. But the sole camera mounted in a corner near the ceiling told him everything he needed to know.

Gloria had removed two bottles from the shelf. On the video screen of the terminals in the pharmacy he watched the technician place two different stock bottles on the counter. The labels looked terribly similar as did the shape and size of the bottles. When Thomas zoomed in the shot, he could read the labels clearly. One was the correct drug… Uribel. The second bottle was the incorrect drug. On the video, Gloria scanned the correct bottle and its barcode using the barcode reader. This prompted the label printer to eject a label. She then opened the bottle and realized it was empty. Someone had placed an empty bottle back on the shelf. Thomas watched her throw the correct bottle away. Then she turned to the second bottle and—without scanning it—began counting the pills.

She then placed the finished—incorrect—labeled prescription into a tray along with the paper prescription and the stock bottle toward Jason's location for checking. It was about fifteen minutes before Jason even got around to checking it. Since it was now September, flu season had begun. As this prescription was being filled, Jason had been besieged by a string of patients requesting flu shots; several phone calls from doctors calling in prescriptions and patient asking questions. Thomas even watched Gloria interrupt Jason three times in the span of five minutes to ask questions.

Finally, Jason picked up the labelled prescription vial for Charles Anderson and began to inspect it. He checked the label to ensure it was for the correct patient, correct doctor and held the correct instructions. All of which were spot on. Thomas watched Jason as he was about to unscrew the cap from the vial to inspect its contents. This is where Jason should have discovered the error.

However, he was interrupted by a patient, a woman, demanding his immediate attention. She was animated and demonstrative with hands and expressions. According to the timing mechanism on the screen, Jason spent a good four minutes plus discussing something with her. He appeared to have calmed her down to the extent that she left.

Jason returned to the prescription bench, bagged the prescription and placed it in the Will Call bin for retrieval by the patient, without ever having inspected the contents of the vial.

"Geez, Thomas. I'm really sorry," Jason said when Thomas had finished his explanation.

The pharmacist held up a hand. "I know you are, Jason. I'm sharing this with you not to punish you. It's to educate."

Jason nodded without saying a word. His features communicated his anxiety.

Thomas went on. "This video shows just how harried we are as pharmacists. Sometimes, we just can't control how many interruptions there are. It's even worse in the big chains." Thomas motioned with his head in the direction of the Walgreens across the street.

Jason sighed, but again, did not speak.

"I have counseled Gloria," he said. "She doesn't remember but she thinks the two different bottles were placed on the shelf one in front of the other like they were the same medication. I have asked her to make sure she reads each label…carefully."

"What about Mr. Anderson?" Jason asked.

"I spoke with him yesterday. He's fine. As we discussed, he did not take any of the pills. And I refunded him his co-pay. I complimented him on knowing what his pills look like. Some patients don't pay attention."

"Is he angry?"

"I don't think so." Thomas shifted in his chair. "So now the question is: how do we help to prevent this in the future?"

Jason turned his palms toward the ceiling.

"I've been reading in the pharmacy journals about a procedure called Show and Tell. We are going to start using it."

"Show and Tell?"

Thomas explained it was a new safety measure. At the time the patient picks up their medication, each vial is opened, and the patient is asked to verify that the contents look familiar to them. Or if it is a new prescription, we show them that the description of the pills on the label matches what's in the vial. This way if something doesn't look right, we can fix it before they leave the sales counter.

"We are starting this today," Thomas declared confidently. "I will be training everyone on the procedure."

$$R_x$$

When Jason returned to work, he paid closer attention to his checking procedure and he promised himself he would not let a prescription leave the pharmacy until he was certain of its accuracy. Though the volume of prescriptions and speed the patients demanded, at times, made this difficult.

Nonetheless, he made incremental progress. The steps were small. Each day he learned something that allowed himself to accomplish his tasks more efficiently...which really meant more quickly. After all, it would take him years to reach the level and experience Thomas Pettigrew had achieved.

The new Show and Tell procedure instilled in him additional confidence that any mistakes that slipped past him could be caught. But Jason was able to observe some of the interactions with patients. He was amazed at how many patients did not pay attention to what their pills look like.

Every day he learned something new about the profession, how to do his job and how to serve his patients. No matter how disagreeable or rude or pleasant they were, it was his job to get them their prescribed medications in the right form, correct dosage and quantities, and with the proper instructions outlined by the physicians. It was also his job to police, in a manner of speaking, the physicians and how they prescribed medications for their patients by looking for possible errors in prescribing, drug interactions, potential allergies and ways to improve their therapies to treat conditions more effectively and to help assure better outcomes. This was called medication therapy management, or MTM.

Jason understood very quickly that a complete transformation would never be achieved. The journey to complete understanding of medications and how they were used and dispensed was a constantly moving target. New therapies were always becoming available. And it would be a lifelong quest to educate himself every day.

He realized, too, that his job to monitor proper prescription writing and get patients the best, most effective treatments was riddled with obstacles. Hand-written, hard copy prescriptions were often laden with poor handwriting that made them difficult to read. A misplaced decimal point or a simple error by the doctor could result in a ten- or hundred-fold error in dosing, a lesson he'd learned many months ago as an extern with Thomas and the elderly man with congestive heart failure. The advent of newer technologies was supposed to avoid drug errors. Many prescriptions were now being sent electronically directly to the pharmacist's computer.

E-prescriptions that were sent securely to the pharmacy's prescription queue were intended to decrease the problem of poor penmanship. But they, too, presented the pharmacist with unique challenges.

Often, the drug selected from the list of thousands presented to the doctor or their nurse who was sending the order by proxy was incorrect or inappropriate. The directions and quantities were sometimes wrong. Often the directions contained multiple directions on the same prescription. This caused Jason to have to send a fax or call the office for clarification, which slowed down the filling process. It was up to the pharmacist to make sure what the doctor's intent was and to dispense the correct medication and directions. If that was unclear, the pharmacist needed to act.

At one point, Jason tried to measure how many times he was required to correct or clarify an electronic prescription. He did this over the course of a two-week period and found that as many as ten percent of prescriptions needed some form of alteration or clarification. The Colonial often filled as many as four hundred prescriptions on a weekday. That meant that up to forty prescriptions a day contained confusing, inaccurate, or incorrect information.

But Jason considered himself lucky. He would talk to other pharmacists, his fellow graduates or career druggists working at large chains when calling to get prescriptions transferred. They constantly complained that they were being asked to fill many more prescriptions with fewer technician hours than Jason was. Many times, when he called a competitor, the phone rang without ever being answered. It was an obvious symptom of not having enough help.

Working at The Colonial, an independent, Jason was given more help and the patients were generally more understanding because all issues went straight to Thomas, the owner. He had the final say. And if he determined that more help was needed, he made the decision then and there. In the large chains, getting change manifested had to go through layers and layers of management. And the bean counters at the corporate offices only cared about the bottom line which meant cutting labor hours or containing them. Most of them had never filled a prescription in their lives. Of if they had, they'd forgotten what it was like on the frontline.

Retail pharmacy was an assembly-line of never-ending prescriptions throughout the course of a mind-numbing, twelve-hour shift and Jason was often confronted with a myriad of complex issues. At a dinner party he attended with Chrissie for one of her functions, he described this phenomenon to someone who managed to succinctly summarize the situation.

"So, you are an air traffic controller for prescriptions?"

Jason nodded and said, "That's a very accurate description."

Pharmacists, like air traffic controllers who juggled many flights at once, had to juggle many prescription balls in any single moment. Jason once googled the job requirements and found that many ATC personnel were "on position" for two-hour periods followed by a thirty-minute break.

The need for this was obvious. Aircraft carried hundreds of customers and a mishap could result in a major loss of life. He scoffed at his own job requirements and those of his colleagues at the large chains. They often worked twelve and thirteen hour shifts constantly on their feet many times without breaks. Lunches, if they managed to eat at all, were bites of a sandwich a few feet from the prescription bench, choked down in between prescriptions. Even at The Colonial, Jason found himself skipping lunch in order to keep up. He continued to be mentally and physically drained at the end of the day.

For the most part though, he found his work rewarding. Most patients genuinely appreciated the product and information he was readily able to provide. The drug seekers, frequent fliers and plain old addicts were sometimes the flies in the ointment.

Mid-way through October with the advent of flu and cough and cold season, the prescription volumes began to ratchet up in number.

With each passing day and week with Thomas's help (Jason often called him on his day off) and that of Gloria and Sarah, Jason had developed his own professional niche. And it happened just in time, the fall which carried with it more prescriptions for antibiotics, cough syrups, steroids, inhalers, and over-the-counter cough and cold medications, plus flu shots, ushered in a whole new level of prescription volume. The aisles were packed with sick patients waiting. Every minute of every shift was a barrage of refill requests, new prescriptions, ADHD medications for kids in school. Jason weathered the onslaught with only a few issues. And those that did occur were resolved with Thomas's guidance and assistance.

The holidays, Thanksgiving, Christmas and New Year's came and went without any major incident. Though Jason experienced two more instances where patients returned medications that had flaws. One was the wrong strength of a cholesterol medication; the other was a medication with the wrong instructions on the label. Jason had typed on the label for the patient to take the medication 4 times a day when the prescription had read three times. In all now, he'd been made aware of three prescription errors since becoming a pharmacist. He calculated how many prescriptions he'd filled since starting with The Colonial in August. On average, he'd worked fourteen days out of every four weeks, filling an average of two hundred and fifty prescriptions each time. With sixty-five shifts to his credit that meant he was responsible for more than sixteen thousand prescriptions in his short career. Only three errors in so many prescriptions represented a fraction of one thousandth of a percent as an error rate. He could think of no other profession where such a low error rate could be achieved. And yet, each time Jason fretted over the errors as if they were cataclysmic events. Because they were. He cared greatly about doing a good job, as did the other pharmacists he had spoken too. Each error drove a dagger through his heart.

But how many other errors did he not know about?

Jason called a couple of pharmacist buddies to go out for drinks one night. The conversation eventually turned to their jobs. Jason broached the subject of medication errors. Each man took turns recounting some of their near-misses and not-so-near misses.

Trent, a fellow classmate of Jason's who now worked at a large chain, said he'd dispensed an anti-depressant for a woman who had been prescribed an antibiotic. The names sounded similar and his technician had entered the prescription incorrectly. Trent missed it because he'd been asked to give four flu shots in a fifteen-minute period. He didn't have enough time to properly review the prescription. He put this is his report but had been told not to blame the workload for his mistakes.

Lance, who graduated a year before Jason, confessed that he had harmed a patient because he mistakenly dispensed an ear drop instead of eye drops. The line items in the computer were on top of each other. His cursor strayed a millimeter too high and he hit the wrong one. It was missed on review. The patient ended up using the ear drops which are not sterile and not Ph-balanced for the eye for five doses. They ended up having to go back to the ophthalmologist and he was currently being sued.

"We go so fast; we end up being robotic in our work because of the volume of prescriptions." Lance's crest fallen visage made Jason ache. "There's so much emphasis put on speed."

"What did the company say?" Jason asked.

"I complained about the number of prescriptions." Lance slugged another mouthful of beer. "The company and me were being sued. I don't have liability insurance because I was told the company would protect me. But guess what, they want me to accept blame. They said if I got out of line, then they would not protect me legally. So, I had to bend over and take it up the ass."

℞

In late January, Jason and Chrissie attended a Super Bowl party at one of Chrissie's friends' place. At halftime, the temperature in the house climbed because of the twenty-odd souls crowded into the kitchen and living room. They both snuck out onto the back porch to get some relief from the growing temperature. She could see something was eating at him.

"What's bothering you, honey?" Chrissie asked, and rubbing his arm.

Jason shook his head. "Nothing."

"Don't give me that," she replied. "You're not yourself. You haven't been for a few weeks now."

Jason admitted Chrissie was right. The intensity of his work; the number of prescriptions had increased by twenty percent at The Colonial and was straining even the well-trained technicians, Thomas and Jason. The immunizations: flu shots, shingles vaccines and all the others, the phone calls, dealing with the intransigent insurance companies, the long hours, the worry about errors was taking their toll on him. Perhaps it would get better as he put more years under his belt, but that notion did little to ease his mind now.

Jason shrugged. "This work is stressful! I work incredibly hard. And I worry about making mistakes."

Jason told her about his conversations with his colleagues.

"What can I do?" she asked.

He rotated his head to peer into her inquisitive caramel eyes. They appeared black in the moonlight. A gentle breeze gently caressed her hair. Jason smiled. "Don't stop loving me."

"Never," she replied, raising up on her tiptoes to kiss him. "Will you love me forever?"

"Always," he answered.

℞

The swelling tidal flood of prescriptions continued through February and early March. As the Virginia winter thawed into spring, the numbers of prescriptions eased, but only slightly. By that time, the job began to feel like a pair of new-but-broken-in, shoes. The strain of the winter season had lightened. Jason relegated his worry about errors for the time being to the back burner of his mind. With the shrinking prescription volumes, Jason was less stressed. Thomas had told him in a moment of candidness that this kind of worry assaulted pharmacists all the time, ebbing and flowing over time.

He and Chrissie continued to see each other at least three or four times a week, often at her parent's house. He worked two days on and two days off and every other weekend on Friday, Saturday and Sunday. Because his workdays were so long, he generally did not see Chrissie when he worked. He'd call her after he had made the night deposit and was driving home so they could catch up on each other's days.

On the days he did not work, he met her at Thomas's for dinner and an evening of watching television or playing cards. Thomas and Eleanor often went to bed early, leaving them alone. Many nights they would sit on the sofa in the darkened living room under a blanket. The only light was the bluish tint flickering from the television. Often, they ignored the screen and explored their bodies. And on the three-day weekends when Jason was off, Chrissie arranged for them to travel to North Carolina or Washington DC. They spent hours talking about life, their work, and dreams of the future.

This blissful cycle of work and leisure continued until May. That was when everything changed. And the bliss turned into a blistering, soul-shredding nightmare.

PHARMACY PHACT:

Nearly, 75% of medication errors have been attributed to [distraction].

Medication and Dispensing Errors,
StatPearls, November 2020

CHAPTER 47

It was the second Tuesday in May. Jason worked the second twelve-hour shift of a two-day stint. The air outside held a pleasant warmth. The spring skies shone bright and clear dotted with a cloud or two floating like cotton candy on a serene cerulean blanket. A cool breeze whipped off the James River, rustling the trees and neutralizing the growing heat of the day.

In every aspect, it appeared this particular day would be no different than any of the hundreds in the last nine months since Jason had started working as a licensed pharmacist. Happy and content, he and Chrissie were approaching their second anniversary of dating. All things were as they should be. A glorious future loomed bright, potent and bounded only by the imagination. Jason had even begun to entertain thoughts about proposing marriage to Thomas Pettigrew's only daughter. His euphoric mood reflected it.

Later, Jason would recall the circumstances of the incident with great clarity. It was one of those images seared into a pharmacist's memory because of the unforgettable, dire and irreversible circumstances.

He was talking to Gloria, the technician, as she worked. He'd stopped for a moment, facing her. He would not remember what topic they discussed, just that they were engaged in conversation. In the late afternoon with the prescription counter stacked with countless baskets brimming with orders and stock bottles, Gloria bellied up to the counter and began scraping white tablets across the plastic counting tray into the cylinder running along its side. She closed the cover to the chamber and tilted the tray so that the tablets slid into a wide amber vial. She pulled the adhesive prescription label from its backing and affixed it to the vial. Then she attempted to push the non-safety cap onto the vial. But her hand slipped causing the vial to fall from her hands.

The white oblong tablets of diltiazem, a heart medication, dropped to the floor and scattered like little white chiclets. Some hopped along the tiled floor, others slid into corners or under the overhang of the drawers.

"Shit," Gloria lamented.

They both ignored the phone and the pile of prescription orders. Jason crouched into a catcher's pose, picking up individual tablets while Gloria dropped onto all fours and began sliding clumps of pills into a pile.

"Of course, it had to be a ninety-day supply, one hundred and eighty damn pills. No, it couldn't have been thirty. I had to drop almost two full bottles worth."

"Take it easy, Glor. It's cool. We'll get it taken care of."

"She looked up at him and smiled. "You definitely have the right attitude for this job," she said.

"Ask me that in twenty years," Jason replied with a smile.

Gloria retrieved a dustpan. They swept up the remainingpills and tossed them into the hazardous waste bin. Then Gloria re-counted another batch of tablets.

"At least," Jason said. "They were not very expensive."

"Ha," Gloria shot back. "Don't tell Thomas that."

When she had finished re-counting out the replacement pills, she passed the basket to Jason. He accepted the basket and the prescription vial from her like it contained a dangerous, highly volatile chemical requiring great care in handling. He pretended to have the basket almost slip from his grasp, but then quickly grabbed it in an overly dramatic display.

"You ass," Gloria said sharply, then smiled. "Do you have this sense of humor with Chrissie?"

Jason grinned. "Yep."

"She's a lucky girl."

"Damn right she is."

Jason took the basket and the vial and carefully studied the label. Diltiazem 240mg tablets. Take one tablet twice daily. Quantity: one hundred and eighty. He compared the markings on the white oblong tablets with the description of the markings written on the label. "White oblong tablets, scored. NT 341. Then just to be sure Jason compared the new tablets to the pills in the stock bottle and to some of the spilled tablets that he'd saved and lay on the counter.

They matched perfectly. It was one of those singular moments that stay etched in a pharmacist's mind. They occur a few times a week. So many prescriptions, labels and pills sweep past them, it was hard to remember every prescription or every patient. Like most pharmacists, Jason checked so many prescriptions daily he often had to go back and re-check certain prescriptions because he could not remember seeing the prescription in his mind. It was one of those obsessive-compulsive actions only another pharmacist could understand.

But when an event such as spilling the tablets occurred or when you filled prescriptions under extreme duress like a patient yelling at you, the images and memories stayed with you, seared into the memory bank of the brain like a white-hot brand.

The name of the patient also added to his ability to recall the incident. Jason read the name on the label. He smiled. Ada Mae Renforth. "I need to make sure this is right," he told himself. For some reason, Jason set the basket and the prescription vial aside. A few minutes later with memory of Mr. Anderson's drug error months ago and a few minor errors that had been corrected since, he checked this prescription a second and a third time.

$$R_X$$

Two days later, Thursday, was Jason's day off. He woke early to the soft chime from his phone. He retrieved it from the nightstand and read the text message.

Love you darling. Had a great time last night!

Jason smiled, rolled over and stretched out on his back amidst the sea of blankets and fluffy mounds of pillows. He'd spent last evening with Chrissie. They'd gone to the Newport News Block party in the City Center and hooked up with some of her work friends and some of Jason's buddies from high school. They sang, drank and ate. Chrissie and Jason danced and partied for hours. Jason had dropped Chrissie off at her parent's house before eleven and driven home.

Today was his second consecutive day off. He was scheduled to work, tomorrow which was Friday and the weekend. Hoping to relax and run a few simple errands at some point, Jason lay in the bed for another ten minutes, then managed to drag himself out from under the covers. His head throbbed from the few beers he'd had last night. He'd stopped drinking about nine o'clock and was perfectly sober to drive. But a low, throbbing headache remained.

He turned on the shower and let it run until the bathroom was clouded with steam. As the water heated, he returned to his bedroom and pulled out some clothes. For some reason, he glanced at the clock on the nightstand. It read: seven twenty-seven. Returning to the bathroom, he climbed in letting the harsh needle-like jets of water clear the mild throbbing and willowy cobwebs. He let the hot water blast away at him for five full minutes, then lathered his hair with shampoo and rubbed the thick bar of soap over his body. Seven minutes after entering the shower, he stepped out and toweled off.

Returning to the bedroom, he ran a towel over his thick hair. Standing naked in his bedroom, he checked his phone and saw that he had another message. He smiled inwardly once more. *She's trying to make sure I'm up,* he told himself.

Jason picked up the phone off the dresser and saw that this time it was a voice message. And it was not from Chrissie's number. It was The Colonial's landline.

Thomas has a question about an issue, he thought. But then he looked at the clock once more. It read seven thirty-four.

Why is he calling this early?

He pulled up the voicemail and pressed play. Thomas's recorded voice was low in pitch and somber in tone. Jason could barely understand the mumbling message. He pressed the phone tighter against his ear. Thomas asked that Jason come to the store as soon as possible.

Jason clicked off, standing confused and transfixed. For some inexplicable reason, Jason's gut twisted into a tight electric knot which swelled and pulsed as he dressed.

Wonder what he wants? He sounds ill.

Jason played the recording once more.

Jason, It's Thomas. I need you to come to the store as soon as possible. It's urgent.

PHARMACY PHACT:

The most common causes [of pharmacist errors] include workload, similar drug names, interruptions, lack of support staff, insufficient time to counsel patients and illegible handwriting.

Medication and Dispensing Errors,
StatPearls, November 2020

CHAPTER 48

Jason sat on the stiff, uncomfortable metal chair in Thomas Pettigrew's office as he had all those months ago. Today he was waiting for Thomas to get off the phone. Thomas glanced in his direction every few seconds. The pained countenance on his face was one Jason had never seen before. It appeared to be one of complete and utter defeat and despair.

His eyes were red and clouded with fatigue and stress. They seemed to have withdrawn deeper into his skull. If Jason wasn't mistaken, it almost looked like he'd been crying and had tried to wipe away the evidence. The skin hung from his cheeks with an ashen cast. It was the visage of a man dealing with some enormous burden. After a minute of grunts and concerned listening, Pettigrew hung up the phone.

"What's going on?" Jason asked. "Who died?"

Pettigrew scoffed and leaned forward in his chair. "Interesting you should ask that question."

"What are you talking about?"

Pettigrew motioned with a flick of his head for Jason to close his door. At that moment, the knot in his stomach which for the most part had dissipated as he drove into Newport News suddenly reappeared, reaching levels of intensity that exceeded the earlier ones. Thomas Pettigrew's office door was always kept open while he was at the store. After a moment's hesitation, Jason twisted his torso and reached out and pulled the door closed. It clicked shut with a loud, metallic air of solemn finality.

Thomas was a man who barreled through life. He did not mince words or meaning. His honesty was blunt and harsh. He told you what he was thinking, sometimes without considering the ramifications. Jason had witnessed it early in his externship. Now, Jason could see the normally bold and loquacious man was searching for the words-the right words-to communicate what was going on. It was an eerie, disconcerting sensation to see his mentor struggling in this way.

After what seemed like eons, he spoke in halting, hesitant words. "Jason...there's...been...I mean...there's been...we have a crisis..."

$$R_x$$

"Is it happening?" Victor asked, already knowing the answer.

Simon and Victor were huddled in the small living area of the tiny townhouse they'd inhabited for almost two years now. This communal room had become their office, their command center and, often, their dining area. Simon's scrawny butt barely dented the worn cushions of the sofa as it hung off the edge. His elbows dug into the thin flesh of his thighs. His arms angled, tapered upward to form a triangle as his hands--balled into fists--supported his bony chin. Victor rested like a reclining bear after a hearty meal across from his partner, leaning against the back of the threadbare armchair, an iced tea balanced on one armrest while his hand cradled the glass. In the other hand between his first two fingers, a cigarillo burned. A curling strand of blue smoke stretched from a curved fingernail of ash toward the ceiling.

"It's happening," Simon replied without looking up from the audio meter flickering on the screen. "This will make up for Italy. We'll be back in the saddle again. I can feel it." The memory of their monumental disaster in Bologna still dangled from their necks like the proverbial albatross—and would until they logged a success—any success. You were only as good as your last op, Simon often lamented. For some reason, Simon's mind revisited the event in Italy from more than two years ago. Victor's silence communicated that, he too, was remembering.

℞

Kidnapping was never an easy endeavor. There were always so many variables for which to account. So many unanticipated things that could go wrong. In Victor and Simon's case, something did go wrong. Terribly wrong.

The apparent simplicity of the assignment was matched only by the massive consequences surrounding its outcome. A clean capture would allow the Americans and their allies the opportunity to bring down the underground railroad of armaments, guns and explosives making their way from Russia to the rebel faction in Syria. A successful revolution there and the resulting governmental instability was one political scenario the Americans could ill afford.

This op could lead to the capture the mastermind behind the shipments. Failure would not only see the continuation of these deliveries of deadly arms, but the targeted individual would be alerted to the fact that he was on the Americans' radar and appropriate measures to secure himself, his family, and his operation would be taken. And two years' worth of work would be wasted.

Nonetheless, this mission was supposed to have been relatively straight forward. After all, the target was not a spy. He was not trained in the procedures of countersurveillance. He was not a government official surrounded by a detail of beefy security men because his father was unaware that he had become a target. He was not even, by the day's societal standards, an adult. He was an oblivious, carefree college student studying Architecture and Engineering at the prestigious University of Bologna who seemed not to have a care in the world. And his name was Giancarlo DeMarco.

Giancarlo Demarco's only sin was that he was the progeny of the powerful and well-connected billionaire businessman Antonio DeMarco. The elder Demarco, an Italian, had amassed a fortune in steel over the last two decades. His conglomerate, Acerias Italianas, owned and operated four steel manufacturing plants; one in Savona, Italy; a second in Katowice, Poland; a third in Belarus; and the fourth and largest in Essen, Germany.

His steel profits had seen a steady decline for years. Shrinking margins and dwindling orders were offset by the illicit deals he was making with a Russian arms dealer named Nicolai Maksim. Multi-million-dollar shipments managed to find their way from ports in Savona, Italy and the Latvian river port of Riga, through the Mediterranean and the Suez Canal and the Red Sea around the Arabian Peninsula and into the Persian Gulf, to Al Qamishli in northeast Syria by way of Iran's Highway 55. This illicit trade route had been on Langley, Virginia's radar for two and a half years.

The CIA operation was a simple one: kidnap Giancarlo, the son, and use him as leverage against Antonio, the father, to turn him on his Russian supplier. Victor and Simon surveilled, tailed and dug into Giancarlo's life for six weeks. With the help of the techno-geeks in Virginia, they hacked into Giancarlo's phone, laptop and school e-mail account, learning his class schedule and the days he worked part-time at a small gelateria a few blocks from the apartment. They tracked and studied his routes to class, his favorite haunts and his daily routines.

Giancarlo lived in a small campus apartment on Via S. Felice in Bologna with a female roommate, Bianca Moretti, a student at the Arts, Humanities and Cultural Heritage school at the same university. The best they could determine the relationship was strictly platonic. The boy and the girl were of similar build, hair color and skin tone. If they hadn't known better, they could have been mistaken for siblings.

Twenty-one days into their surveillance, it was decided that they would grab Giancarlo along the Via Nordella as he rode his Vespa toward class on a Tuesday morning. On the morning in question, Giancarlo exited the apartment in his A.S. Roma football club hoodie with its distinctive red and gold color scheme and iconic shield. He wore it frequently, at least two or three times a week. With its red hood pulled tightly over his head, he also toted a black nylon bookbag also adorned with A.S. Roma's stickers slung over his shoulders.

On the appointed day, Victor and Simon sat in the parking area of the Basilica di San Francesco, a church of French gothic design just north of the apartments and watched Giancarlo's building as they had for the last month and a half. But this time instead of the small Fiat 500, they spied him from a small delivery truck. When the young man emerged, they knew something was amiss.

In fact, they noticed three things. Normally, Giancarlo, much like his father, operated with the timing and precision of an expensive Swiss timepiece. This morning though, he'd emerged from his apartment ten minutes after his class was supposed to have begun. Second, instead of the Vespa, Giancarlo began walking south in the direction of the school of Architecture. Victor and Simon guessed it was at least thirty-minutes on foot. So, they surmised, Giancarlo was not going to his Tuesday class or he was going to be extremely late. Third, Giancarlo's usually leisurely gait was hurried and rushed.

In hindsight, they should have postponed. But time was of the essence and Langley needed the boy taken. So, they pressed on. He appeared to be heading toward the school of Architecture despite his tardiness. They followed him in the small truck closing the distance to about thirty meters as he approached the snatch point. Then, Simon gunned the engine and they pulled even with Giancarlo who walked with his head down and no situational awareness. When the truck skidded to a halt, Victor, the stronger of the two spies, jumped out, grabbed the smallish Giancarlo and threw him in the cargo hold of the truck, climbed in with him and tossed a blanket over him. The whole maneuver took less than twenty seconds.

Victor forced the boy face down into the floor of the truck bed, wrapped duct tape around his mouth and head without bothering to look at him or even pull off his hood. Then he secured his hands and feet with the duct tape. They drove south out of the city along the Via del Colli for an hour into the hilly farm country. He sat on him the entire way as Giancarlo grunted, groaned, and tried to flail in protest. But the massive Victor had no trouble keeping him subdued. Past Paderno, they pulled into a deserted farmhouse and garaged the truck in a barn.

It was when they dragged the blanket-wrapped student into the house, they realized their problem. Their captive was not Giancarlo. It was the girl, the roommate, Bianca Moretti. After ten minutes of shouting and screaming in exasperation at her and at their monumental bad luck, she was permitted to explain.

Giancarlo had allowed Bianca to borrow his hoodie and backpack because he was staying home sick. She needed something to keep her warm because she had left her coat and backpack at school.She explained that her items had been left at school because she had received an emergency call from her mother stating that her father had been taken to the hospital. They thought he was having a heart attack.

She wasn't headed to the school of Architecture but to the school of Arts and Humanities located nearby. She was going to retrieve her belongings.

Bianca had made immediate plans to return to her hometown near Rome. But as it turned, her mother called three hours later saying everything was okay. Her father had simply had a bad case of indigestion and was being released that same day.

Simon and Victor reported to their case office in Milan that Giancarlo had not shown himself that day and that the roommate had been taken by mistake. The case officer shouted all sorts of invectives and insults at Simon over the phone. Finally, he questioned them at length. Simon tried to explain as calmly as he could what had happened. The case office told them to sit tight. After much consultation and deliberation with Langley, they decided to release Bianca. Simon and Victor dropped her at the same location where she'd been taken and threatened her not to tell anyone about what had happened.

But the girl had returned to the apartment and done exactly the opposite. She breathlessly shouted at Giancarlo what had happened to her. The kidnappers thought she was him and were asking a lot of questions.

Giancarlo immediately phoned his father, explaining that he would have been kidnapped were it not for the fact he'd taken ill. He'd come down with a fever and a severe cold and decided to skip class that morning. The next day, three large men in dark suits showed up, carried his belongings to a large black sedan and Giancarlo became a ghost. Bianca, they learned later, did not see nor hear from Giancarlo for three months.

The failed kidnapping had tipped off Antonio Demarco. The op had been blown and Victor and Simon had become the scapegoats.

With their careers in tatters, they were banished from the field and recalled to Langley where they were assigned menial, inconsequential tasks like decrypting electronic messages of insignificant ops taking place somewhere in the bowels of Equatorial Africa.

A year later, with the Agency suffering from budget cuts, dwindling resources and desperately short on manpower, the Deputy Director had directed Carl, their new case officer, to get Victor and Simon involved in the op watching and reporting on The Colonial Pharmacy and its employees.

"You're lucky," Carl had told them. "This one will be extremely hard for you to fuck up!"

Simon heard Thomas explain to Jason that he would drive him home from The Colonial after the devastating news had been delivered. As the conversation between the pharmacist and his new staff pharmacist paused, Simon relived the events from earlier that morning. Simon and Victor had met with Thomas Pettigrew for ninety minutes to discuss how he could avoid losing his pharmacy. It was simple, fire Jason Rodgers and speak to no one about it. Sign a letter of intent to sell The Colonial to their company and they would pay the family and the whole matter would disappear. Fail to do so and he would be sued and probably lose The Colonial. At least, Thomas Pettigrew would have to time to arrange a proper sale. But that was better than going through an expensive lawsuit and losing.

Pettigrew said he needed to speak to his attorney. They left Pettigrew stunned and confused. Feeling good about their chances, Simon then quickly dropped Victor off at the apartment and drove to his hastily arranged conference with Ada Mae Renforth's daughter for the second phase of their operation.

"Thank you for seeing me," Simon had said, delivering the words with great empathy and compassion. Their op depended on compensating the family while keeping the real lawyers and the regulatory agencies like the Board of Pharmacy out of the picture. It required the speedy delivery of a generous settlement offer and an equally speedy acceptance of that offer. "I know this is a difficult time."

Ada Mae Renforth's eldest daughter, Charlotte Knox, nodded and choked back another episode of tears. "What's so important that it couldn't wait until after my mother's funeral?" She was a petite woman with small breasts, sandy blonde hair with wisps of gray creeping along the temples. Her gray-blue eyes held deep sadness.

"I do apologize again. What I have to say is urgent and must be decided upon in short time frame." Simon knew that Renforth was scheduled to be buried in three days. The body had barely gone cold before Simon had rung Renforth's daughter and the promise that his message was urgent.

"You're an attorney?" Her tone was stiff and clipped as if Simon's profession represented all that was wrong with the world.

"Yes, ma'am. I am."

They were in the dead woman's kitchen inside a modest home with dated décor, yellowed linoleum, and aging appliances. Simon glanced at her husband, Kurt, as the man pulled out a chair. He was much taller than his wife, standing about six-one. His broad shoulders and thick arms were the result of years on construction sites. His attractive, but weathered features were accentuated by his tanned skin. The expression he now wore communicated an extreme distrust at the most inconvenient timing. Of course, Simon knew all this because the couple, their family dynamic and relationship to the deceased had been thoroughly investigated and studied by the folks in northern Virginia.

Ada Mae Renforth had borne three children into the world; a boy had been sandwiched between two daughters in span of five years almost four decades earlier. Charlotte was fifty-two, lived locally and had married well. As a stay-at-home mother, she had raised three children of her own with her husband, Kurt, the owner of a small construction company.

Ada Mae's two younger children had departed the area years ago and left the chore of looking after their mother to Charlotte. In return, Ada Mae made Charlotte executrix of her estate and bestowed upon her all sorts of powers of attorney. Simon, again with the assistance from the legal department at Langley had collected a thick stack of documents.

Simon interrupted the awkward silence. "I am an attorney with a law firm in Virginia Beach." Simon removed a business card from the breast pocket of his recently purchased gray Joseph Abboud vested suit and slid it across the table. "I know this is quite inconvenient and I promise to not take too much of your time."

"You lawyers always come out of the woodwork at the most inappropriate times," Kurt, the husband chimed in.

Charlotte placed a restraining hand on her husband's forearm.

After another long interlude of uncomfortable quiet, Simon cleared his throat feigning an uneasiness he did not feel. The consummate performer, Simon said in a low, hesitant tone. "I'll come straight to the point. It has come to my attention that your mother's death…was not due to…let's say…natural causes."

Charlotte Knox's brows furrowed. Thin lines crinkled at the corners of her strong, wise and skeptical eyes. Thicker ridges puckered her forehead. "What?"

Simon nodded, acknowledging her confusion. "Her death never should have happened."

"Are you telling us that someone killed her?"

Simon swallowed involuntarily. He knew that Ada Mae Renforth had been murdered. Even as a spy, it was difficult to mask his reaction to her statement. He knew full well that his team and someone hired by them had, in fact, deliberately conspired to end the old woman's life. He ignored his own visceral reaction and recovered instantly. These two civilians were not trained to see through him. He proceeded in a smooth, calm tone of voice possessing a soothing, yet matter-of-fact air. "In a manner of speaking, yes. Your mother died because of a mistake made by one of her pharmacists at The Colonial Pharmacy on Jefferson Avenue."

Charlotte regarded this well-dressed intruder with a look of profound misunderstanding as if he'd spoken to her in a foreign tongue. She then glanced at her husband whose eyes had been trained on the tabletop. He swiveled his head towards his wife,

It had been decided that Simon would undertake this part of their operation alone. As a former lawyer. Simon possessed the interpersonal skills to connect with Charlotte. The presence of anyone else, especially Victor would detract from his ability to connect with her.

After thirty seconds, Charlotte Knox's eyes welled with tears. Her face swam through a storm of rapidly evolving emotions while dredging up the more recent ones. The two men watched her for nearly a full minute. She swiped at her wet eyes with the back of her hand then stood and retrieved a paper towel from the counter and dabbed her eyes. "Oh, Jesus," she gasped. "You mean, Thomas, the pharmacist made a mistake. I've known Thomas for almost three years. I don't bel--"

"It wasn't Thomas Pettigrew," Simon interrupted. "It was his staff pharmacist, a man named Jason Rodgers."

"What happened to his other pharmacist. I think his name was… Kevin?"

"That would be Kyle. Kyle Griffin. He left The Colonial's employ several months ago."

"So you're an ambulance chaser?" The husband interjected in an acid-laced tone. "Looking for a juicy case to take on so you can sue?"

Simon inhaled slowly and forced a smile. He leveled a patient gaze at the husband who was leaning forward. His eyes were laser beams trying to penetrate the CIA agent's placid veneer. Simon answered slowly so as not to allow his mounting anger to seep through. "No, Mr. Knox. As a matter of fact, we represent The Colonial. Thomas Pettigrew acknowledges that the mistake resulted in Mrs. Renforth's demise—"

"Demise?" Kurt Knox blurted. "Demise? Let's call it what is really was. It was her death!"

Charlotte again put her hand on her husband's arm. "Kurt, please. He's just doing his job." She turned back to Simon. "I'm not sure I want to think about this right now. I have a lot of things to do in the next three days."

The husband leaned back in his chair and pushed out an extended breath. He stroked his forehead with a hand and stood. He turned to gaze out the kitchen door into the back yard.

Simon removed a handkerchief from inside his suit and wiped his brow. "Anyway, The Colonial recognizes that the error caused your mother's …death. They want to avoid a log drawn out legal proceeding. I have been authorized to make her estate an offer."

Kurt Knox turned from the door. "This ought to be good," he hissed. "You want to make this go away."

That's true," Simon replied. "Thomas Pettigrew does want this to go away."

Kurt Know crossed his arms across his chest. "And you want to make it as inexpensive as possible, right?"

"I believe the offer is more than fair."

Charlotte spoke up. "Maybe, we should call the attorney for mom's estate."

Simon paused. "That's certainly understandable. But this offer has a very short expiration."

"Oh yeah?" Kurt said. "How short?"

"It expires the moment I walk out that door."

That's not much time," Charlotte remarked.

"No, it's not," Simon agreed.

"So what's the offer?" Kurt demanded.

Simon lifted his briefcase off the floor and laid on the table. The locks snapped open like two gunshots. He removed a five-page document and placed in front of him.

"Let me explain the basics of how a case like this works. In personal injury cases, your mother's estate would hire an attorney and a complaint would be served on The Colonial. That could take a month or longer..."

Simon went on to explain that after the complaint was served the pre-trial process would begin. Both parties would ask each other for evidence and witness information in discovery. Then they would appear before a judge to inform him or her as to how the case is proceeding and to determine if the parties would agree or not to arbitration or to set a trial date.

If arbitration is not agreed to, and Simon told both Charlotte and Kurt that arbitration would be highly unlikely, then depositions would be scheduled. More court appearances would be scheduled. Those trial dates would be delayed or continued numerous times. Discovery, he told them, could take a year or longer.

As the case inched closer to trial, both parties would have to participate in mandatory settlement conferences. Motions would be made to determine which evidence would be allowed at trial. If they managed to go to trial, a jury would need to be selected followed by a trial of several days.

"And as the attorneys representing your mother's estate spend time on this case, expenses would pile up and the attorneys would take forty percent of any judgment or settlement plus incurred expenses."

"What's a typical settlement?" Charlotte asked.

"That's hard to say," Simon replied. "It can vary greatly. But please bear with me." Simon raised a hand toward Kurt. "I'm going to explain to you the case in legal terms. It's going to sound callous and unfeeling.

"Your mother was an elderly woman who lived a rather long life. She was ill and retired. This is not to dimmish the value of her life. But her perceived value would be lower than say, if the injured party were a person in the prime of her life or a child, the judgement or settlement could be much higher. But each case is different."

"What do think a case like this would…I mean…how much a judgment would be?" Kurt asked in a more inquisitive and cooperative demeanor as he retook his spot at the table.

Simon tilted his head this way and that, then said, "I would guess about a million. But after legal fees and expenses, the estate would net about five hundred thou. But, again, every case is different."

"And your offer is better than that, I take it?" Charlotte Knox asked.

"Much better."

"Well?" Charlotte continued.

Simon reached into his inside breast pocket and withdrew a cashier's check made out to Renforth's estate in the amount of two million dollars. He laid it on the table and slowly turned it so the pair could read it. They both leaned in. Their eyes widened as the figure registered. They exchanged surprised glances. "And, of course," Simon explained. "No fees will be taken out of this amount. And since this is a settlement for a personal injury case, it is non-taxable."

Simon continued his explanation. "We were involved in a case recently in North Carolina. A young child died as a result of a drunk driver hitting the car. It was settled but the parties agreed to one point eight million. But again, fees and expenses came out of that. The plaintiff pocketed just over nine hundred thousand."

"What do you think?" Charlotte asked her husband.

Kurt rubbed his chin and said to Simon after a few moments. "Would you give us a minute?"

Simon stood as the chair squealed against the kitchen floor. "I'll wait outside."

He retreated to the back porch. Kurt said, "We'll just be a minute," as he closed the door behind him.

Simon placed both hands on the peeling railing of the back porch. He could hear their muted voices. Kurt's was deeper and more forceful while Charlotte's was more hesitant and questioning. Then the voices became softer as they became barely audible as if the pair were conscious that Simon might be able to hear them. Simon did the only thing he could. He removed the Mont Blanc pen from his shirt pocket and began deftly twirling it as he waited.

He checked his watch every thirty seconds or so. After six interminable minutes, the door opened, and Kurt asked Simon to come back in. As Simon lowered himself into the chair, Kurt addressed him.

"We appreciate your offer. But it's not enough."

"Not enough?" Simon replied as if he was insulted. "Two million dollars is a lot of money. Mrs. Renforth's heirs will do quite well with two—"

"Three," Kurt demanded.

"Three?"

"Make it three million and you have a deal!"

Simon peered at Charlotte who was studying her hands. "And you both are in agreement?"

Charlotte lifted her gaze and her eyes steeled as she returned Simon's look. She nodded slowly. "Yes."

Simon studied both as he moved his eyes back and forth. "I'm not authorized to go over two." He understood. Renforth had three children. They wanted a million for each.

"Call someone," Kurt insisted.

"If I can get this approved, you will sign the document today?"

"Yes," Charlotte answered. Kurt nodded.

Simon withdrew to his car and pretended to make a call. Carl had authorized him to go as high as four million. So Simon just saved the Company a million dollars. He held his phone to his ear and acted like he was demanding that the request be approved. His head bobbed emphatically and a hand stabbed at the air. It was for effect. He suspected one or both was watching him through a curtained window. After five minutes, he lowered the phone and pretended to make some notes. Then he returned to the front door and rang the bell.

Simon amended both copies of the contract, adding a clause that stated the amount would be raised to three million. He would leave the check for two million and have another mil transferred within twenty-four hours. The Knoxes agreed. They signed the settlement agreement and gave Simon their mother's bank account information.

"Again, I'm sorry for your loss," Simon repeated. They shook hands and Simon was back on the road in ten minutes.

$$\mathrm{R}\!\!\!/x$$

Between them sat the old, distressed coffee table pocked with dings and scratches on which rested Simon's laptop. The coffee table always held a computer or some other electronic gadget, a thick file folder or a rumpled newspaper or magazine. It had become their de facto command center. The computer screen was angled so that both men could see it. On it, an audio recording program registered a conversation taking place inside The Colonial. More specifically inside Thomas Pettigrew's office. It recorded the conversation taking place at that very moment between Thomas and his young pharmacist, Jason Rodgers.

The first tiny bug that had been placed many months ago and had captured countless, monotonous hours of Thomas Pettigrew on the phone with suppliers, other pharmacists, state legislators in Richmond, his wife, Eleanor or his daughter, Christine, as well as private one-on-one conversations with employees including Kyle Griffin and the two technicians, Sarah and Gloria. This was the second listening device they'd placed in Pettigrew's office. The first had stopped transmitting two months back.

They'd used the same ruse to insert the new device as they had to place the first. They jammed the electronic signal coming from the server in Thomas's office. Without delay, Thomas Pettigrew immediately called his service provider. Using the same call cloaking program used previously, the call to the provider was re-routed to the phone at the townhouse. Simon answered posing as a male receptionist. Thomas reported the problem and Simon promised to have a technician at the store within the hour.

Victor, dressed in a dark blue pullover with the logo stitched over the breast and tan khakis, appeared thirty-five minutes later. He was directed to the server in Thomas's office and made a show of performing a diagnostic using his own laptop and connecting to the server. Thomas, pre-occupied with dealing with the backlog of prescriptions, allowed the man to work in his office unattended. Victor disassembled the handset of the landline on Thomas's desk and inserted the bug in less than forty-five seconds. The bug captured both ends of any phone call placed from Thomas's phone and any conversation taking place in the room with excellent clarity.

"How did it go with the daughter?" Victor asked.

On the audio, Thomas Pettigrew laid out the situation for Jason Rodgers. Victor's question went unanswered as they leaned in and listened, transfixed by the drama playing out in the office. When Thomas stopped speaking, Victor repeated the question.

"The daughter?"

"Yes," came Simon's reply, stopping the twirling of his pen and placing the cap's finial between his lips "I contacted the daughter after the body was discovered and told her that I'd been contacted by someone from the hospital morgue who'd overheard a doctor's conversation with a concern and a theory as to what happened. I met with her and the husband. I offered them two million to settle immediately. They balked and the husband said they wanted three. I made a show of looking upset. But then agreed. They signed. I wired the funds to their account an hour later." Simon waved the contract, flapping the pages in the air.

He continued. "The funds came from our accounts in Geneva, but they think the money came from Pettigrew and The Colonial. It took some convincing, but they have agreed not to pursue a lawsuit. They gave me power of attorney to handle the matter quietly for them and signed a waiver. And we have agreed to pay for the burial."

Prior to becoming a spook, Simon had worked as a lawyer in a mid-sized Washington personal injury firm.

"Your legal experience is going to be invaluable in the days ahead," Victor said. "Let the games begin."

CHAPTER 49

After Thomas had delivered the devastating news, Jason lost all sense of time. His mind disengaged from the real world, unable to assimilate information gathered through any of his five senses. His next conscious realization occurred in the parking lot. He found himself sitting in the passenger seat of his car. A metallic rattle caused him to swivel his head at an agonizingly slow pace. He witnessed Thomas inserting the key into the ignition and starting the engine.

He did not remember getting up from the stiff unbearable chair in Thomas's office. Nor did he recall his trudge from Pettigrew's office through the cramped, darkened hallway past the pharmacy department and down the two steps. He shuffled past Gloria, zombielike, as Thomas guided him by the elbow, down the pair of steps and out onto the sales floor.

He did not remember the door opening or the tinkle of the bell hanging from its frame. It was only after he was outside as he stepped off the curb that a flash of white-hot sunlight briefly roused him from his fugue. But his mind quickly blotted out the brief interlude of illumination and retreated to an amnestic state.

The engine clunked to life. As it pitched higher and the car moved forward, Jason peered through the cruddy windshield seeing nothing but an obliterated future. Pettigrew, appearing gargantuan in the driver's seat of the small car, bumped it out of the parking lot and onto Jefferson Avenue. The rhythmic rumble of the tires on the pavement and the uneven hum of the engine jarred Jason back in time to ten minutes earlier, causing him to relive his earlier conversation with his boss.

The image of a crestfallen Thomas sitting across the desk delivering news that had shattered Jason's world...and Thomas's.

You are on paid leave until we can figure all this out.

When Thomas had first informed him of the situation, Jason sat dumbfounded and speechless. With halting words and an emotionally laden tone, Pettigrew had delivered the message no pharmacist ever wanted to hear. The few minor errors Jason had committed during his brief time in Pettigrew's employ had jarred him to his core. But Pettigrew's comments numbed Jason into a horrific wasteland of anguish.

A medication error occurred, Jason...you made an error.

Initially, Jason was concerned. His chest filled with nervous electricity. *Okay*, Jason had told himself. *We'll figure out what happened and fix it going forward.* But then, the fact that Thomas had called him into the store on his day off combined with his mentor's crestfallen visage communicated to Jason that this time it was more serious... much more serious.

Okay, Jason had said aloud. He recalled how the word quavered as it passed his lips. *What...happened?*

It's Ada Mae...she's dead.

What?

That was the only word, the only question, the only syllable that he could manage from his parched throat and dry lips.

Thomas explained that one of their beloved patients, one Ada Mae Renforth, was gone. It had been determined rather quickly that one of her prescriptions, the diltiazem 240mg—her heart medication—had been filled incorrectly. Whatever had been filled in its place had caused her heart to seize.

His lawyers and those of the family had visited with Thomas twice to discuss the situation. Unlike in the other areas of his business which were well run, The Colonial was under insured. A lawsuit would ruin Thomas Pettigrew and cause him to shutter its doors. Somehow, Thomas went on, the family agreed to a quick out of court settlement. Deep in his subconscious Jason sensed there was more to the settlement than Thomas was letting on.

Thomas had had to repeat his explanation three times. Each time Jason's response was slightly more forceful, but his mind's inability to wrap itself around the words Thomas had spoken in willowy and hushed tones was manifested in two simple phrases. "No, that can't be" or "No way". He then repeated: "That can't be."

I'm afraid it is, Jason. Effective immediately you are on paid administrative leave. My lawyer says this is the way it has to be!

Jason had sat shocked on the small, hard chair. The lines and angles in the room, the file cabinets, the desk and the framed certificates on the walls seemed to waver as if the space was being rippled by an unseen wave. Then the whole room began to spin uncontrollably. Jason braced himself, grabbing the desk and thrusting his head between his knees.

Thomas continued laying out the restrictions being placed on him. His next words hurt him almost as much as the devastating news the Old Man had already delivered.

You cannot discuss this with anyone, especially Christine. You are to have no contact with her starting right now.

What? For how long?

"Until I tell you," Thomas barked. "The lawyers tell me it's crucial."

"I have to tell her something!" he groaned, lifting his head and sitting up slightly.

"I'll handle that," Thomas said.

He slouched in the chair again seemingly taking on its dimensions like a deflated balloon.

"Lawyers?" The word "lawyers" sent another jolt of fear and anxiety through him. The words felt like a shot of adrenaline. He sat up so fast his head swam.

"I've been on the phone with them all morning. I had to call Kyle Griffin in to cover my shift. He happens to be off from his hospital job. Even if I had time to fill prescriptions, I wouldn't be able to concentrate."

Jason remembered seeing Kyle at the prescription bench when he'd arrived. But he was on the phone and pre-occupied. Beads of sticky perspiration popped onto the skin of Jason's forehead. They were soon followed by an outbreak all over his body. "Oh my God!" He whispered, lowering his head once more.

At that moment, he had closed his eyes and clutched the chair like it was a life preserver and he was alone in a vast, stormy sea being pelted by a monsoon of fear. A loud squeal reverberated off the walls of the office. This was followed by the shuffle of shoes on the tile floor. Jason did not recognize what these sounds represented until he felt the sensation of Thomas's long, powerful hands on his shoulders, then his arms embracing him. The sound was coming from inside him.

Jason, I'm sorry. Give me a few days and I will have more information. Now you should go home and get some rest. Try to relax.

Relax? Jason scoffed.

Jason pushed himself up from the chair. But before he was fully erect, his arms failed him, and he toppled to one-side. Thomas's arms cradled him, stopping him from hitting the floor. Pettigrew pushed him back in the chair. "I'm going to take you home."

Thirty-five minutes later, Thomas pulled Jason's Honda to a halt in the Jason's driveway.

"Are your parents home?"

Jason lay back in the partially reclined passenger seat with a hand over his face, struggling to breathe. He croaked out a reply. "No, they're both at work." He thought a moment then said, "How the hell am I going to tell them?"

"Just tell them you're sick for now," Thomas said. "Let's get you inside."

The Old Man pressed the garage door opener. He alighted from the car and circled to the passenger door and practically lifted Jason from the seat. Thomas managed to locate the key to the door. The tall, aging apothecary guided him to his bedroom. Jason fell more than sat onto the freshly made bed. Then without warning, he bolted upright and ran past Thomas into the hallway bathroom where he retched, emptying the meager contents of his stomach into the toilet.

Several minutes later, he returned to the bed and lay face down. The sunlight filtered through the gaps in the blinds. Then as his eyes closed the glow slowly faded into blackness. He was not asleep yet. He did not remember Thomas telling him he'd be in touch. Nor did he hear the soft click of the bedroom door closing.

He laid on the bed, despondent and paralyzed with fear. Thomas's words returned to him as if carried on violent, hurricane-forced winds. Jason closed his eyes, trying to block out the sound of Thomas's voice in his head. The final message Thomas delivered had nearly sent a dagger through him.

They have agreed to a quick settlement…On two conditions. You must leave The Colonial and never return. And you must not have any contact with anyone associated with me or the business…ever again…including Chrissie You are sworn to secrecy…forever.

Thomas hesitated to allow his words sink in.

I know you love her, Jason. But if you stay, I'll lose The Colonial. This is the hardest thing I've ever had to say…I'll leave the choice to you. But I know you'll do the right thing.

As Thomas's final words returned to him, the enormity and consequences of their meaning registered. Then unable to deal with what they meant; Jason descended into the depths of unconsciousness.

℞

After Jason had emptied the contents of his stomach and returned to the bed, Thomas found a throw blanket on a chair in the living room. He returned to the bedroom and covered Jason. He studied the young man, watching the rise and fall of his rib cage as he lay face down on the comforter. The boy looked gaunt and green with shock. Satisfied that Jason was asleep, he left the keys on the dresser and moved to the door.

"God help us, Jason," he said. "God help us."

He closed the door and departed the house. Using his cell phone, he called a cab to take him back to The Colonial.

CHAPTER 50

Chrissie dialed Jason's number for the fourth time in the last ninety minutes. She peered out the window from her cubicle in the large sea of cubicles at the accounting firm of Collins, White and Casper. The sun hovered over the tree line in a glorious golden hue. It would disappear in about thirty minutes. She checked the clock on her phone; twenty minutes to seven.

It had been a long, grueling day. She had spent a good portion of it working a combined trial balance for a chain of local restaurants. When Jason had not answered her first two calls, she had been mildly annoyed. But the work on the trial balance consumed her so she had not dwelled on the issue.

Her repeated attempts had all been met with silence. Now she was concerned. She could not remember a time when Jason did not return her calls. Chrissie pulled up her call log and her texts. In addition to the phone calls, she had texted him three times.

It was his second day off in a row. He was scheduled to be back at the store tomorrow which would mean he would be working twelve or thirteen hours. They had spent a wonderful evening at the block party listening to music, dancing and having a grand time with friends last night. She'd texted him good morning earlier and Jason had responded. Since then, there had been nothing.

They usually spent the evenings before he went back to work having a quick bite after she finished up at the office. Time, like the sun, was slipping away. If they didn't make plans soon, they would have to forgo dinner. She needed to be back at the office early in the morning.

She tried his cell phone for a fifth time. It rolled to voicemail after five rings. She clicked off the call without leaving a message and immediately dialed the Rodgers's home line, Jason's father, Edward, answered.

"Hi Edward. It's Chrissie."

"Hi Chrissie. How are you?'

"Okay…I guess. I'm a little worried. I've been trying to reach Jason and he's not answering. Have you seen him?"

"Yeah, he's in bed. I don't think he's feeling well."

"He's not answering his phone or his texts."

"Do you want me to get him?"

"Just for a moment, please," she said. Irritation mounted. *What the hell was going on?*

Chrissie heard Edward Rodgers place the phone down. Then she heard fading footfalls. Five seconds passed. Then she heard Edward's muffled voice. She could not make out the words. But the intonation in his voice told her he'd asked a question.

When he returned to the phone, he said, "Chrissie, I'm sorry. His phone's been on silent. He's been asleep. He looks and sounds awful. Can I have him call you tomorrow?"

"Ah…yeah. That would be fine. I hope he's feeling better."

℞

Edward Rodgers placed the cordless phone back on its base. After pausing for a moment, he walked back to Jason's bedroom door. After he'd knocked on the door a moment ago, he'd heard a weak, hoarse version of his son's voice. This time he did not bother knocking.

He entered the darkened room and stood beside the bed. "What's going on, son?"

"I told you I don't feel well."

"You also told me that your phone was on silent. But I've heard it ring at least four times in the last two hours. Are you and Christine having problems?"

"No, Pop, we're fine."

"That's bullshit. If you don't want to see her anymore, man-up and tell her!"

CHAPTER 51

What the hell was he going to do?

Jason had been awakened by his father's impatient knocking. Now, he lay on the bed in his darkened bedroom. His father had departed, closing the door firmly. Jason had been awake for an undetermined amount of time, frozen in place, afraid to move. He looked at the bedside clock. It was approaching seven o'clock. The normally small act of lifting and turning his head tonight was a titanic effort. The movement reminded him that this was not just a bad dream. It was more than that. It was a cataclysmic nightmare. It was all real.

The sliver of sunlight that had sliced through the blinds earlier was gone, replaced now by a grayness that seemed to suck at his soul. He was adrift on a night sea with no boat, no oars and no life vest. He bobbed uncontrollably, his mind racing, water trying to overtake him. Sinister thoughts bounced against the inside of his skull, colliding like violent, crashing waves on a rocky shoreline. Despite the agitated state of his mind, his muscles were frozen, paralyzed with fear about a future that was suddenly, extremely uncertain.

What the hell do I do now?

What do I tell my parents?

What do I tell Chrissie? Wait! I'm not supposed to speak to her. How do I handle that?

Rolling onto his back, he fretted like this on the bed for several endless minutes. Then his mind, unable to endure any more anxiety, temporarily pushed back the uncertainty and replaced it with a tenuous episode of fragile calm.

This can't be happening! This is all a joke. Tomorrow, it will all be cleared up, he told himself.

Then reality burst forth once more, shattering the fragile temporary peace of his mind and churning it, once more, into turbulent, wind-swept swells.

Administrative leave!

A patient was dead…a sweet, little old lady had died because of a mistake he'd made!

What was going to happen?

Would he lose his job?

What about his license?

Shit!

And so, it went for the rest of an endless night. His mood and outlook oscillated, teetering back and forth questioning the reality of it all and then realizing it was true. He lay in the dark asking questions. Questions that, at the moment, held no answers.

Hours ago, his future had been bright, concrete and assured. He had been carefree and ebullient, excited about the days, weeks and years to come. As a newly anointed pharmacist, a glorious, lucrative career lay ahead. Then in a flash, one phone call had changed everything. Thomas Pettigrew's emotion-cracked voice spilled forth hesitant words, explaining that he had to stop working immediately. His excitement about the future, his future, had evaporated in an instant.

One damned phone call had changed all of it.

What was he going to do?

$$R_x$$

Chrissie slipped through the back door into the two-story Colonial-era home her father and mother had owned for nearly fifteen years. Light glowed throughout the small but comfortable downstairs. The full, rich voice of the Italian tenor Andrea Bocelli consumed the kitchen. The aroma of chocolate, flour and sugar hung in the air. A batch of freshly baked cookies sat on a tray cooling on the counter as her mother, Eleanor, stood nearby, mixing more batter in a large, clear bowl, humming to herself.

The small television on the countertop was tuned to the Hallmark channel but largely being ignored; it was some syrupy movie about love and redemption. Eleanor turned at the sound of the closing door as she wiped her hands with a towel.

"Hello dear," she said, her voice brimming with affection. Eleanor was always at her best when doing for others. "How was yo..."

Eleanor stopped as Chrissie forced a half-hearted smile. Her mother knew her better than anyone. And Chrissie could see in her mother's eyes that she knew something in Chrissie's world had shifted violently on its axis.

Chrissie lifted a hand, showing her palm. "Not now, Mom."

"What's wrong?" Eleanor persisted. "You look ill. So does your father. Are you both getting sick?"

Chrissie marched past, sucking in a lungful of air, communicating silently her frustration at her mother's persistence. Chrissie shook her head, left the kitchen and headed upstairs.

She stormed into her bedroom, closing the door with a frustrated bang.

What the hell?

Slamming her bag on the bed, she kicked off her pumps with un-characteristic abandon and disrobed, allowing her skirt and blouse to lay where they fell. Chrissie padded into that bathroom adjoining the bedroom and opened the tap full blast. Hot water. She needed hot water. A minute later, a cloud of steam had turned the bathroom into a sauna. Chrissie's mind returned to the vortex of emotions that had swirled within her throughout the day.

Something was wrong.

She knew it. She sensed it with every fiber in her body. She and Jason had been dating exclusively since they'd gone out on their first dinner date, almost two years ago. In that time, she recalled Jason being sick only twice. On those two occasions, he had sounded terrible and begged off, saying he wasn't up to getting together. And on both of those occasions, Jason had communicated with her through texts and phone calls, telling her he was not well. They'd spoken to each fondly and lovingly like couples in new relationships did, expressing their de-sire to see each other even though the circumstances meant it would not happen. Chrissie had even volunteered to come visit and sit with him while he lay in bed or on the couch at his parent's home. Jason had politely deferred, expressing sincere regret.

Chrissie didn't know how sick he was tonight. But he had com-pletely blown her off. He had never acted in this manner. After the first three unanswered texts, Chrissie became irritated. He had never ignored her like this. It was his day off after all. When she texted him while he was on duty at The Colonial, sometimes, he did not respond for hours. She understood this. Jason was busy filling prescriptions and often had his phone on silent.

He had no such excuse for his behavior today. After more unan-swered texts, followed by two more unreturned phone calls, Chrissie's concern had morphed into something more than irritation. It was exasperation. As the day gave way to early evening, that vexation had blossomed into a combination of full-fledged worry and bouts of stymied anger. As night fell, she found herself sitting in her cubicle working through the trial balance, not seeing the numbers and unable to focus. She had pounded the keyboard, punishing it with each keystroke. With no reason to expect she'd see him tonight, she stayed at the office two hours longer than usual.

In the final unanswered call, she had plead with Jason to call her telling her he was alright and when that call did not materialize, the realization set in that she would not be seeing him tonight, her mood now was a monolith of ire and fear. By seven o'clock, she had experienced a conversation with Jason's father in which she was told he was not feeling well.

As darkness sifted through the window at work, her anger had subsided long enough for a thought to creep into her mind. It was a thought that at the beginning of the day would never have crossed her mind. *Was Jason blowing her off? Was their relationship teetering on the brink of collapse? If so, why?* Her anxiety erupted into a trip to the ladies' room where she sat in a stall on the toilet silently weeping. She recovered quickly and prayed that Jason was not going to end it.

There was a good reason he was not calling her, she told herself. There better be or, she promised herself, Jason Rodgers would be wishing he were dead.

Now, she sank into the hot bath and stayed there almost an hour. She ran a bar of soap and a luffa over her skin, scrubbing away most of frustration, leaving a residue of mild annoyance. Finally, she lifted herself out of the water, put on her thick, white robe and wrapped her hair in a towel.

In the bedroom, the digital clock on the nightstand read just past nine-thirty. She went to her closet and laid out her outfit for tomorrow.

Then she laid on the bed, picked up the remote and turned on the television resting high on her bureau. She clicked the remote every few seconds, changing channels, completely unable to find any show or movie that would distract her. She stopped on an old episode of the X-files and watched for a moment. David Duchovny and Gillian Anderson sat in there their offices, engaged in deep conversation, mulling over some global extraterrestrial crisis when three rapid and solid knocks rattled her bedroom door.

"Come in."

The door creaked open and her father slipped inside. "Hey sweetie," he said. His voice was soft and timid, holding a concerned timbre like nothing she'd ever remembered.

She muted the television. In the flickering light, Chrissie noticed that her father appeared drawn and sallow. Her mother had been right. He looked ill. In all her life, she had never seen her father looking so… unhealthy.

Chrissie bolted upright. "Daddy? What is it? Are you okay? You look awful."

Her father tried to smile. But it was nothing more than a pained smirk. "Chrissie," he said, motioning for her to make room for him on the bed. She swung her legs over the side and allowed Thomas to sit beside her."We need to talk."

CHAPTER 52

Chrissie woke the next morning, utterly exhausted. Her mood reflected her fatigue and her frustration. She'd replayed her father's statements over and over in her head all night long in an endless loop while she tried to sleep, and they did so again now.

"I have asked Jason to take some time off from his job," he'd said.

"Why," she'd demanded. "What's going on? I've been trying to reach him all day."

"I told him not to call you. It's better…I mean…I can't discuss it right now. I need to you to understand."

Chrissie sighed. Her loud exhalation quavered as it passed her lips.

"Understand? How can I understand. I have no clue what's happening. How long?" She did not allow her father time to respond. "What's going…what the…hell…is going on?"

This time it was the aging druggist's turn to sigh. "Chrissie, he's going to be away for a while…indefinitely, in fact."

"What did he do? I deserve to know!" Her voice brimmed with emotion and worry. Her eyes searched her father's. She could see defeat and pain in them. It unnerved her. She'd never seen him like this.

"I can't really discuss it," he'd repeated, then he immediately followed it with another bomb. "I've told Jason to stay away. He's not going to call you. And I don't want you to call him."

"What?!"

"Please for his sake, do not contact him."

Chrissie recoiled from her father like he was spewing some sort of contagion, then anger reared in her.

"Like hell," she spat. "I will do no such thing! You have no right to ask me to do that."

"I do. And I am asking you, as your father. My business is at stake."

His business is at stake!

Now, she climbed out of bed with the awkwardness and infirmity of an old woman. Questions. She had nothing but questions. Questions without answers. She had been confounded by Jason's silence yesterday, her father's dreadful appearance last night and her own anxiety over the last fifteen hours. But his request for them not to communicate with each other was totally incomprehensible to her.

Oddly enough, Chrissie was partially relieved to learn that Jason had not contacted her because her father had told him not to. *Her own father!*

This knowledge eased her fears in two ways: it told her that there was a good explanation for why Jason had not returned her calls and assuaged her worry that Jason had blown her off. It helped but only to a minuscule degree. His desire for them to be apart merely added to the growing list of unanswered questions.

Then a new barrage of concern assaulted her and had done so throughout the night and early morning. She'd managed to doze for brief snippets of time, but there was no satisfying, meaningful interludes of rest. Her mind raced with fear and worry. The status of their relationship had now taken a back seat to the troubling notion that Jason was in trouble. *What was happening?*

That morning, a Friday, Chrissie bathed again, this time with a shower. When the mirror had fogged, she stepped in, letting the searing needles of water blast her skin.

Normally, Chrissie was an efficient bather. She would put shampoo in her wet hair and allow the lather to sit for a minute while she glided the soaped-up luffa all over her body. Then she would rinse, towel dry and get dressed. She'd once timed the whole process. Five minutes. It was a trait in which she took great pride. She had never been one of those lingering women who took ages to get ready.

But today, she stood under the shower for an eternity, allowing the blistering jets to wash away the horrible visions her mind had conjured during the night. It was the second time in less than twelve hours she'd tried to wash away her anxiety. Both times her attempts had been incomplete and would be temporary.

As she stood under the water, she tried to make sense of everything; a fruitless task considering what little she knew. Her father had temporarily assuaged her angst with his cryptic statements. But something had happened to or with Jason. Something so bad that her father had ordered him to stay away from the pharmacy and have no contact with him or her. Even though, she was no longer angry with Jason for not calling her, now she was equally worried for him. And her frustration and anger had found a new target, her father.

Why had her father had told him not to contact her?

What could be so bad that it could cost him his pharmacy business?

And in the end, she ended up back in the same place, worried about whether she and Jason still had a relationship.

Chrissie turned off the water. She had stayed under the shower so long the water had turned cold. She toweled off and stepped out of the tub. After wiping a curved swath in the fogged mirror, Chrissie gazed at her reflection.

Her eyes belonged to a stranger. They were swollen, drawn and puffy. And at the same time, they seemed to have sunk deeper into her skull. She'd seemed to age several years in less than twenty-four hours. Then her anger flared once more.

No, she told herself. *This was not good enough! To hell with her father.* She was going to get answers. And she was going to get them today.

Ŗ

Chrissie burst through the front door of The Colonial and marched up the center aisle towards the pharmacy. The shower, two cups of coffee and an English muffin with jam on which she had only nibbled had temporarily pushed back the tidal wave of emotion. Going through the mundane motions of the morning, making the bed, getting dressed, and eating breakfast had temporarily halted the torturous slide back into the black abyss.

She saw evidence that something was amiss immediately when she spied an unknown pharmacist behind the counter. *Where was her father?* Then she remembered this would have been Jason's day to work.

An awful gnawing sensation crawled over her skin.

She had called out sick from her own job today. She'd spoken to a junior accountant who also reported to Beatrice the Beast. Luckily, the founding partner was in a meeting and told everyone she was not to be disturbed. She explained to the underling that she didn't feel well. She did not have to mask her voice with feigned illness. Its tone and timbre communicated her horrible physical and mental state.

A teenage cashier was plucking items out of a blue tote and adhering small yellow price stickers on them. The girl was relatively new, and

Chrissie did not remember her name. She greeted the teenager with a tense smile. The cashier nodded at her as she stepped behind the counter and climbed the two steps to the pharmacy.

The relief pharmacist shot her a quizzical, concerned look until Gloria said, "Relax Doc. She used to work here… she's the boss's daughter Hi. Chrissie."

"Where's my father?"

Gloria cocked her head in the direction of the backroom. Chrissie angled towards the entrance to the dark hallway and heard Gloria mumble something about a meeting.

Gloria followed and drew near. She whispered, "What the hell is going on?"

"I intend to find out," she replied.

A small light fixture on the ceiling in the hallway burned naked and tried unsuccessfully to illuminate the narrow space. The resultant effect was dank and hollow, reflecting her mood. Boxes of files and old prescriptions lined the left side, climbing halfway up the wall, leaving a narrow walkway through which one had to angle one's torso to get by. The left wall held no doors. That common wall was shared with the rear of the pharmacy department. On the other side of it sat shelves and bays of drugs totaling almost a million dollars.

The right-hand wall sported three doors. All three were closed. This sight stunned Chrissie. It was an unusual sight and signaled to her the tense and awkward state in which The Colonial found itself. The first door, a supply closet storing vials, paper and other assorted necessities required for operating a pharmacy business, was always open. The third door, a bathroom that her father managed to keep semi-clean, was by necessity always closed. When Chrissie worked here, she tried her best to not use it and refused to clean it. She often used the bathroom at a nearby restaurant where they often ordered sandwiches.

The second door, the middle door, was the object of her focus and the source of her surprise. Her father's office. It, too, was closed. He never, ever closed it. It was literally an open door. Chrissie stepped gently to it, placed her ear on the metal panel and listened.

Muffled voices filtered through the metal from within. But she could not make out anything intelligible. The inflection of the voices behind it were hard and serious. She thought about knocking. But the simple fact that the door was closed told her he would be furious if she did. She hesitated, then retreated to her old workspace at the head of the corridor where she once reconciled invoices and paid bills. That chore had been given over to a new bookkeeper who'd occasionally consulted with Chrissie about procedures and locating certain paperwork. That woman was not here. So, she sat in her former swivel chair and waited.

Gloria saw her sitting there with her hands on her bag sitting in her lap like a patient in a waiting room expecting bad news. Their eyes met. Gloria gave a sympathetic smile and walked over to her in between prescriptions.

"What the hell is going on?" Gloria asked again in a hushed tone.

Chrissie shrugged. "I was hoping you could tell me."

"He's been back there for forty-five minutes," Gloria said. "Yesterday, they were back there for almost two hours."

"Whos' with him?"

Gloria shrugged this time. "Three suits."

"If I find anything out, I'll let you know," Chrissie said.

"Is Jason alright?" Gloria asked.

"Why do you ask?"

"Thomas called him in yesterday on his day off. They met in the office after the suits left. When Jason came out, he looked like a zombie. He had that stare."

"What stare?"

"My grandfather was in Vietnam. He told me about the thousand-yard stare his buddies would have after seeing combat. Jason had it yesterday."

"Really?" Chrissie's heart skipped a beat in her chest and leapt into her throat. Suddenly, the contents in her stomach welled, threatening to explode forth. But she swallowed hard and sucked in some deep breaths.

"I gotta get back to work. We're way behind," she whispered. "This mutton head the relief agency sent doesn't know his ass from his elbow."

Chrissie forced a smile. Gloria went back to the counter while Chrissie continued her vigil.

Thirty minutes later, she was still sitting in the chair. She stood and moved toward the break in the counter leading to the sales floor.

"You leaving?" Gloria asked.

Chrissie nodded.

"You want me to give him a message?"

"Yeah, tell him I'll be back."

℞

Chrissie mashed the doorbell and waited. Thirty seconds later, the door swung open. Jason's mother, Evelyn, peered at her through the screen. "I'm here to see Jason," she said, her voice held the demanding air of someone repressing roiling emotion.

"Hi Darling, come on in," Evelyn replied sympathetically, squeaking open the screen door. Her expression radiated bewilderment and concern.

Chrissie edged past her into the living room and stood rigidly.

Evelyn Rodgers sidled close to Chrissie and placed a gentle hand on her shoulder. "What's going on? We can't get anything out of him," she whispered.

"That's why I'm here," Chrissie said. "I'm trying to find out."

"Follow me," she said.

She led Chrissie down the hall to Jason's closed bedroom door and rapped lightly three times.

"Jason, Chrissie's here to see you."

Silence.

Evelyn tried again, knocking more forcefully. She called to her son louder this time. When there was no answer, she turned to Chrissie, raising her eyebrows and shrugging. "He's been like this since yesterday."

Chrissie moved forward. "May I?"

"Be my guest."

Chrissie stepped in front of Evelyn and knocked a third time. Then she turned the knob and pushed open the door. Light from the hallway illuminated the darkened room like the rotating beam of a lighthouse lantern, revealing dishevelment and disorder. Clothing lay strewn along the perimeter of the bed. An open can of soda, Jason's cell phone and a television remote rested on the nightstand beside a digital clock sitting at an oblique angle. The rumpled bed covers revealed an unmoving human form beneath.

Both women moved to the bedside. Evelyn reached down and shook a bent leg under the sheet. "Jason, get up! Chrissie's here."

Slowly, an arm moved through the air, becoming visible from beneath the comforter and folded it back. Jason's tousled hair and swollen, sullen face came into view in the stark light spilling from the hall.

"Oh, my," Evelyn gasped. Then she sighed. "I'll give you two sometime. I'm going to make some coffee."

When Evelyn was gone, Chrissie sat on the edge of the bed, almost afraid to crowd Jason's space. "Jason, what's going on?"

Jason did not respond for a long, excruciating moment. He lay in profile. His face partly visible. Chrissie watched his chest rise and fall as his eyes studied the wall or something farther beyond. It was as if an invisible force had hold of his gaze and prohibited it from rotating in her direction. A whoosh of breath, a querulous sigh escaped his lips. Then he turned over, laying on his back and, with apparently great effort, moved his eyes toward her.

The sight of him startled her; his red-rimmed eyes fresh with tears; his face and cheeks were puffy; his whole countenance was gripped with anxious fatigue. He looked into her eyes. But it was as Gloria had told her. It was a faraway gaze. The thousand-yard stare.

Chrissie was not seeing *her* Jason, the Jason she'd known just two days ago. This Jason was alien, someone altogether different.

"I'm not supposed to talk about it," he whispered.

"Says who?" She demanded, already knowing the answer.

"Your father. I can't talk about it...not yet."

"When then?"

Jason shrugged and moved his head from side to side. "I don't know."

"Goddammit, Jason. It's me. I'm not going to say anything. Not even to my father. Just tell me what the hell is going on!"

Jason lifted the covers off his body, swung his legs over the side of the bed and stood with enormous effort. His muscles seemed to creak. He wore a rumpled pair of pajama pants and a t-shirt. A pair of jeans, a Polo pullover, a pair of tennis shoes and socks lay scattered around the bed in addition to clothes laying on it.

With leaden legs, he shuffled toward the hall bathroom.

Chrissie raced to intercept him. "Jason! Talk to me!"

He stopped, glaring at her in confusion and irritation like she was a stranger coming up to him on the street. He started to open his mouth, stopped himself and shook his head. He brushed past her and stepped into the hall. She stayed with him, a step behind, refusing to relent.

"Jason!" Chrissie grabbed his arm and tried to swing him around. He yanked his arm away violently, continued his march to the bathroom and closed the door with frustrated force.

After a minute, she heard the toilet flush and the water running in the sink. Evelyn reappeared at the doorway, smoothing her dress and engaging Chrissie's stare with a concerned one of her own. Jason reemerged from the bathroom and padded back into his bedroom.

"Are you going to talk to me or not?"

In the bedroom, Jason pulled back the curtains, allowing the spring sunshine to slice in dagger-like. He stared out the window and spoke to her. "I can't. Not right now! You have to leave."

"What the hell?" Chrissie moved to him and forced herself between the window and Jason. "Jason!"

Jason placed both hands on her shoulders and marched her through the bedroom to the door and into the hallway. Evelyn who had come down the hall had to move quickly out of the way lest she be knocked over. Chrissie faced him, anger brimming. She felt color filling her face. Her hands balled into fists.

"It's bad. Don't ask me again! I'll call you when I can," he hissed. Then he slammed the door in her face.

CHAPTER 53

When Chrissie returned to The Colonial, it was almost noon. Her father's door was now open and the men who had been here earlier had apparently left. He sat alone behind the dented metal desk...sitting slumped and looking forlorn staring at the wall. His focus was miles away.

"Dad?!"

Thomas Pettigrew continued to stare. Chrissie repeated the word. "Daddy?!"

Finally, with tortured slowness, like a battery-powered robot whose charge was fading, Pettigrew rotated his head in her direction.

"Tell me what's the hell is going on!" She demanded with an air of resignation. "I deserve to know." Her words quavered. She swallowed hard, pushing back tears.

Chrissie had wept as she drove from Jason's. Tears flowed with every mile, sometimes like a wide-open spigot. Other times, they dribbled. But they were always present. She had to wipe them away every minute or so just to see the road. She knew she should have pulled over. But the not knowing, the lack of information ate at her, driving her for answers, any answer. So, she kept her foot on the gas, refusing to relent, and blundered her way back to the store.

The behaviors she'd witnessed and were continuing to see from Jason and her father told her something awful, dreadful had happened. It was as if she'd been locked out of a glass room and was being subjected to the torture of watching her loved ones inside being persecuted by an unknown, unseen demon.

When Thomas Pettigrew moved his eyes in her direction, it was the slow and labored movement of a man who might have been drugged. His eyes were distant, unfocused orbs. She had never seen her father like this. Again, fear mounted in her.

He had always been sharp, focused and undeterred in everything he did. Even when Chrissie knew he was dead wrong. There was nothing that could stand in his way. He had been a giant, a hero of a man who had answers to every question and a solution for every problem. But now he was as distracted and as sullen as Jason.

When his gaze finally settled on her, he hesitated as if trying to conjure words but unable to put letters and syllables together coherently. "I can't talk about it, honey." He finally whispered. His voice trailed off.

Chrissie tried again.

Thomas shook his head. "I can't talk about it!" He repeated more forcefully. "Go!"

℞

Simon, Victor and Carl gathered in the small townhouse located in the drab neighborhood a mile east of The Colonial. The laptop rested on the distressed coffee table as they drank in every utterance of the conversation between the distraught Thomas Pettigrew and his confused daughter.

Simon and Victor, still dressed in their dark, expensive, lawyerly suits looked out of place in the dingy apartment with its aging, faded furniture. They looked like men who should be sitting in thick leather chairs around a massive and polished board room table discussing settlements and payouts, not eavesdropping on the anguish of a father and his child. Their shiny, new black briefcases, rested on the threadbare carpet beside the sofa, as out of place as Waterford Crystal in a trailer park.

Over the past forty-eight hours, they had met with Thomas, posing as attorneys for their aggrieved client in two long sessions that totaled more than five hours discussing, lecturing and instilling in the pharmacist a sense of how bleak his future appeared if he did not agree to their demands. Simon, the attorney from another life, had taken the lead in the conversation, using daunting legal terms like "judgments", "punitive damages", "negligent acts and complete indifference or a conscious disregard for safety"; and "high probability of injury or death". Victor stood, resting a bent arm on a filing cabinet in the cramped office and looking dour and serious as if the world might end any moment.

Pettigrew suggested that he should reach out to Ada Mae Renforth's family. Simon cut him off and told him that would be worst possible he could take. From a legal perspective, Simon had told Pettigrew, admitting fault was not advisable. Pettigrew simply sighed. Simon steered the conversation in another direction. Of course, the last thing their op needed was Pettigrew talking to the family.

Carl had monitored their conversation with Pettigrew from the apartment and congratulated the two men upon their return. He assessed their performance. "Simon, you were the consummate lawyer in there. Victor, you jumped in at the right times for emphasis. You repeated the demands that Rodgers was to have no contact with anyone associated with The Colonial and they were not to talk to anyone about the situation themselves. Well done!

"I especially liked how you threatened them with us contacting the Board of Pharmacy which would result in Rodgers losing his license and that Pettigrew would face a lawsuit and the loss of his business I must admit you both exceeded my expectations."

Victor and Simon exchanged congratulatory glances.

From Pettigrew's vacant and mystified demeanor during those interminable meetings and by what they were hearing now on the laptop, they knew he was scared shitless. Pettigrew's attorney had also been present in the tiny office. And the constipated look his face told them Pettigrew's situation was unsalvageable.

"Pettigrew said he needs to talk to his attorney tomorrow," Simon explained.

"I know," Carl replied. "I had one of the agency's attorneys reach out to Pettigrew's partner while you were in with them yesterday. He explained that there's not enough liability insurance to cover him in this scenario. Pettigrew's lawyer seemed genuinely concerned. There were no histrionics, no counter demands, no threats to fight it.

"It turns out," Carl continued, "that Pettigrew's attorney had been begging him to increase his coverage. But Pettigrew stalled."

"So now what?" Victor asked.

Carl nodded. "Okay. Well done. Let him stew for three days. He said Jason Rodgers has been placed on leave and instructed not to talk to anyone. On Wednesday, we will go in get him to sign the letter of intent. And we go from there."

℞

Three days elapsed, wearing on like slow, creeping lava burning a hole in her. It was now Thursday. Chrissie woke as she had done every day for the previous week: in a foul mood. She laid in the bed staring up at the ceiling but not seeing it, still focused on the unknown. The fingers of her mind clawed at the bumpy, uneven walls of the deep cave into which Jason and her father had thrown her. Her fitful sleep was anything but restful. When she did manage to doze off, the brief episodes of unconsciousness had been punctuated by harsh, ugly nightmares which caused her to jolt awake in sweaty, breathless spasms.

After fifteen minutes of laying on her back, she summoned the emotional and physical energy to face another day of uncertainty. She dragged herself from under the bed clothes with great difficulty and padded to the bathroom. She ran another steaming hot shower. *How many times had she tried to scrub away her fear and worry with scalding water?* she asked herself. Though her body was as clean as angel's ass, her mind was littered with the devil's detritus of darkness and doubt. When she emerged and toweled off, she went to her phone and saw she had received a phone call from...him.

The message was emotionally void and flat-toned as if any vestige of personality had been scooped out of his soul, "Call me when you get this."

In the last seventy-two hours, Chrissie's life had become a series of perfunctory tasks that held no meaning or purpose. To say she was a basket case was like saying Bill Gates was just another millionaire. Her work at the accounting firm suffered. She lacked focus and clarity. On Wednesday, Beatrice the Beast finally inquired. She told him she was dealing with a family emergency.

"You should have told me, Christine." Without hesitation and uncharacteristically, she followed with, "You're more efficient than some of my fulltime accountants. Take the rest of the week off."

Chrissie apologized, gathered her purse and stuffed some files into her leather bag. "Thank you. I'll get some work done at home."

At home, she logged a few hours on her laptop, but truly little of value had been accomplished.

She went by the pharmacy every day, taking extended lunches so she could attempt to pry information from her father. With whatever crisis was gripping everyone, he was at the store even on days he wasn't scheduled to work. He rebuffed her questions more forcefully each time she asked. Finally, his anger and frustration boiled over.

"Christine, mind your own business, please!" He'd blurted.

The words and their harsh delivery stung. Her father had never spoken to her in that manner in all her years. They still rang in her ears now as she punched up Jason's cell, hoping against hope to get him on the phone. He answered after five rings.

"Jason?" She said quickly, thinking he might hang up.

His words were slow, unhurried, the response cold, resigned.

"We need to talk," he said. It was a statement not a question. "I'll pick you up in two hours." He did not wait for a response. The line went dead.

℞

"What?"

Victor let the word hang in the air. He had uttered it as if he'd not understood the statement that had preceded it. The portly spy was on the phone with their case officer Carl in Langley, Virginia who had returned to his office two days ago. Victor and Simon had watched Thomas Pettigrew sign his letter of intent to sell a few hours ago. It was sitting on the coffee table.

Then the words of the man on the other end of the line began to sink in. Victor's first reaction was to check that the small, round red light on the phone was illuminated, signifying that their call was being encrypted. His second reaction was a question, harder and more accusatory in nature.

"Are you fucking shitting me?"

The words slipped from Victor's lips in a higher pitch but were still the words of a man who was having trouble believing what he'd heard and trying to absorb their incredulous meaning.

Victor's harsh, rude question caused Simon who was in the kitchen leaning on the counter sipping a from a tumbler filled with iced tea. He had raised his glass toward his mouth when Victor's second question prompted him to push himself off the counter and march into the living area.

Simon mouthed the words, "What's going on?" He removed the Mont Blanc pen from his shirt pocket and began twirling…rapidly.

Victor regarded his partner then rolled his eyes with a combination of disgust and frustration. Simon could hear Carl's muffled, unintelligible words coming through the handset pressed to Victor's ear. The tone was that of a supervisor explaining a hard but unpopular choice.

Victor interrupted Carl in mid-sentence. "We just ruined this guy's life. We just had a woman killed! How the…"

Victor stopped speaking, his anger consuming him.

"What's going on?" Simon asked again this time in a full-throated voice.

The pitch of Carl's voice through the phone ratcheted higher. Again, Simon could not make out their meaning. But the rapid nature, tone and timber told him that Carl was lecturing his partner about who was in charge and that a decision had come down that Simon did not like but he must accept.

Victor listened to the tongue-lashing for a full minute before replacing the handset on the base.

"So?" Simon demanded again.

Victor ran a frustrated hand through his thinning hair front to back then scratched his scalp rapidly as if trying to dislodge crawling creatures from it. He finally cast his eyes toward Simon.

"What did he say?" Simon demanded.

℞

The two hours had elapsed torturously. They were the longest Chrissie had ever endured. Seconds ticked by like decades. The large wall-mounted clock's minute hand appeared to be struggling against a clear, viscous liquid inside its glass, fighting to make its arc around the circle. She brooded in the living room on the couch that backed up to the large picture window. Her arm rested on its back as she gazed out onto the street.

"Chrissie, honey," her mother said, appearing from the kitchen. "What is going on with you...and your father? Both of you are acting like zombies!" Her voice was clogged with uncertainty.

Chrissie ignored the question and continued to gaze out the window. Then her mother's footfalls faded away. She did not know how much time had passed but eventually her mother said she was going out. Chrissie thought she heard her say where she was going and when she would be back. But the words had not registered.

Beyond the large picture window in the parlor, a clear, gorgeous sun-soaked day yawned. The cloudless azure sky floated above the loblolly pines and the maples. Two weeks ago, she would have marveled at its beauty and headed off to a job she loved, her work filled with spreadsheets and numbers and the promise of a carefree evening caressed by a warm spring breeze as she ate dinner with the man she loved. The same man who over the last week had ignored her like a pedestrian avoiding a panhandler on the sidewalk. When she'd pressed him, he snapped at her to get away and leave him alone. He had even physically put his hands on her and pushed her out of his bedroom.

Now, he wanted to talk. Chrissie scoffed audibly as a wry smile curved up one side of her face.

The words he'd spoken held no hint of hope or reconciliation. It held not even a pinch of remorse. Chrissie feared this meeting with Jason would only make her life more tortured.

Outside the large window cars had slid past, their engines pitching high, then fading in a low drone as they disappeared. Joggers ran by their footfalls silent through the glass. A small postal van slipped from mailbox to mailbox like a squirrel scurrying from tree to tree. Life continued, she thought. No matter what, life continued. No one else knew or cared about her suffering. The world was oblivious to her pain.

The wait on the sofa had been one long stretch of anxiety-filled desperation. The urge to weep had swelled several times. But she steeled herself, pushing back the raw emotion. Thank God her mother had left. She did not want her to see her like this. She did not want to answer any more of her questions.

Though most of the wait was unbearable, for brief interludes, hope sparked within her. Maybe, she told herself, they can get past whatever the hell is going on...and start again. She just needed to get Jason to talk to her. After all, he did say, they needed to talk. But then her paranoia would well once more, forcing her hopes down like a hand pushing her head under water, drowning her.

Finally, two hours and eleven minutes after they spoke on the phone, she saw Jason's Honda slip into the driveway. He honked twice. But Chrissie had exited the house before the second blast. She started down the front walk at a quick, anxious pace, then forced herself to slow down. Her legs were two numb cement logs smashing along the concrete.

The first thing she noticed was his face. It was in worse shape than when she'd last seen him. His eyes were leaden and rheumy. The eyelids more swollen. Dark pockets hung beneath his eyes. The fun, the gleaming sparkle was gone. Jason Rodgers was a ghost with skin.

Chrissie climbed in.

℞

"Are you fucking shitting me?" Simon spat, repeating Victor's words from minutes ago. He'd repeated those words at least four times in the short interval since Victor had informed him of the news.

Victor repeated his statement to his partner as if her were trying to convince himself it was true. "The operation is over.!"

They both took seats on the dilapidated, threadbare furniture, Simon on the sofa and Victor on the recliner. A long, leaden silence ensued.

After what felt like an eon, Simon spoke. "This is so much worse than Italy," he croaked.

"I don't like it either," Victor agreed. "But we were only following orders. We're spies. We do some nasty and ugly stuff. We don't decide what actions are taken. We only carry out the orders."

Simon glared at his partner. "We were responsible for an old lady's death. An innocent old lady who did nothing except be a patient of The Colonial."

"Yeah, but we didn't actually kill her," Victor declared as if this fact alone would absolve him.

"No," Simon replied somberly. "Is that going allow you to sleep at night?"

Victor shook his head as both lapsed into another state of shocked contemplation. They had killed before. But their victims had always been corrupted or evil men who stood in the way of the greater good. Men like the Argentinian dictator, Cesar Garcia.

They hadn't liked killing an old woman. But they were on shaky ground because of their fiasco in Bologna. They had justified their actions with the fact that the woman had lived a long life and her family would be compensated handsomely. But now, they learned that their actions and the plan to bring down Thomas Pettigrew was being scrapped for some unknown reason that was above their pay grade.

"How do these assholes on the seventh floor live with themselves?' Victor asked rhetorically.

The pair had put in motion the plan to "eliminate" Ada Mae Renforth and make her death look like a drug error committed by Jason Rodgers, the-pharmacy-student-turned-druggist. They had been responsible for taking a life and ruining one. They had employed-with Langley's approval-a reliable contract killer who had replaced Renforth's diltiazem pills with a different medication, pilocarpine which causes excessive salivation. The pilocarpine had been obtained from an agency contact in northern Virginia.

The assassin had snuck into the victim's house and forced her to swallow several tablets of the pilocarpine. He subdued her for several hours while the medication took effect. Renforth lived alone and had already checked-in with her family for the evening as was her custom. The killer waited for the old septuagenarian to finish her call then broke in.

The woman was frail and weak. He had no trouble forcing her into the bedroom. He tied her to her bed with her head and neck hanging over the foot and her feet pointed toward the head. Using restraints cushioned with small pads so as not to create ligature marks, he held her in her bedroom, petrified beyond belief, as he waited for the pilocarpine to take effect.

When her salivary glands began producing their product, he aided the process by producing a bottle of artificial saliva. Hyperextending her neck over the end of the bed, he secured it by the forehead with a soft, cotton-lined cloth so that her throat was exposed. Without the aid of drugs or anesthetics, he produced an intubation kit and slid a plastic tube down her throat.

The assassin forced the artificial saliva into the tube that had been passed by her trachea and into her lungs. The old woman gagged and sputtered as he carefully removed the tube. She coughed and gurgled as she began drowning.

The killer then used his gloved hands to clamp her mouth and nose closed. He applied pressure for nearly a minute suffocating Ada Mae Renforth and making it look like an apparent laryngospasm secondary to aspirating her own saliva.

Simon peered at Victor. "Why is the operation cancelled? Did he tell you?"

"He refused to go into specifics. He just said that the intel the Agency had received about the infiltrators into this area and the sleeper cells they were forming was erroneous. Proven to be invalid. So the op is over. He wants us to pack up and be outta here in forty-eight hours."

Simon shook his head as nausea clawed at his throat. There was only one string of words that came to his lips. He sighed the words that in the last minutes had become a mantra with a solemn resignation. "Are you fucking shittin' me!?

℞

Jason did not speak. He had simply shifted into reverse and backed out of the driveway. As Jason drove, he never took his eyes off the road. Except for a brief glance over at her as she entered the car, he never set eyes upon her.

"Where are we going?" She asked.

Jason's lips scrunched into a frown. He lifted his shoulders in a pseudo-shrug but did not respond. Chrissie tried three more times to engage him with questions. Each time Jason let them slip by without a reply.

"Fine," she finally said. "if that's the way you want it." She folded her arms in front of her and stewed. Her anxiety and anger multiplied with each mile.

Jason turned off West Mercury Boulevard just before they reached the James River Bridge. He parked the Honda in the small parking area north of Huntington Beach at the junction of the bridge and the shoreline. He turned off the ignition and said, "Let's walk."

He walked ahead of her, slowly, like a man going to his own execution. Chrissie trailed a step behind and to Jason's right. Then he realized he was ahead of her and paused to wait. He removed a hand from his pocket and reached it out.

Chrissie glared at it the extended palm like it held a deadly virus. Jason held it there. Chrissie finally extended her hand and placed her hand in his. The temperature outside was warm, probably near seventy, she thought. But his skin was cold and clammy. At first, her hand and body were rigid and unreceptive. They walked for fifteen yards. Then, involuntarily, she interlaced her fingers with his.

Despite the tension between them, it felt good to finally touch him. They had not touched each other meaningfully for two weeks. They had been so busy the week before all this, whatever this was, they had not seen each other. Then seven days ago, something had happened and the Jason Rodgers she knew and loved had vanished.

It was May. Springtime in Virginia was a bright, warm brilliant explosion of sunshine and warmth. And today was no exception. The clear, cloudless sky floated over the choppy, blue-brown wavelets of the James River. The breeze rustled the trees as they trudged along a paved path to a flat swath of green land perched above the east bank of the river. Jason veered to his left onto the grassy expanse.

Chrissie could not bring herself to look at Jason as they walked along under the shade of the wide oaks and tall maples. Her gut somersaulted with each step. She could not feel her feet inside her white tennis shoes connecting on the soft lawn. She focused instead on the line of trees in the distance on the opposite bank of the river. Five miles west lay the heavily wooded shoreline of Isle of Wight County where Jason and Chrissie had driven over the bridge almost two years earlier to the Vintage Tavern restaurant on their first date. That evening seemed like another era, a bygone yellowed, faded chapter of their lives. Chrissie felt as if she were outside her own body, observing with an impartial, detached mien, but feeling everything. Every movement, every caress of Jason's cold skin sent shivers of pulsing emotion through her. It was like she was watching a surgeon operate on her without anesthesia...and feeling every tug and cut.

He led her to an iron bench in the center of the expanse, the idyllic scene lost on both. They sat. Then he turned and faced her. But he did not look at her. He took both of her hands in his. But instead of gazing into her eyes, he studied the two pairs of hands resting on his knee. Then Jason peered out over the water. Tears welled in his eyes.

Without warning, Chrissie's eyes watered as well. After a moment, she started to sob. The fear, the not knowing what Jason was going to say and at the same time, knowing exactly what his message would be, felt like a hanging judge passing sentence, a death sentence. She clutched his hands tighter, steeling herself. Then she floated a desperate notion, hoping it would explain his actions and bring everything send everything back to the way it had been.

"Tell me this is a joke. Tell me it's your way of punking me. The way I did you those times. Please tell me that's what this is." Chrissie's eyes pleaded with him. "If it is, it's one sick joke. But I'll forgive you."

Jason blurted out his next statement with the urgency of a message that would evaporate if the words weren't delivered in a rushed torrent. Each syllable spilling forth from his lips became a bullet piercing her heart. "It's no joke, Chrissie. I don't want to see you anymore. I'm leaving The Colonial too. I can't stay. I'm...sorry."

Hearing the words spoken aloud caused the air to be sucked from her lungs. Suddenly, she could not breathe. She tried and failed to pull sweet oxygen into her chest. and gasped. It was as if the earth's atmosphere had suddenly been sucked into outer space. She continued to wheeze, clutching at her belly which had seized with spasms.

She couldn't know for sure how long her episode of suffocation lasted. But it felt eternal. Eventually, minute wisps of air seeped into her lungs. "Jason," she choked as rivulets of tears streaked down her face. "Why? Talk to me....Please....talk....to me!"

Chrissie squeezed his hands with hers, she did not want, could not release him. *It couldn't end this way. What had happened?*

They sat for a long time on the bench, hands interlocked. Both were crying. Both racked with sobs. And yet neither of them could summon the strength to speak.

Finally, she whispered. "I don't understand...I don't understand."

Jason sat motionless; his eyes averted. As anger flared, she ripped her hands from his. She'd lost count of how many times anger had filled her in the last week. "Take me home," she demanded in a low, wounded growl.

Jason reached into his jacket pocket and removed something. He lifted her hand and placed something round and smooth in it. When he removed his hand, Chrissie saw the polished crimson Heart Stone she had given him in Myrtle Beach after he'd passed his pharmacy board exam. That night on the beach had been the first time she confessed her love for him.

Up until this moment, it had been a talisman representing her feelings for him. She had used it to demonstrate to him all the feelings and love she possessed. But in this instant, it looked like a crimson nugget of radioactivity, spewing unseen rays of hatred and anguish.

Chrissie regarded the small, polished rock with disgust. She reached out and grabbed his hand and placed it back in his palm. "You keep it."

The three simple words were laced with disdain and delivered through a curtain of tears.

In the years that followed, Chrissie would forever remember the pain and torment of this day. But the actual events, the minutiae of what happened and in what order, would become blurred and fuzzy. The sharp stab of pain, though dulled, by time would never leave her. She did not remember the walk back to the car or the drive back to her house in Newport News. Jason's words and actions, especially today's, numbed her. Her surroundings and her passage through them did not register in her confused brain. Chrissie had shut down, her mind trying to protect her. She sank into an anesthetic chasm, oblivious to the world around her.

This episode, whatever it was, would also driving a lasting wedge between Chrissie and her father. It would spawn an obsession in her father that would doom his relationship with his only child.

When Jason's Honda bumped over the end of the driveway, she was jolted out of her paralyzed state. Fury outmuscled despair. Though every fibrous strand in her body screamed for her not to, Chrissie put her shoulder into the door. It squealed in protest when it swung open and she climbed out. Every inch that she moved farther away from Jason, her heart plunged miles into a bottomless hole.

She pushed the door closed to another equally agonizing squeal and leaned in through the open window. Her watery feelings mounted one last charge.

"Don't do this! I love you!"

For some unknown reason, Chrissie focused on his throat. Jason did not look at her. His eyes were down cast. His Adam's apple bobbed as he swallowed a moment before he spoke. The fact that Jason would not look at her through all of this, hurt as much as, if not more than, his spoken words. He spoke to her... for the final time with his eyes still riveted on his hands wrapped tightly around the steering wheel.

"I'm sorry, Chrissie. I really am."

Then without warning or another word, Jason jerked the gear shift lever into reverse and gunned the accelerator. Chrissie backed up a moment before the car began to move. She watched the Honda recklessly back into the street. The tires squealed as he sped off. The car paused at the stop sign at the end of the street. The brake lights flared, burning through her like a laser. Turning right, the Honda shrank into the distance, and the gnarled, hulking mass that had taken up domicile inside her seemed to explode.

She trudged toward the front door, once again enveloped by the darkness of the numbed, inky cavern enveloping her. When the front door clicked closed, it signaled the moment of release. The sluices of emotion opened their valves and released her pent-up tension blasting through the spillways. Chrissie collapsed onto the cold, tiled floor in the small foyer and wailed.

℞

Jason drove trance-like along the busy roads of Newport News. He had hesitated at the stop sign at the end of her street, but he had not come to a complete stop. He'd allowed his eyes to move to the rear-view mirror. The image vibrated under the rough influence of the aging engine. In that shaky reflection, Chrissie stood in her driveway, facing the Honda. He could not make out her face, her eyes or her mouth. But in the low hunch of her shoulders, Jason could see the massive dose of pain he'd delivered had begun to manifest itself.

Tears flooded his eyes. Chrissie's image seemed to dissolve before him in the small oval of glass. Jason wiped them away with the knuckle of his left hand and she reappeared. He stepped on the gas. Then the sight of Christine Pettigrew slipped from the mirror.

He did not remember anything about the trip home. He did not remember stopping at any of the traffic lights along the route to his parents' home in a tree-lined section of lower York County. He would not remember what songs played on the radio. He did not recall getting out of the car or unlocking the front door. The sensation of hitting his bed shocked him back to the now. As his head hit the soft, cool pillow on his freshly made bed, Jason remembered the one time he'd sneaked a glimpse at Chrissie's face while they sat on the bench on the escarpment overlooking the river.

The image would remain branded in his mind: her face contorted with pain; the eyes scrunched closed as tears streamed down ruddy cheeks; her beautiful soft lips thrust forward and pursed as if by an invisible drawstring; her lower lip quivering as the tears leaked over them. Then the image was quickly replaced by the image he'd seen in the car's mirror. The slumped sullen carriage of Chrissie's body was reflected, vibrating in the clear glass oval.

Jason wept, sobbing like a small child as he lay on his belly, his cheek pressed against the pillow. His sight partially obscured by the pillowcase. He saw only a Dali-like image of his dresser and open closet.

His life had been destroyed. One day his life had been perfect, poised for a rich and vibrant future. In the next, it was in flames, descending through Dante's nine levels of hell. For the last seven days, he'd been subjected to emotions and feelings he'd never wish on his worst enemy.

How had all this happened?

How would he recover?

The questions assailed him again like feral dogs nipping at a carcass. Tearing little chunks of flesh from his mind. The thousands of pin pricks of sharp teeth stabbed at him. As the answerless questions barraged him, Jason wrapped his arms around his head, shielding himself from the attack.

He screamed, the sound of his voice echoing inside his head. Then there was silence.

Jason, too, in the years to come would question the mistake he'd made that had led to Ada Mae Renforth's death. When the pain and shock of this moment subsided, Jason would remember the day Gloria had spilled Ada Mae's pills all over the floor. He would recall how they had gathered up the scattered tablets. And how they'd thrown the tablets out and replaced them. Then he would recall how he had double, and triple checked the prescription for accuracy. In the years that followed, Jason would come to question if he'd, in fact, committed the error as Thomas had described. It would be a question that would haunt him for more than a decade.

In fact, it would be thirteen years before another set of untoward events would lead him back to The Colonial and allow him to scratch away at the truth. Only then would he begin the journey to the truth. And even then, he might never truly know everything.

But, right now, in the epicenter of emotion and hurt and despondency, Jason did not have the ability to summon the memory of that day or the logic to question what he was being told. Right now, all he could do was fight off a tidal wave of numbing anguish.

Then, finally, another question came to him, whispered and devilish, sounding like a death knell in his mind. It did not attack him. It was not accusatory. But it, nonetheless, held great torment.

Would he ever see her again?

It was a simple query, soft and mild. But the response was only a haunting, eerie silence.

Enjoy this excerpt from *The Cyclops Conspiracy*,
the sequel to David Perry's *The Extern*.

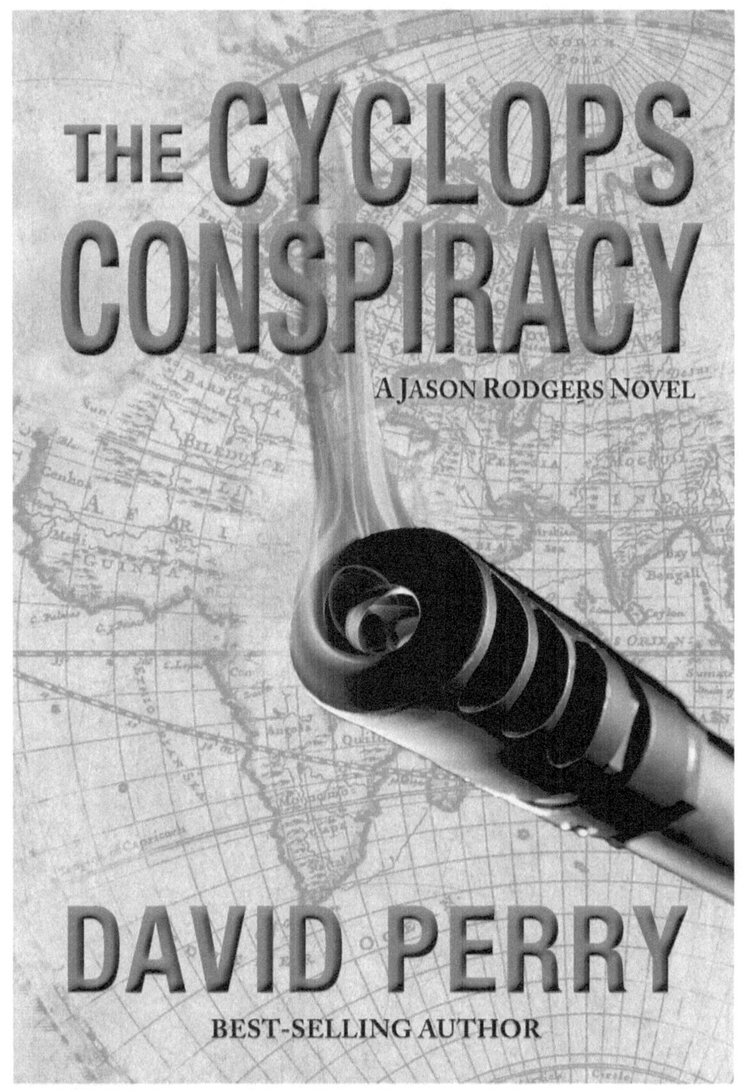

CHAPTER 1

Jason waited for the door to his tortured past to swing open.

Having just rung the bell, he fidgeted on the stoop. His secret had haunted him for thirteen years. Separated from it now by only a thickness of wood and glass, he couldn't believe he was actually standing here, once again, after all these years.

The door opened, and a hunched old woman peered at him. "I'm Jason—Jason Rodgers," he said, the words catching in his throat.

"Chrissie warned me you might be coming by," croaked the elderly woman in a heavy Italian accent. "Please come in." Her voice was filled with kindness, but her eyes penetrated Jason Rodgers as if she were already familiar with his history.

"Over the years, the deep pain had faded, leaving only hollow regret. His secret had been confined to a dull ache in the recesses of his analytical mind. Every once in a while though, a sight or a sound would trigger an agonizing flashback. He'd remember the pained look on Chrissie's face. Or the hangdog visage of his mentor, Thomas, Chrissie's father.

Those ghostly memories never really went away, and now, stirred as Jason stepped through the door into the Newport News, Virginia, colonial-style house. It had been Thomas Pettigrew's home for thirty-plus years and where he'd picked Chrissie up for their first date. His lungs seized, unable to push out air.

Though not responsible, Thomas had been at center stage in the episode that nearly ended Jason's pharmacy career before it began—and at the same time—doomed his love affair with Chrissie. The man's tutelage had shaped Jason's pharmacy career. In the thirteen years since he'd left, Jason felt as if he'd failed both of them. The least he could do was attend the funeral of the man who'd given him his start.

He'd seen Chrissie graveside. It was an awkward reunion, one that Jason highly anticipated and deeply dreaded. Thomas was, after all, her father. She had every right to be pissed off at Jason. Her first reaction was a nervous smile and a stiff hug. They exchanged a few words, and then she made an offer that shocked him: to join her at her father's house for the funeral reception. His internal struggle was a monumental one, but in the end, Jason knew it was an invitation he would not decline. Nonetheless, he was daunted by the thought of actually setting foot in this house again; of actually talking for the first time to the only woman he ever really loved.

Long ago, his actions had blindsided her, in an excruciatingly painful way. Of course, he hadn't been around to see the pain he'd caused. But Jason knew how deeply Chrissie had loved him. he could deduce from the agony he himself had suffered that Chrissie's pain was magnified by unanswered questions. For many reasons, and for many years, he'd hoped and prayed for the opportunity to make her understand his actions.

The old woman had said "warned". Despite the ominous implications of the word, a question nagged him. Had Chrissie been thinking about him after all these years?

"Did you find the house alright?" asked the old woman, her voice chalky and exhausted by life.

Jason nodded. "Yes, thank you," he replied, unable to force more than a whisper past the lump in his throat. I've been here before! he thought.

She offered him a hand spider-webbed with blue veins. "I've been Thomas's neighbor for five years. "I've been helping Chrissie with the funeral. I'm experienced with this sort of thing—my Giuseppe passed last year."

Jason frowned, unable to muster any sympathy for the woman. "I'm sorry," he said mechanically, looking over her shoulder to the small gathering of mourners.

"You and Chrissie were lovers many years ago, weren't you?"

Jason's gut clenched, and she saw his reaction.

"I see the pain in her eyes when she speaks of you. These eyes," she said, tapping her temple and then her chest, "and this heart have seen a lot." She leaned closer. "What happened?'

Jason stepped back, too stunned to answer her question.

"I know it's forward of me," she said, touching his arm as if keeping him from running away. "But I'm an old lady who doesn't have much time left. I speak my mind. No time for bullshit! And I see it in Chrissie's eyes—she truly loved you. Whatever you did wrong, you might still have a chance with her."

Jason felt his eyebrows lift at the audacity of the woman's words. What stung more was their accuracy. It had been more than a decade since Jason dumped Christine. And only one other person on this earth had known why. Thomas, Chrissie's father, had sworn Jason to secrecy. But Thomas was gone now.

That left Jason holding the secret like a rucksack filled with the weight of a thousand universes.

Was he released from his obligation now that Thomas was gone? Jason had asked himself that question a hundred times in the last few days.

The old woman waved a hand. "But there are more pressing matters today, no?"

"Yes," said Jason, relieved the conversation was veering in another direction.

"Thomas's death was so tragic and so sudden," she said, placing a hand to her cheek. "He was un uomo buono."

"What?"

"A good man." She leaned in once more. "I'll tell Chrissie you're here. There's food and drink in the kitchen if you're hungry." She winked a paper-thin eyelid. "Good luck! Tread lightly!"

Jason shook his head slowly as he watched her shuffle through a klatch of mourners. He waited nervously in the foyer. Guests cast him sideways glances. He avoided them and studied the once familiar surroundings.

The décor hadn't changed. This house had been his second home during their courtship. The familiar layout was thick with painful memories. The sparkle in Chrissie's eyes as she descended the stairs on their first date. Bacon, lettuce and tomato sandwiches at the kitchen table. Late night movies on the television, ignored in the darkened living room as hands probed hungry flesh beneath blankets.

Outside, the house had not seen a fresh coat of paint in years, though Jason noticed a small satellite dish sloppily attached to a downstairs window. Apparently, Thomas had made a weak attempt to enter the new century.

The six-foot portrait of Thomas and his wife Eleanor still hung on the same wall in the foyer. No one who entered could miss it. Thomas stood regally behind his wife as she sat in an ornate chair, smiling stiffly.

The gilded frame's tiny crevices were caked with dust. Surrounding the piece, the wallpaper's glow had faded to a dull matte finish.

Jason overheard a woman whispering about the tragic circumstances of Pettigrew's death. The word "alcohol" reached his ear as if Satan himself had hissed it. Jason glared at the woman, ready to walk over to her and set her straight. But she was too engrossed in herself to notice him. His outrage rose another few degrees. There was no way he'd driven drunk! Not Thomas Pettigrew!

It was then that he spied Chrissie in the living room speaking with two older women. Probably acquaintances of Thomas. She was not facing him, but he studied her face from an angle. To say Chrissie was attractive was a gross understatement. She was drop-dead, you're-in-heaven-before-hitting-the-floor-gorgeous. Her chestnut hair cascaded to her shoulders, curling behind petite ears. Sexy and understated, the style framed a perfect face and reminded you that a brain that crunched numbers like a supercomputer resided beneath. Her conservative dress, a tan blazer with matching skirt and low brown pumps, and an ivory blouse open at the neck, could never hide the firm curves of ample breasts and sleek hips.

Her cherubic appearance and rambunctious, passionate nature had, most certainly, been tempered by the travails of life. Travails to which, he was certain, he had in no small part contributed. What had happened in her life? What had he given up? The sight of her told him one thing: she was not a frail, broken woman crushed by the weight of a failed love. Hers was a tested, demure confidence set in an unflappable foundation of femininity.

Christine caught his eye, excused herself from the women, and walked toward him. As she approached, Jason's stomach flipped as if her were on the first death-defying plunge of a roller coaster. God, she's still gorgeous, he thought.

Her lips formed a thin line. "Jason," she said. "I'm glad you could come." Her eyes were rimmed in red as she forced a smile and took his hands in hers.

Her voice sparked something in his chest. "I'm so sorry about your father, Chrissie. He was a great man, and a giant in pharmacy," he said softly. "He gave me my start."

"I remember, Jason. I was there," she replied, releasing his hands. "Come into the kitchen."

They faced each other from across a small island.

"How are you?" she asked stiffly. "Are you still over at Keller's?"

Her eyes alternated uncomfortably between the counter and Jason.

"Actually," he replied. "I'm sort of between jobs right now." He didn't mention that, only three days ago, he'd resigned from his position as pharmacy manager at Keller's Food and Drug. The poor and potentially dangerous working conditions, which he'd tried so hard to redress, had finally defeated him.

"Really? Daddy told me a year or so ago that you seemed to love it over there."

"How would he know? I hadn't spoken to him in years."

"He had a lot of connections in pharmacy. He kept tabs on you, I'm sure. So, why the change?"

"Well," he said, ignoring the question. "I'm not completely out the door yet. They're trying to lure me back."

"Interesting." The word had an ominous tone. Unasked questions and issues floated beneath the surface like submerged icebergs.

"The question is, how are you?" asked Jason. "I know how hard all this is." He meant to sound solicitous. But after all this time and his lengthy absence, it sounded lame to his own ears."

"Thanks. It's a lot easier than it looks."

"What do you mean?"

Christine waved the question away. The old woman returned with a glass of iced tea for Jason. "Would you like some Swedish meatballs or finger sandwiches?" she asked Jason.

"No, thank you." Jason set the glass on the counter and ignored it.

The woman looked between them. "Christine, if you need anything, I'll be in the living room."

"Thank you, Mrs. Liggieri."

"She seems like a big help," he said, when they were alone again.

He thought about the woman's earlier comments and cringed.

"You have no idea. The night Daddy died—" She choked. "I came to the house looking for him. When I couldn't find him, I called the police. Mrs. Liggieri came over to make sure everything was alright. Later, after we found out he was—dead—she helped me with everything. I think she enjoys it. She knows how to bury someone properly." Moisture glistened in her eyes.

Jason smiled and said, "Old people always do."

Christine chuckled, blinking back tears. He wanted to reach out to her, to comfort her. But he was too far away, physically and emotionally, so he stood frozen in place.

Mrs. Liggieri reappeared. "Christine, honey," she said, "Ms. Zanns and her doctor friend have stopped by."

On the heels of the old woman strutted a small, elegant woman dressed in a navy business suit. She wore no expensive jewelry or rings, yet wealth and authority oozed from her. Her prim ensemble contrasted oddly with an ancient-looking amulet hanging from her neck. Wisps of gray dotted her temples, but her smooth skin gleamed like tan porcelain. The woman appeared irritated at the slow gait of Chrissie's neighbor, as if she were late for a meeting and did not have time to be held up.

Close behind the new woman followed a tall, lithe, and much younger woman. They were introduced to Jason as Lily Zanns and Dr. Jasmine Kader.

"Please," Zanns instructed Jason when he used their last names. "It's Lily and Jasmine." Zanns turned to Christine. "I apologize, Christine, but Sam couldn't be here. With your father's passing, we have a hole in our staffing. He's covering the pharmacy until we can find a suitable replacement. Of course, I don't think anyone could replace your father." Her thick Mediterranean-French accent was roughened by a guttural throatiness.

Christine forced another tight smile. "Thank you, Lily." Mrs. Liggieri motioned to her once again. "I'd better go see what my neighbor needs. Excuse me."

Kader, Zanns and Jason smiled stiffly, enduring a pregnant awkwardness.

Jason broke the silence. "So you own The Colonial now?" It was more a statement than a question. Thomas Pettigrew had sold The Colonial to this woman three or four years earlier. Pharmacists Jason had spoken to over the years had given her stewardship mixed reviews.

"Yes," replied Zanns. "For three and a half years now."

"And Thomas stayed on to work for you?"

"Yes, he said he wasn't quite ready to retire." She paused, then added, "His death was so…tragic."

Jason nodded solemnly. Jasmine Kader caught his eye. They shared an awkward smile.

"And how is it that you knew Thomas?" Zanns inquired.

"I was a pharmacy student of his."

"Of course. The pharmacy profession, like most, is a small community, isn't it?"

"Yes, it is. In fact, I work at Keller's, and I've filled many of the prescriptions your colleague Jasmine has written."

Zanns's dark brown eyes suddenly seemed to become alert with possibility. "I see," she said slowly. Then she quickly excused herself and moved off to speak with someone who was waving at her. Jasmine wandered in the direction of the food, leaving Jason alone.

The urge to bolt was formidable; he felt as if his sins against Chrissie were being broadcast on a moving teletype across his chest, like sports scores, for all these strangers to see. And naturally, Chrissie was distant, distracted and in mourning. *She just buried her father,* Jason thought. *Had you truly expected…?*

He ambled through the house, trying to shake off his uneasiness. The mere act of walking eased his anxiety slightly. The dining room table was covered with potluck platters, which were being largely ignored. He scanned faces, hoping for a friendly port in which to drop a conversational anchor. But he was miles from shore, and the seas were choppy. He circled twice.

On his final lap, he noticed a tall man who looked as out of place as he did, standing alone in a corner. With a gray, fuzzy ponytail, a fraying tweed jacket, and cratered skin, the man looked like a cross between a beardless Abe Lincoln and Willie Nelson. His eyes darted about, studying everyone, and locked on Jason's. They each nodded, kindred souls stuck in the abyss of social awkwardness.

Jason was about to drift over and strike up a conversation with the fellow misfit, when he spotted Christine, moving through the kitchen into the dining room. She was alone, trying to find some privacy. Tears lined her cheeks. She was overcome with emotion. Jason entered from the living room. Though it was not his to give, he wanted to offer understanding, support. A small voice inside him cautioned him to leave her alone, but he ignored it, intercepting her near the oak buffet.

Christine spotted him, wiped her eyes with the heel of her hand, and avoided his eyes. She let out an exasperated sigh, communicating with a wave of her hand what words could not. Jason reached for a paper napkin from a stack on the table and handed it to Chrissie. "Come with me," he said. He grasped her hand, and an electric jolt coursed through his body. He led her out the back door onto the porch, and sat on the top step. He patted the spot beside him. "Sit."

Chrissie complied. They stared out at the backyard in silence for a long moment as Jason tried to organize his thoughts. "I remember how hard it was burying my father five years ago," he began. "He had a massive heart attack. Died where he was standing and was gone before he hit the floor. I know how you feel, Chrissie."

Chrissie studied the steps and did not speak. Jason saw her lower lip quivering. "Jason, why did you come by today?"

"You invited me when I saw you at the funeral. Remember?"

"I know that. I didn't think you'd actually accept."

"I guess I owed it to your father...and you," Jason replied. He turned to look at her. "Why did you invite me?"

Christine sighed. "Seeing you at the funeral brought me back to happier times. At least, they were happier until you..." Her voice trailed off.

Jason scanned the backyard. The lawn was dying, yellow, and overgrown, sprouting weeds. He wanted to crawl into it and die himself.

"Maybe someday I could explain it all to you. But I know now's not a good time." He removed a Keller's business card from his suit and scribbled his cell number. "When you're ready, let me know."

Christine accepted the card and turned it in her hands. "We'll see," she whispered.

Jason cleared his throat and changed the topic. "I hadn't spoken to Thomas in years, but I think of him every so often. Was he in good spirits before the accident?"

"I wouldn't know," she replied. "Daddy and I weren't close in the last few years."

"Really? Why not?" Jason remembered how Chrissie had adored her father and hung on every word he uttered.

"Daddy changed. It got worse with each month that passed."

"I know it's none of my business, Chrissie, but I have a hard time believing what I read in the papers. The article said he was drunk and ran off the road. Is that what you're talking about? Because that's not the man I knew."

"Tell me about it. I grew up with him. I got all the Southern Baptist lectures." Christine squeezed her nose with the napkin. "I'm not talking about drinking. There were other things about Daddy that were strange." She placed her hand on Jason's arm. Her touch was magnetic through the sleeve of his suit. "I'm talking about his obsession."

"What obsession?" What are you talking about? Your father wasn't the obsessive type."

"Daddy changed. It's complicated—and somewhat embarrassing. I can't get into it here. I have to get back to my guests," she said.

"I understand." Jason studied her swollen eyes. "Chrissie, if there's anything I can do…"

Christine held up the card he'd just given her. "Maybe we'll have that conversation and we can talk about…the past. And I could tell you about Daddy's transformation, as disconcerting as it was. But it would be much easier if I showed you."

Read what happens to Jason and Chrissie, check out *The Cyclops Conspiracy* and the entire *Cyclops* series at www.davidperrybooks.com or wherever books are sold.